Guardian Angels

Guardian Angels

Heartwarming Stories of
Divine Influence and Protection

Martin H. Greenberg, Editor

CUMBERLAND HOUSE
NASHVILLE, TENNESSEE

GUARDIAN ANGELS
PUBLISHED BY CUMBERLAND HOUSE PUBLISHING, INC.
431 Harding Industrial Drive
Nashville, Tennessee 37211

Cover design by Karen Phillips
Page Design by Mike Towle

Library of Congress Cataloging-in-Publication Data
  Guardian angels : heartwarming stories of divine influence and protection /
  Martin H. Greenberg, editor.
      p. cm.
    ISBN 978-1-58182-124-6
    1. Angels—Fiction. 2. Guardian angels—Fiction. 3. Christian fiction,
  American. I. Greenberg, Martin Harry.
  PS648.A48G83 2000
  813'.0108382353—dc21   00-064422

Contents

Introduction

Mankind has always been fascinated with the guardian angel. The idea that God has thousands of supernatural assistants ready, willing, and able to assist mortals in their hour of need appeals to many people and gives the idea of a divine being and Heaven a little more credence.

To believe in the existence of guardian angels is the ultimate step of trust in one's faith, for it means taking control out of human hands and giving it to something that may or may not exist. For those who believe, it is a self-fulfilling choice, for if God's power derives from belief in him, then his angels also benefit in the same way and are thus able to help those who call on them, consciously or not.

The debate as to whether angels exist has probably gone on for as long as religion has existed. Skeptics and naysayers claim humanity has free will, and each one of us should get out of the mistakes we blunder into. They dismiss the idea of angels as ludicrous in this rational, scientifically guided world and say that those people who believe in the idea of a higher power existing to help mankind is nothing more than a self-deluded fantasy.

But there are thousands of people who claim to have been helped by a presence they could not define except as . . . otherworldly. For these people, this is often a life-changing event, a signal that there is something out there, tangible evidence that a higher power does exist. A recent survey showed that more than two-thirds of the population of this country think angels exist in some form, which only proves that belief in angels shows no sign of wavering any time soon.

Of course, the idea of angels has been passed down for centuries, from the angel staying Abraham's hand in the Bible to much more recent interpretations of angels in films such as *It's a Wonderful Life, City of Angels,* and *The Preacher's Wife,* and on television with *Touched by an Angel.* Guardian angels have been with us for a long time, and their popularity shows no sign of slowing.

When all is said and done, the guardian angel is a symbol of what is good and right in the world, a protective power sent from above to guide mankind when, for whatever reason, we've strayed from the righteous path. That is what we've collected for you in this book, eighteen stories celebrating the guardian angels as they walk among us, lending a hand wherever they can. As always, whenever a group of authors is given a specific topic, the resulting stories are as varied as they can be. Susan Sizemore introduces a newspaper columnist who's just wandering through life after the death of his wife, until he meets the most unangelic angel ever. Neesa Hart takes us on a journey that explores the power of belief and how it can divide a father and his son, until a little help from the divine appears in the form of a man who appears in the right place at the right time. Tim Waggoner tells a story about an angel who discovers that even he needs a guardian of his own, and from Ken Wisman comes the story of a man who looks after his son, even after his death, and the lessons they both learn from his tenure as a guardian angel. Finally, we are pleased to bring you a story by fantasy master Stephen R. Donaldson, whose epic tale of good versus evil illustrates perfectly the role guardian angels have been playing for humans for centuries.

So relax, and settle in for these tales of guardian angels doing what they do best—helping men and women when they need it most. For sometimes, when problems seem insurmountable, when all hope seems lost, the best help can only come from above.

Guardian Angels

Star of Wonder

Neesa Hart

The day Augustine Max arrived in Brisby, Mother Nature put on her best show. It was one of those perfect late fall days—the kind where the air is cold enough to keep your cheeks red, but not so cold to demand a jacket. Laughter and voices carried farther than usual that day, borne on the crisp, clean breezes that tickled their way down Main Street. An azure blue sky formed a canopy, and against its cloudless backdrop, every color appeared clearer and brighter. Russet and saffron leaves whistled a merry tune in rhythm with the winds and in counterpoint to the nut-laden squirrels that dashed from branch to branch. Occasionally, a leaf would break free in a mad, autumnal dance until it settled somewhere along the wooden sidewalk. The steady whisk of shopkeepers' brooms beat a cadence on the weathered planks, but the leaves seemed to be winning.

And everywhere, in every door, on every face, in the storefronts and the schoolhouse and along the tree-lined avenues there hung a sense of anticipation. Something was going to happen, something bigger than Brisby had seen before, and, perhaps, something bigger than Brisby itself.

Today was the day. Hank Avery had promised that today, Brisby would find itself on the map of scientific history.

1

So no one was surprised when a loud popping noise preceded a quick flare of the lights in the brief second before the power went out in Brisby.

From his perch at the counter of Bud's Pharmacy, Augustine Max smiled softly, then took a long sip of his milkshake. Hank Avery, it seemed, had done it again.

In that short window between realizing the town's transformer had blown, and the laughing acceptance most of Brisby's residents now had for Hank's mad-scientist methods, life had ground to a halt. The waitress had paused in the act of pouring a cup of coffee. Beside Augustine, Charlie Danver's newspaper had slowly lowered to the counter. Conversation at the lunch counter had ceased.

Charlie broke the silence with a slight laugh and a snap of his paper. "Hank's done it again," he said.

Beth Ann, the young waitress, shook her head and finished pouring the coffee. "Wonder how long we'll be without power this time."

Augustine placed his glass on the counter. "This kind of thing happen often around here?"

Down came Charlie's paper. "You new to this town, or passing through?"

"Er, passing through. But I'll be here for several weeks, I think."

"Then you might as well get used to it. Every year, about this time, Hank Avery fires up all that equipment he has. Brisby's generator can't handle it."

"Equipment?" Augustine swiveled his chair for a better look at the patrons. Most seemed oblivious, or at worst, mildly amused. Not what he'd expected.

Beth Ann moved closer to his position at the counter. "Sure. Old Hank is part scientist, part movie producer—"

"Part Merlin the Magician," Charlie added. That won a collective laugh.

"You don't say?" Augustine propped his elbows on the table. "What's he working on?"

Charlie folded the newspaper and propped his hands on it. "Well, for as long as I've known Hank, which is most of his life and all of mine, he's had this fixation—some folks call it an obsession—with the Star of Bethlehem."

"Really?"

Beth Ann shook her head. "It's not a star, Charlie, it's a conjunction of planets. Didn't you listen to Hank's lecture last December?"

"I've been listening to Hank's lectures for the last fifty-two years," Charlie retorted.

A woman and her preschool son had made their way over to the counter. She patted Charlie on the shoulder. "Now, Charlie, don't you go giving this man such a sour impression of Hank Avery. He's a very nice man."

"He's a nut," Charlie insisted. "A decent, kind-hearted kind of nut, but still a nut."

Augustine stifled a smile. "About this equipment—"

"Oh, that," the newcomer shifted her son on her hip. "Hank has built a kind of planetarium out of pieces and parts of stuff he's salvaged from all over the country. It's his dream to recreate the Star of Bethlehem," she glanced at Beth Ann, "or the conjunction of planets, or whatever happened, on Christmas Eve. He's been working at it for most of his life."

Beth Ann propped her elbows on the counter and rested her chin in her hands. "According to Hank, he's got the actual events of the first Christmas pinpointed to April 17, 7 B.C."

Augustine's eyebrows lifted. "Really?"

"Yes," Beth Ann continued, obviously warming to the topic, "He's done all this research. You should see it. It's like a library's worth of stuff."

"Years," the other woman said. "He's spent years on this."

"And he promised," added Beth Ann, "that once he gets all his equipment working, we'll be able to go up to his barn where he's built the planetarium and he can show us what the sky looked like on that actual night."

"It's foolishness," Charlie muttered.

"I think it's romantic," insisted Beth Ann. "My boyfriend, Tommy, and I are planning to go."

"You'll be disappointed," Charlie said.

"I think he's going to do it," Beth Ann retorted. "It's going to be wonderful."

"It would be," concurred the mother, "but I'm afraid Charlie's right. Even if Hank could get his equipment calibrated, he'll never solve the power problem."

"That seems a shame," Augustine said. From the corner of his eye he saw a gentleman making his way from the far end of the lunch counter. "I'd like to see the show if he gets it working."

"You into that kind of thing?" Charlie asked.

Augustine didn't bother to hide his smile this time. "You could say that." He dug into his pocket and placed enough coins on the counter to cover his bill and the tip.

Beth Ann cleared his glass and started wiping the counter. "I meant to ask you earlier, mister, what brings you to Brisby? We don't get many visitors other than passers-through."

The other man had almost reached them now. He had a sturdy build, and the angriest eyes Augustine had seen in years. Augustine reached for his light jacket. "I suppose," he explained, "you could say I'm an avid observer of celestial matters."

Charlie frowned. "You a scientist or something."

"No." He shrugged into his jacket. "Just a fan."

The man now stood a few feet behind the young mother. "Well, take my advice, mister. If you're counting on Hank Avery for a show, you might as well forget it. That old man is nothing but a fool, and he's wasted his entire life chasing this pipe dream. If you let him, he'll make a fool out of you, too." He tossed some bills onto the counter, nodded at Beth Ann, then exited the pharmacy in long, ground-eating strides.

Augustine stared after him, a deep frown marring his forehead. At the touch on his sleeve, he turned to look at Beth Ann. "Don't mind him," she said quietly. "That's just Hank's son."

AUGUSTINE MADE THE LONG climb to Hank Avery's house, stopping along the way to admire the magnificent view across the valley. No wonder, he mused, Hank's mind dwelled on heavenly things. If he lived here, amid this natural splendor, he'd find it easy to focus on the wonders of God. Augustine found a wide, flat boulder and sat down. Since that encounter at the pharmacy, he'd been feeling the need for a little guidance.

The nice thing about his job, he thought with a wry smile, was that he didn't need to phone in to talk to the boss. He was just a thought away.

Staring out over the rolling landscape, he opened his mind. "I thought I knew why You wanted me here," he explained. "I thought Hank Avery needed my help in realizing his dream. But now, I'm not so sure. I think this has something to do with Hank's son. Is that why You sent me?"

Augustine sat and listened, as he had a thousand times before over the course of several millennia. The answer came, as wise and as mysterious as always. Not as an audible voice. He'd never heard it that way, though he knew some who had, but as an increased consciousness of will. *Wait,* the Answer said. *Wait, watch, and employ common sense.*

Augustine grimaced. Waiting. He hated that part. Prime directives were always easier.

With a sigh, he levered himself off the rock and started back up the hill. He'd been looking forward to meeting Hank Avery since he'd first heard about this case a week and a half ago. No sense in putting it off any longer.

A knock at the weathered farmhouse door garnered no response, so Augustine made his way around to the barn. Picking a path through the scurrying chickens and cats, he followed the clanging and muttering noises through the barn doors, up the stepladder, and into the shadowed interior of what was once the hayloft. Hank Avery, Augustine decided, fulfilled every expectation he'd had—and then some. Short, stocky, with a shock of white hair and a beard that would have made Saint Nicholas proud, the old man was fiddling with a mass of electrical wires that looked tangled beyond redemption. He wore faded bib overalls over a buffalo plaid shirt. One boot was unlaced, and the other had a hole in the toe.

Augustine advanced into the loft with a sense of joy. This was one of his favorite parts of his job. "Hello," he prompted. "Anyone up here?"

Hank dropped the wires and turned with a start. "Oh, hello there. Didn't hear you come up."

"Sorry, didn't mean to startle you."

"You didn't. It's these dratted wires again." Hank rubbed his plump hands on his ample belly. "Suppose you're here about the power?"

"Uh—"

"Don't worry. I don't think I did any real damage. Just threw a breaker, maybe. I wasn't even testing the entire shebang. I just wanted to turn on the projector and see how she's working."

"Actually, I—"

Hank frowned. "Don't tell me we lost the transformer again?"

"Well, yes."

"Drat. I didn't think I'd run nearly that much juice through the system. I suppose you're here to give me another summons?"

"No. I'm not—"

"You power company boys take yourselves way too seriously, you know. Next thing I know, you'll be showing up here with the sheriff."

"I think you misunderstand."

"In fact, if you're going to arrest me," he held his hands out in front of him, "why don't you just do it and get the matter over with."

Augustine laughed. "I'm not with the power company, Mr. Avery. And I'm not here to arrest you."

Hank dropped his hands and gave Augustine a quizzical look. "Oh. Well, who are you?"

Augustine advanced the rest of the way into the loft. "Augustine Max is my name." He handed Hank a business card. "I'm here because I'm interested in your work."

A shaft of sunlight illuminated the cramped space. Dust mites bobbed and danced on the beam. Hank leaned closer to it and held the card up for inspection. "Augustine Max," he read. "Celestial Observer and Planetologist." Hank glanced at him. "Somebody pays you for a job like that?"

Augustine smiled. "Sort of." He turned to look at the various telescopes, planetariums, and star charts. "Impressive array of stuff you've got here."

Hank stuffed his hands into the pockets of his overalls. "Sure is. I've spent years collecting all this." He moved forward to lay his hand on the large barrel of a telescope. "This is my latest acquisition. Got it from Duke University when they upgraded their stuff. It's the most powerful telescope I've had. Saw Venus with it night before last.

"Venus? Really?"

"Yep." Hank ran his hand along the barrel. "I'd seen it before, of course, but not this close."

"I understand your special interest lies with the Star of Bethlehem."

That made the older man's eyes twinkle. He leaned forward and said to Augustine in a conspiratorial whisper—as if the information were too important to spare on the cows milling below—"It wasn't a star, you know?"

"I've heard that."

"It was a conjunction of planets in the Aries triton, paired with a lunar eclipse of Venus. That would have told the Magi something big was happening in Judea—actually, given the relative positions of Mars and the Sun, there was no way they could have mistaken the sign for anything other than an announcement of the birth of a king."

Augustine was impressed. So very close. "Fascinating."

"It is," Hank exclaimed. "And I've been able to pinpoint the actual events to April 17, 7 B.C. Now if I can just get this stuff working, and the power company to cooperate, I can project the exact image as it appeared on that first Christmas night."

"I heard in town that you're planning to do just that on Christmas Eve."

Hank chuckled, which made his ample belly roll beneath his overalls. "I am. I am. Can you think of a better way to celebrate Christmas?"

With a shake of his head, Augustine unbuttoned the cuffs of his dress shirt. "No, I don't suppose I can." He began to roll back the white cuffs. "But I suppose we'd better get started on these wires."

Hank tipped his head to one side and studied him in the dim light. "You're here to help me?"

Augustine knelt on the loft floor by the tangled mass. He shot Hank a wry smile. "Why else would I be here, Mr. Avery?"

SUNDAY AFTERNOON AFTER CHURCH presented Augustine with his first opportunity to speak to Hank's son, Bill. He hadn't seen the man since that first encounter in the pharmacy, but when the services ended, Augustine discovered that Bill Avery was the deacon in charge of greeting new visitors. With a slight tip of his head, Augustine acknowledged the Lord's sense of humor and timing in matters like these. Bill's wife, Lana Avery, whom Hank described in glowing terms, had greeted Augustine near the door of the church. "If you don't have any lunch plans," she'd told him, "we'd love to have you join us." She cast a glance at her husband's shoulder. He was deep in conversation with the pastor. "I know that you must know something of what's going on between Hank and my Bill."

"A little."

"I—well, if you don't want to come, I understand. But we'd love to have your company."

"I'd like to have yours."

Lana smiled at him, a warm smile that made the sunlight seem a little brighter. "Bill's as stubborn as his father, and I can't guarantee what kind of reception you'll get."

Augustine laughed. "Never fear, Mrs. Avery. I've weathered far worse, I assure you."

"Great. Let me give you the directions."

So here he was outside Bill's house. As he walked up the sidewalk, he noted the stark difference between Bill's home and Hank's farm. Where everything on the farm had a homey, Americana kind of look, Bill's house was the most contemporary on the street. The stucco facade, even the perfectly manicured bushes, had a tale to tell to anyone who knew Bill Avery's father. Bill seemed to have tried to sever every link with his past, right down to the boxwoods.

His knock on the door brought Bill's son, Grant, to the door. Augustine knew from his conversations with Hank that the ten-year-old boy had been born shortly after the death of Hank's wife. Bill's resentment of his father had burst into bloom then, and Hank had been allowed little access to his grandson. Unbeknownst to his father, however, Grant had taken to sneaking off to the farm. He and Hank were developing quite a rapport. Augustine feared that a major confrontation was brewing in the Avery family. He extended his hand to the younger Avery. "I'm Augustine Max. I've heard a lot about you."

Grant beamed at him. "I've heard my share about you, too. I saw Hank the other day when I stopped by the farm." He glanced over his shoulder. Seeing the coast was clear, he continued. "You weren't there, though. You really going to help Hank get the planetarium working?"

"That's my goal."

"I can't wait," Grant assured him.

"Neither can I."

"Grant?" Lana's voice came from inside the house. "Grant, is that Mr. Max at the door?"

"Yes, Mom."

"Well, bring him in. Don't make the poor man stand on the porch. The weather's turned cold these days."

Grant ushered Augustine into the house. An open-floor plan and towering cathedral ceilings gave it a sense of airiness. Lana came out of the kitchen wiping her hands on a dishtowel. "I'm so glad you decided to join us."

"I never turn down a home-cooked Sunday lunch," Augustine assured her.

Lana laughed and turned to her son. "Grant, go wash your hands and call your father. Dinner's ready."

He and Lana chatted briefly about the sudden cold snap in the weather, then Bill came down the curved staircase. "Mr. Max," he said gravely. "My wife told me you'd be joining us for lunch."

Not the most gracious of greetings, Augustine mused, but he'd had worse. "She was generous enough to invite me after church this morning."

"We've been so eager to visit with you," Lana assured him. Bill gave her a sharp glance. She ignored it, but slid her hand through the bend of his elbow. "How are you enjoying working at the farm?"

"Very much. Hank's a character."

Bill's frown deepened as Grant came bounding down the stairs, slinging the water off his hands. "Ready, Mom."

She beamed at Augustine. "Let's eat, then."

WITH THE FOUR OF them seated at the dining room table, Bill said the grace. Augustine sent up several silent pleas of his own, hoping for guidance a little more specific than the common sense rule. Not surprisingly, Grant gave him the opening he needed.

"Mr. Max," Grant said, dropping an enormous spoonful of mashed potatoes onto his plate, "what exactly are you doing for Hank?"

Bill gave his son a cross look. "Grant—"

Lana headed him off. "I'd like to know, too. I'm sure Hank's keeping you busy."

Bill snorted. "Running you ragged is more like it. You figured out yet, Mr. Max, that he's not going to get the fool thing to work?"

"I think it's going to work, Dad," Grant insisted.

Bill stabbed at a piece of steak on his plate. "I thought so, too, when I was your age."

Augustine leaned back in his chair. "He's got all the right components. I think it just needs a little tinkering."

Bill frowned. "He's been saying that for forty years. You'll understand if I'm a little skeptical."

"Of course."

Lana placed her napkin next to her plate. "You have to understand," she told Augustine, "Bill's father has been pursuing this project for as long as Bill's been alive. It's had," she paused, "an effect. On all of them."

"He can't stand it," Grant chimed in.

His mother gave him a sharp look. "Grant."

"Well, he can't."

"That's enough, Grant," Bill said. "You don't know what you're talking about."

"But, Dad, you don't even talk to him. If you'd just—"

"Grant." Lana's voice was firmer this time.

"It's all right," Augustine assured them. "I didn't mean to intrude."

"If you're going to work with my father," Bill tossed his napkin down, "then you might as well know the truth."

"I take it that you don't approve of your father's commitment to the project."

Bill snorted. "I don't approve of the way my father spent every cent he and my mother ever had chasing after this stupid idea. When my mother was dying, they couldn't afford the treatment she needed because their life savings were tied up in some prehistoric piece of equipment in their barn. I've put up with this for forty-two years, Mr. Max. The man's the laughingstock of this entire town."

"That's not true," Grant said angrily.

"Yes, it is, Grant." His father looked at him. "And you might as well know it. Every person in this entire town thinks Hank Avery is a nut."

Grant shoved his chair back from the table. "That's not true. I don't think he's a nut! You're not being fair. You don't even talk to him."

Lana held out a hand. "Bill—"

Her husband interrupted her. "Someone has to tell him, Lana. It's not going to be you."

Grant glared at his father, then raced from the table. With a mumbled apology, Lana followed him. Bill took a deep breath and leaned back in his chair. He pinned Augustine with a piercing look. "If you don't mind my asking, Mr. Max, just what are you trying to do here? I don't know who you are, or why you're in Brisby, or why you're working with my father, but what's in this for you?"

The fierce anger that Augustine had sensed that first day was still there, radiating from a pair of brown eyes that closely resembled his father's. "Truth is," he said slowly, "I've got nothing invested in this but curiosity. I heard about your father's work and wanted to take a look."

"Then you're wasting your time," Bill assured him. "He's been claiming he's on the verge of getting the thing to work for as long as I can remember. He's invested every penny he has in that project, and he's no closer to success now than he's ever been."

"I don't know. I like to keep an open mind about these things. You might be surprised."

"Hah!"

AUGUSTINE HAD THREE WEEKS to ponder Bill's frustrations, Hank's insistence, and the anger that hovered between the two men. As fall faded into winter, and the Christmas decorations began to appear along Main Street and in the storefronts, that phenomenon that Augustine referred to as the December Miracle began to spread through Brisby. Folks found reasons to go out of their way for each other. More people smiled. More people whistled. The mood of the town brightened, and the first snowfall of the year turned Brisby into a winter wonderland.

In the weeks that had passed since his visit with Bill and his family, Augustine had seen Grant several times. The boy often stopped by on his way home from school. He was full of questions and curious about his grandfather's tinkering. The sun set earlier these days, and Grant's visits were growing shorter—the short bike ride to his home was best completed before dark.

Augustine and Hank stood at the barn door one afternoon where they watched Grant ride down the hill.

"He's a good kid," Augustine said.

"Great. Smart as a whip, too. Like his daddy."

This was the first time Hank had left the door ajar for a conversation about Bill. "Hank—I've been meaning to ask—"

"About Bill?" Hank asked as he pulled the barn door shut. He headed for the loft. "What's to tell? I'm sure Bill's told you why he's so angry with me."

"Something about his mother?" Augustine followed Hank up the ladder to the loft.

"Is that what he said?" Hank began packing away the tools. "I'm surprised."

"You think there's something else."

"Sure." He latched the top of the toolbox, then turned to face Augustine in the fading light. "When my Betty died," he paused, "that was the worst day of my life. She and I had decided that she didn't want to spend the rest of her life in terrible pain, practically incapacitated. She told me before she went to the hospital that I couldn't let them hook her up to a machine. She wasn't willing to suffer like that—and I wasn't willing to let her."

"Bill thinks—"

"I know what he thinks. He thinks I let his mother die because we couldn't afford any more treatment. He stopped speaking to me that afternoon."

"Did you tell him about his mother's request?"

"No." His jaw squared. "He didn't ask. He didn't want to know. And he was angry at me before all that started anyway."

"Hank—"

"He was. Bill always resented the time I invested in this project." With a sweep of his arm, he indicated the equipment in the loft. "I'm not going to lie to you and tell you that I was a perfect father. I made my share of mistakes. Sometimes, I'd get wrapped up in research, and I wasn't there when Bill needed me. Betty was good about keeping my feet on the ground."

Hank's eyes drifted shut, and Augustine waited while he collected his thoughts. When Hank looked at him again, he looked older, somehow. "Augustine, why are you helping me?"

Augustine blinked. "What?"

"Why are you doing this? I'm not paying you. I'm not even sure it's going to work."

"I told you—"

Hank shook his head. "I know, you told me you were curious. But you've been here every day for three weeks doing nothing but running my errands and wiring my contraptions. I'm sure Bill told you that I've tried to get this to work every year for most of my life. Since Betty died, it's the only thing that's kept me going—particularly since Bill won't have anything to do with me. Then you show up out of the blue one day, offer to help, and the next thing I know, I'm telling you things I haven't told another living soul. Who are you?"

Augustine hesitated. If he revealed the truth too soon . . . "I'm here to help you, Hank. Does it have to be anything more than that?"

"Why?"

"Because when you get all this to work," he said slowly, "it will show people something miraculous. Something that has pointed the way to God, and truth, for almost two thousand years. I think things will change in this town the day they see this. And I want to be a part of it."

Hank considered him for long seconds, then shook his head. "You're a strange man, Augustine."

"So I've heard."

With a sigh, Hank shoved his hands in his overall pockets. "Well, we're out of daylight now, and it's cold. No sense trying to work up here any longer."

Augustine reached for his jacket. "I think I'll head off, then."

"I've been meaning to ask you," Hank said as he switched off the dim overhead lights. "Where are you staying?"

Augustine headed down the ladder. "Oh, I've got a little place outside town. It suits me."

"I didn't know there were any rentals around here."

Augustine waited until Hank had joined him at the bottom of the ladder. "I was just lucky, I guess," he said. "I found exactly what I needed."

AUGUSTINE GLANCED UP FROM his desk. His long-time friend and
fellow angel stood at the entrance to his office. "You're working
late," Gary said.

Augustine glanced at the clock. Two in the morning. "Had a
few things I wanted to get down on paper."

"How's it going in Brisby?"

Augustine shook his head. "I don't know. Hank and Bill are
two of the most stubborn men I've ever met. They're hurting, but
neither one will make the first move."

"Is Hank going to get that contraption to work?"

"I think so."

"What about the power problem?"

Augustine gave his friend a slight smile. "I've got a plan,
Gary."

Gary laughed. "I don't know why I doubted it. Wish I could be
there for the show."

"You've got your own problem to worry about. Any progress
with Sue and Rick?"

"I think so. They finally talked about the baby this afternoon."

"Good." Augustine switched off the lamp on his desk. "That's
a great first step."

They exited the small office together and made their way
down the street, chatting companionably as only the oldest of
friends can do. They were round the corner near Augustine's
house when Obadiah, one of the youngest of their kind came
racing down the street.

"Augustine!" He waved his arms over his head. "Augustine,
come quick. You're needed down under."

Augustine handed his notebook to Gary. "Take care of his for
me?"

"Of course. Good luck."

"Thanks." Augustine took off after Obadiah at a run.

"HANK?" AUGUSTINE SHOOK HIS friend's shoulder. "Hank, can you
hear me." The heavy smell of liquor, and the papers strewn across
the living room told a grim tale. Augustine cursed himself for not
trusting his instincts earlier. He hadn't wanted to leave Hank
alone, but Hank had insisted. "Hank, wake up."

Hank's eyes cracked open. "Wha—"

"Hank, are you all right?"

The older man's head bobbed on top of his neck. "Too much—"

"Too much to drink. I know. Do you want me to call an ambulance?"

"Not that much," Hank assured him with a bleary smile. "Can't make it to bed."

"I'll help you."

"Why—you're here."

Augustine sensed Hank's confusion, but didn't choose to explain. He slid one arm around Hank and levered him out of the chair. Hank swayed unsteadily on his feet. "Hold on to me," Augustine told him. "I'll help you walk back to your room."

Hank leaned his full weight on Augustine's shoulders. "It's what she wanted," he muttered. "I told you it's what she wanted."

"I know, Hank."

Hank stumbled as they neared the hall. "Bill doesn't believe me."

"I know." Augustine kept him moving until they reached the back bedroom. "It's okay. Everything's going to be okay."

"Why didn't he ask?" Hank demanded as he fell heavily onto his bed.

"I don't know." Augustine started to unlace his boots. He pulled off, first, one, then the other. Swinging Hank's legs onto the bed, he pulled the quilt over his large frame. "I don't know, Hank."

Hank gave him a pained look. "He should have asked," he mumbled as his eyes drifted shut again.

Augustine watched him for long seconds, then headed back to the living room to straighten up the mess. At least the next few hours would give him the opportunity for a long talk with the Boss. He felt sorely in need of a little guidance right now. With Christmas just a week away, and Bill's planetarium nearing completion, Augustine had a strong conviction that this might be Bill and Hank's last chance. He was sure that God had sent him here for this reason, but didn't begin to know what to do about it.

He dumped the remains of the liquor down the sink, then set about straightening up the living room. Since he'd left him that afternoon, Hank had, evidently, been taking a walk through his memories of Betty and Bill. Scrapbooks and photos were strewn about the room. A wedding picture that showed a younger, happier Hank and a beautiful young woman sat on the table by Hank's easy chair. Augustine collected the photos and slipped them back in the empty shoebox. He was busily shelving the scrapbooks when the letter drifted to the floor.

He picked it up, thinking he'd slide it back in the book, but that voice of common sense—the one he'd been waiting on since the day he'd arrived in Brisby—told him to read it.

Augustine sat down on the floor. He sensed that this letter represented the most private moment of Hank Avery's life, and before he read it, he asked God to give him enough wisdom to know what to do with it.

Satisfied, and a little nervous, he spread the yellowing stationary and read:

Dearest Henry,

I haven't told you yet, but I feel that I know where this is leading us. I've lived in this body for sixty years, and I know what it's telling me.

Henry, I wish I could make this easier for you. But I think that you still have many wonderful things left to do. One day, you'll show the world what, until now, you've only seen in your mind. And it will be wonderful, darling. Don't give up that dream. No matter what happens, don't give up that dream.

And even though I know it's going to be hard for you, I want you to know that I'm ready for what we talked about. I'll miss you dreadfully, and I know you'll miss me. But you'll have Bill. And I'll be waiting, out there among the stars you love so much, to see the miracle you're going to bring to Brisby and to the world. I love you, Henry. And I thank God every day of my life that He gave you to me.

Don't lose heart, my love. The day you see the Star, you'll also see me again. I'll be smiling down on you.

Love always,
Elizabeth

Augustine carefully folded the letter and slid it into his jacket pocket. He leaned his head against the bookshelf and prayed earnestly for direction.

As the sun peaked above the horizon, and a pink wedge of light slipped through the windows to illuminate Augustine's spot on the plank floor, he found his answer.

AUGUSTINE GLANCED AROUND THE insurance office where Bill Avery had built a successful business on the principles he'd learned from his father: hard work, compassion, and creative risk taking. Bill's secretary gave him a warm smile as she hung up the phone. "I'm sorry, Mr. Max. Friday mornings are always so busy around here— and with Christmas just around the corner, well, you can imagine."

"I certainly can. And I'm sorry to stop by without an appointment. I just thought Mr. Avery might be able to squeeze me in."

"I'm sure he will, if you don't mind waiting for a while. He's with a client right now."

"No problem." Augustine sat in one of the comfortable padded chairs. "I've got plenty of time."

A half-hour passed before Bill emerged from his office. He shook hands with his client, then gave Augustine a quizzical look. "You here for insurance, Mr. Max?"

"No." Augustine stood. "Something else."

He noticed the way Bill's jaw set into the same stubborn square he'd seen on Hank. Bill looked at his secretary. "Hold all my calls, will you, Christine?"

"Sure, Bill."

She smiled at Augustine as he walked past her toward Bill's office. Bill shut the door with a decisive click. "I assume you're here about my father."

"More or less."

Bill motioned to one of the chairs across from his desk. "I thought I made it clear," he said as he rounded the desk, "how I felt about that."

"You did. But there's something I think you should know."

"You aren't here to give me a speech on how Hank's just a lonely old man and I should cut him some slack, are you? I hear that from my wife once a week."

Augustine took his seat. "You're wife's a very nice woman."

Bill studied him from across the desk. "Yeah. Why are you here, Max? Plenty of people have tried to meddle in this over the last ten years. What makes you think you're going to be any different?"

Augustine hid a smile and produced Betty's letter from his jacket pocket. "I'm better at this kind of thing than most," he assured Bill. "I thought you should read this."

Bill looked at him skeptically, then took the letter. He spread open the stationary, then glanced quickly at Augustine. "This is my mother's handwriting. Where did you get this?"

"From Hank."

"Does he know you have this?"

"No."

Bill paused, but finally looked at the letter again. He traced a finger slowly over the curves of his mother's elegant script. By the time he looked at Augustine, his expression had softened. "Thank you for showing me this."

"I realize it doesn't make up for the past."

"No, it doesn't."

"But I thought if you knew what your mother was thinking—"

"It helps," Bill assured him. "I don't think we can just put all this behind us, but it really does help."

"Bill," Augustine said carefully, "has it occurred to you that you aren't hurting anyone more than yourself by staying so angry at your father?"

Bill didn't respond. Augustine forged ahead. "Don't get me wrong. Hank's not exactly blameless in this. I know he never told you that he and your mother had already decided to decline any further treatment before she went into the hospital for the last time."

"He's stubborn."

"Like father, like son?"

Bill managed a slight smile. "You could say that."

"He loves Grant, and you, and Lana."

"I know."

"Do you know Grant goes by to see him some days after school."

"Yes. Grant doesn't think I know, but I do."

"Why didn't you put a stop to it?"

Bill shrugged. "I don't know."

"Really?" Augustine prodded.

Bill glanced out the window. "At least I knew someone was checking on the old man. I didn't like the thought of his staying up there day after day by himself."

"So you left the responsibility to your son?"

"Lana calls him twice a week," Bill said. "She doesn't think I know that either."

"I guess the question is, Bill, is it really worth it? All this anger?"

Long seconds of silence ticked by. Bill spoke first. "I wouldn't even know where to start to begin again."

"Do you want to start?"

Bill glanced at the letter. "I guess so. Mom wanted it."

"Hank's got a real chance of getting the planetarium to work, Bill. With a little help from you, I think it could happen."

"Me? What have I got to do with it?"

Augustine smiled at him. "I thought you'd never ask."

CHRISTMAS EVE DAWNED FULL of promise. A fresh snow covered the ground. The air was crisp and clear, and bright sunlight made the world glisten. Augustine headed up the hill toward Hank's farm feeling confident and energized. News had been spreading through Brisby for the past week. This year, even the skeptics seemed to think that Hank would finally get his planetarium to work.

Augustine hadn't spoken to Hank about that night he'd found the letter, or what he'd done. They had concentrated on the work in the barn and hadn't discussed Bill or Augustine's visit. As far as Augustine knew, Hank was completely unaware of what was happening, even now, on his behalf.

Grant had gladly taken on the task of distributing the flyers Augustine and Bill had designed. There wasn't a household in Brisby that didn't at least know what was supposed to happen that night. The heightened sense of anticipation brought back fond memories for Augustine. Christmas Eve generally did. Magical, wonderful things happened at this time of the year, and he loved his job more during the Christmas holidays than at any other time.

The hours passed quickly as nightfall approached. Augustine and Hank checked and double-checked every circuit and every line. Hank was still concerned that they'd drain too much power from the town's transformer, and that, at the last minute, despite their preparation to the contrary, there simply wouldn't be sufficient amperage to fire up the planetarium. Augustine did his best to reassure him, but knew Hank was worried.

The sun had set, and the sky had faded from a dull winter gray to a fathomless black when the first of the torches appeared near the edge of town. Augustine watched the bobbing lights for several seconds. "Hank," he called. "Is everything calibrated?" Hank stuck his head out from behind one of the instrument panels. "Yep. As long as the power holds this time, it's gonna work. I've waited my entire life for this, Augustine."

"I know."

"I couldn't have done it without you."

Augustine just shrugged. "It's going to be spectacular, Hank. I was glad to help."

"When you see it—" Hank shook his head. "I can't even tell you what I think it'll be like to stand and look at the heavens and know that's exactly what wisemen and shepherds and angels saw on the first Christmas."

Augustine felt a warm glow spread through him. "I'm sure it will be breathtaking," he said, and wondered if Hank would notice the husky note in his voice. He turned again to look at the sea of torch lights, then pointed them out to Hank. "Looks like you'll have a good crowd, too."

"I'll be," said Hank. "What do you reckon that is?"

"It looks like firelight."

Hank watched as the number of orange flames grew and moved closer. Scratching his head, he frowned. "That makes no sense at all."

"Maybe they're headed this way—you know. To see the show."

"But why—" Hank looked at Augustine. "They turned off all the lights in town, didn't they?"

Augustine shrugged. "Why would they do a thing like that?"

A slow grin spilled through the frame of Hank's whiskers. "This is your doing, isn't it?"

Augustine shook his head, glad he could be truthful. The torch procession was closer, now, and Bill, accompanied by

Lana and Grant, led it. "Nope. I planted the seed, but Bill made it work."

Hank looked at his son walking up the hill, leading a group of merry, laughing Brisby citizens. The entire town, it appeared, even the skeptics, had turned out for the event. Augustine saw a tear slide down Hank's weathered cheek as Bill drew closer. "When's the show, Dad?" Bill called. "We're ready."

Hank wiped his eyes, rubbed his hands together, and looked at Augustine. "As soon as we can get everything fired up."

"Actually," Augustine said, pulling his jacket on, "I've got to go into town. I think Grant can help you. He's seen us do it every afternoon this week."

Grant nodded vigorously. "I know exactly what to do. Man, this is gonna be cool."

Lana laid her hand on Augustine's sleeve. "You're leaving?"

Augustine looked at Bill. "Somebody has to go throw breakers that control the streetlights and other non-emergency systems for the town. Otherwise, the power drain will overload the transformer."

"But if you leave," Grant insisted, "you're gonna miss the show."

Bill continued to hold Augustine's gaze. "After all," he said quietly, "isn't this what you came for?"

Augustine shook his head. "Nope." He glanced at Hank who was happily welcoming the sea of visitors. "I came for you, Bill."

Bill nodded. "I sort of figured."

"Thank you for organizing this voluntary black-out," Augustine added. "I think people agreed because you supported the idea."

"It felt like the right thing to do." Bill glanced at his father. "We still have a lot of work to do."

"Yes. But this is a first step. After tonight, he'll have a little more time on his hands."

Lana laughed. "Oh, Lord. I don't know what the man is going to do with himself when he doesn't have this to plan all year."

"Don't worry," said Bill, shaking his head. "I assure you, he'll think of something."

"Just make time to talk to him. He's hurting, too," Augustine advised.

"I know." Bill wrapped his arm round his wife. "I'm going to try. I promise."

"That's all I ask. Merry Christmas, Bill."

"Merry Christmas, Augustine."

"Now," Augustine looked at the growing crowd. "I'd better hurry. Looks like it's time to get this show on the road."

Lana slid her arm around her husband's waist. "I really hate for you to miss the show. Especially after you've worked so hard. Maybe we could—"

"Don't worry about it," Bill said, giving his wife a quick squeeze. "I really don't think he minds."

Augustine tipped his head back and gazed at the inky night sky. "I really don't," he assured them. "I'm glad to do this." He glanced back at Bill and gave him a slight wink. "Take my word for it, though. You'll really enjoy it when you see it. It's like nothing you've ever imagined."

"You sound pretty sure," Lana said.

"I am," Augustine answered with a slight smile. He walked away. Just before he was out of earshot, he turned and said one more thing. "After all, I saw it the first time."

Her Angel

Stobie Piel

T hings have always come easily to you, Gabriel—this should be no trouble. Piece of cake." God, the Father of All, sat back, reclining comfortably in what He had arranged as a lounge-type chair, smiling innocently at one of his infinite children, and today, the most enraged.

Gabriel studied his assignment, a young woman still living on Earth, a woman he had encountered only briefly during his own life. When he drove through an intersection too fast, she had slammed her tiny car into his lovely Porsche, crushing it, and killing him. And that was all he knew of her.

God waved His hand at Gabriel, idly. "You remember her, of course?"

A shrug acknowledged that he did. "How could I not? She escaped unscathed, and I was killed."

"Unscathed, except for her broken back."

Gabriel remained unimpressed by her fate. "She is certainly better off than I am."

He retained annoyance at his thwarted life, because it had held so much success and enjoyment. From the dawn of his existence, Gabriel had loved to entertain others, and he was quick-witted, personable, and naturally beautiful enough to do it. When

23

not manifesting a physical form, his soul sparkled with a bright magenta color, to which over time he had added bits of other bright energy, from violet to green to orange, and all the qualities those colors possessed were now his; pride and intelligence and daring. His soul, his essence, was vibrant and bright and colorful, and yet somehow he felt all that he lacked was an undefinable depth. A depth he could only find, he felt sure, by living again.

Gabriel waited for God to speak, assuming it was time to discuss his next venture into human existence. God said nothing, so Gabriel seized the initiative. He had grown impatient waiting to begin again. "A soul evolves over many lifetimes, I know, Sir. The chances I missed in my previous life will be more than made up for in the next."

"You had much glory in your life, Gabriel. Riches, women, praise, success."

"I worked hard for it, Sir." His talent with music might have been minimal, but his skill at performing was unmatched, and at still a young age, Gabriel had become one of the most popular rock stars on earth. It annoyed him only slightly that he had missed the Millennium celebration in which he was to star, dying on its eve. Celebrating the Millenniums had become something of a ritual for him. As a younger soul, he had celebrated the Jewish year 2000, which had occurred in 1700 B.C., as well as the Chinese year 4698, whose year 2000 was in 698 B.C., and he had every intention of performing in some starring capacity for the Muslims, whose year 2000 would commence in 2579. But before that time, there were worlds to be conquered, glory to be had, and life to be lived to its fullest.

"I have great plans for my next life, and I'd like to get started."

God considered this quietly. "It is your choice to begin again, of course. But before you commence, there is this matter you must resolve."

He eyed God. "I'll handle it when she gets here. Apologize and all. But I'd like to get started on something new, since she cut me off back there."

"You, my son, cut her off."

Gabriel's being filled with suspicion. "So, I kept this girl from some sort of important event?"

God gestured widely, a flamboyant move clearly done to amuse Himself. "These are the sacred events, Gabriel. Some big,

widely known across the world, some small, known only to the
individual involved—but all equally great in importance to Me. In
a lifetime, only a few moments are set. You shoot them like arrows
before birth, and they are destined to land and to then be dealt
with as you see fit. These are the most treasured gifts from Me.
Rarely, almost never, is that arrow waylaid, usually because one of
the parties involved 'chickens out' and destroys it. But when you
sped through a traffic light and hit a dreamy woman in her small
car, you interfered with a sacred event."

God paused, fixing all His attention on Gabriel, until Gabriel
squirmed with discomfort. "I didn't mean to." He sounded sullen,
and felt embarrassed by his tone. This was not the most favorable
way to deal with God.

"You interfered because you were so fixated on your own
journey that you could not see another's."

"So . . . what do you want me to do?"

"Go back and guide her to the moment you stole."

"Guide her? I thought only the very old spirits became
Guides."

"You're old enough." God assessed him again, long and
thoughtfully. "Is there anyone you care enough about to guide
throughout their lifetime? You have never made the request of
Me. By the amount of lives you have lived, your age, most souls
have found themselves deeply connected to another, perhaps
many others, and wish to watch over them in their lives."

"Sure. There have been . . . some." He couldn't think of a
single person or entity he wanted to spend that much time with.
"You know, I check in on people sometimes."

"There is one you have avoided for centuries."

Gabriel's bright colors darkened as if a cloud settled over
him. "I will never visit *her* again."

"Your vision has clouded so much that you can't even see
her." The white of God increased until it cast Gabriel as a shadow.
"What do you remember of her?"

He felt cornered. "That I disliked her intensely, that she made
me a fool . . . and that she was very fat."

"Indeed? And did you ever love her?"

"No. Never. I did not."

"Do you remember the last time you saw her?"

"No."

"Do you remember her hands?" God's voice turned quieter, almost hypnotic. Gabriel began to wish he could leave. "Were they small, or very large and bony?"

"Small. Too small."

"Did she ever hold your hand when she was afraid?"

"No . . . Never. She did not." Fingers closing tight around his . . . *Don't leave me . . . Go, for all I care . . . I am not afraid . . .*

"Did you find her beautiful?"

"She was ugly. I didn't like her at all."

"She was strong-willed, like you."

"I hated her."

"Other men, did they find her beautiful?"

Gabriel darkened until his bright energy was swallowed in shadow.

"Yes." He moved from God's light, angry. He didn't ever want to think of that *one* again. He had blocked her from his light and his life for many lifetimes now. "What do I have to do for this girl on Earth, anyway? Point her in the right direction? Fine. And then I can live again, right?"

"That is your choice, as always. Once you have set this matter straight, and given her—and Me—what the accident denied her."

"What is it, exactly, that I must restore?"

"She was on her way to a meeting that would have changed her life."

"She was, what, a musician? Plays the cello?"

"Violin."

"I suppose she missed out on the glory she might have had . . . That doesn't sound too hard. So when I set this girl straight, I can start a new life?"

"What you ask for, I shall grant you, as ever."

Gabriel felt drained. He left the mystic, domed audience hall, and headed for the golden arch. He hesitated before departing, then glanced back at God, who had already turned His attention to another matter. "You have said, Sir, that everyone has a soul mate."

God glanced back, uninterested. "Yes. One being, lonely, twists into two to know itself, like a cell dividing, and in so dividing, creates infinity. It happened once, and now happens forever, and forever after."

Hope came upon Gabriel unawares. At last, he had found the loophole that might spare him all the grief of his own existence. "What about you, then, Yahweh? Where is your soul mate?"

The white that was all color glistened until Gabriel winced with its brightness. Then God smiled and said, "I Am."

SOMETIMES, SHE FELT TOO tired to ever touch a violin again. Amy Hart sat in the garden room of her Maine cottage, looking out across her garden, and a bright red cardinal settled on her bird feeder. The bird surveyed the area, then snapped up a black sunflower seed. After a few seeds split and dropped, the cardinal's paler mate perched tentatively beside him and ate, too.

Amy watched for a moment, then started to turn away. A sharp squawk snapped her back. The female attempted to steal one of her mate's seeds, and he pecked her viciously. The female recoiled, then flew away, angry. For reasons she didn't understand, Amy's eyes filled with tears. The male ate sullenly, glutting himself, then flew off, too.

She went to the open window and looked out across her garden to the pine tree on the far side of the brook. The two cardinals sat on opposite branches. They hopped, one after the other, back together, as if drawn despite themselves. Then they sat huddled, heads turned away from each other.

Then, at last, the male deposited a seed in his mate's mouth, and the two birds flew away together.

Amy went back to her music room and waited. Another student would arrive soon, a new one this time. She would start again, listen to his faulty music, set him in the right direction . . . She loved her life and she loved teaching, but today she felt weak and a little shaky.

Her doorbell rang, and her old Sheltie barked twice, a bored alarm to an oft-repeated entrance. Molly was getting old now, but she seemed to feel the doorbell insufficient as an alert. Amy patted her head as she reached for the door, and she gave the dog a cookie.

She opened the door, her tired smile already in place. "Welcome, Mr. . . ." Curses! She'd forgotten her new student's name.

He stood there, tall and proud, looking bored already, and a little impatient. "Gabriel Saint Pierre, Mrs. . . . Miss . . . ?"

Amy straightened. He didn't remember her name? Everyone in the world of classical music knew her name, and he had enlisted her as a teacher. Perhaps he was just nervous—many of them were, but Gabriel Saint Pierre didn't look nervous. Best to combat using his obvious weakness. Polite manners.

"Ms. Hart." She held out her hand, almost lovingly, and motioned him into the front room of her cottage. "Mr. Saint Pierre. How good of you to come!"

His green eyes slanted as if he instantly recognized her sarcasm, despite the sweetness of her voice. "I'm here."

She resisted the impulse to shout, "*Ta da!*"

He was a handsome man. In another time, that strong, lean body, those sparkling eyes, the perfect, classic bone structure might have set her feminine heart fluttering. His immediately obvious arrogance put all that aside at once. She looked him up and down with a critical eye. "You're a little . . . older than the students I normally take on."

His lips curled in a confident smile. "I think you'll find my ability worth the trouble. Now, let's get started." He walked into her cottage as if he owned it, then settled himself on her most comfortable armchair. He crossed his long legs and massaged his ankle as if . . . as if he wasn't used to feet.

Amy eyed him doubtfully, then seated herself on a stiff captain's chair and offered a polite smile. "Arthritis?"

He glared. She smiled even more sweetly, then sat forward to offer him iced tea. He shook his head before she spoke. "Let's get started, Ms. Hart."

"I'm afraid we're overlooking something rather important."

He stopped rubbing his ankle. "What?"

"Your audition."

Those green eyes darkened and his well-formed jaw tensed. "I sent you a . . . tape. You accepted me. What more do I have to do?"

She stood up, seized her violin, and passed it to him. "Play."

He fingered it as if he'd never seen a violin before. "I see no need . . ."

"A tape, Mr. Saint Pierre, can be faked. I assume you know this?"

The green of his eyes sparkled with anger. He didn't look away from her, not for a second, and he began to play. He played until her heart ached, until she filled with forgotten anguish, of all the love, and all the dreams, and the terrible heartache and terror that came when you are alone. He played until she cried.

He set the violin aside and Amy stood up. She went to her window and stared across the garden. "Mr. Saint Pierre, we may begin now."

⌒

AMY HART WAS THE most irritating woman Gabriel had met, in any lifetime. No matter how brilliantly he played her stupid instrument—and he was brilliant because he had mastered it well—she expected more. She would take it from him, and in her tiny, perfect hands, it would sing. She always looked a little smug when she passed it back, and said with feigned weariness, "Try again."

He'd gotten nowhere. After three weeks, what he knew of her was still minimal. After her accident, she'd given up concert performances and taken to teaching, instructing heaven-knew how many young musicians on their way to glory, while never mentioning the glory she might have had herself.

Every summer, she came to Maine and stayed in her idyllic cottage with its pretty garden, its wisteria-covered walls, its swift little brook running through the pine trees and into oblivion. Every summer, she took the best students from around the world and taught them what she herself had given up—the road to glory. Everyone she had taught was now in a major orchestra. She was in a little cottage alone.

He wanted to tell her he had been famous in his day, in his lifetime, but not only would she not believe him, he was certain she wouldn't care. So he tried to focus on his purpose, and the future glory this success would insure.

He had learned very little about the night he had died, nothing terribly helpful. He had been on his way to another night of glory at Madison Square Garden, the star of a Millennium concert, and she had been on her way to an audition for a tiny, unknown orchestra in Brooklyn. He was late, and being impatient, refused to wait for his driver . . . They collided, ending his life, and apparently, knocking hers permanently off course. He could only assume that her sojourn with that orchestra would have brought her to the attention of a more prominent conductor, and then to glory.

Well, there was still time. She had obviously made her reputation as a teacher somehow, so she must have the contacts to earn
her a better position.

"So . . . you must get sick of this, right?" Gabriel sat across
from her at her small, round breakfast table, anticipating another
day of torment. "I mean, you don't get out much."

She looked up at him over her fried eggs and ham, doubtful.
"Before she died, I took Molly for a walk every day, I fetch my mail
and the newspaper, I feed the birds, and I weed my garden."

He sat back in his seat, having already finished his eggs and
ham. "My point is made." Maybe if he took the direct approach . . .
Gabriel sat forward, and she frowned when his elbows implanted
on her table. He refused to move them. "Look. You're a beautiful woman, you're incredibly talented. Why not pick up where
you left off before the accident, and get yourself a reputation of
your own?"

She stared, open-mouthed, then puffed a surprised, and perhaps offended breath. "How do you know about the accident?"

He hesitated, then shrugged. "God told me" probably
wouldn't go over too convincingly. "Um . . . everyone must have
heard of that."

Her bright eyes narrowed. "I have never spoken of my accident to anyone."

Great! Gabriel's jaw shifted to one side and he popped his
lips. "No one?"

"No one." Her soft, melodious voice had hardened, and her
small, beautiful face radiated suspicion.

Gabriel nodded. "Well, these things get around." He shifted his
weight in his chair, then got up and cleared the table, a first during
his tenure as Amy's student. He shuffled the plates into her sink
and attempted to wash them. Something cracked, which he hoped
she didn't notice. "Car accident, right? You broke something . . ."

"My back."

"You were on your way to an audition." He glanced over his
shoulder, but she didn't respond. If anything, she looked a little
guilty. "Right?"

"That is where I was supposed to be going, yes." He sensed
more but had no idea which direction to pursue.

"So . . ." He sponged out a cup, added too much detergent,
and created a small mountain of soap in her sink. "So it must

have taken you quite awhile to recover, broken back and all. Really set you back from your career."

Amy stood up and left the room. Gabriel shook the suds from his hands, rinsed them, then followed her, dripping on her oval rug. She was standing, staring out her garden window as birds flocked to her little blue feeder. The soft summer wind blew through the open window and lifted her hair, and it danced around her neck and shoulders.

Sometimes, she seemed more an angel than he ever could be.

Gabriel hesitated, then placed his hands on her shoulders. She felt small and vulnerable, delicate . . . and the power of her soul radiated through his skin, piercing into his heart and all through him. "It's not too late."

She closed her eyes, but he saw tears. This sign of emotion was helpful, at least. She must care, she must regret the glory she had lost.

"It is for him."

"For who?"

She turned so that she stood close to him, face to face. The tears in her blue eyes glistened and fell to her cheeks. "For the man I killed."

Gabriel groaned, stood back, and clamped his hand over his eyes. "Is that it? Are you feeling guilty about the guy who died in the accident?"

She stared in amazement, but he shook his head, then laughed. "I should have known. Well, don't. It wasn't your fault— it was his. He drove into you, not the other way around. So get on with your career, and forget about him. He's fine."

"He's dead." Her voice sounded very small, as if she was thinking he was crazy.

"These things happen. I'm sure he felt no pain." He paused. "Do you know who he was?"

"He was Indigo Crisp, a famous rock star."

Gabriel cringed at the name. Most horrifyingly, it hadn't been a made-up name, but chosen by his hippie parents who were "clearing chakras" when he was conceived, and eating breakfast cereal. In his spirit form, he took the name Gabriel, because it had been his many lifetimes ago, before he met *her*, before he knew she even existed, when she was felt and not known.

He refused to think of *her* now. He had more important matters to consider. "Well, you know, I'm sure he forgives you."

Amy eyed him doubtfully. "That's very comforting." She looked out the window again. He was struck once more by her beauty, by her small nose, her clean, arched brows, her soft lips. But he had his own future to think of now.

"There's nothing you can do about . . . him. I'm sure he'd want you to get on with your own life."

She drew a long, patient breath. "You really don't understand, do you?"

He wanted to say, "of course," but he had no idea what she meant. "No."

"My life changed that night, yes. And I did decide not to pursue a public career. But not for the reasons you think."

He hesitated. "What reasons?"

She closed her beautiful eyes, her expression soft as the wind caressed her face. "There is so little time . . . I could have raced about throughout my life, as he did. Giving nothing, feeling nothing. It was all so important then, to succeed and to have fame and glory. I wanted more."

He stood dumfounded. "What *more?*"

She smiled, an ageless smile. "To give and to share. To love, Mr. Saint Pierre. Don't you know?"

He felt suddenly cornered, as if the walls closed in around them and Amy Hart held the key with which to lock him in forever. "But you are alone. You've never married . . . or even had a date from what I can see."

"I've given all I've had, for all my life. I've taught children, and some older gentlemen like yourself, and shown them the beauty of music that they carry within. That is love, to share, isn't it?" She looked away again, wistful but at peace. "I have never shared my most inner soul, that's true, but I have held love as sacred, and maybe that is too much."

He gulped and didn't know why he felt so scared. "Look at yourself, Amy. You couldn't be more beautiful. Men must flock to you."

She looked at him quizzically, then laughed. "Is that so? I know old Pete at the local supermarket has suggested an evening of bingo . . ."

"Old Pete?" Gabriel shook his head. "You could have any man you want. You're speaking as if your life is over."

Her lovely head tilted to one side, her lips curled as if in confusion. Very gently, almost as if against her will, she reached and touched his face. "But, Gabriel . . . My life is over. I am an old woman. I'm eighty-seven years old. I'm dying." She paused, confused. "Didn't you know?"

HER NEW STUDENT WAS obviously crazy. When she had reminded him of her age, Gabriel Saint Pierre had choked back a horrified gasp as if in shock, backed away, then burst out her door and ran off . . . heaven-knew where.

When he called her beautiful, she almost felt it was true. She assumed at the time that he was flattering her, or maybe he recognized her own classic bone structure, her bright eyes, the wave in hair that once was full and glorious.

He truly seemed shocked, as if some veil had been pulled over his eyes, then snapped up inadvertently. If she had known it was there, she might have left it in place.

Amy sat in her favorite chair, having seized the opportunity in Gabriel's absence. She sipped tea and watched the sun setting on the pine trees through her window. The birds retired for sleep, and their soft songs filled the evening. She knew she would sleep soon, too, and this time, forever.

She expected to die. Her life had been full, and she had taken every gift offered to her and made the best of it. She had fulfilled her dream to teach others and used her talent to its best advantage, remembering her mother's wisdom, "*Talents are God's gifts to man, Amy. What you do with those talents are your gift to Him.*"

Throughout her life, she had taught her students to use their gifts well, and they had found joy. Gabriel Saint Pierre was an exception, but she'd known from the moment he burst into her cottage that he was different.

He hadn't returned since he left that afternoon. She had no idea where he was, and the night was closing in. Despite herself, she felt a little afraid. She finished her tea, then got up and walked around her cottage, arranging pictures and books on their shelves, vases on the mantelpiece. She went outside for one last walk around her garden, and her heart ached with the beauty of it.

She stood for a while by her dog Molly's grave. The little sheltie had died a few nights after Gabriel arrived. He had dug her grave, and Amy, crying, had planted the geraniums that now bloomed. Her heart fluttered, and she felt shaky, light-headed, so she went back inside.

Where are you? I am so alone, and I'm scared . . . scared.

GABRIEL WALKED INTO THE house, and found Amy lying in her bed. She looked weak and pale, but he had to have an answer. "Why didn't you tell me?"

She struggled to sit up, and she adjusted her robe to cover breasts that he could have sworn were full and round. "What? That I'm old? Gabriel, this may surprise you, but I thought my eighty-seven years were obvious. At least, seventy-two of them."

He had no idea what she meant. She rolled her eyes and laughed. "It was a joke. I thought I might pass for seventy-two." She paused. "Get it?"

He sat on the edge of her bed and stared. "You're dying."

"So much for my joke."

"I thought—I thought it was only a few years ago . . . The accident." She looked predictably confused, but he couldn't explain. He was beyond words and emotion threatened him in a way it hadn't in many long years, in lifetimes beyond count. "Amy, you're dying. I can't help you. Why did He send me here?"

Tears welled in his eyes and burned so hot that they stung. She touched his face again, soft and gentle. "You're not who you seem to be, are you?"

He swallowed tears and bowed his head. "No." There was no reason to hide the truth now. "I'm an angel."

She nodded, but didn't seem surprised. "Somehow I missed that." She smiled, then drew a quick breath as if she felt weak. "What do you want from me?"

He glared, despite his anguish. "I don't want anything from you. I came here to help you."

"How?"

"I don't know. I thought that because I had run into you, you missed some opportunity that was . . . set."

She stared, her mouth open. It was a beautiful mouth, even if she was eighty-six. Why couldn't he see her age? Or was she lying? "You . . . you were Indigo Crisp?"

"I prefer Gabriel."

She nodded. "Agreed." She paused. "So I killed you?"

He smiled, but the tears wouldn't leave his eyes. "No hard feelings. Look, I'm sorry. Somehow I screwed up your life by running into you, and I assumed it was because I kept you from that audition."

She clasped his wrist and squeezed. Her hands were so small. So small, and so cold. "Gabriel, I wasn't going to the audition."

"Where were you going?"

She closed her eyes for a moment, then drew her hand from his and folded them tight on her lap. "I was supposed to be auditioning, yes. It was a small orchestra, but my first big chance. But there was something I wanted more."

"What?"

She looked up and into his eyes, and he felt as if she had looked at him this way a thousand times. "I was going to see you."

Chills ran through him. He wanted to run, and he didn't know why. "Me?"

"Indigo Crisp. In concert, singing at Madison Square Garden on the Millennium Eve." She stared at her little hands, embarrassed. "I had won a backstage pass from a radio station. I skipped my audition to meet you."

They stared at each other. *An arrow* . . . And then he knew, he had known her all along. He stood up from her bed and stared down at her. "You have caused me so much pain."

She looked up at him. "I know."

"You've tormented me for centuries."

"I know."

"It was a trick—His trick—to make me see you again. I defied his cursed 'arrow,' and he tricked me!"

"I know."

She knew. Gabriel turned and walked through her door, leaving her there. He heard her whisper, as quiet as the wind through her windows. "I am so afraid."

Oceans and oceans of memory flooded through him, and he stumbled to his knees as it assailed him. He saw her, he saw himself, lifetimes ago—some wild barbarian culture enveloped and defined them, and they were fighting, because she was strong and he was strong, and they loved each other too much. Fear came opposite love, and anger from fear, and they were fighting. He raged at her, and she at him.

Don't leave me . . .

Go, for all I care . . .

I am not afraid . . .

When he came back, finally, after being away at war, their village had been destroyed, and she was dead. She had died alone, without him. Gabriel staggered to his feet and returned to her. She lay quietly on her little bed, her tiny hands folded over the lace coverlet. He lay beside her, and curved his body around hers to protect her.

"Amy, I will never leave you. Never."

Her fingers found his and she squeezed tight. "I am afraid."

"I am sorry, I am sorry, for everything, I am sorry." He was crying, because he had left her and he had been so angry. He had left her, and she had died alone, and for all those centuries, he couldn't forgive himself. Because she was part of him, he hadn't forgiven her, either.

She opened her blue eyes, struggling to hold onto her life that was over. "If you had known that I was going to be killed, would you have left me?"

"No, love."

"Did you really think I was fat and ugly?"

"You are the most beautiful woman, the most beautiful being, that has ever lived."

"Where will you go, next time? Will you have more glory than Indigo Crisp?"

"I will go with you, next time and forever after."

She smiled and sank into his arms, surrendering her body to its quiet end. He held her and sobbed, and felt his own body slipping away.

Her voice came as a whisper of the soul, the last words she spoke. "Gabriel, do you know who you are now?"

"Yes, love. I know. I know now." He kissed her forehead, and felt his soul at last mingle and join with hers. "I am."

Letting Go

Ken Wisman

Alex Layton floated in the far corner of the tiny New England church where he had come each Sunday for most of his adult life.

His wife Lois, his daughter Jen, his son Billy, and his son Eric sat in the first pew just below the podium on the altar. Billy and Jen looked grim. Lois kept dabbing at her eyes with a white handkerchief. But little Eric just stared up at his father floating in the far corner where the sun threw shadows, his father who sparkled like streaks of sunlight on the bottom of a pond.

Hello, Eric, Alex Layton said.

"Hello, Daddy," Eric whispered.

A crowd of people sat behind the family. Relatives Alex Layton hadn't seen for years. And old friends.

To the left of the altar, at the podium, the minister stood and spoke in solemn tones: "How do you measure a man? By how tall he stood? By how strong he was? By how much money he earned? Or do you measure a man by how much he loved?"

Alex had loved the old minister. Alex was glad he was delivering the eulogy. It would be straight from the heart. Not like what was usually said at such affairs.

"So sorry he passed on . . ."

"It's so terrible knowing he's gone . . ."

The pastor continued, his voice quavering with the emotion: "If love is the measure, then Alex Layton stood tall, the richest of men, and the strongest."

Sweet man, Alex thought. The minister could very easily have been delivering the eulogy for himself.

Alex floated down and hovered just above the coffin. Without emotion he looked through the closed case. *Passed on? Gone?* To everyone there—save one.

Little Eric smiled at Alex.

Alex smiled back.

"Don't leave, Daddy," Eric whispered.

Not on your life.

A FEW SHORT DAYS before, Alex Layton had felt the tightness in his chest like a huge mailed fist closing around his heart. A moment of pain and fear and he was floating free, watching his wife and two sons and daughter being consoled by the doctor.

And then he was floating away and outside the hospital. It was like dropping down a long dark tunnel. A light waited on the other side.

The light showed him things. It showed him his life like one long thread from end to end. And though there was no judgment in the light, it dwelled on moments of love and happiness and times shared.

Then the light showed him another light like an ocean. And Alex was asked to join the light that seemed to sing to him with a music that wasn't like any earthly music but a music that sang through everything. And Alex felt an overwhelming urge to go into the light and beyond it to see what was there and the meaning of death.

But Alex was sad and there was something that held him. And when he looked back, he saw a thin connecting thread that stretched all the way back through the tunnel to the Earth that was like a speck in the universe . . .

THREE DAYS AFTER THE funeral, Alex Layton hovered above the headpost on Eric's bed. Lois and Jen and Billy sat on the edge. Eric, being the youngest, was in his pajamas and ready for sleep.

Lois spoke to the children in soft tones: "It's been a few days now, kids. And I know it's hard, but we've got to put some of it behind us and get on with our own lives. I'll be going back to my job tomorrow. I want you all to return to school."

Billy put on a brave face. "Okay, Mom." It wasn't hard to see that he, being the oldest, felt he was the man of the house now. How old was he? Eleven.

Jen, nine and the most emotional of the three kids, felt no restrictions about holding back her feelings. "I miss Dad," she said, her voice cracking.

Lois put her arm around her and Jen sobbed. Then Billy leaned his head onto his mother's shoulder and buried his face. He cried silently, embarrassed by his tears.

Eric crawled out from under the covers and hugged his family affectionately. But he shed no tears.

Later, when Jen and Billy were asleep, Lois returned to the room and, seeing Eric awake, sat on the side of his bed.

"Sweetheart," she whispered, "it's okay to cry."

Eric stared at her with his huge, brown eyes. But he said nothing.

"What I mean is it's all right to mourn for your father," she said.

And Alex knew Eric was on the verge of telling Lois the truth. *Don't tell her, son. It would only upset her more,* Alex said.

Later, when Lois went away, little Eric spoke to where his father glowed in a corner of the ceiling. "Daddy, are you like the angels Mom used to tell me about. Are you my guardian angel?"

You bet.

"G'night, Daddy."

'Night, son.

But Alex no longer needed sleep. Instead, he played the whole scene back and thought about his family.

His wife Lois. Sensitive. But on the inside strong and drawing on that innate strength now to pull her family together.

His daughter Jen. She most likely taking the longest time to forget the pain. But in the end as strong if not stronger than her mother. His son Billy. He would weather it best perhaps.

The truth was that, once the pain was forgotten, each would find his or her niche in life. For Jen he had had great expectations. A doctor perhaps with her compassion. Billy, a leader. Lois—with necessity motivating her—rising to a high position in her job.

And Eric?

Little Eric. There was the rub.

. . . AND POISED BETWEEN LIFE and death Alex Layton had hesitated. Then Alex asked the light to repeat certain scenes from his life, and the light complied.

And suddenly Alex was there in the delivery room with his wife looking down at the tiny frail infant. Alex knew without the doctor telling him that something was wrong. And Alex wasn't at all surprised later when the doctor told him about the complications and the heart murmur and how the boy would need extra care until he was old enough to be operated on and the problem could be corrected . . .

ALEX FOLLOWED ERIC TO school. When Eric got to the schoolyard, most of the other kids ignored him. Alex, who could see much clearer into people now, saw that it wasn't unkindness that kept the other kids away. No, they were a little afraid of Eric. He was the kid whose father had died, and death was a mystery they were all just learning about.

Eric didn't seem to mind the isolation. He smiled and whispered: "Are you still there, Daddy?" And Alex, who was invisible to his son in daylight, said back: *Still here.*

Then the bell rang and Alex followed his son inside.

Eric's teacher, Mr. Hodkins, was a tall, thin man with a sour face. And the very first thing he announced was a spelling bee.

"We'll use the words we've been studying the past two weeks," the teacher said. "Let's split up into two groups."

It was, of course, unfair since Eric had missed a week. And especially unfair since Eric was quite good at spelling and this bee counted as a test.

But the spelling bee progressed well for Eric. He went through the first five rounds with ease whereas everyone else was eliminated save one boy in his group and two girls in the other.

"Mountain," Mr. Hodkins said, pronouncing the word distinctly. He gave it to Rachel Childress who was on the other side. Rachel missed the word and Mr. Hodkins gave it to Jimmy O'Neill, who was on Eric's side. Jimmy missed and the word bounced over to Judy Nelson.

She any good? Alex asked.

"No one's ever beaten her," Eric whispered.

"Mountain," Judy said. "M-O-U-N-T-A-I-N." She smiled with supreme confidence at Eric. Obviously Judy Nelson wasn't above flaunting her superiority and taking advantage of being Mr. Hodkins's favorite.

"Excellent," Mr. Hodkins said.

Alex could see that Eric was nervous. In the last two rounds they had entered unknown territory and Eric had stayed alive by blind luck.

Then Alex saw something he didn't like. He could see down into the souls of people and knew things about them and what they were thinking.

Mr. Hodkins was eager to get the bee over with. It was a foregone conclusion that Judy Nelson would win it and they were already fifteen minutes into the history lesson. Mr. Hodkins did not look at the list when he chose the next word.

"Eric, spell—uh—chrysanthemum," Mr. Hodkins said offhandedly.

There was a slight murmur in the class. Those who had studied knew it wasn't a word on their homework list.

Your teacher isn't playing fair, son, Alex said. He was surprised that he could still feel so much anger. *Let's even up the sides.*

"I don't understand, Daddy," Eric whispered.

"What was that?" Mr. Hodkins said, smiling and glancing at the clock.

Repeat after me, said Eric's father.

"C-H-R-Y-S-A-N-T-H-E-M-U-M," Eric repeated.

The class gasped, A few clapped.

Mr. Hodkins looked puzzled. He recovered and gave Judy Nelson an easy word which she spelled but not with her usual bravado.

Mr. Hodkins thought a moment. "Pterodactyl," he said.

The class groaned. An impossible word. A word beyond the ability of a mortal man to spell.

And yet Eric called out unfalteringly: "P-T-E-R-O-D-A-C-T-Y-L."

The whole class clapped and cheered. They were totally behind Eric now.

"Uh—bounty," Mr. Hodkins addressed Judy Nelson.

The class laughed. A few booed and jeered.

Judy's face burned with shame. "I don't know that one, Mr. Hodkins," she said.

"Try," Mr. Hodkins said with unnecessary sternness.

Judy broke into tears. "I don't know it," she said. She sat in her seat and buried her head in her arms.

The class held its breath.

"B-O-U-N-T-Y," Eric called out.

And half the class rose to crowd around him and pat him on the back.

. . . AND AFTER ALEX HAD asked the light to play back the scene of Eric's birth, Alex asked to see the nights that followed. The nights Alex lay in his bed listening for the monitor alarm, hating the sound of it yet listening with all his being because it was the only way to know that Eric's breathing had stopped. And Alex watched those nights when he ran with all his might into the room to snatch his son up to breathe life back into his chest.

And something passed between Alex and his son then. Something like love but deeper than love . . .

ALEX FOLLOWED HIS SON home after school. Eric had no friends. He was shy and felt his difference—the years on the monitor, the illnesses, living on the edge of death had made him an introverted child. And every attempt on Alex's part to break him out of that mold had failed.

On this particular spring afternoon Alex was enjoying the day through his son, who walked at a slow pace. Eric laughed a lot and talked in subdued tones to his father. Many people passed, but Eric was young enough that talking to himself wasn't such an oddity, and these people only smiled.

Then Eric came to the middle of a block where large oaks with low branches grew. He threw his books down, turned, and waited.

What's up? Alex asked.

"You'll see," said Eric.

Soon a small figure came around the corner. And Eric ran to a branch on the oak and hung upside down. The figure came to the spot, stopped, and looked at Eric.

Pretty, Alex said. He chuckled to himself. Kids grew so quickly. He himself didn't show interest in a girl till he was twice Eric's age.

"Hi," Eric called to the girl.

"Hrrmp," the girl said, turning away.

Doesn't seem to be impressed, Alex said to Eric. *Not surprised. Hanging from a tree isn't exactly an original idea.*

The girl yawned and appeared on the point of making a quick departure.

Let's show her something really good, Alex said. *You game?*

Eric giggled and nodded. And suddenly he was doing slow loops around the branch. The loops increased in speed and suddenly Eric was hurtling up to the bough above.

Eric whirled around the bough, changed direction, and whirled around again.

Get ready, now, Alex said. *Here comes the grand finale.*

Eric laughed and closed his eyes and hurtled into space, turned three impossible somersaults, and stood on the branch of an oak twenty feet away. Eric tight-roped the thin branch, reached the end, jumped up, somersaulted, and landed on his feet on the ground—right next to the girl.

Ask her if you can carry her books, Alex said,

"Can I carry your books?" Eric asked shyly.

The girl, her mouth agape and eyes glassy, handed over her books without a word.

⌒

. . . AND ALEX HAD ASKED the light for one more set of scenes. Of the time when Eric was old enough for his operation.

And Alex was watching there in the hospital with his son in an oxygen tent and still unconscious but Alex wanting to be there when his son woke up.

"Don't leave me, Daddy."

"Not on your life."

And how Alex got special permission to stay in the hospital to be near his son. And how Alex took a leave of absence from work to be home with Eric until he recovered.

"I'm afraid, Daddy."

"I'm here, son. I won't leave."

And it was to show the light that Alex called for these memories and to ask the favor . . .

ON A PARTICULARLY BRIGHT Sunday morning Alex followed his son out of the house and into the garage where Eric mounted his bike. And Alex followed his son like a kite attached as the boy cut through the breeze of the fine morning that smelled like clean sheets and fresh milk and grass grown richly green.

Feet up, Alex said to his son.

Eric giggled and raised his feet, and his father pushed the bike along at a fast clip so that the wind cut cool and exhilarating around his face. Then Eric came to the park where a group of boys were gathered—some from his class, some from a grade or two higher.

"We can't play," one of the boys was saying. "You need eighteen and we still only got seventeen."

This elicited a series of suggestions that were each voted down. Then one of the boys noticed Eric watching from a distance. "How 'bout that kid?"

"Naw," said a boy named Bingo Honneger. He stood a head taller than everyone else and apparently was one of the team's captains. "He stinks. Besides he's too short."

But Eric seemed the only solution around, and some of the other boys disagreed.

"He never plays anyhow." Bingo Honneger looked contemptuously at Eric.

Eric was about ready to remount his bike but Alex said, *Tell them you'll play.*

"I'll play," said Eric.

"Not on our side you won't," Bingo Honneger said.

The other captain conferred with his other players. "Look. We put the shrimp out in right where he can't do much harm. And we let him bat last."

There was a sound of reluctance. "You got a better idea?" the captain said. And the game began.

Eric's team took the field first. Eric borrowed a mitt from someone on the other side and ran out to right field.

Alex hovered above his son. *How'd that big kid get that nickname?* Alex asked.

"Fighting," Eric whispered. "He always tries to pop the other guy in the nose. When he does, the kids standing around yell, 'Bingo.'"

I knew kids like that when I was a boy, Alex said. *I always wished there was someone around to take them down a peg or two.*

The first batter got up and hit a grounder right at the first baseman and was out. The second kid struck out and, after a lengthy altercation, sat down. Then the third batter hit a grounder between the shortstop and the third baseman, who collided. And before things could be sorted out, the kid was on second base.

Fourth up, batting cleanup, was Bingo Honneger.

If anything's hit your way, put your glove out, Alex said. Then he floated in and above Bingo Honneger and home plate. The boy was eyeing Eric out in right and taking his practice swings pointed in that direction. He knew where to hit it.

Bingo connected with the first pitch. The ball arced up, but for Alex it was all in slow motion. He grabbed the ball and steered it, and from his bird's eye view he watched his son below.

Eric ran, his head up, his glove out. He ran, his legs striving and straining. He closed his eyes, knowing he'd miss, but trying with all his might nonetheless. Then he heard the thwack in his glove and looking down he saw it resting like an egg in its nest.

"You little turd," Bingo Honneger said to Eric as he ran in. "Really lucky catch." And he tripped Eric by sticking out his leg.

Eric picked himself up and dusted himself off. A couple of the other kids on the other side laughed as they took the field.

Don't worry, son, Alex said. *We'll nail this guy.*

But the first inning didn't produce much for Eric's side. Just two quick singles and three quick outs.

The game proceeded apace. The fielding got a little shakier, the arguments louder. Eric, who was at the bottom of the order, got up two times but had no opportunity to hit the ball. Bingo Honneger, who pitched for the other side, claimed sudden lapses in control and threw the softball at Eric. Bingo hit Eric once in the shoulder and once in the leg.

Then it was the bottom of the ninth. Bingo Honneger's side was winning, 9-6. The middle of the order was up for Eric's side. But the first batter grounded to the first baseman and the second batter struck out.

Then the third kid hit a clean shot over the shortstop's head. The fourth was hit by the ball. The fifth was on by an error. And Eric was up.

If ever there was a setup for a grand-slam home run, this was it.

Bingo Honneger was too crafty to hit Eric a third time and force a run in and pitch to the lead-off man. No, he would pitch to the kid and go home the hero.

Bingo lobbed one in and Eric swung. It was a weak swing, but it connected. And the softball flew across the ground as slowly as a butterfly flies on an August afternoon.

Bingo Honneger felt like a hawk feels when it sees a mouse in the grass and yards away from its hole. He flew from the mound and pounced on the ball. But the ball seemed to take a bad bounce and arced over his head.

Bingo had good reflexes and he turned and lunged at the ball where it had come to rest ten feet behind him. He covered the ball with his mitt, scooped it up, and reached in with his right hand to throw to first—except the ball wasn't there.

"Behind you," the shortstop called.

Bingo looked around, spotted the ball, dove for it, and threw it to first. The ball sailed six feet over the first baseman's head. The first baseman rushed to retrieve it. Meanwhile, Eric ran around first and was on his way to second and one run was home.

The first baseman threw the ball to second base. But Bingo Honneger was on the run to back up the second baseman, and Bingo somehow lost his footing and collided with the second base-man. The ball sailed past third base. Meanwhile, Eric ran around second and was on his way to third and two runs were home.

By the time the third baseman got to the ball, three runs were home, and Eric was rounding third. The third baseman threw home and hit the cut-off man, Bingo Honneger. Bingo caught the ball easily enough, but it dropped out of his mitt. Bingo dove for the ball, but wherever he put his hand, the ball wasn't—it seemed to have a mind of its own.

Finally, the captain of the other team went out to Bingo Honneger on the field. The captain bent and picked up the ball and looked at Bingo Honneger as though he were crazy.

"Game's over," the captain said, and he dropped the softball into Bingo's mitt.

. . . AND WHEN THE LAST scene had been shown, Alex explained to the light why he couldn't leave the Earth as yet. There were things still left undone. Troubles he had not helped Eric weather and work through; things he had never told his son.

And the light had let Alex follow the thread back . . .

AFTER THE GAME ALEX followed Eric to his bike and they pedaled through the neighborhood. Around suppertime, Alex had his son head for home.

Eric was walking his bike by the lot with the oak trees, when Bingo Honneger pushed his way out of the bushes.

"Been waitin' to talk to you, turd," Bingo said, He pushed Eric's bike down.

Eric, a head and a half shorter, stood his ground.

"I don't know how you done it," Bingo said. "But what you done was real stupid."

He pushed Eric down.

"I'm gonna smash your face in if you even dare to stand," Bingo said.

I want you to stand slowly, Alex told his son. *And I want you to repeat everything I say. Let me do the rest.*

Eric stood, and Bingo Honneger lunged for him. But Eric sidestepped, stuck out his leg, and the bigger boy went sprawling.

Bingo rose in a rage, his arms swinging. Eric's arms blocked each punch deftly, now left, now right.

Then Eric slipped his right hand under Bingo's belt—and lifted Bingo two feet off the ground.

"Bullies come in all sizes, in all ages," Eric said. "Every once in a while they pick on the wrong person. I'm the wrong person. Don't do it again."

Bingo was terrified. His legs and arms paddled like an overturned turtle's. Eric let him drop to the ground. Bingo stood and ran and never looked back.

. . . AND THE LIGHT HAD followed Alex to the earth. Alex could sense the light waiting just at the entrance to the tunnel. He could sense it watching, observing but never interfering with what Alex did . . .

ON MONDAY, ALEX FOLLOWED his son back to the schoolyard. Bingo Honneger was there with some of his cronies. Bingo talked loudly in earshot of Eric. But when Eric came close to the group, Bingo broke from the circle and ran a little way off.

The other kids laughed. Some gathered near Eric, who was encouraged by their laughter. He walked toward Bingo. Bingo backed away. Eric ran ten steps. Bingo ran twenty.

That's enough, son, Alex said.

"He deserves it," Eric whispered. "He deserves it good."

Eric stomped his feet and Bingo Honneger turned and ran down the road to the jeers and taunts of everyone on the playground.

The bell rang and once inside, Mr. Hodson took the class through the reading assignment. Then he announced a surprise quiz in arithmetic.

Eric wrote his name on the top of the paper passed to him and paused.

What's wrong? Alex asked.

"I didn't do my assignment," Eric whispered.

Why not? Alex asked.

"Help me, Daddy," Eric said.

I can't, Alex said.

"You did before," Eric said.

That was different, Alex said.

"If you don't, I'll flunk."

Alex sighed and helped and swore it would be the last time.

Later, at lunch, the boys in the class chose up sides for three-inning softball. Eric's reputation had preceded him, and he was one of the first ones picked. He was put at shortstop, a position of status.

Eric's side was up first, and he was third man in the lineup. The first batter was on through an error. The second batter hit a clean double up the middle. When it came to Eric's turn, he just stood at the plate and let the first ball whiff by without a swing.

"Help me," Eric said under his breath.

You can hit it without my help, Alex said. *Eye on the ball. Level swing.*

Eric took a swing and missed. Strike two.

All right, but this is the last, Alex said.

And the next ball Eric hit cleanly through the second baseman's legs and reached first safely.

In the field, Eric whispered, "Help me with the grounders, Daddy. I'm real bad with grounders."

Not this time, Alex said. *You're on your own. He moved off and away from his son.*

Eric, who couldn't see his father in daylight, closed his eyes and put down his mitt.

The first boy up whacked a vicious grounder straight at Eric. The ball hit a stone, bounced, and struck Eric in the forehead. He fell unconscious to the ground.

⌒

. . . AND NOW IN THE second week on the Earth the light drew toward Alex where he hovered in Eric's room near the unconscious boy's bed.

It wasn't supposed to happen like this, *Alex said to the light.* You saw him. He was turning into a bully. And a cheat.

The light said nothing. Instead, it showed Alex scenes from his life.

In the first scene, Alex was holding Eric's hand as the boy walked along. And suddenly Alex let go and Eric took his first few steps. And before falling down, Eric smiled with such a look of triumph and accomplishment that it brought tears to Alex's eyes.

In the second scene, Alex was following behind and holding the back fender of Eric's first two-wheeler bike. Eric fought to stabilize the handlebars, and when he looked back, Alex let go. Eric went down the block and back again and the same look of triumph was in his eyes.

In the third scene, Alex held his son's hand as Eric boarded the bus for the first time for kindergarten. There was no look of triumph this time as he let go. But when the boy returned that day the smile was there and the sense of accomplishment.

I understand, *Alex said to the light.* I understand.

WHILE THE BOY WAS unconscious, Alex entered his dreams. He appeared to Eric as he had appeared in his prime—tall, strong, handsome. The boy went to him and hugged him. Then Alex held the boy at arm's length.

"Listen to me, Eric," Alex said. "Some of what I tell you now might not make sense right away. But later when you're older, it will."

"You're going to leave me, aren't you?" the boy said and hugged his father.

"I can't take every test for you, Eric. I can't hit every ball. If I rob you of your chance to lose, then I rob you of your chance to win. I can't go through your lifetime giving you what you've got to earn for yourself."

"I'll do my homework next time," Eric said. "I promise, Daddy. I promise."

"I know you will," Alex said.

"Don't leave, Daddy."

"I'd only be cheating you out of your own life," Alex said. "Remember, Eric. Remember. Sometimes loving is letting go."

Alex faded in the dream. Eric grabbed at the air and suddenly he was awake.

Lois smiled at him. "You got quite a bump on the head."

"He's gone, Mom," Eric said.

She looked puzzled.

"Dad is gone," Eric said. He burst into sobs.

She smiled through her own tears, happy that Eric was at last able to let go, sad for his pain. "Your father loved you so much," she said. "You will always have that, Eric. But he's gone now. And sometimes even though you love someone, you've got to let go."

Eric nodded. "That's what he said, Mom."

"Then you know it must be true." And Lois drew him to her and surrounded him in her arms.

I'm Not Making This Up

Susan Sizemore

What are you doing with your writing, channeling Ambrose Bierce? What is your problem, McCarthy?"

I considered my editor's words, and despite her tone, I chose to take them as a compliment. "You flatter me. Bierce was a fine and funny Victorian journalist."

"His nickname was Bitter Bierce, and he was so sarcastic he was toxic. Why are you going that route, Dan? You used to be the funniest man in the world. And nice. Dare I say it—inspirational?"

That made me want to gag. "I take it you're not happy with my column."

"Your nastiness is hurting circulation. Do you know what kind of letters you're getting lately? Not to mention the e-mail."

"I don't have time to read fan mail."

"I wouldn't call it fan mail if I were you. And," she added the words I'd been expecting, "you have heard the word *deadline*, right? Know the meaning of it?"

"I've still got two years on my contract with the *Journal*," I answered. "I'm sure I'll turn in something in that time. You have other concerns, talk to my agent."

I hung up the phone. Then I unplugged it. Then I threw it out the window. It hit the swimming pool and floated gently on top of a green coating of algae. This reminded me that I should do something about the house, like maybe clean it up, or make a house payment. There'd been something in the mail about overdue electrical bills. I half hoped the electricity would get cut off. Then I couldn't turn on the computer and I wouldn't have to write column inches to turn in to a snotty editor that my so-called-where-were-they-when-I-needed-them fans would hate anyway.

I sat back in my chair, closed my eyes and ignored Paisley when the big black and tan mutt butted her head against my thigh and whimpered. The last thing I wanted was a dog feeling sorry for me. I didn't want anything or anyone—except Alison. "Ali is dead." I made myself say it out loud. I made myself say it at least once a day, when I was alone and the pain tearing me apart squeezed my heart so hard I had to make a noise or die.

When the doorbell rang I ignored it like I always did lately. A lot of stuff got delivered to my home office. The FedEx and UPS guys had learned to just leave whatever they brought, cause I wasn't going to open up for anybody. The package would get brought in by the kids whenever they came home. They'd leave it on the growing pile on the hall table and that would be that.

Except that this delivery person was a persistent sucker. The doorbell kept ringing. After a while he gave up on the doorbell and a heavy hand started pounding on the door. Paisley began to bark, and the dumb dog *never* noticed anything. Her complete inability to behave like a watchdog was one of her saving graces. Not this time. Dog not only started barking, but running back and forth across my office like a crazed wolf. She let out a howl to wake the dead. Whoever was pounding on the door set her off to the point of making me nervous.

I should have let it go. Why should I care if some delivery person made a fool of himself and bruised his knuckles on the door, or that the dog was going wacko? Eventually, though, just to make the noise stop, I got up and went to the front door.

That was my first mistake.

~

The McCarthy Zone
Meet Mr. Jordan

THE GUY AT THE *door was the size of an L.A. Lakers center, and he wasn't exactly the neatest dresser in the world. I've seen homeless people with better tailoring. His shirt was plaid, his baggy pants were striped pajama bottoms. Several days' growth of stubble covered his dark-skinned face. Big brown eyes glared at me from under a heavy brow ridge. There was a misty rain falling on this spring afternoon, which didn't help. In fact, he smelled like a wet chicken. You know I'd never lie to you, gentle readers. Maybe to the IRS, but not to you. He smelled like a chicken cause his wings were wet. Of course, they also looked like they could use a good cleaning.*

Yeah, I said wings.

The angel held up a newspaper in one meaty hand. "Your biggest fan is pissed as hell at you," he said as he backed me into the house. One of his wings caught on the doorframe for a moment, then he was inside the house and the door slammed behind him. He was oversized, massive. His presence filled the room. His eyes flashed with a fire I wouldn't exactly call divine. Insane, maybe, but not divine. "When I say hell *I am not being figurative. You get my drift?"*

I nodded. What else could I do? There was a stinking wet angel the size of Shaquille O'Neal standing in my living room waving a newspaper at me. It didn't occur to me to call the cops until much later, and by then it was way too late. So I kept nodding.

The angel—let's call him Jordan—went right on talking, hitting me repeatedly on the shoulder with the rolled-up newspaper while he spoke. "What the hell is the matter with you, McCarthy? Don't you know God put you on this earth to make people smile? To make 'em see that life is serious but that they can't take themselves seriously all the time? Maybe you once thought you were put here to make fart jokes, but the Light's got different ideas about your purpose. You're not fulfilling your purpose. You used to make God laugh. God's not laughing at you anymore, boy. I'm the one who has to bring the Eminent One the Sunday newspaper and I'm getting really fed up with the thunder and lightning that happens every time the Holy Presence reads your latest column. Singed me good, last week. Not to mention what getting coffee and orange juice thrown at me is doing to my wings." He jerked a thumb at his feathers. "These things need to be dry cleaned, did you know that?"

No, I didn't, but Jordan didn't give me time to point this out. It occurred to me that I had the bad luck to have my column syndicated in whatever newspaper God read on Sundays.

"God reads all of 'em."

A mind-reading seven-foot angel was stinking up my house. Great. I would have told myself it was all a hallucination, if it hadn't been for the smell.

"Something has to be done," Jordan went on. "I'm here to do it." He looked around the living room. "I've got a little vacation time coming and I'm taking it here." He looked at the couch like he was measuring it for fit. Then turned that dark glare back on me. "You've got a gue-stroom, right?"

If I'd said no would he have politely left? I didn't think so. Besides, lying to him didn't cross my mind at the time. Mostly I kept thinking, there's a seven-foot angel in my living room. I did not for a moment doubt that he was an angel. I hadn't been drinking. I wasn't on any controlled substance, though I vaguely remembered having a couple of aspirin earlier in the day. I was not hallucinating. There was a seven-foot angel in my living room.

Telling me to shape up. Telling me he was moving into my house.

I'm not sure which I resented more.

At the time I couldn't think of anything to say.

The yelling didn't start until later.

The McCarthy Zone
The Fire of Heaven

"JORDAN'S MAKING PANCAKES."

I didn't know if it was Saturday morning or afternoon, or even if it was Saturday. But the kids were home and the angel was cooking, so I made the assumption it was morning. I would like to tell you that the angel had left. That he was a figment of my imagination, a symbolic manifestation—but, gentle readers, symbolic manifestations do not do to bathrooms what this uninvited houseguest did. Nor do they shed feathers all over the house. Nor do you leave the room whenever they take off their shoes.

Now he was cooking.

"Oh, God."

"Daddy?"

I lifted my head from my hands to find Missy standing in the office doorway, looking nervous. She'd grown, I noticed, and it seemed like I hadn't seen my thirteen-year old daughter for a long time. We shared the same house, she and Danny and the dog and I, but not much else since Alison's car went off the road late one night and there was no Alison to share anything with any more.

"He says you call him Jordan," Missy went on before I could say anything. "Is he like a nanny, or something?" She put a skinny hand on a non-existent hip. "And what's with the wings?"

"What's with the pierced nose?" I asked in turn. "Who told you you could get your nose pierced?"

"You did."

I didn't deny it. There were a lot of things I couldn't deny doing or not doing recently. Was that a faint glimmer of parental guilt? Whatever it was, I knocked it down hard and looked at the carpet. It hadn't been vacuumed for a long time. That only made it more interesting, though it looked more like a carpet of Paisley fur than the color I vaguely remembered picking out with Alison. At least Paisley could always be depended on to clean up any dropped food.

It wasn't until I smelled the grease fire that I became actively involved in the morning's activities.

It did not help that the damned angel was excitedly flapping his wings and fanning the fire as I ran into the kitchen. Missy was shrieking. Danny stood by the glass door to the deck silently watching. Paisley was unconcernedly licking up a bowl of spilled pancake batter. The flames were licking up around the range hood by the time I grabbed the fire extinguisher—and discovered the damn thing was empty.

Swearing, I pulled everything out of a cabinet by the stove until I found some flour, and used that to douse the fire.

"What is all this stuff?" I asked once I noticed the contents of the cabinet scattered on counters and the floor. Alison would know.

Then I turned on the angel. "What do you mean by endangering my kids?" I'd never been so angry in my life. I hadn't felt anything but pain for an endless time and now this new furious, protective, reaction took me so hard it left me shaking. I wanted to gather Missy and Danny up in my arms and hold them tight. Only, they were on opposite sides of the big kitchen (Ali loved her big kitchen) from me, and there was this huge winged creature looming before me.

The angel didn't notice my mood. He was wearing MC Hammer garage-sale, tiger-striped parachute pants and an orange muscle shirt. The effect was frightening. The pancake dough on his shirt and the dusting of flour covering his face and chest didn't make him any less menacing. He looked down at me and asked, "Don't you feed these children anything but Pop Tarts?"

"They like Pop Tarts."

"How would you know?"

A can rolled off the counter and hit me on the foot. I barely noticed the excruciating agony this set off. Paisley started licking flour off the floor in front of me.

From his spot by the door, my fifteen-year-old son demanded, "Yeah, how would you know?"

That's my boy. Honest to a fault, and sassy and surly as hell. When I look at him I see myself at fifteen. It's a wonder my parents didn't leave me in the woods to be raised by wolves. It briefly crossed my mind that maybe I should leave Danny to be raised by an angel. Then I looked at the angel. I'd been ignoring my son's barbs for weeks now. They'd just become background noise, but for some reason this time his words stung.

I looked around at the mess. For an instant I felt like a man for having saved the day. That passed with the recognition that the mess went deeper than a little grease fire and the contents of a cabinet strewn around the place. The angel had turned back to the stove and was ladling pancake dough into a skillet full of smoldering flour. Missy was dancing from foot to foot, her gaze nervously on the angel's wide, winged back. I could feel Danny's gaze boring angrily into me. He was like me that way too, angry cause his mom was dead and I was there and the world wouldn't go away and leave me—him—alone.

Smoke started billowing up from the skillet. The angel's wings fanned the smoke. He began to whistle, so off-tune it was painful to hear.

"Come on," I said to the kids. "Let's go to McDonald's."

It didn't occur to me until later that the first small miracle, that first small baby-step back into the responsible adult world, came because I was driven out of my house by impending smoke inhalation.

The McCarthy Zone
The Curse of the Pharaohs

GENTLE READERS, MY EDITOR *recently accused me of being inspirational.
I'm not sure what I inspired other than possible severe nausea in my crit-
ics, but there you have it. She called me inspirational. And nice. I'm not
'nice,' all right? That's worse than calling a guy 'cute.' We will not go
into the things Alison used to call me, but occasionally she did refer to me
as cute, an appellation no red-blooded American male wants to hear.*

*I recalled such a devastatingly embarrassing incident of being called
cute while engaged in the manly act of grilling steaks on the patio in front
of a half dozen of my male peers. She called me cute because I was wearing
a matching apron and chef's hat that she had given me, I had hated, that
she knew I hated, but that I'd worn because she had given it to me. For
her I would do any ludicrous thing, even be cute.*

*If she were here in bed beside me now, I thought as the windows and
walls rattled around me, I'd let her call me cute. But Ali wasn't here. I
was alone. Even Paisley had deserted my room to sleep with Jordan. It's
said that all dogs go to heaven, and I think Paisley was trying to make
points, just in case the matter of those two rabbits she'd caught when she
was a pup got brought up when she reached the pearly gates.*

*I was lying in bed wide awake as I frequently did. This time with a
pillow over my head, but it didn't help much. I was trying to stay still
and numb and unthinking, but was too irritated to reach my preferred
state of uncaring detachment. Still, I didn't notice anyone was in the
room until I got a hard poke in the shoulder.*

"Daddy?"

Missy.

*I pretended to be asleep. She poked again. Harder. Then pulled off the
pillow. I cracked an eye and looked at her in the dim moonlight coming in
the open window.*

"Jordan's snoring."

*This was, to say the least, an understatement. The whole neighbor-
hood knew he was snoring. Either that, or I had a 747 warming up for
takeoff in my guest room. Jordan was, I knew, God's secret weapon for
raising the dead come judgment day. I don't know why no one had com-
plained or called the cops yet. Maybe Jordan's presence was some leftover
biblical plague that only the McCarthy family was being made to suffer—
though I didn't think we were related to any Egyptian pharaohs.*

"Daddy!"

I sat up. *"What?"*

Missy pointed toward the door. *"Daddies are supposed to do some-thing."*

"Is there a monster in your closet?" I asked her.

Missy stamped her foot. With her fists on her skinny hips. *"Daddy!"*

It's amazing how many nuances a kid can get into that one defining word. Missy was suddenly using it to demand the right of every child to the privileges and protections she was entitled to from a male parent to a dues-paying kid. She was telling me to make him stop. To make it better. That she might have entered puberty, but I still had to take care of her sometimes.

We hadn't been into that parent-child thing lately. I'd forgotten how. The kids ignored me. I ignored them. We rambled around the house each locked in our own lonely silence. Silence had become a habit. But the place wasn't silent tonight. A couple of days ago I might have told Missy to go away, to live with the discomfort—or some other bitter fool thing—but with Jordan making that ungodly racket I simply couldn't work up any indifference to the situation. I got up.

"Go back to bed," I told my daughter. *"I'll take care of it."*

When I left the room I took the pillow I'd been using to cover my head with me.

Funny thing was, Jordan was snoring, but he wasn't asleep. At least, he opened his eyes, sat up, stretched out his cheesy wings and looked at me when I walked into the guest room. *"Thanks for the extra pillow,"* he said, and took it from me—though I was standing in the doorway and he didn't actually leave the bed on the other side of the room. Angels have long reaches.

I had been planning on stuffing it over his face. *"You're bothering my kid."*

He crossed his arms. *"I'm keeping you up."*

"That too."

"You don't sleep much anyway. You keep going over how it's all your fault she's dead. How if you hadn't been coming home from doing a lec-ture tour your wife wouldn't have had to pick you up at the airport. If she hadn't been on her way to pick you up at the airport she wouldn't have gotten killed. If you weren't a famous writer you wouldn't have been on the lecture tour. If you hadn't been away from home—"

"I don't need to hear this."

"So you haven't been away from home since the funeral. Like that's going to bring her back."

"I work at home."

"Wallowing ain't working. Being angry at your readers for daring to make you popular isn't working."

"It's coping."

"Yeah, right." He snorted, and settled back down on the pile of pillows with his wings folded forward forming a blanket.

I wasn't ready to give it up yet. "That's cheap pop psychology, you know."

"I'm a cheap angel."

I slammed the door and stalked back to my room, where I settled down seated on the edge of my bed. Who needed to sleep? At least he didn't start snoring again, that was one mission accomplished, one little victory. I didn't notice that Paisley came with me until she jumped up on the bed and put her head in my lap. "Why am I angry at thousands of people I'll never know?" I asked the dog. Alison would have said that it was stupid. "Why be mean?" she'd have said.

"Why indeed?" I asked. Why indeed, gentle readers? I didn't know, but I did lie down and finally go to sleep alone in that big empty bed. It wasn't any less empty when I woke up . . . but I did notice that the sun was shining for once.

The McCarthy Zone
Come Here Often?

IF THERE'S ONE POSITIVE *thing I can say about Jordan it's that he makes good coffee. Every now and then a feather might drift into a cup, but we've lived with Paisley's shedding in this house for long enough not to be too picky about what was in our food.*

But on another front, I tried not to breathe as he sat down across the kitchen island from me and concentrated on wolfing down a plate full of scrambled eggs. Watching him eat eggs kind of bothered me. Seemed cannibalistic somehow, what with the wings and all . . .

Finally, I had to have some air and my nose grew somewhat numb. I took a deep breath and said, "You ever hear that cleanliness is next to godliness?"

"I'm on vacation."

The kids had made the excuse that they had to go to school just to get out of the house. The place was quiet. It was quiet a lot these days, but I noticed for once. And I noticed that I missed Missy and Danny's presence. She was shrill, he was surly . . . but they were mine. Mine and Alison's. Alison'd be pissed at my behavior toward them lately. Realizing that made me squirm inside. It was a good guilt. Necessary.

I glared at the angel. "This is how you save people? By making them miserable?"

"This is how I spend my vacations." He finished the eggs and drank some coffee. "I like hanging out with writers."

I thought about this for a while, and said, "So you're why Hemingway killed himself."

"It cured his writer's block." Being an angel, and honest, he confessed after a moment. "I've never met Hemingway. The last writer I hung out with was Ambrose Bierce. Man had a bad attitude."

"He disappeared in Mexico and was never heard from again."

The angel leaned close and whispered, "He joined a monastery. Don't tell anybody. It was our little secret."

"I won't tell a soul."

All right, gentle readers, I'm telling you, but if Ambrose "Bitter Bierce" Bierce is currently rolling in embarrassment in a Mexican grave I don't figure it's our problem. Besides, I know I can count on you not to tell a soul.

"I'm going to work," I told the angel and headed for my office. First, though, I decided to make a bathroom stop. Which got abruptly interrupted when I opened the door. I backed out, closed the door, and went back to the kitchen.

"Who's that woman cleaning the bathroom?"

"Maggie."

"A name is not an explanation. What's she doing here?"

"She's your new housekeeper."

"Housekeeper!"

"She's homeless. You're helpless. It's a match made in heaven." He smiled, and I noticed that he had very sharp teeth. It occurred to me that he really wasn't an angel. "Angels have to be helpful. That doesn't mean we have to be nice."

I was tempted to go into a self-pitying tirade about how it was just my luck to end up with a smelly, cranky, slovenly, free-loading member of the heavenly host. Then it occurred to me that maybe we get the angel we deserve, and I didn't have the fit I wanted.

He nodded sagely at my restraint, and said, "But I make great coffee."

A housekeeper. He'd brought some homeless woman—a young woman with clean but worn clothing and shining black braids and a hopeful expression in her big brown eyes—into my house! To cook and clean and whatever else it was that women did to keep civilization going while men played with riding lawnmowers and gas grills with thousands of BTUs . . . whatever those were. I wanted to be outraged at the notion of having some stranger looking after Alison's house. Gone or not, home-making was the job she took great professional pride in. Then I thought about how Alison would hate that her house was gone to hell and that her kids weren't getting ironed clothes and hot meals and figured wherever she was she was pretty teed off at me.

"Housekeeper," I said. I punched Jordan on his big, beefy bicep. "Good idea. He gaped at me and almost dropped his coffee cup in surprise.

I got a lot of satisfaction out of that.

⌒

The McCarthy Zone
Fly Away Home

"THE SCHOOL CALLED," MAGGIE said. She looked worried. She had good reason too.

"I know. Where's Danny?"

"Out by the garage."

I was boiling mad or I would have figured that out for myself. And it didn't help when Maggie added, "with Jordan" as I headed out the patio door.

Danny'd been spending more and more time with the angel in the last two weeks. It turned out that he'd been spending less and less at school. The principal had decided it was time to stop cutting the kid slack because his mom had died. Missy liked the idea of having Maggie in the house, but Danny pitched a fit. That was when he took to spending time with Jordan outside. I knew exactly where to look for them when I went out. There's a basketball hoop over the garage.

They were there all right, gentle readers, sweating and shouting and shedding chicken feathers. I have to admit there's nothing more seductive than the slap thwap sound of a basketball being bounced. The swish of the ball going through the basket is heavenly. Danny's my kid. He inherited the love of the game from me. It was a beautiful day. The sun was shining down, glaring off the concrete of the driveway and the yellow siding of the garage. Small bits of Jordan's feathers flew through the air like cottonwood fluff in May. Danny and Jordan were blocking and dancing around each other under the net, Danny in a Raptors jersey, the angel in his usual bad-taste mixture of stripes and plaids and Hawaiian prints. Parental outrage cooled as I spared a moment to take in the pleasure the pair took in the game. A quick glance toward the street showed me that no local traffic was slowing down at the sight of a big angel playing basketball with my kid.

Danny's grown like a weed lately, but this was the first time I noticed that he was filling out as well as growing up. He didn't look bad, but he was still a skinny little twerp next to the Shaq-sized angel. One of the angel's palms was bigger than Danny's whole head. The basketball looked more like a tennis ball in his grasp. For Danny to play against the angel at all was a brave act, but my kid showed no fear.

Which didn't stop me from being terrified when Danny got the ball, swerved around a shoulder block from Jordan, headed for the basket and made a leap—

"Danny!"

The kid went up, stuffed the ball, grabbed the rim, spun around in a circle from his own momentum, and went down. Hard. The sound his knees made against the concrete of the driveway was one of the ugliest meaty thuds I've ever heard. Danny howled in pain. The sight and sound nearly ripped my soul out.

The next thing I knew I was kneeling on the ground next to Danny, helping him to sit up. I checked him over quickly, my heart trying to pound out of my chest. Bruised and scraped. Nothing broken. Assured that my son was going to live, I took my first breath in a minute and lit into him. "What do you think you were doing? Do you know how danger-ous that was? You could have killed yourself? What do you mean trying to slam dunk in the driveway—"

I went on and on like this, with Danny staring at me like he didn't recognize me. After I yelled at him for a while, I hugged him. That really surprised him. He protested, and squirmed, but after a while he hugged me back. He was warm and solid and real, alive.

And a snotty fifteen-year-old. Eventually he pulled away and demanded, "What's your problem? Why do you care if I get hurt?"

"I'm your father, that's why."

He sneered, but he couldn't hold it for long. His lip started to quiver. "Oh, yeah?"

"Yeah."

"Jordan's more fun. He can dunk."

"Of course he can dunk! He's got wings!"

Jordan had been calmly bouncing the ball at the end of the driveway during this. He joined in now to say, "I've got skills."

"Danny's got skills too!" I shouted at him. "But I don't want him to die before he has a chance to develop them!"

"You don't?" Danny asked. "Like you notice I'm around."

This statement reminded me of the reason I'd come looking for my son in the first place. "Speaking of being around—no more skipping school." I pointed a finger at him and gave him a lecture that my own father would have been proud of. In fact, I could feel myself turning into my father even as I spoke. I was half tempted to search in my tweed jacket pocket and pull out a pipe. Except that I don't own a tweed jacket, or smoke. I laid down the law. I laid down rules. I set limits. I praised and I threatened. I might even have mentioned something about military school and "in my day."

Whatever it was I said, it certainly had an effect on my wayward fifteen-year-old. When I was finished he said, "Okay."

"Okay?"

He shrugged. "Sure."

"Sure what?"

"Sure I'll go back to school. If you'll drive me and pick me up sometimes. And come to games. And I'll catch up on my homework—but you gotta help."

I stared. "You want me around? Don't I embarrass you?"

"Sure. But that's your job."

Which I hadn't been doing lately. I glared at the angel and capitulated. "Okay, I'm busted. You," I pointed at the house, "go do some homework." Danny left without arguing. "I'll be in to check it in a minute." He knew this was an idle threat as I have the comprehension of a clam about all the computer stuff he's into. Still, it sounded suitably fatherly.

I looked at the angel. He was grinning. "What?"

He tossed me the basketball. He checked his watch. "Vacation's over. My work here is done," he declared. "Father and children reunited . . . blah, blah, blah." He waggled a huge finger at me. "Just make sure you start writing funny columns again, or I'll be back."

Then he was gone. But he left a suspiciously brimstone and flatulence aroma behind. The neighbors are still complaining.

Gentle reader, I do take the angel who came to visit at his word. I will endeavor to bring you my opinions in as entertaining a format as I can manage. I've spent the last few columns being rather self-indulgent, relaying to you how my family and I came to begin recovering from the grief of losing our wife and mother. I don't apologize for having to tell about an angel visiting my house, but I do beg your indulgence. I've come to the conclusion that being a widower and single parent isn't going to kill me. The world didn't end when Alison left it—it just stood still for an empty while. It isn't easy, but we're together, and we'll be fine. Next week I'll go back to talking about politics and the economy and whatever world news that strikes my fancy.

But that's next week. Right now I'm going to make sure Danny and Missy have finished their homework. Then we're going to walk the dog and watch a videotape.

Nothing with angels in it.

"WHY DON'T YOU DO a couple more angel columns?"

I sighed at my editor's suggestion. "I can't."

"It's a great storytelling device. The stuff you've been doing lately is so touching and personal, but the angle of having an angel in your house causing all these problems helps distance the reader from the very real pain you've exposed. It's good you've worked through Alison's death this way," my editor added, tempering her enthusiasm with sympathy I knew was very real. "But the response to Jordan is great. People want more."

I picked up the long, scraggly white feather sitting on my desk and twirled it through my fingers. "Sorry," I said. "Can't do."

She sighed. "Well, keep him in mind."

"I will," I said.

I'm going to have the feather framed and hang it over my desk.

The Stars Look Down

Tim Waggoner

An instant of vertigo followed by the disturbing sensation of being suddenly encased in flesh; surrounded, *subsumed* by it.

Jalil didn't have to open his eyes (*his* being a term of convenience—*hers* or *its* would work just as well and be equally as meaningless). The host's eyes were already open; all Jalil had to do was begin to see through them. The five senses these creatures possessed were barely sufficient to help them maneuver through their environment, but Jalil had had long practice with the sense called sight, and he took in his surroundings quickly.

It was night, though he could see well enough. His host stood in a gravel parking lot awash in blue-white fluorescence, car keys clutched in his right hand. Jalil saw the car ahead of him, an older vehicle, dented, with rust nibbling at the edges. A stray residue of thought in the host's mind informed Jalil that this was a Ford P.O.S., whatever that meant.

Jalil pushed the thought aside. That this was a pivotal moment in the host's life was a given, else Jalil wouldn't have been drawn to him here, at this particular time. The trick, as

67

always, was determining exactly what needed to be done, and Jalil didn't have long. What his people called the Confluence, the juncture of circumstance and probability when they could act, lasted only a few minutes, sometimes mere seconds. If one of the *Chhaya* misinterpreted the task set before them—or worse, failed to act altogether—it could have disastrous consequences for their host.

Not that Jalil particularly cared one way or the other; he wasn't exactly fond of the limited bags of meat and bone that called themselves *humans*. Still, he believed being a *Chhaya* carried a certain responsibility, and he always did his best to help the creatures he found himself inhabiting. If for no other reason than so he could return home all the sooner.

As Jalil's essence became more acclimated to his host's form, he realized that the man's hand was trembling, causing the keys to jingle softly in the night air. Jalil took in a breath through borrowed nostrils. It smelled like early spring, but his host's body felt warm, almost feverish. He glanced at his host's arms, chest: the man wasn't wearing a jacket, just a simple T-shirt emblazoned with the words *Dick's Last Resort*, and which sported various food and drink stains. The body should have been cool enough, but it wasn't.

Jalil turned, the host's form performing the motion sluggishly, like an overladen barge trying to reverse course on a cramped waterway. Jalil saw the building he assumed his host had just left, neon sign humming in the darkness: *Rowdy's Roadhouse*. With his free hand, he grabbed a fistful of his host's shirt and brought it up to his nose. He inhaled, scenting the harsh, acrid stink of alcohol. He let go of the fabric with a shudder of disgust. The situation seemed obvious enough; the fool had imbibed far too much drink this evening and had been about to climb behind the wheel of his car when Jalil was drawn to him. The *Chhaya* had no special abilities to peer into the future, but Jalil didn't need the powers of a seer to have a good idea what would happen if his host had been left to continue his course of action. Far too impaired to operate a bicycle, let alone an automobile, the man would have driven away from the bar and gotten into an accident—one that almost surely would have meant his death (else why would Jalil be here?) and most likely the deaths of others.

As much as they might have liked to effect a more permanent change, the *Chhaya* had only a limited opportunity in which to act, so there was nothing Jalil could do about his host's drinking. For all Jalil knew, being this drunk was rare for the man; but knowing human nature as he did, the *Chhaya* doubted it. In any event, he could at least make sure the idiot didn't kill himself or anyone else tonight.

He directed his host's body to turn toward the edge of the parking lot, where a small grove of trees stretched forth from the ground and toward the night sky. Jalil drew his arm back and hurled the keys toward the foliage. They arced up and through the air and disappeared into the trees with a rustle of leaves and a metallic jingling. *That should do it,* Jalil thought with satisfaction. Not only wouldn't his host have any memory of what had occurred while he had been inhabited by Jalil, even if he did somehow think to look for his keys among the trees, he'd never find them, not as inebriated as he was. At least one life saved, perhaps more. Time to move on and let his host return to his miserable, alcohol-soaked excuse for a life.

Jalil closed his host's eyes and waited for the first sensations of detachment. Once their work was done, the *Chhaya* were drawn out of the human bodies they so briefly inhabited and pulled back to the Empyrean, the realm of pure light that was their home. There they compared notes about their experiences, shared information on what they had learned, debated whether the actions taken with any particular host were correct and proper, and struggled to understand the limited, physical world, which, for some unknowable reason, they constantly found themselves drawn to.

Jalil wasn't one to participate in the discussions, and he didn't care to learn more about the human plane—all he wanted was to be free once more to swim the pure seas of light and fire that made up the Empyrean. So he waited, eager to be released from his human host. And waited. And . . .

He opened his eyes. Something was wrong; he had never remained so long in a host after his task was done. Had he perhaps misinterpreted what needed to be accomplished? It wasn't unheard of. The differing probability streams that combined to make a moment of Confluence weren't always easy to read. He likely had only moments to determine where he had gone wrong and correct things, else he would be drawn back to the Empyrean, his task unfinished. Jalil wasn't overly concerned about what might happen to the human—as far he felt, the creatures deserved to face the consequences of their own actions—but he didn't relish returning home a failure, and he certainly didn't want to have to face the disapproving questions of his fellow *Chhaya,* most of whom took their interventionist role very seriously.

His thoughts spun: should he retrieve the keys and get into the car? Return to the bar and see if he was needed there? Or should he—

He broke off. The hairs on the back of his host's neck stood up, and he detected a faint, leathery sound, as if a large piece of burlap were sliding across the ground. No, not sliding; *slithering,* like a serpent. And not just one—Jalil sensed several presences coming toward him from different directions. He was surrounded, and they were closing in quickly.

Loknoth! A half dozen, perhaps more.

Jalil suddenly regretted discarding his host's car keys. He could have used a vehicle just then.

Without further thought, he began running, his host's inebriated form performing the action clumsily, stumbling, swaying, threatening to pitch face-first into the gravel at any instant. Jalil had to get away; if the *Loknoth* caught him, they would rip his essence free from his host and devour the luminescence that was his being. His host would be unharmed, but that would be little comfort to Jalil in the bellies of the *Loknoth.*

He heard them coming up behind him, giving forth a dark, snuffling hyena sound that was equal parts hunger and amusement. Felt the chill of their encroaching presence, like a sudden, unexpected blast of winter wind driving tiny shards of ice into his skin.

Jalil left the parking lot, stumbled out into the street, saw headlights blazing before him. He turned toward them, waving his arms for help, hoping the light would keep the shadowy *Loknoth* at bay.

The shrill blast of a horn, the screech of tires desperately trying to grip asphalt, then impact.

Jalil experienced a confused jangle of sensations that his host's body, impaired by alcohol and stunned nerves, was unable to process. When he was able to make some sense of his host's input again, Jalil realized that he was lying on cold, hard ground, looking up into a moonless night sky sprinkled with pinpricks of light. He fancied the stars were in truth holes poked into the fabric of reality, allowing small portions of the Empyrean's light to shine through. He imagined his fellow *Chhaya* looking down, clucking their nonexistent tongues in disapproval and disappointment.

He heard the *chunk!* of a car door closing, the tap-tap-tap of shoes against road surface, then the starlight faded and he heard no more.

" . . . MOSTLY JUST A FEW scrapes and contusions. I'll know more once we run some tests, but if you ask me, it's more likely he passed out from all the booze he drank than from any injuries he sustained in the accident."

Jalil was confused. Why was everything dark? The Empyrean was Light itself, and thus had never known the stain of darkness. And those guttural sounds were hardly the sweet, lilting symphony of voices that comprised the endless conversation of the *Chhaya.*

"Thank you, Doctor."

A human's voice, Jalil realized. A woman, her tone one of gratitude and relief. He opened his eyes, blinked as they struggled to adjust to a light that was at once far less and far more intense than that of the Empyrean.

Jalil saw a middle-aged human woman who had once likely been considered attractive by the standards of this place and time, though she now showed definite signs of her age. Her raven-black hair was threaded with gray, and wrinkles radiated from the corners of her eyes. Her lipstick was garish red, her eyeshadow a strange pale green. She was well fleshed, though not fat, and wore a green blouse the same color as her eyeshadow and green slacks a shade or two darker. Her hoops earrings were too large, and she sported too many bracelets and rings. The overall effect made her resemble an ambulatory Christmas tree.

Standing next to the woman, dressed in a white coat, was another female, this one of Asian descent, and young enough to be the first's daughter. A doctor, the other woman had called her. Most likely a resident.

Jalil realized then what had happened. He had run into the street to avoid the *Loknoth* and been struck by a car. He hurt in a dozen places, but at least he still lived, as did his host. Evidently the accident hadn't been that serious, and the car's headlights had driven off the *Loknoth*, at least for now. But they would be back.

He tried to sit up, the motion drawing the immediate attention of the two women.

"Whoa, there! Take it easy," the doctor said. "You got banged up pretty good tonight." She moved to push Jalil back down, but he gently, if firmly, brushed her hands away.

"Thank you, but I am fine." The voice was that of his host— low, husky from too much smoking—but the words, their cadence and rhythm, were Jalil's. He finished sitting up, paused for a moment to allow his head to clear. When he realized it wasn't going to do so any time soon, he slowly swung his feet over the edge of the bed and attempted to stand. He nearly fell, causing the doctor to grab one elbow, the Christmas-tree woman the other, but he managed to keep his feet beneath him.

The doctor scowled. "You really shouldn't be standing here like this."

"I concur." Jalil pulled away from both women and began walking away from the bed.

"You can't do this!" the doctor protested. "You could be suffering from internal injuries, and you might have head injuries that could result in death if left untreated. You should—"

Jalil turned and cut her off. "I will survive." He gestured at the other beds in the emergency room, nearly all of which were occupied. "Surely there are others here who need your assistance more than I."

The doctor's scowl deepened until Jalil feared it would permanently crease her skin. Finally, she sighed. "I suppose I can't keep you here if you don't want to stay." She turned to the Christmas-tree woman. "Make sure he signs the proper release form at the nurses' station, though, stating that he is leaving against medical advice. I don't want him coming back here and trying to sue me." With that, she turned and headed off to a bald man whose right hand was swaddled in a blood-stained cloth.

The Christmas-tree woman took his arm and looked at him with kind, concerned eyes. "Are you sure you feel good enough to leave?"

"Believe me, I am quite ready to depart," Jalil said. "In fact, I'm well overdue."

The woman cocked her head and gave him a puzzled frown. Then she smiled. "How about I help you check out?"

Jalil was going to decline the woman's offer, but he realized he had no clear notion of the procedures required to removed one's self from a hospital. If this woman could expedite that process . . . He moved his host's lips in what he hoped was a fair approximation of a smile. "Thank you."

"Don't mention it." Her own smile grew wider. "After all, it's the least I can do since I creamed you with my car."

THE CHRISTMAS-TREE WOMAN, whose name turned out to be Linda Daniels, steered him through the check-out procedures with an ease of someone long used to dealing with bureaucracies. Much sooner than he had anticipated, Jalil found himself standing on the sidewalk outside the emergency room entrance, Linda beside him.

It was still night, though he had no clear notion of the specific time. He thought of asking the woman, but decided against it. What did it matter what time it was?

"I am grateful for your assistance."

"Like I said, it was the least I could do."

A silence fell between them then, one that Jalil had no idea how to break. He had decided to nod once, turn and walk away when she said, "Do you need a ride anywhere? Maybe back to the bar to pick up your car?"

Jalil frowned. "While I appreciate your continued concern, your debt to me is discharged. You are free to go your own way."

The woman laughed; a rich, earthy sound. "Honey, I'm a social worker. Picking up and helping strays is my business." She took his arm and began to steer him toward the parking lot. "C'mon."

Jalil knew he should have more forcefully declined the woman's offer, but his host body still ached from alcohol abuse and the accident, and he had no idea what city he was in, let alone what country—though from the language and accent of the humans here, he guessed he was somewhere in America— and, if he were to be completely truthful with himself, he was afraid. He didn't know why he remained trapped within his host body, and he knew it was only a matter of time until the *Loknoth* tracked him down.

So he let Linda Daniels steer him through the parking lot to her car, while he pondered how he might survive long enough to regain his freedom.

⁓

"IS THERE ANY SPECIAL reason why you want me to drive with the inside light on?"

Linda's car was a disaster area: the backseat was crammed with cardboard boxes full of files stuffed to overflowing with papers, and the floor was covered with empty cardboard coffee cups and crumpled fast food bags. It appeared as if her vehicle functioned as a combination mobile office and compost heap.

"It makes me feel more comfortable," Jalil said. He rolled the passenger side window down halfway, felt the breeze wash over his face. The sensation was unexpectedly intense, but not altogether unpleasant. No, not at all.

He noticed an object dangling from the rearview mirror; it appeared to have been knitted from some thick, colorful thread. It was a crude representation of a humanoid form with blonde hair, a white robe, and bird wings. Jalil watched as the figure swayed back and forth as if it were flying.

He nodded toward it. "An angel," he said.

"Yeah," Linda said. "I'm a big angel freak. Didn't you notice my bumper stickers when we got into the car? One says, *Miracles Happen,* and the other says, *Angels are Watching Over Me.* I've got a ton of angel stuff in my apartment: figurines, pictures, books, videos . . ."

"I take it you are a religious woman, then." From the bits and pieces of knowledge the *Chhaya* had gleaned from their millennia of fragmented experience on earth, they had learned that humanity had developed a multitude of belief systems to explain the universe and their place in it to themselves, and beings like the *Chhaya* figured in virtually all these religions. The *Chhaya* believed humans somehow retained a subconscious memory of those moments when the "angels" intervened in their lives, and it was from these scraps of memory that all the religions of humanity had been woven, much like the threads that were knitted together to make up the tiny figure dangling from the rearview mirror.

"I don't consider myself religious, per se," Linda said as she slowed for a stop light. "More like spiritual. While I believe in a higher level of existence, I don't follow any particular religion. I don't know if I think angels are literally real; for me, they just sort of represent the spiritual side of life." She turned and flashed him a smile. "Besides, they're fun to collect."

Jalil smiled back. He wondered what she would say if she knew she had collected a real angel tonight.

Not long after that, they pulled into the parking lot of Rowdy's Roadhouse. There were fewer cars than when Jalil had last been here, but the lot was far from empty.

"Which one's yours?" Linda asked. "I'll park next to it."

Jalil struggled to remember. The moments before the accident were hazy and jumbled. He pointed to a car that he thought belonged to his host, and Linda pulled up next to it and turned off her engine and lights.

"Do you feel good enough to drive?" she asked. "I can follow you home, if you'd like, make sure you get there okay."

"No, thank you, I should—" Then Jalil remembered: the keys. He had thrown them into the trees in order to keep them out of the hands of his drunken host. Not that he supposed it mattered; he had no idea how to operate a car, and he wasn't certain he'd be able to draw on his host's memories in order to do so.

"I can't find my keys." Not quite the whole truth, but it was close enough.

"Maybe you lost them during the accident. Neither the paramedics nor the police said anything about them, though. Maybe they're still back at the hospital, and they just forgot to give them to you when we checked out." Linda thought for a moment. "I suppose they could still be in the parking lot, somewhere, or maybe alongside the road." She started to open the door. "C'mon, let's go take a look."

Jalil grabbed her arm to stop her. He didn't relish the prospect of walking around in the pale-white illumination of fluorescent light. He already knew the cool, soft light was no deterrence to the *Loknoth*. They had attacked him here once already, and they could surely do so again.

"That's all right," he said. "I think I'd rather just go home and return for my car tomorrow. I'm . . . tired." This latter was true enough; while the *Chhaya* never knew weariness, the human body Jalil currently wore certainly did.

Linda hesitated, then closed her door. "All right, but I have to warn you, I was on my way to visit a few clients when I hit you, and—"a quick check of her watch—"it's starting to get late. I really need to at least see one or two of them before I can drop you off."

Jalil thought he heard a faint, leathery rustling from outside the car, as if something—or some*things*—were creeping slowly closer, struggling to catch a scent.

"That's fine," he said quickly. "I can always doze in the car."

Linda looked at him for a moment, and over her shoulder, Jalil thought he saw something dark and sinuous rear up outside the car, something made entirely of shadow with black-red eyes like angry, blazing coals. He fancied it made a *ch-ch-ch-ch-ch* sound, a noise like that of a . . . *rattlesnake*, his host's mind supplied.

"Okay, then." With a smooth motion, Linda turned the key in the ignition and flicked on her lights. Jalil heard sharp, furious squeals as the *Loknoth* fled back into the darkness, but if Linda heard anything, she gave no sign.

She favored Jalil with a smile as she backed out of the parking space. "I don't know what you do for a living, but you're about to experience the wonderful world of social work. Your life will never be the same."

As she drove through the lot and pulled onto the street, Jalil turned and looked through the rear window. He saw ribbons of darkness like great serpents sliding along the ground in pursuit.

"I imagine not," Jalil said softly.

THEY STOPPED FIRST AT a homeless shelter where one of Linda's clients—an elderly man in a wheelchair—was watching a medical drama on a small black and white TV set in the shelter's common room. While Linda spoke with the man, seeming more like she had dropped by for a pleasant chat instead of working, Jalil looked around the room. He had expected the air to stink of unwashed bodies, the people to gaze vacantly into the distance, obviously mentally deficient. But the people here seemed like people anywhere else. Oh, there was an atmosphere of depression, but hardly one of despair. These people chatted, read books, did crossword puzzles, worked on writing resumes . . .

Next, they stopped at an all-night donut shop to speak with a waitress. The woman, Jalil learned, was a single mother with four children as well as a recovering alcoholic. The place wasn't especially busy, and her boss let her take a break to talk with Linda. As they spoke, Jalil sat at a nearby table with a cup of coffee and a cruller. He marveled at the taste and texture of the food and drink, the sweetness of the donut contrasted with the bitterness of the coffee. While he had been drawn to help human hosts for thousands of years, this was the first time he had ever had a chance to experience the simple act of eating. He found the sensations nearly overwhelming.

While he ate, he watched Linda work. He noticed how cheerful the woman was, how easily she laughed, how she periodically would reach across the table and touch Linda's hand with obvious affection. This woman was stuck in a dead-end job that barely kept food on her family's table, yet she somehow managed to remain positive and upbeat.

As they drove away from the donut shop, Jalil said, "How do you do it?"

"How do I do what?"

"Your work. Talking with those people . . . I think it would be demoralizing."

Linda glanced at him and smirked. "Nothing personal, pal, but from what I can see, you are one of 'those people.'"

"I meant no offense," Jalil said, "I am merely curious. I—I have done similar work myself on occasion, and . . ." Jalil paused, ashamed to admit what he had to say next. "You treat them as if they were ordinary people, no different from yourself."

Linda shrugged. She flipped on her turn signal and executed a right turn. "That's because they aren't. Their circumstances might differ, the choices they've made, the situations they have to deal with, but in the end, we're all human, right?"

Jalil looked out the window, watched the streetlights blur as they passed. "I have had . . . difficulty remembering that."

"Don't get too down on yourself. It's easy to start looking down at the people you help as if they were a lesser species, as if you are so far above them that they ought to kiss your feet for being so gracious as to allow them a few minutes in your magnificent presence. It helps put distance between yourself and them, helps you feel better about your own life and the choices you've made."

Jalil turned to Linda and smiled. "It sounds as if you speak from experience."

She laughed. "Unfortunately, yes. When I was younger, I acted like I was better than my clients. Oh, I cared for them, but it was the same way a vet cares for animals. I felt sorry for them, pitied them, tried to help them, but I didn't respect them, didn't see them as equals."

"What happened?"

She grinned. "I got over it. You talk to enough people, after a while you start to get to know them, and you begin to see that there's really very little difference between you and them, and what little there is, isn't really worth talking about."

Jalil looked at Linda for a long moment before replying. "I'm beginning to see what you mean."

Linda slowed and put on her turn signal. "Last stop," she said, then pulled into the parking lot of a small apartment building. She found a space, parked, and killed the engine and lights. The lot was badly lit, merely a single fluorescent light above the rear entrance of the building, and Jalil found himself tensing, listening for the tell-tale leathery rustling that announced the *Loknoth*'s arrival.

"You might want to stay in the car this time," Linda said. "The couple I'm here to see have a tendency to get a little . . . agitated when I show up."

Jalil only paid partial attention to Linda's words. He was listening for the *Loknoth*. "I'd rather accompany you, if you don't mind."

"If you're sure that's what you want."

There was suddenly something different about her tone, as if there were a hidden subtext to her words. Jalil noticed it, considered asking, but decided not to. He just wanted to get inside where it was light.

They exited the car, crossed the lot to the rear entrance, and went inside. If the *Loknoth* lurked somewhere out in the darkness, they gave no sign of their presence. Jalil found himself hoping that he had spent so much time inside his host that the shadow hunters had lost his scent.

The foyer of the rear entrance was cluttered with trash— crumpled newspaper, candy and fast food wrappers, a broken popsicle stick. Linda picked her way through the trash to the stairwell, and Jalil followed. The stairs were cramped, and they creaked and groaned alarmingly as the two ascended. The building's atmosphere was stifling, and the air smelled like cabbage and soiled diapers. As they reached the second floor, Jalil could hear televisions playing behind cardboard-thin doors, babies crying, people talking in loud voices, not quite arguments, not yet, but well on their way there.

Linda led him halfway down the hall, to apartment 2D. Country music blasted inside, so loud it sounded as if the stereo speakers were shoved right up against the door. Linda knocked once, twice. When there was no answer, she pounded on the door with her fist.

That got results. The door opened a crack to reveal a woman's bloodshot blue eye, a curve of cheek framed by a strand of greasy blonde hair. The mouth remained hidden behind the door. "Whoozit?" The word was slurred, the eye struggling to focus.

"Linda Daniels." She smiled as if she were greeting a long-lost friend. "We spoke a couple weeks ago?"

The woman didn't reply.

"It was about your husband applying for disability benefits?"

That got even faster results than pounding on the door had. The woman quickly undid the chain, opened the door and stood aside so they could enter. The apartment was small, almost an efficiency, Jalil's host-mind supplied. There was little distinction between the main living room and the kitchen. In the latter, a thin man in shorts and a white T-shirt sat at a cardboard table, holding a beer can and staring at a CD player on the counter. The man was in his mid to late twenties, had shoulder-length brown hair and several days' growth of beard. Now that Jalil looked more closely, he could see the man wore some sort of back brace beneath his shirt.

The woman closed the door and walked past them into the kitchen. She was roughly the same age as the man, shorter and pudgier. She too wore shorts and a T-shirt, though hers was pink and urged Jalil to VISIT JAMAICA! at his first opportunity.

"Hon? That woman's back, the one from social services?" She reached out and touched the man's shoulder. "She wants to talk to us about your disability money."

The man didn't remove his gaze from the CD player, so the woman walked over and shut it off. Jalil found the sudden silence to be a blessed relief.

The man looked up at her, face clouded with anger. "Now why'd you go and do that for?"

The woman scowled. "Linda's here, hon. From social services?"

The man turned to them, suddenly startled, as if they had just materialized out of thin air. He smiled, displaying nicotine-stained teeth. "Well, hell, whyn't ya say so?" Then he looked at Jalil and scowled. "Who's yer friend?"

"Someone I'm training," Linda replied. "He's here merely to watch and learn."

The man looked at Jalil for a moment more before finally nodding. "All right, then. Tell me about the money. I ain't had no work since I hurt my back on that construction site, and that was months ago. Worker's comp's ain't gonna last much longer, and Ruthie here only makes so much down at the dry cleaners." He smiled again, this time tentatively, as if he were afraid to. "I hope you've got some good news for us, ma'am."

Linda took a breath, and Jalil knew that the man's hope was destined to go unrealized.

"I'm sorry, Alex, but your claim's been denied. Again."

"Dammit!" The man called Alex slammed his fists down onto the flimsy card table, making it jump. He rose to his feet, face red and edging toward crimson. "Why the hell for?"

"Now, hon, simmer down." The woman stepped closer to her husband, reached a hand toward him, but didn't make contact. Jalil wondered if she were afraid to.

"Your doctor didn't fill out the proper paperwork—" Linda began.

Alex pushed past his wife and stood directly in front of the social worker, leaning his face toward hers, scowling, jaw thrust out. "You got the gall to come into my home, tell me that I'm not gonna get my money, and you bring this guy along to watch!" He jabbed his chin in Jalil's direction. "Is this how you social workers get your jollies? I suppose once you leave, you're gonna have a good laugh about the idiot who was stupid enough to think he was gonna get what's coming to him!"

This was going badly. It appeared that Alex, angry and drunk, might lose complete control of his temper and hurt Linda. Jalil couldn't allow that. He took a step forward.

Linda raised her hands in a placating gesture. "I assure you, Jalil and I only came here to—" She broke off suddenly.

"You said my name."

Linda didn't respond. She looked at Jalil, worry in her eyes. Alex no longer looked upset; in fact, he looked quite calm, more, he was completely devoid of expression, as was his wife. They were like puppets whose strings had been suddenly released.

"I never told you my name," Jalil said.

Linda forced a smile. "Of course you did, back at the hospital. You told it to me when we filled out the release forms."

Jalil shook his head. "I used my host's name." And he had gotten that from the driver's license in the man's wallet. "I never told you my true name."

Linda sighed. "I don't suppose you'd believe me if I said I'm just a really good guesser."

Jalil looked at the young man and woman. Their faces remained slack, but their eyes had been replaced by black-red coals. He understood then; this was some sort of trap set by the *Loknoth*, and Linda was in league with them, might even *be* one of them.

Without another word, Jalil turned and fled the apartment. Linda called out after him, but he couldn't make out what she said over the pounding of his footfalls, and the twin sounds of his terrified breathing and his pulse pounding in his ears. Soon, they were joined by another sound—that of a leathery rustling coming up fast behind.

He took the stairs two, three at a time, stumbled, nearly fell, reached the exit, shoved his way through, and plunged into the night. The stars blazed down, far larger than they should have been, bloated, swollen orbs, like the abdomens of monstrous fire-flies hovering overhead.

Light, Jalil thought frantically. *I have to find light!*

But before he could take another step, a shadow reared up out of the night in front of him. Vaguely human shaped, it swayed bonelessly before him, like a serpent fashioned out of pure darkness. The air grew chill in the thing's presence, and Jalil shivered, as much from terror as from the cold. He backed away, turned to flee in a different direction, and found his way blocked by a second *Loknoth.* He looked to his left, saw another *Loknoth*; looked to his right, saw the same. He turned slowly in a circle, counting. One, two . . . a dozen, perhaps more, ringed around him, forming a barrier through which he could not pass. He was trapped.

One of the shadow-creatures flowed forward, transforming as it came, solidifying, taking on human form. It was Linda.

"I'm so sorry, Jalil. It wasn't supposed to happen this way. You'd think after all the times I've done this, I wouldn't make such a simple mistake, but in the short while we've been together, I feel as if I've gotten to know you—more so than I usually get to know your kind—and I kept thinking of you as Jalil, and I guess it just finally popped out."

She smiled, shrugged, the gestures so genuine, so *human* that Jalil found it hard to remember this was a *Loknoth* standing before him.

"I guess it goes to show that even we aren't perfect, huh?"

Jalil's mind raced. There had to be a way out of this. Perhaps he could appeal to Linda, or maybe if he ran fast enough, he could . . . No, he was deluding himself. There were a dozen of them, and only one of him. He was bound to a human form, while they had no such restrictions. Now that they had him well and truly trapped, there was no escape.

"Very well. You've got me. Go ahead and do it. But if you have any feelings for me at all, you'll at least be quick about it."

Linda laughed a small, sad laugh. "Oh, Jalil. We're not here to hurt you. We're here to help you."

Now it was Jalil's turn to laugh. "Do you truly expect me to believe that? You are *Loknoth*, the devourers of Light. Your only reason for existence is to prey on the *Chhaya.*"

Jalil heard a snuffling sound and realized that the *Loknoth* that surrounded him were laughing.

"Really?" Linda said. "And how do you know that? From tales told by those *Chhaya* who manage to elude us and return to the

Empyrean with their stories of shadow demons. That is, in fact, why you perceive us the way you do now. Because of those stories. You expect to see shadow demons, and you do. But these—" she gestured to the others—"are not their true forms, any more than *this*—" she tapped her own chest—"is mine."

"If you are not demons, then what are you?"

"A better question might be: What are the *Chhaya*?" Linda countered.

Jalil was taken aback. "I . . . we are beings of Light who are drawn to humans in times of need. We are their protectors, their guardians."

Linda put a hand on Jalil's shoulder. To his surprise, he did not draw back. There was no chill, no surge of fear; just a simple, human touch. "It's a lovely fantasy, Jalil, but that's all it is. The *Chhaya* aren't superior to humans at all. They are . . ." She paused, as if searching for the right words. "On a lower rung of the ladder of existence."

Jalil drew back from Linda's touch, shaking his head in disbelief. "That is not possible."

"Is it so difficult to believe? The Empyrean may be a wonderful place in its way, but it is a stable, safe environment that doesn't promote growth. It has remained the same since the dawn of existence; the *Chhaya* as a race have remained the same. This world, this level of reality, is messy and unpredictable and full of an infinite variety of experience." She smiled. "It makes a far better school house than the Empyrean ever could."

Linda's words seemed to resonate somewhere deep inside Jalil's being, but he still couldn't bring himself to believe them. Earth . . . a higher level of existence? Impossible!

"Haven't you ever wondered why your race is constantly drawn to earth? Haven't you ever wondered what happens to those who come here and never return?"

"We have many theories—" he began.

"Which are all wrong," Linda said. "You come here because *this*—" she made a sweeping gesture with both arms—"is the next stage in your spiritual evolution. You enter humans during moments of crisis as a sort of . . . audition. It's a chance for you to experience corporeal existence, an opportunity for you to come to terms with some of its less-pleasant aspects before you make the transition."

"Transition to what?" Jalil asked, though he already knew how Linda would answer.

"To a human life, of course. Your time has come, Jalil. That's why you didn't leave your human host when you were finished helping him." She smiled warmly. "You're ready to be born."

"I . . . It doesn't make sense. Why do they allow us in? The humans, I mean."

"They were *Chhaya* once themselves. On a subconscious level, they are just returning the favor that was once done for them. Plus, it helps them get ready for the next phase of their spiritual existence."

"The *Loknoth*?"

Linda nodded. "Think of us as midwives. We try to ease the transition to corporeal existence for your people, but unfortunately things don't always go as smoothly as we'd like. You insist on seeing us as demons, no matter what we do, so we create scenarios designed to ease your fears, help you come to terms with humanity so you're ready to move on." She smiled sheepishly. "Back in the apartment, you were supposed to intervene and stop Alex from hurting me. My hope was that action would cement your relationship to a human, help you see their race as something more than lower lifeforms that need the *Chhaya*'s help from time to time."

"That's . . . just what I was about to do." And the truth was, Jalil had come to the realization of which Linda spoke. Remaining in human form for an extended period, getting to know her, seeing her work with her clients, coming to truly care about her enough that he wanted to protect her, not merely perform a quick task so he could flee this plane and return to the Empyrean . . . all of these experiences had effected a profound change in him.

"Then perhaps I didn't mess things up too badly," Linda said. She held out her hand. "Are you ready?"

"What, now?"

She grinned and the other *Loknoth* laughed—not a dark, snuffling sound this time, but a light, warm sound unlike any he had ever heard before. He looked away from Linda, turned his gaze to her fellow *Loknoth* and saw—

He saw beauty that made the Light of the *Chhaya* seem as mere candleflame to the sun. He then looked up, expecting to see the swollen stars of his earlier vision, but they were gone, replaced by . . . replaced by . . . Jalil couldn't grasp what he was looking at, no matter how hard he tried. It was beyond him.

"They're something, aren't they?" Linda whispered. "We don't know much about them; they're the next rung on the ladder above the *Loknoth*. I can tell you this, though; they're smiling at you. At all of us."

With an effort, Jalil turned his face away from the sky and faced Linda once again. In a small voice, he asked, "How many rungs are there, do you think?"

She shrugged. "Who knows? Does it really matter? The point is to keep climbing."

Slowly, Jalil nodded. He then took a deep breath and held out his hand.

"I'm ready."

Linda took his hand, and gently, with love, led him toward tomorrow.

Pas de Deux

Michelle West

The lights dimmed in the crowded theater, soothing away the harsh edges of brilliance that glimmered off glossy programs. At that signal, silence spread across the crowd; people turned away from conversation to watch the stage. The conductor, replete in standard black tuxedo, stood beneath the glare of a spotlight and bowed to scattered applause. Heads rose in expectation, some bored, some pleased, some ready to suspend the outside world for a moment to watch the dancers as they made their way onto the stage.

For Maia Anderson, it was more than simple ballet—it was magic; the wisp of a dream too fragile to grab onto, but too solid to ignore. She had perfected a happy, distant smile, a becoming manner, and a fashionable style; they hid the emptiness from the casual prying of strangers.

Tonight, to celebrate the start of the season, she wore a special dress—one that she had purchased to please no one but herself. It was a black, elegant drape of cloth that fell from shoulder to knees like comfortable shadow.

She was alone.

She drew her breath in unevenly as the ballet corps came onto the stage. Sighed once, a gentle noise that was lost to the woodwinds. She had given up on the dream of belonging on that stage years ago, but it still stung; it always stung.

She had started so young. Like many girls, she loved the elegance and grace, the essential femininity of the dancers, their willowy limbs and the ethereal lightness of their beautiful steps across the stage. Some girls fell in love with horses, some with teen heart-throbs. She had chosen the ballet.

Her first encounters with dance were simple; her later encounters painful. The point shoes had hurt her toes and her legs, and she could not understand how the dancers could smile and look so joyous through the pain they must have felt. But that hadn't stopped her.

Not that.

If I were smart, she thought, *I'd* . . .

Leave? No. She'd purchased her ticket. She'd paid.

They danced and she watched, forgetting to smile.

FROM WHERE HE SAT, he could see her perfectly. Even had he been in the very top of the back balcony, he would still have known where she was. His elbows rested lightly along the armrests of his chair; the tips of his fingers brushed the line of his chin. It had been a long time since he had come here, and it had not been in shadows and darkness.

But the shadows and darkness held promise. Here, people came to watch, to dream, or to hide.

Sometimes all three. He came to watch, and to dream, but it was not necessary to remain hidden. She would see him in her own time and in her own fashion, or she would not see him at all.

While she watched the dancers, her forehead creased, her lips bent at corners in a grimace that she could not—quite—smooth away. He watched as well, seeing in the altering width of her eyes the echoes of the movements of the dancers.

THE DOOR TO HER apartment was jammed again. The humidity of the rainy week had swelled the old wood just enough that the bowed frame rested a little too snugly against it. She twisted the key in the lock just so, her arms moving forcefully, but gracefully, to the sound of distant music. The door, obstinate old piece of poorly painted wood, lifted slightly in its frame and creaked open.

There was no one to watch her, so she danced into the small hallway on her toes, lifting her arms and hands in a gentle sweep above her head. Lost in her reverie, she didn't see the furry body that shot, unerring, toward her legs until it hit her and she was falling.

The floor met her with an audible thud, breaking her mood and its spell.

A pink, dry tongue began to assiduously clean make-up off her face.

"Stupid dog," she murmured, without any rancor. The little brown terrier-and-something mix wagged its tail in a friendly fashion; it always amazed her that anything moving that fast didn't just snap off. "You're lucky you're all I've got, or you'd be out that door so fast I'd dislocate my arm throwing you." He licked her face before she stood, taking it safely out of his reach.

"Idiot."

He wagged his tail, trotted toward the kitchen, and stopped to make sure that she was following.

"Complete idiot."

His tail went faster; his tongue started its friendly loll. She was certain he thought every word she said had something to do with food. The can-opener was lying in the sink along with the morning dishes; she retrieved it quickly and set about getting Winston dinner.

"Sorry I couldn't take you with me," she said, as she placed his tray on the ground in front of his face. "I'd've bought you a ticket if I could afford it, but they don't let funny men dressed in dog suits into the Hummingbird Centre."

His answer was pretty simple: He ate. He could always eat.

Winston had been a stray, much as she often felt she was. Straggly, suspicious, and underfed, he'd sort of bumped into her when she was walking the half-mile from the subway to her apartment. It was raining, she remembered that clearly, because it was the one day that week that she'd forgotten to take an umbrella.

If he'd been a friendly, perky dog, she would have been tempted to kick him—which would have been very bad, as she'd only just gotten the cast removed from her left knee, and had been strictly ordered not to do anything more strenuous than a gentle walk.

She certainly hadn't been told to get hit by a mangy dog, slip in a rain-slick street, and land—as awkwardly as possible, on her side in a vain attempt not to hit a knee that had only recently stopped being agonizing.

But he hadn't been friendly, and he'd looked about as bad as she felt. Worse, even. He was the kind of dog that went to the humane society and never got taken home by anyone—just sat in a cage until someone decided to put it to death in a merciful fashion. She found herself kneeling down, in the rain, her knees scraping cement as she tried to distribute her weight intelligently. It hurt. After about five minutes, her knee started to tingle; she hadn't been certain she was going to be able to stand up again.

Anticipation of pain made it easier to be patient, and after fifteen minutes, she was rewarded by a scruffy, mangy dog who'd decided to test the waters by sniffing her outstretched hand.

They didn't become fast friends right away. Winston was, as she suspected, much like her in that regard; he was willing to take a chance, but he took it at his own pace. He condescended to follow her home, and that night, for the first time in two months, she had company when she crossed her threshold.

Food was the great bridge.

Once he realized that she was going to keep feeding him, he stopped growling like a rabid pit bull whenever she walked too close to his dish. He stopped shying away from her hands when she bent to pat him, and eventually, he found his way to the foot of her bed. It was only a short trip up to the center of the bed itself.

And it's not like anyone else is going to be there.

"I'm going to take a shower. Be good."

AFTER THE SHOWER SHE felt more comfortable. She slid very quickly into her bathrobe because she didn't want to have to look at the scar on her leg for a second longer than she had to. It had faded with time, but not as much as the doctors had said it would. Or perhaps her vision of the scars reflected their effect on her life.

Winston had made himself quite comfortable waiting for her; he was sprawled out across her bed, happily shedding bits of himself all over the comforter that she'd barely managed to get clean after he'd decided that bull-rushes might be food.

"You'd better not have eaten anything indigestible," she said, mock-severe.

He wagged his tail, licked her face, and then allowed her to crawl under the comforter.

"I went to see Giselle tonight. Want to hear about it?"

He wagged his tail.

"Is that a yes, or do you think I just said something about f-o-o-d?" *Great. I'm talking to a dog. I can't believe my life.* But she wanted to talk about what she'd seen. Talking out loud was almost like sharing the experience. She wasn't always good with words—emotion tended to make her incoherent, and more than one sentence trailed off into silence—but she managed to convey almost everything she felt. A hint of an old dream colored her words with truth and all the longing that time and circumstance had made so bitter.

HE WATCHED HER FROM a corner of her room, unseen and unrecognized. The dog sat up and whined, lifting its wet black nose, its dark unblinking eyes seeing what she did not.

"Winston?"

He turned his head back to her, let his tongue hang out over either edge of his jaw.

She hugged the dog. "Let's go out for a walk," she said softly. "I'm not getting any sleepier."

THE WALKS HAD BEEN the hardest part of her life to adjust to. Newly come from surgery, her knee—or what was left of it after reconstructive surgery—made even necessary exercise unpleasant. The occupational therapist whose responsibility she was had pushed and prodded more and less gently, and found that she was stone-walled either way. Maia told her, point blank, that she didn't have a lot to get better *for*.

But Winston had other ideas.

And in the end, having dragged him from a life on the street by some intuitive stubbornness she both regretted and was thankful for, she surrendered to the inevitable and began to walk. Not to overdo it—she tried that once, and the three days being cooped up with a sulky, bored dog was plenty of incentive not to do it again—but to simply walk. Morning and evening, the hours that sandwiched work so neatly, became their private time. If the word *private* could describe forays into a world crowded with people, houses, cars, and the noises that all of these things made when you jumbled them haphazardly together.

As she became use to his schedule, she occasionally demanded that he accommodate hers.

Late at night, when the world was as quiet as a city ever got, she would leash Winston, who waited with head cocked to one side as if listening to the jingle of the chain, and she would make him go for a walk.

Tonight, the sense of regret as strong as it had been in years, was one of those times. She got dressed again, fought with the door briefly, and left the relative safety of her apartment.

HE FOLLOWED HER WHEN she left her apartment. He had done it before, but in the end he had not found the opening he sought. She was careful, carefully defended. But the ballet and its aftermath had opened a small hole in those defenses, and he knew that if he was to reach her at all, it was during this particular walk.

He followed her.

She lived above the Don Valley, and she could walk out the front door of her apartment building, turn a corner, and descend from the heights to the floor. There, a bike trail, a river, and a few solitary travelers were all that broke the illusion of forest and wilderness.

She stopped at the sloping height of Pottery Road. In the valley, mist was rolling in, like white smoke spreading from some lightless fire.

She hesitated just a moment and then began her descent.

IT WAS A PERFECT evening. The mist rolled in like a shroud across the valley. It was cold and wet, but not so thick that it obscured all vision; just thick enough that it offered the illusion of privacy. Maia Anderson sauntered along the bike path, and he stepped in front of her, waiting. But she did not bump into him, did not pass him, did not approach.

The dog, little perceptive creature, stopped moving and began to growl. She tugged gently at his leash three times; his response was simply to growl more deeply. He could see her frown as she squinted into the distance.

"What's wrong, Winston? Winston, *cut that out.* There's nothing there."

"Oh, but there is," he said. "Hello, Maia. I've been waiting for you."

SHE LOOKED UP. ANYTHING she might have said to an intruder, any cry she might have raised, was trapped between lips that almost refused to let breath pass.

She saw him as he had once appeared; tall and glorious, arms outstretched in a nimbus of soft, warm light. His face, pale and beautiful, seemed marred by the pain of a distant loss, but no other blemish, no other scar, troubled him. His eyes, blue and clear, regarded her as if from a lofty height. He cast light the way anything else cast shadow.

"Maia," he said, in a soft voice that nonetheless managed to fill the valley. "Come, child." He held out one hand and she gazed at it a moment in confusion, but his words pulled her slowly forward. She pushed Winston gently but firmly to one side; it was actually harder than the difference in their weights would have suggested. The dog was stiff and shaking.

But it was impossible not to approach the stranger. She had been taught, directly by her parents, and indirectly by experience, not to trust strangers; to find them slightly threatening in the way only the unknown can be.

But the known in her life wasn't all that comforting, and although she knew it was shallow she couldn't feel threatened by someone who looked like this man. She could, however, feel inadequate. Small, crippled, old, even ugly.

She stopped moving, and he covered the distance between them, reaching out to touch her chin gently.

"Maia," he said, pulling her face up, forcing her gaze to meet his, "I have been watching you."

She wanted to ask, *Are you an angel?* But the words wouldn't come. Instead, she waited. It seemed to her, as his gaze brushed her face, that all she had ever done was wait—and now, it was impossible to do anything else.

He nodded, as if agreeing with the things she would not say. "Three years ago you suffered an accident."

Her gaze became subject to gravity; it fell to the leg that track pants now covered. But cloth or no, she could suddenly see every detail of the scar and the ugly white web it made of her knee. It seemed a signature, in some language that she had learned by immersion and experience, that had certified the death of her dreams, had cut her loose from the future that she had worked so hard for.

She nodded dumbly. All of her hard-won acceptance fell away as if it were sleep. Waking was hard.

"No one should have to live without their dreams."

Are you an angel? She thought it so loudly she was certain he must have heard it.

He only smiled. "This accident didn't kill you. There are days when you wish it had. Evenings, like this one." He turned toward the asphalt bike path that led into mist. "Will you walk with me? I walk seldom. It is . . . pleasant."

"I—yes. Yes, I'll walk. Are we going anywhere?" His words were stark, but they were not cruel—there was something behind them, around them. An insane hope flared to life, luminous and brilliant.

He laughed. "Almost anywhere you like," he said softly. "But it is best, when you travel this way, to travel unencumbered." His gaze fell to Winston and rested there like a judgment. But it was not unkind. "Little friend," he said, "I think you have almost served your purpose. Run along now; your master and I have much to discuss, and she cannot afford the distraction."

Winston growled. His belly was low to ground, his ears flat against his skull. Which shouldn't have been possibly, given his ears.

"I don't believe he likes me," the stranger said.

"I—he's not the friendliest dog in the world." She bent down. Fiddled with his collar for a moment, while chain links chimed against each other in time with her shaking hands. "Go on," she whispered.

He whined.

"No, go on. I'll find you on the way back."

But as she said it, she knew she was lying. She hesitated.

"Maia," the stranger said softly, "we have little time; there are so many people who require my aid."

She stiffened. "You can go and help them if you've got someplace you'd rather be."

His smile was indulgent. She had seen a smile like that on her grandmother's face when she was four, but that was the last time she had seen it. "Unlike many that I see, you have never forgotten your hope and your dream. I saw it in you tonight, at the ballet. I see it now, in what you remember."

She said nothing.

"Am I an angel?" He smiled, but the smile was peculiar; it was warm, but not friendly; it touched everything but his eyes. "For now, say that I am a keeper of dreams, and a maker of them, if they are strong enough." He placed a gentle hand upon her shoulder.

"Will you travel with me for the night? There are things you must see, and a choice you must make. We have far to go if you are strong enough."

She looked around the valley; it seemed diminished in grayness and shadow, almost squalid when compared to his shining countenance. *This is a dream.*

"Perhaps *the* dream." He took her hand in his.

She could not stop hers from shaking, and it made her angry—but not angry enough that she could let go. Some stubborn, foolish part of her mind had always believed in the mystic. She wanted magic. There was so little magic in her life. "Where—where are we going?"

"Back, child. Back three years, two months, and ten days. Come." He began to walk and, hand trapped in his, she followed; the mists rolled in, thicker than any mist she had ever seen.

Like, she thought absurdly, the dry ice on the stage of the ballet.

"DO YOU KNOW THIS place?"

She shivered and nodded.

She had never liked crowds—or rather, had never liked to be in the middle of one. Dancing in front of a crowd had always been different; people were contained, one to a seat, the chaos of their numbers reduced by rows. But there were no seats here, and order in an amusement park was a matter of manners and patience. It was a beautiful day.

Maybe, she thought, that was why she liked the rain now.

In the background, the tinny drone of amusement park music played in her ears like a nightmare serenade.

"Come. There are people here that you know. Let us find them."

She followed, afraid to lose him in the crowd. Afraid of what would happen if she did not lose him. *Get a grip,* she told herself. *What could happen? What could possibly happen that could be worse?*

"You will not lose me here, Maia. Only yourself; only what this place has made of you." His grip on her arm was sure and steady as he began to help her through the crowds.

She wondered what he meant.

Then a man passed by, laughing. She recognized his gait first, the easy way he walked, the length of his stride and the confidence of his step. Even at a distance, when height, weight, and detail was obscured, the way he moved was distinctive. He wasn't at a distance now. She looked up quickly enough to clearly see his face. Neil's face. Beardless, smooth, a little too shiny.

"Yes," he said quietly. "Shall we follow him?"

She had already begun to do so. She could not have said why it had become so important, but it was. He stopped where she knew he must stop and joined a group of his friends. In the harsh light of this perfect day they were . . . perfect. Slender, not too pale and not too tanned. They had hair and clothing that was three years out of date—but so was everything she owned with the exception of a perfect black dress.

"They can't see me."

"No."

"Good."

Sharon's face came into view as she moved around Neil, as if he were a pillar, just another geographical impediment. And another—Andrew's. The former looked very annoyed, although all of that emotion was contained in the edges of narrowed eyes, the thinning of lips. Andrew was smiling, at ease; it had been his practice to ignore anything that resembled anger, anything that might lead to messy confrontation. It didn't matter. She found them all magnetic, although she hadn't seen them in . . . years.

"Keep looking," he said softly, but it wasn't necessary; she wasn't certain she could have looked away had she tried.

Because, at the end of the group, she came face to face with herself. Also laughing, talking, maneuvering her way through the crowd that she so disliked. She froze.

"Do you recognize her?"

". . . yes . . ."

"She cannot see you." He watched her a moment, smiling evenly. "But she has your dream. It isn't as strong as yours because she can take it for granted. Do you know what's about to happen?"

She started to shake her head, and then stopped. Whirling around, she saw the looming shadow of the log ride. The log ride—what did they call it? The sudden weight of water against the surface of her eyes blurred color, smudged the distinct lines of the colorful sign. But the shape of this harbinger was unmistakable.

The log ride. The one where you got those ridiculous rectangular boats pulled by those ominous grinding chains . . . the boats that weren't quite wide enough to touch both sides of the slide that contained them . . . the log ride, where the ground was so slippery and the boats just kept moving no matter what was caught beside them . . .

"Yes," he said quietly. She didn't hear him.

Unable to stop herself, she ran forward, seeing time slip between her fingers. They were in line—she was in line—for the ride; they were so close to being on it. Neil was beside her—Neil was drunk. Horsing around, with just a little edge of menace to make it not quite fun. Nudging her. Pushing, grabbing.

"No!" She let out a cry—reached out to grab herself and saw her hands go through the image as if she were a ghost. As if one of her were a ghost.

"Child, this can change." He raised one arm. The scene froze.

And when it started again, she saw herself frown at Neil's antics—and *pull away*. Only this time, this time, when Neil went to grab her in a wild spin, he missed. He missed, he stumbled—he fell flat on his face. But it didn't matter what happened to him.

She saw her younger brow furrow in momentary disgust; saw the way she forced it down—saw her leg, whole, not trapped to one side of that insidious, horrible ride. And she felt fire suddenly bite into her own leg. She cried out in shock and in a little pain—but heat became warmth as it radiated out in waves.

She looked up at her companion—her angel—very slowly.

"Don't be afraid of me. Never of me. You have a dream, and I the ability to fulfill it. Let us walk back to your time. Let us see what difference this one small act has made."

This time, when she took his hand, she didn't hesitate.

The amusement park faded, the sounds of laughter lingering longest.

"WHAT? WHERE ARE WE?"

"This, child, is your home now."

She looked at her bedroom. She knew it had to be a bedroom—there was a bed in it. But if it was hers, it had grown by about two hundred square feet, and windows had taken over the east wall completely. Her bed was no longer the old futon frame that she'd rescued from somebody's garbage; it was long, wide, and beautifully antique. Something she might have bought had she ever had the money.

"You have it now," he said. "Come, will you not look out?"

Half afraid that it would vanish, she shook her head.

He only smiled. "As you wish, although you chose this place because of the view. We both like heights. But you must hurry. Tonight is to be a special performance—your first as principal ballerina. Would you miss it?"

. . . *principal dancer* . . .

Those words brought an odd flush to her face. For an instant she closed her eyes, her imagination making the details solid, welcome. Then they jumped open again as she realized the glaring flaw in the dream. "But I don't know how to—I don't know which—I don't—"

His face, as he smiled, was beautiful. "But you do, child. You've been doing this constantly and steadily for the past three years. It's been your whole life." He held out a hand. "You've a car you can use, or if you prefer we can travel together."

She took his hand eagerly. Everything was rushing in toward her—all the hopes and plans that had been lost in the dead years. Yes. That's what it had been like—death. But now, if what the angel said was really true . . . She wanted to shout for joy, wordless and loud. Words were too small to contain all that she felt.

He frowned as she suddenly stopped.

"Where's Winston?"

"Winston?"

"My—my dog."

"Ah. The animal." He bowed his head for an instant, concentrating. When he met her eyes, he was frowning slightly. "Was he important to you?"

Something about the way he asked the question stopped her from answering.

"I see. Child, the day that you met this animal, you were returning from the hospital."

She nodded automatically, and then her eyes widened. She looked down at her knee—her smooth, unscarred leg was visible.

"Yes. You never had your accident."

She opened her mouth to speak, closed it, and opened it again. "Do you—do you know where he is?"

His frown was almost painful; it was as if the light left his face. "It was you and your loss that drew me. A dog seldom has dreams of loss, and if it does, they are not the type of loss that I can address. Dogs don't look back." His grip on her hand tightened. "Now come. You'll be late."

"I'll know?"

"When you start to dance, Maia, the life that you should have led and the life that you did lead will blur. You'll remember all of your decisions in both lives, and you will value what you have in *this* one all the more for its loss in the other."

She hesitated for a moment, and then nodded. *He survived without me before. And it isn't my fault that we couldn't really meet in this life.*

But she felt a little hollow as the room melted away beneath her feet.

"MAIA!"

SHE SPUN AROUND at the sound of the unfamiliar voice.

"There you are! Thank God—Jarrett's been having seven kinds of fit!"

Without waiting for a reply, the large woman grabbed her by the arm and began to drag her through the cramped halls. It took Maia a moment to realize where they were, and when she did, her feet failed her and she stumbled.

"We're—we're backstage—"

"No kidding." The woman rolled her eyes. "This is *not* the time to weird out on me, Maia. Come on. you've got to get changed, and you've got to get prepped." The woman laughed. "Y'know, if you can be late for this, it must be true."

"What is?"

"You can be late for anything." She shrugged philosophically as they came to a closed door. "Well, at least you won't have time to be nervous—which is good because if you were, he'd kill you."

Maia barely heard her. She touched the knob of the door with wonder.

"Hey," her unfamiliar friend said. Maia turned around and was quite surprised when the woman wrapped her in a tight hug. "Good luck, kid. This is your night. You've earned it."

Before she could answer the door swung open.

"Enter, little one."

Maia looked up to meet his eyes; in the confusion, she'd almost forgotten he was there.

"This is your triumph—but it is also mine. Enter now; you've little time."

She took a breath, closed her eyes, and pushed the door inward. It opened on chaos and cacophony—bodies rushing back and forth bearing make-up, clothing, glasses. She didn't have time to take it all in.

"Maia!"

She jumped and someone laughed. It was not the man who grabbed her arm.

"Where the hell have you been? Don't just stand there gawking—get to wardrobe!"

HE WATCHED, NOTING THE flush of her cheeks and the unnatural glimmer of her eyes. She was transformed before him from the ordinary Maia into the lovestruck young girl of the first act.

ONLY WHEN SHE WAS ready did she turn back to him, her eyes showing doubt.

His smile stilled it. "You will know what to do when you touch the stage. Trust me." He touched her cheek gently. "Have faith in your dream." He had time for no more as she was guided out of the room.

Jarrett, his calm returned to a small degree now that he was sure she would be on stage on time, led her into the wings. He kissed her cheek, which surprised her.

"Knock them dead, kid."

THE CORPS WAS ON stage, waiting in their elegant poses for her dance onto the stage; for her spins and turns as the simple, fragile peasant girl who loves both willfully and foolishly, and pays for both youthful crimes. Without knowing how, she felt her feet and arms begin to move of their own accord, as if somehow the music had become her master. The stage loomed before her like a cliff, daring her to fly.

It all felt so right somehow. This is what she had cried herself to sleep for for three years. This is what the scar, so fine and ugly and white, had deprived her of.

She belonged here.

With a wide smile that said more than it had ever said, she began to let the music take her. She took a step forward, graceful and elegant, the orchestra pulling her along. Another step, quick and more sure, brought back a hint of memory. Yes, of course she could do this. Hadn't she been working so hard and so long for it? Her arms framed her face; she took a full, deep breath and lifted her chin to the sound of . . . barking.

Barking?

Startled, she looked back into the wings to see Winston bristling beside her angel. Winston, all scruff and ire, was trying to run toward her.

Not now, Winston—I—she fumbled a moment, her feet misstepping. He'd said Winston wasn't here. She looked up at his pale face, but for once, he was not looking at her. Rather, he was staring intently down at the dog. Before she could move, he raised one arm—one glorious arm—and brought it down. It fell like lightning, striking the terrier's back with blinding speed.

"NO!" The music was gone. Her feet were her own as she spun around and began to run back.

"Maia, *stop.*" This was a voice used to command; it rained down around her as she obeyed. "This animal has no place in our lives from here on. I have given you your dream. You have but to walk onto the stage and all that you have seen will be yours; you will have no memory of anything else."

Her dream. Unable to stop herself, she turned back to see the lights on the props of the stage.

"Yes. But time is short. Go now."

Almost, she turned, but Winston whimpered quietly, drawing her attention. She met his eyes as he lay immobile.

"What do you owe to an animal? If dogs are important, you can buy another—but this chance will never come again. If you prove false to your dream, it will die."

Die. Like the dead years. *No. God, he's only a dog!*

For a moment, she raged against it—against the lifelessness that she'd faced for so long, against the emptiness that had been everything to her until—

Until that one rainy night.

She closed her eyes, suspended on a very fine line between everything she had ever wanted and the only thing that had ever completely accepted her. It was sharp, this line, and the longer she stood upon it, the more it threatened to slice her in two.

She stepped off.

And as her left foot touched the ground, her knee buckled. She bit her lip to hide the pain as she crumpled to the floor of her small, dark room. No longer a ballerina. Her peasant costume became track pants, her shoes, with their hard, ungiving toes, simple runners.

She looked up. The tears in her eyes were more than her knee could have caused at its worst.

"Maia Anderson," the stranger said softly. His face was different. Beautiful, but . . . different. Ah, that was it. Transparent. He was leaving, she thought.

All she could say was "Why?"

"Why?" His voice was warm. His smile was ineffably gentle.

"Why did you try to kill my dog?"

"Did I?" He was fading as she spoke. But he lifted a hand, and pointed.

Winston was sitting, as she'd left him, belly down on the path. His ears were turned down, his lips drawn up over yellowed teeth. His head was cocked to one side in curiosity, and his fur was slightly bristling. But he was not whining. He was not . . . broken. Not dead.

She pushed herself up off the damp ground. She collapsed again, but this time Winston was not content to watch. He ran across the path and licked her face. He had the *worst* breath. Obviously she was no longer dreaming. Her leg throbbed in protest at the damp, damp evening.

"Why did you come here? Why did you make me that offer? Why did you—"

"Because," he said softly, "in the end, there is no going back. The past *is* the past. Maia—if you were a different person, I would have spoken differently. But we give what we must give, and if our lessons are harsh, they are never cruel.

"You were trapped in a past that no longer existed. And there were things in the present that you could not acknowledge you valued." He bowed; the light was fading so quickly.

So was the fog.

"You have a life ahead of you that is not the life you thought you would live." His smile was peaceful. "And I?" He lifted a hand, and in it, for just a second, burning like the soul of fire, was a blade. "I saw the fall of Sodom. I offered the mercy of an old, old god. I have learned to value what I have, as well." He bowed. "Mercy is your greatest gift. Use it wisely, and grant it first to yourself."

She crossed her arms, tight, against her chest. Alone, she let the tears fall. It didn't matter if Winston saw them—he'd seen them for years; it wasn't anything new.

"You s-s-stupid dog," she said, as she reached out blindly for him. "You moron." His tail thudded back and forth and she buried her wet face into his fur and let the tears bleed themselves dry.

And then, as she sat, she heard it. The music played, softly at first as it always did—a hint of the dream that had died three years ago.

Or had it?

Using Winston's back, she forced herself to her feet again as the strains of music coalesced, growing louder and more certain. This time, her wobbly knee held.

"I didn't miss it," she said, her voice shakier than her leg. "I—I didn't." With effort that she knew she'd regret in the morning, she lifted her friend by his two front paws, and they loped in the growing clarity of a perfect summer evening.

...Next on Channel 77

Lucy A. Snyder

Tom Wilson woke in the gray early-morning light to the smell of coffee percolating and the sound of dishes rattling. A moment later, he realized that his girlfriend Myrna was still sleeping beside him and his heart jumped like a rabbit: *Oh, shit, there's a burglar in the apartment—*

—and then he heard a woman's voice humming "Strangers in the Night."

Aunt Fran? No. It wasn't possible. She was back in Barlow Gap, Montana. No way she'd suddenly show up in downtown Chicago at this hour.

"Thomas! Coffee's ready!" Fran called.

I'm still asleep, he thought. *This is a dream.*

He slipped out of bed and found his jeans. Myrna mumbled a sleepy protest, then rolled over and started snoring softly. Tom pulled on his pants and crept toward the living room.

His eighty-year-old grand-aunt Francine was standing in the tiny kitchen that adjoined the living room. She was wearing her favorite Sunday-go-to-church outfit: her lilac dress, white pearl-buttoned gloves, and white straw hat. She was carefully pouring

105

coffee from his stained pot into a pair of her best antique china teacups on her silver serving tray.

"Aunt Fran?" He slowly stepped toward her. She looked the same as when he'd said good-bye to her at the bus station in Barlow Gap nine years before. She'd been the only member of his family to see him off. "What—what are you doing here?"

"Good morning, Thomas! Do you still take cream and sugar in your coffee?"

"Uh, yes, ma'am . . . but what are you doing here in Chicago?"

Her blue eyes twinkled mischievously. "What makes you think we're in Chicago?"

The room rippled, changed. Cracked beige paint became crisp striped wallpaper, dingy hardwood turned to tidy cream-colored carpet.

They were in Fran's living room.

"What the—" Tom began.

"Come, your coffee's getting cold." Fran was sitting on her couch, the china tea service sitting on the coffee table in front of her. A black plastic RCA TV remote lay beside the tray. She poured a splash of cream into one of the cups, then smiled at him and patted the cushion beside her. "Sit down, sit down! I'm not going to bite."

Dazed, Tom sat beside her. She passed him his cup, a silver spoon, and a tiny plate stacked high with sugar cubes. He hadn't seen anyone use sugar cubes in years.

He stirred two cubes into his coffee and took a tentative sip. Yep, it was real joe. If all this was a dream, it was far more realistic than anything his mind had churned out in a while.

"Let me see your hand," she said.

"My hand?" *What the heck does she want to see my hand for?*

"Yes, your right hand."

He held it out. She put on her spectacles and peered down at his index finger. She lifted it and waggled it back and forth. "Well, your dialing finger isn't broken. How come you never call me, boy? The comic book shop's doing pretty well these days; you can afford a few calls back home."

Tom blushed deeply. "I—I'm sorry, Fran, I just—you know, got busy. But I think about you lots and I meant to call—" he stammered, then stopped. "Hey, wait a minute, how did you know about the comics shop?"

Tom had helped Myrna open her comics shop, the *25th Century Five and Dime*, on North Halsted a little over two years ago. It was finally seeing a profit, partly due to the coffee bar they'd added. Until recently, Myrna had been financing the shop with money she'd inherited from her grandfather.

"You'd be surprised what you learn once you're dead," Fran replied primly, sipping her coffee. "The future and the past both become clear."

"D-dead?"

"Well, not *dead* dead . . . my heart's still ticking away, but my brain checked out last night after the stroke. So my body's still warm and breathing in the hospital, but I'm not in it anymore. My heart's going to go soon, though, and then they can put me in the ground."

She paused. "Dying's not so bad. The hard part is having to leave so many things undone. There's so *much* I wanted to do that I just never had time for. Never *made* time for. And then there's some things I dreamed of doing that I simply never *could* do, just because of the time and place and family I was born into.

"Did you know that, ever since we got our first TV back in 1960, I wished I could be a TV news reporter? No, of course you didn't, because I never told anyone. It was impossible; women didn't become TV reporters back then, especially not forty-year-old housewives. I might as well have dreamed of becoming an astronaut or a fairy princess."

She picked up the TV remote and clicked the power button. The big console TV in the corner came on, the screen fuzzing bright blue before the image resolved.

Fran was on TV. She wore a smart green suit and held a microphone with a round "77" logo on the front. In the background, Tom could see the Barlow Gap Community Hospital.

"Luckily for our ALTV-77 viewers," said smiling newscaster Fran, "many dreams *can* come true in the afterlife. But will *all* my dreams come true? Will my favorite nephew attend my funeral? As my body lingers inside this hospital, young Mr. Thomas Wilson must decide to telephone his estranged family to make arrangements to pay his last respects to his loving aunt."

Fran clicked off the television. "It's very important that you be at my funeral. I *need* you to be there. I expect it'll be next Tuesday. Call your mother; she'll be awake soon."

God.

Tom hadn't talked to his mother since the day he left home. She'd been stoned on tranquilizers that day, as usual, and acted as if he were just going down to the store or something.

Acted as if he weren't really leaving home for good.

As if she didn't care about him.

Which she likely didn't. She hadn't seemed to care all that much for him once he was too old to be a cute attention-getter down at the grocery store. And when he left, she had his two little sisters to keep her occupied. With a seven-year-old in pigtails and frilly skirts and a cute-as-a-button babe in arms around the house, Tom was the unsightly teenage stain of the family. No one besides Fran seemed to want him around, and even she agreed it was best he leave for the big city.

The first few years after he'd left, Tom sent his mother Christmas cards, a few letters, Mother's Day cards and such, but he never got a reply, so he stopped sending them. Ever since, he'd been so angry at her for so long, he didn't know what to say to them—or if he *had* anything to say to them.

"But—" Tom began.

"I know it's going to be hard. But please promise me you'll come?"

"Okay . . . okay, I'll come."

She patted his knee. "You always were a good boy . . ."

Fran and her living room faded into the gray dimness of his and Myrna's apartment. Tom found himself sitting alone on their old tweed sofa. He still held Fran's teacup, the coffee inside it hot and steaming slightly in the cool apartment air.

He drained the cup in one gulp and held it in both hands. The eggshell china was a delicate rose pattern of pale pinks and greens and a little interwoven gold-leaf filigree that had rubbed off in a few places. The lip of the cup had a small chip, and age had spiderwebbed the glaze. The cup had to be at least as old as Fran . . . was.

He glanced at the clock in the wall. It would be just past six in Montana. And his mother always awoke at 5:30, no matter how many pills or glasses of wine she'd had the night before. Growing up on a farm made her an incurable early riser.

He stared at the phone and felt dread building in the pit of his stomach. After nine years, what was he supposed to say? *Hi, Mom, still hooked on Valium? Dad still an unbearable jerk?* Sheesh.

Why had he agreed to go back? He'd washed his hands of his parents, and apparently they had done the same of him.

At least it would be nice to see his sisters, Lisa and Joanie. He hoped they remembered him. He hoped they'd had a better time of it than he. His father always went out of his way to belittle him; Tom chalked his behavior up to some weird Freudian competitiveness. Probably his siblings' being female would take the edge off his father's temper.

He stared at the phone.

The phone stared back: *Well, ya big wuss, you gonna call your mother or not?*

"Crap," he sighed, then picked up the receiver and punched in the number.

After a few rings, his mother answered. "Hello?"

"Hello, Mom?"

"I think you have the wrong number."

Click.

Tom stared down at the receiver. *Oh,* this *is going well. Once more, with feeling . . .*

He punched in the number again, and when his mother answered, he quickly said, "Wait! Don't hang up! This is Tom, your son. Remember me? I was just calling to see how you all are doing."

"Oh. *Tom,*" she said, sounding supremely surprised. "Hello. Well, uh, we're fine. Me and your father and your sisters, we're all . . . fine."

"How's Aunt Fran doing?"

"Well, she ain't doing too well, actually. She had a stroke, and . . . well, she don't have much time left. A day or two at most."

"I'd like to come to the funeral," he said, "but it's going to take me a few days to get out there. The bus ride'll take about a day and a half."

"Well . . . it surely would be great to see you again. You, uh, you can stay here at the house if you want. I turned your old room into a sewing room, but you're welcome to one of the couches."

"That'd be great, Mom. Thanks. I'll call you when I find out when I'll be getting there, okay?"

"That'll be fine."

"Good. Talk to you soon. 'Bye."

Tom hung up the phone and leaned back on the sofa, idly playing with Fran's empty teacup. *I can't believe I'm actually going back there . . .*

Myrna shuffled out of their bedroom, cinching her blue satin bathrobe around her narrow waist. "Who was that?" she asked.

"You want the single, or the dance mix?"

"Gimme the single. It's too early for dancing."

"That was my mother. My Aunt Fran's dying. I need to go to Montana for her funeral."

"Wait, wait, I gotta sit down for this." She plopped down beside him and pushed her dark red hair out of her eyes so she could stare at him. "Lemme get this straight. You hear *nothing* from your family for close to a decade, and now you're gonna drop everything and spend beaucoup bucks on a plane ticket to go home for a funeral? What, exactly, have they done to deserve you spending *any* amount of time and money on them?"

"Two things: first, I'll take the bus, so the bucks won't be beaucoup. Second, I'm not doing this for them, I'm doing it for *Fran.* You know how much she helped me out when I first came here. I'd never have made it without that two grand she gave me. At the very least, I owe her the courtesy of showing my respects at her funeral."

"I understand wanting to do it for Fran . . . but it's not like she's really going to know you're there."

"She'll know," Tom replied, staring down at the teacup. "Trust me on this one."

Myrna sighed. "I suppose I can cover most of your shifts myself. I can probably sweet-talk Ralph into working the coffee bar."

Tom set the teacup down on their paper-strewn coffee table and pulled her close. "Tell you what . . . when I get back, I'll work the shop for a few days. You can watch movies, catch up on your reading, take bubble baths. And then we'll both take a day off, go out for breakfast at the Melrose, catch a matinee, and then do whatever we want. Sound good?"

She giggled. "Sounds good. Just be careful in Montana . . . I wouldn't want you getting hurt in a freak cow-tipping accident."

THREE DAYS LATER, TOM stepped off the Greyhound as the sun was setting behind the mountains. It was a gorgeous sunset, all pinks and oranges and purples, and the sun was a gigantic ruby. He'd forgotten how pretty it was out here.

He shouldered his duffel and garment bag and went into the station to look for his mother. He scanned the people in the narrow yellow plastic chairs; none looked familiar. He walked toward the pay phone to call for a cab.

"Tom?"

He turned. Two girls, one close to ten and the other about sixteen, stood by the snack machine staring at him uncertainly. The younger girl had short blond hair and wore overalls and a blue corduroy 4-H jacket. The older girl had long, straight honey-blond hair, green eyes, a smattering of freckles, a long, graceful neck, and a great figure that she was apparently trying to hide under a floppy sweatshirt and loose jeans. Her eyes were rimmed red, as if she'd been crying for a long time. Something about her stance reminded him of his mother.

"Lisa? Joanie?" he asked.

The younger girl broke into a wide smile. "See, Lisa, I *told* you it was him! He's just like in the picture, only he's bigger!"

He stepped toward his sisters. "Wow, you two look *great*. You girls really got pretty while I was gone."

He leaned down and gave each of them a quick, awkward hug. "Where's Mom?"

"Uh, she wasn't feeling well," Lisa replied, looking embarrassed. "So she sent us to pick you up."

"You've got your driver's license now? Oh, man, I *have* been away a long time."

The girls led him out to Lisa's little Dodge Neon.

"The funeral's tomorrow morning," Lisa said as they loaded his bags into the trunk. "It's supposed to storm, so we might not be able to do the graveside service."

Her lip began to tremble, and a tear slipped down her cheek. She pulled a wad of Kleenex out of her jeans pocket and turned away from him. "Sorry. Just give me a minute."

Deciding it was best to give her space, Tom climbed into the back seat. Joanie crawled onto the seat beside him and started telling him all about 4-H (which she'd apparently just joined) and about the lamb she was raising as her first project. The girl's words tumbled over each other like eager puppies. But one look at her eyes told him she was just as sad about Fran's death as Lisa was, but she clung to her pretense of cheer as though everyone depended on her to be the Designated Happy Child.

Lisa finally got into the driver's seat and took off without another word, content to let her little sister's chatter camouflage the heartbreak that hung between them all.

It took them half an hour to get to the family ranch. According to Joanie, their father had sold off their cattle and most of their grazing land to a neighbor. They still had the good hunting land around the creek and a few wooded acres in the foothills that Joanie liked to ride her horse in.

Lisa parked the car in front of their old two-story house and they all piled out.

The teen was the first one through the front door. "I made some fruit salad and ham sandwiches; they're in the fridge. We left you a pillow and a blanket on the couch in the rec room." She was blinking fast, as if she were about to burst into tears. "I, uh, I gotta go."

With that, Lisa bolted up the stairs like a scared cat.

Joanie tugged at his sleeve. "I gotta go feed Bo. Wanna come out and see him?"

"In a minute. I better say hi to Mom and Dad first."

"'Kay." She ducked back outside, the screen door slamming loosely behind her.

Tom stood alone in the foyer. Dueling TVs blared from the kitchen and the darkened living room. Yep, home was just the way he remembered it: TVs on in practically every room, conveniently removing the need for conversation and real human interaction.

Tom heard his father's cough and the creak of him getting up from his recliner. The elder Mr. Wilson shambled out of the living room like a groggy bear. He wore a pair of old denim overalls and a white T-shirt. His face was puffy, and he'd gained about forty pounds. His hair had gone almost entirely gray. He loosely clutched a longneck in his left hand; the old man had probably already killed three or four of its brothers this evening.

"Hi, Dad," Tom said.

"Well. You're back." His father looked him up and down, then shifted from foot to foot.

"Yep. I'm back," Tom agreed. "For a few days."

"You look good, son. Real good. Got tall. Still got that faggy earring, though."

"Yeah." He touched the silver ring in his left ear. "My girlfriend really digs it."

His father grunted and gestured toward the living room with the longneck. "Ya wanna grab a beer and come watch the ball game with me?"

This, Tom knew, was as close to a warm welcome as he was likely to get. "I'm kinda stiff from the bus ride, so I'd like to walk around outside first, if that's okay?"

"Uh-huh," his father grunted, then turned and shuffled back into the living room. "Got ham sandwiches if you're hungry."

Tom went down into the basement rec room. Even the TV down here was on; he turned it off and surveyed his quarters. The air was musty and smelled like old sneakers. The pool table was stacked high with old board games and paper bags of magazines. He wondered if anyone used the room for anything but TV these days. The old red Naugahyde couch had been cleared off and supplied with a pillow and a neatly folded blue blanket. Tom set his bags on the couch and headed upstairs to the kitchen.

HIS MOTHER WAS SITTING in a faded pink housecoat at the kitchen table. The old portable black-and-white TV on the counter was deafeningly loud; some kind of medical drama was playing. His mother's eyes were glazed, staring unblinking at the flickering screen. A half-empty bottle of red wine and a Looney Tunes juice glass sat on the table beside her left hand. A forgotten cigarette was burning down to a gray tube of ash in her right hand. She'd only recently turned forty-three, but she could've easily passed for sixty.

"Mom?" Tom called. "Mom!"

No response. She didn't even move.

He went to the TV and turned it down a few notches. She gave a little start, then blinked.

"Oh . . . *Tom*," she slurred, then smiled wanly. "You're . . . how was your trip?"

"It was fine. A little long." He leaned over the table and gave her a quick kiss on her forehead. The smell of alcohol clouded around her like cheap perfume.

"I'm sorry I couldn't meet you at the bus station. I wasn't . . . feeling well." Her eyes focused on him, then unfocused as they suddenly brimmed with tears. "You've gotten so big. My little boy's gone. All gone."

"Shh, it's okay, Mom," he said, trying to comfort her. She seldom got maudlin when she was drunk, but this was a welcome change from her usual zombielike stupor.

She wept into his shoulder. "I'm so s-sorry, Tommy. I wasn't . . . I'm not . . . much of a mother."

You're a fine mother, he willed himself to say, but the lie stuck in his throat and refused to come out. So he just held her.

"I wanted you to stay," she sobbed, "but I didn't know how to ask. I didn't know what to say."

"I couldn't stay and watch you kill yourself. God, Mom, why do you *do* this to yourself? Why do you do this to *us*?"

He knew the answer; he'd known it in his heart for a long time. She'd married too young and had a child too early by a man who didn't know how to give her the love and attention she needed. And so she crawled into the nearest bottle to escape the stress and loneliness she didn't know how else to cope with.

Her grip on his arm was starting to loosen, her eyelids fluttering. "I . . . didn't know . . ."

She slumped back in the chair, snoring softly.

Just like ol' times, Mom, he thought, shaking his head.

He knew from experience that she'd wake up in an hour or so and put herself to bed. He quietly took the bottle off the table and poured the rest of the wine down the sink. Then he went to the fridge and found a plate of plastic-wrapped sandwiches on the bottom shelf. He took one and a can of ginger ale and went outside to find Joanie.

The cool, humid evening air was a welcome relief from the stuffiness of the house. He took a deep breath of country air. It was oddly comforting to be smelling hay and manure instead of diesel and garbage. No matter how much he loved Chicago, Montana still felt like home.

He popped open the soda and munched on his sandwich as he walked around the house to the barn. Two half-grown kittens were stalking something in a loose pile of hay by the door. Inside, he could see the soft yellow glow from an electric lantern.

Tom stepped inside the barn, straw crackling beneath his feet. Two horses in stalls to his left chuffed and peered at him curiously. A few yards away, Joanie was sitting on a milking stool in the middle of a chickenwire pen. She was bottle-feeding a sturdy-looking lamb and brushing his woolly coat with a curry comb.

"Hi, Joanie," he called.

"Hi! Come meet Bo!" the girl called back.

Tom walked to the pair and stepped over the yard-high pen wall. "That's some lamb you've got," he said, his eyes watering from the smell. He'd forgotten how powerfully sheep stank, even clean ones.

"Isn't he great? He's just a few months old; he was born premature and his momma died. They didn't think he would live, but I fed him and kept him warm and now look at him! If he gets big enough, I'm gonna show him at the next county fair. He gets awful dirty, though, even when he's just here in the pen. You know what I use to wash him?"

"No, what?"

"Woolite!" She laughed, but her smile didn't make it as far as her eyes.

They were both quiet for a moment.

"I'm really sorry about Aunt Fran," he said gently. "She meant a lot to me, so I know she must've meant a lot to you and Lisa. And . . . I'm sorry I left you girls. I hoped things would be better for you two than they were for me . . . but I guess they haven't been. Anyway . . . I'm sorry. Things got so bad between me and Dad, I just didn't know what else to do but go away."

"S'okay," Joanie replied, her eyes downcast. "I think Lisa was mad at you for a long time, but I wasn't. It would've been cool to have a big brother and all . . . but I want to leave, too, sometimes. Mom and Dad . . . they're here, but they're someplace else most of the time, you know? It was Aunt Fran who took care of me when I was little. Her and Lisa."

A tear trickled down her cheek. She wiped it away and forced another one of her patented cheery smiles. "I just don't know what's going to happen now. It feels like everything's broken, and if I let myself get sad, it'll all just fall apart."

Slate-black storm clouds steadily built on the horizon during the graveside service the next morning. The preacher had to raise his voice to be heard over the rising wind. As they lowered the brass-handled casket into the ground, the first cold raindrops splattered down on Tom and his family.

As soon as the service was completed, everyone hurried back to their cars. The rain was pounding down by the time they got back to the house. Once they were inside, the Wilson family silently scattered to their various havens: his mother and Lisa to their rooms, his father to his beer and TV in the living room, and Joanie to her lamb in the barn.

Tom was left alone in the kitchen. The table was crowded with casseroles and pies the ladies from the Presbyterian church had brought by that morning before the funeral. Most of the church ladies adored Fran, but none cared to stay very long at the Wilson house.

Well, now what? Tom thought as he sat down at the table. Fran had been adamant about him coming all this way, but to do what? She hadn't made an appearance at the funeral. *Why am I here?*

Tom jumped as the kitchen TV switched on. As if possessed, the TV's dial ratcheted around until it landed on Channel 77.

"Welcome back to ALTV-77, your channel for the Guardian Angel Network's news from the afterlife." Fran was wearing a beige pantsuit and a Jackie Kennedy-style pillbox hat with a black veil. She looked a solid twenty years younger than when she'd visited him in his apartment. "Many viewers still don't realize that suicide is a leading cause of death of North American teenagers. Teens are particularly at risk after the death of a loved one."

Tom felt his blood run cold.

"You need to talk to your sister, Thomas, and do it now."

The TV switched off.

Tom pushed away from the table and hurried to the stairs. When he got to Lisa's room, he put his ear to the door to listen. She was sobbing. He rapped on the wood.

"Lisa, can I talk to you?" he called.

"Go away."

"No, I won't go away . . . I really need to talk to you."

Panic scrabbled at the back of his throat when she didn't answer. He tried the knob. It was locked.

"Look, if I have to kick the door open, I will!"

He heard the floor creak as she moved toward the door, then the click of her unlocking it. The door swung in. He stepped inside.

"What do you want?" Her tone was nervous and surly. She was holding something behind her back.

"What have you got there?"

"Nothing." She backed up, but he grabbed her arm. "Let go! It's none of your business—"

She had a bottle clenched in her fist. He pried her fingers open, and a bottle of pills fell to the floor.

Their mother's tranquilizers.

He released her arm and picked up the bottle. It was only half full.

"Oh, God. Please tell me you didn't—" he began.

"No. I didn't." She sank to her knees on the bare floor. "I was *about* to . . . I'd been psyching myself up to do it for the past half-hour."

"But *why?*" he asked, kneeling beside her. "You've got your whole life ahead of you—"

"That's bullshit and you know it!" she flared, then started crying anew. "*What* life is it that I'm supposed to have ahead of me, huh? I got no friends at school; everyone thinks I'm some kind of freak loser on account that everyone knows my parents are a couple of lushes. School's boring, and my grades suck because the work just makes me want to scream, it's all so stupid. And the other kids—*God*! They're either cowboy jerkoffs or they're running around in baggy jeans listening to rap and pretending to be these little white gangstas. Gangstas! Here in Montana! What a freakin' joke! This whole place is a joke. And I'm the biggest joke of all, 'cause I don't fit in and nobody but Aunt Fran cares whether I live or die. And now she's gone. So I might as well die and save everyone the trouble."

"*I* care, Lisa."

"You do *not*," she snapped. "Tomorrow you're going back to Chicago, and you'll forget all about me like you did before."

"I'm sorry I let you down, Lisa. The last thing I wanted to do was hurt you—I just wanted to get away from here."

"Yeah? Like I *don't*? All I think about is being someplace besides here . . . but I'm too scared to leave. I can't go off by myself like you did. God. I am *such* a *loser*!"

"You are *not* a loser. Number one, you are a very pretty girl— now, don't give me that look, you *are* very pretty; you'd have to beat the boys off with a stick in Chicago. If the yokels around here are too dumb to see what a beautiful person you are, that's their loss.

"Number two, you are a smart girl, too smart to throw it all away like this. Number three, think of how bad you felt when I went away—now how do you think Joanie would feel if you went and killed yourself, huh?

"And number four, I felt just like you do now when I was your age, and I can tell you that *it does get better*. There's so much more to life than high school. Everyone's got this idea that high school is some kind of carefree golden age of youth, but the truth is that for most of us, it's a hell you just have to endure to get that diploma. And, speaking as a guy who dropped out, *not* having that little scrap of paper is a major pain.

"You've stuck it out for sixteen years; what's two more?"

She sniffled and wiped her eyes. "But . . . what then?"

"Okay," he said slowly, "how 'bout this for a plan: you apply to colleges in the Chicago area, then come to live with me and Myrna while you go to class. Or, if you don't want to do the college thing right away, you can come out to Chicago, stay with us, and we can show you around. I know the big city can seem kinda scary—but man, it can be *so* much fun, you wouldn't believe it! We'll help you find your own way. How's that sound?"

She smiled; it was like seeing the sun come out from behind the clouds. "You promise?"

He crossed his heart with his index finger. "I won't let you down again."

He helped her to her feet. "Why don't we go downstairs, and I'll fix you some iced tea. Then maybe we can find Joanie and go out for ice cream or something?"

"Okay."

They headed down to the kitchen. Rain pelted the windows, and the wind was lashing the branches of the big trees in the front yard.

The kitchen TV clicked on.

"Welcome back to ALTV-77," said Aunt Fran.

Lisa's eyes went wide. "Ohmigod, that's—"

"Shh!" he said, putting his hand on her arm.

"We have a special weather report for our viewers in the Wilson Farm area. A funnel cloud has been sighted near Thorny Creek; it's scheduled to become an F2 tornado in the next half hour. Bo got loose, and Joanie's looking for him by the creek. She'll be in the tornado's path when it touches down."

"*Shit!*" exclaimed Tom. "Let's go!"

The pair raced out of the house and across the field toward the tree-lined creek. Tom could see the funnel cloud dipping down from the huge black wall cloud not two miles away from them. The violently changing wind threatened to knock him off his feet, but he ran on, willing his legs to move faster.

After five minutes of running down the nearly dry creekbed screaming the girl's name into the rising gale, they found Joanie and Bo in a small stand of alpine spruce on a rocky rise. The girl had tied a rope leash around the lamb's neck and was fruitlessly trying to pull the terrified, bleating little beast along with her.

"Joanie!" Tom shouted. "What the heck are you doing out here?"

"Bo got loose while we were gone," she yelled back, looking like she was starting to panic. "The thunder scared him and he ran off."

Tom and Lisa hurried to her.

"We've got to get to lower ground!" Lisa's face was white with fear.

"He won't move!" Joanie dug in her heels and pulled. "He's too heavy—!"

The wind rose to a freight-train roar. The hairs rose on the back of Tom's arms and neck as he heard the rumble of the new-born tornado.

Touchdown.

"I can carry him." Tom grabbed the leash and scooped up Bo. The wriggling lamb was surprisingly heavy, but once Tom had him firmly in his arms he quit struggling. "Come on!"

The trio pelted down the hill, their sneakers kicking up gravel. They jumped down into the narrow cleft of the creekbed and threw themselves flat in the muddy sand.

Tom could hear nothing but the roar of the twister. He squeezed his eyes shut, covered his head with one arm while he gripped the lamb's rope with the other. *Please sweet Jesus, don't let us die out here . . .*

And then it was over. As quickly as it had come, the tornado sucked back up into the sky. Tom lifted his head and peered up at the clouds. The black clouds were already starting to break up.

Tom rolled over and got to his feet on rubbery knees. "That was *way* too close for comfort."

Joanie burst into tears, letting out all her pent-up and long-denied sadness in huge, wracking sobs.

"Hey, kiddo, shh," Lisa said, crawling over to her little sister. "We're safe now."

"Let her cry," Tom said. "We all need a good cry sometimes."

So they held their little sister, rocking her back and forth until, at last, her tears seemed spent.

"J-jeez," she hiccuped, "We're *filthy*. Mom's gonna kill us."

Tom looked down at himself. The front of his shirt and jeans were completely covered in mud. And he smelled very strongly of Bo.

"She won't kill us if we take care of the laundry ourselves," he replied. "But next time Bo runs off in the middle of a thunderstorm, *tell someone*, okay?"

She sniffled, her lower lip quivering. "But he's my responsibility—"

"And you're *our* responsibility. You could've gotten killed up there!" He stopped himself, tried not to sound angry. "We need to *talk* to each other when bad stuff happens. We'll do a whole lot better trying to work out our problems together than by trying to go it alone."

He helped his sisters to their feet and handed Bo's leash back to Joanie. The lamb was nibbling at a dandelion growing in the sand, the terror of the storm already forgotten.

"Think you can take him from here?" Tom asked.

She nodded, smiling.

"Good," he said, a mischievous smile spreading across his face, "because first one back to the house has dibs on the shower!"

And the race was on.

A few hours later, the freshly showered trio sat around the kitchen table, eating Neapolitan ice cream and giggling. The washing machine and dryer were a comforting hum in the background.

Tom wasn't surprised when the TV clicked itself on.

"This is a special report for our viewers at the Wilson Farm," Fran said from the screen. She was standing just outside their kitchen window. Over her shoulder, Tom could see himself sitting at the table.

Joanie's eyes went round as saucers, and she nearly dropped her spoon. "Whoa. That's *Aunt Fran!*"

"You did good today, kids. I love you, and don't you ever forget that. I can't be with you, but I'll always be watching over you. Be good to each other."

She straightened her shoulders. "This is newswoman Francine Wilson signing off for now. But I'll be back when you need me on ALTV-77, your channel for the Guardian Angel Network's news from the afterlife."

The screen went dark.

"How did she *do* that?" Joanie whispered.

"She's always been an angel," Tom said. "I guess God decided the job suited her pretty well."

Lisa reached over and touched his hand. "Are we going to be good to each other?"

"I'll call you, every Sunday night. And you can call me anytime you want to talk. And I'll come back for Thanksgiving. And the Chicago offer still stands." He paused. "Sounds good?"

She grinned. "Sounds good."

Tom heard floorboards squeak. He turned and saw their parents standing in the doorway. Mr. and Mrs. Wilson peered around the kitchen as if they'd never seen their children before.

"What're you kids doing?" their father asked.

"Eatin' ice cream," Joanie said. She pushed the carton toward them. "Want some?"

"Think I might," her father said.

Tom passed his parents spoons and bowls. "We were thinking of going to a movie later . . . would you two like to come along?"

"Well. That'd be fine," his mother said.

And then she smiled.

It reached all the way to her eyes.

Sparrow Falls

Jane Lindskold

O utta here. That's it. I'm outta here."

Rob spoke by necessity to himself, but even that less-than-unbiased listener could hear the slurring in his voice. He spoke louder, as if volume could make up for lack of clarity.

"What else am I gonna do? Stan' here and face the music? Not Mama Dunning's fair-haired boy. He's too smart for that."

The tiny corner of Rob's mind that wasn't jazzed on uppers or numbed from the shots of whiskey he'd been using for a chaser noticed the deliberate distancing of speaker from self. That happened more and more frequently these days. It only made sense. Robert Dunning didn't really know himself anymore.

Rob stuffed his tongue into the bottom of the shot glass to lick out the last drops of the amber liquid, then shook the bottle, but it was empty. He scowled, staring at the bottle for a long moment before blinking blearily and remembering his purpose.

"I'm outta here," he muttered.

Grabbing his gym bag from the top of his desk, Rob headed for the door. Before leaving, he paused by reflex, glancing around, checking that everything was in order for the next day.

The usually tidy office was a *mess*. File drawers were pulled half-way out, papers hung raggedly from the folders within. The

123

cabinet where he kept his back-up computer disks was almost closed, but a corner of something bright red and plastic jammed it ajar. The desk top itself was pristinely clean, but only because he'd swept everything that usually sat upon it—penholders, telephone, crystal clock, pictures of himself with various famous people—onto the floor.

"I'm outta here," he said more firmly.

Rob strode to the door, squared his shoulders, and put a practiced smile on his face. Maddie, his part-time secretary, was on vacation. Still, someone might see him as he exited the building.

It was so important to make a good impression.

FINGERS TWISTING AROUND THE strap of her purse, Samantha Dunning sat on the edge of her chair and waited for the officer to finish his phone conversation.

She decided that she liked Officer Shaeffer's appearance: tired, friendly, and just a bit sad—like a basset hound in human form. She liked the experienced way his hand moved as he jotted down notes. It matched the calm confidence in his voice when she'd spoken to him on the phone this morning.

Surely Officer Shaeffer could help her. For the first time since the terrible phone call from Maddie Blake earlier that week, Samantha felt a sense of peace, an assurance that everything would be all right. The noise of the large squad room eddied around her, waves beating against a rocky shore on which this one man stood as her personal lighthouse.

Shaeffer hung up the phone, then swiveled his chair to face her. He smiled a weary smile and scrubbed a hand across his right cheek.

"Sorry about that. I told the desk to hold my calls, but that was about a little boy who had been missing since Thursday."

"You found him?" Samantha thought this was a good omen for her own case.

"We did." Shaeffer's smile looked less tired. "Custody dispute. Father had snatched him. Kid's okay. Parents have agreed to talk."

He looked rather forlornly at his empty coffee cup.

"Coffee, Mrs. Dunning?"

She didn't really want any—her nerves were rattling already—but she could see that he did.

"Please, lots of cream and sugar."

Shaeffer was back almost instantly, balancing two mismatched mugs with admirable efficiency.

"Now, ma'am, you're reporting a missing person."

"Yes." Her throat tightened as if the next words would strangle her. "My son, my eldest, Robert."

"He's been missing . . ." Shaeffer prompted, ready to take notes.

"Since Thursday, like that other little boy."

One of Shaeffer's bushy eyebrows, the hairs in it salt and pepper gray, shot up despite its owner's efforts at polite impassivity. She saw him glance at her gray hair with its brave frosting of blond, at the lines on her face and place her age squarely where it was—early sixties, well preserved, but no mother for a little boy.

"Excuse me, ma'am," he said, never letting his surprise into his voice. "Are we looking for a child?"

Samantha managed a weak smile.

"I'm sorry. It just slipped out—I guess every mother thinks of her . . . No, Rob's forty-two. I brought some pictures."

As she slid them across the desk—most of them snapshots taken at a family picnic a few months before—Samantha found herself looking at them as if through a stranger's eyes. She was startled by what she saw.

When had Rob's once golden hair dulled? For that matter, when had it retreated quite so far back along his forehead? She noticed for the first time the deep lines in his tanned face, the tightness around the brilliance of his smile. Robert Dunning was still a handsome man, but no one but his doting mother would think he compared favorably to the surfer boy who still remained iconic in her memory.

"Tell me when your son was last seen," Officer Shaeffer prompted after a glance through the photos.

"Last Thursday," Samantha replied quickly, relieved to have an escape from her own astonishment. "He had lunch with my second daughter, Mary. She said he seemed fine to her, mentioned that he might be going away for the weekend."

"Did he say where?"

"No, just away."

Samantha managed another smile, this one apologetic. "I don't see him very often, with him here in L.A. I'm a widow—I live in Arizona. My children are all over the country; even Mary was only in L.A. on business. She lives in Idaho. I can give you her phone number if you'd like."

"That might be useful. When did you become worried about Robert?"

"His secretary—part-time secretary—Maddie called in a panic Tuesday afternoon. She'd been on vacation. When she came into the office . . ."

Despite her best efforts, Samantha heard her voice quavering like an old woman's. She straightened, took a deep breath.

"The office had been ransacked, stuff was all over the floors, drawers pulled open, all the rest. Rob usually made his first visit to the office later in the day. He'd often have meetings with clients in the morning or at lunch, but when Maddie tried to call him, she couldn't find him anywhere. He'd missed . . ."

This time Samantha didn't try to control the quaver.

"He'd missed appointments on Friday, Saturday, Monday, and Tuesday morning—Maddie found some pretty nasty messages on the voice mail when she checked. She tried him at home, at some friends. Then she thought there might have been a family emergency and called me."

"And you hadn't heard from him."

The statement was mere confirmation.

"That's right. I called all the other kids. Except for Mary, no one had heard from Rob for weeks. I took a few days from my job—I work for the state—and flew out here on Wednesday morning. I went to Rob's condominium—the manager let me in. We'd met a few times before when I was visiting, and she said that she'd seen Mary when she was out here last week."

With the help of a sip of milky coffee, Samantha fought and won her battle with the sudden hot tears that flooded her eyes.

"The food in the fridge was spoiling. The mail hadn't been picked up since the previous Thursday. I drove over to Rob's office—his car was still in the condo garage—and spent all that day making phone calls to everyone in Rob's address book. Then I called the hospitals, the police stations. No one had heard anything. A few people—clients—weren't all that happy. Rob had missed appointments or failed to answer phone calls."

"His clients?"

"Rob runs an agency for actors. I don't know the details. He started it a few years ago." Samantha stopped to make a mental count, was surprised at the total. "Ten years. I think he does pretty well."

Officer Shaeffer nodded. "This is the right town for that type of work."

"A couple of my other kids offered to come out and help, but it made better sense to file a missing person's report. None of us know L.A. and we might be wasting valuable time. I keep thinking about how Rob's office looked—like someone had torn it to pieces."

"You've done the right thing," Officer Shaeffer assured her. "With your permission, I'd like to send someone around to your son's office and apartment. They might find some indication of where he has gone."

"Gone?" Samantha felt a bit blank.

"He's missing, ma'am," Officer Shaeffer said gently. "We need to find out if he's made himself missing or whether someone did it for him. Then we'll have a better idea where to start looking."

Samantha stared at the kind face with its basset hound eyes, all the comfort she'd felt in Officer Shaeffer's presence vanishing as suddenly as it had appeared. His words opened doors she hadn't wanted to contemplate. Rob dead, Rob sick, Rob victim of some mysterious crime—all those she had considered with various degrees of fear, pain, and hope.

Rob on the run was a new thought. One Samantha didn't want to consider at all.

She rose woodenly. Gave Officer Shaeffer her hand, heard herself promising to make certain doors would be opened to the police. Officer Shaeffer even took the time to walk her to the squad room door.

Samantha noticed that the police officer's phone was ringing again even before he had returned to his desk.

ROB DUNNING LAY ON his back on a lumpy bed in a room in a roadside motel in what he thought was probably Arizona. He was stiff and sore from a long drive in the car he'd bought for a few thousand cash from a questionable secondhand dealer. In an attempt to distract himself, he set himself to tracing back through his life to the days when everything had started going wrong.

Not this immediate problem—not that. Rob had a pretty good idea what had started his current financial and professional ruin. It had been when he'd used the June Woodrow money to pay off the Alys Randall contract. Everything had cascaded from there. He didn't want to think about those events. They were over and done with. There was nothing he could do to fix the damage.

No, the bigger problem was what fascinated him, the question of when he had stopped believing in himself.

Had it been five years ago when Tansy Hopper left him for another agency, saying she could do better—and had been right?

No. Rob was in a mood to be honest with himself, helped by the whiskey he was nursing to keep the inevitable hangover at bay. It wasn't very good whiskey—in fact it tasted like raw alcohol with orange food coloring added for form's sake—but it kept the buzz on. The problem was, he was out of uppers—never should have mixed those with booze anyhow, but he'd managed to win that gamble once again—and eventually he'd fall asleep and when he woke . . .

Rob shivered at the imagined hangover. Rather than contemplate anticipated pain, he went back to wondering where he'd gone wrong. Ruthlessly, he turned through his private memory book, looking at his now—though the clients didn't know it—defunct agency, his divorce(s), his years as a model, before that, back to the last days he remembered as unmitigatedly happy.

Twenty years ago—more than twenty—the years when he'd been a swimmer. He'd started swimming young—learned to paddle about unassisted at five years old during a visit to his grandparents.

They'd had a pool that had seemed as big as the ocean. Grandpa had urged him away from the side, holding Rob by the tips of his fingers, showing him how to kick. Then he'd held Rob below the tummy, moving his arms through the rudiments of a crawl stroke. By the end of the visit, kick and stroke had come together.

How the other kids had been envious! There'd been Paul, then, and Terry, though she hadn't gotten beyond the "suck on the thumb and stare adoringly" stage. Mary had been a baby. John wouldn't come for a couple years yet, then there'd be Catherine.

Baby after baby after baby. His only refuge from them all, from a house that stank slightly of diaper pails and sour milk, that resonated with screams and wails, had been swimming. Swimming had become the one constant in a life too full of change—a seemingly endless succession of brothers and sisters, new houses and new schools as the family moved to follow his father's construction work, new friends.

Funny how he remembered swimming better than he did school or just about anything else. Rob could remember every coach he'd swum under, starting with several kindly faced, rather plump mothers, progressing to Sue, his first real coach.

Now that he thought back, he realized that Sue couldn't have been any more than a high school student—though at the time she'd seemed like a real grown-up. She'd coached him from middle school through junior high. Brother Andrew had taken over when Rob started high school. After that had come Rob's final coach, Coach Wilson, the man who had been grooming Rob for the Olympic tryouts.

And then the accident had happened—torn muscles a week before the Olympic tryouts. Rob had been forced to resign his place and that had killed him, just torn the heart out of him.

From the sidelines, he'd watched other swimmers no better than himself make the team. He'd watched the Olympics on television, imagining himself in every race, imagining himself with the gold around his neck. And from his place on the sidelines, Rob had blamed Coach Wilson for pushing him too hard, for wearing him out so that his body finally gave under the pressure.

As soon as the doctors said it was safe—and even a bit before—Coach Wilson had encouraged Rob to get back in shape, but Rob had lost heart as well as muscle tone. He couldn't handle going back, rebuilding skills he'd been developing since he was hardly more than a baby. Oh, he still swam, but now it was more like splashing around, no more sprints, no more distance pushes, no more striving for perfect form.

Rob had worked as a pool guard that summer and on that job he'd discovered something that he'd missed in his obsession with swimming.

Girls.

At first Rob couldn't believe that the shy smiles, the flirtatious glances, the languorous oiling of limbs were all for him, but he caught on pretty fast. He dated one teenage goddess after another. Eventually Coach Wilson stopped asking him to try out for the team. Rob tried not to be hurt.

Soon after that, the family moved to California so his father could be night foreman on some big construction project.

Rob took up surfing. He went to one of the sprawling California universities, majored in parties, girls, and getting by. His grades were never what Terry would earn or even what John managed years later, but they were good enough.

Even better, the body he'd built in all those years of swimming—and which he maintained with what he now recognized as the ease of youth, rather than any skill or inclination—got him a modeling contract. More such contracts followed. Through college and immediately thereafter Rob grew complacently accustomed to seeing his face—along with various body parts, usually more undressed than dressed—in national magazines.

He even acted a little, small roles in several television shows and movies, usually as a friendly bartender or a handsome thug.

Eventually, the modeling contracts trickled to an end. Rob was never quite sure why. He guessed he'd been getting too old to model jockey shorts and tight T-shirts. All that fun in the sun did leave its mark on the skin.

He'd saved money more by luck than by inclination. One day a girlfriend asked him to introduce her to someone he knew from his acting days. That had led to a job for her. Grateful, she'd mentioned him to someone else, invited him to a couple of parties where he'd met other people.

Somehow Rob had drifted into agenting. He'd never much liked the paperwork—contracts, bank balances, all that—but when he was flush he could hire people to take care of that stuff. What he did like was the social life, the parties, the power lunches, the dinners in expensive restaurants where someone else was eager to pick up the bill.

Then Tansy Hopper had left him for another agency. Rob still burned when he thought of the letter she'd sent him. She'd said he drank too much, took too many pills, and was a useless leech.

But the real problem hadn't been Tansy. She'd been a sweet kid, just led astray by bad people. It wasn't her fault—or Rob's—

that rumors had started with her departure and his client base had begun eroding. Rob didn't fight the decline. Something else would come up; something always had. Only this time it didn't.

As Rob saw events in the grand context of his personal history, the person who was to blame for the gradual disaster of Rob's life was Coach Wilson. He'd set Rob up, giving him dreams of glory, then broken his spirit along with his body. If it hadn't been for Coach Wilson and his obsessive training, Rob would have gone to the Olympics, been famous, won the gold.

Never realizing when well-worn fantasy slid off into dream, Rob fell asleep. The liquor bottle held loosely in his hand tumbled to the floor. Not even the ants were interested in the contents.

"MRS. DUNNING?"

THE VOICE on the other end of the phone was vaguely familiar. After a second, Samantha identified it with dread. Rob had been missing now for a week and half and she no longer hoped for good news from that source.

"This is Officer Shaeffer from Los Angeles."

"How are you, Officer? Do you have any news about Rob?"

She struggled for calm. She'd come home the day after she'd made her report, knowing she could do little more than worry and wanting to be where the other children could reach her more easily. In any case, her vacation time wasn't infinite.

"Some." he paused. "I have the report from the officers sent to go through your son's belongings. It took them a while to build a coherent picture. Things were missing or destroyed. The secretary wasn't much help."

"Maddie," Samantha said apologizing, though she didn't really know why, "had only been with Rob for a few months and only part-time. His last secretary left to get married."

"Actually," Officer Shaeffer spoke carefully, as if he might be quoted, "she left because her salary hadn't been paid in full for six months. Mrs. Dunning, Rob was in considerable financial difficulty. I can forward you a copy of the report if you'd like the details, but essentially he was in arrears in his payments to most of his clients. There is some evidence that he was kiting checks between accounts."

"Oh."

Looking almost blindly into the living room, Samantha saw her own reflection in the mirror over the sofa, her face a mask of pain. The hand that still held the receiver pressed to her ear seemed nerveless—the phone a dead weight she held from reflex rather than volition.

"Mrs. Dunning," continued Officer Shaeffer's kind voice, "you could learn this easily enough, so I may as well tell you—several of your son's clients have filed complaints against him. There is a warrant out for his arrest. Although Missing Persons will continue to search for him, other departments will now become involved. If you hear from your son, you should report that information."

"Rob's a felon?"

She asked the question in the flat tone of one looking for information.

"Let's just say that he's wanted for questioning on several matters."

Samantha didn't remember the rest of the conversation except for a vague awareness that she had assured the officer that she and her other children would, of course, cooperate with the law. After hanging up the receiver, she sat with her head pressed into her hands.

Where had they gone wrong? Rob had been such a good boy, so athletic, so hard-working. It must have been the influence of the people he met in Hollywood, the modeling people, the actors.

Rob had done well enough in college, been so popular, so sweet. If that modeling job hadn't come along, then he'd have done okay.

Hours later, after calling the other kids to let them know the worst, Samantha still sat numbly next to the phone. Various local friends—doubtless alerted to the crisis by one or more of her children—had called and tried to comfort her. Nothing could get through the fog in her head, nothing but a sense that as miserable as she was, she was also angry.

The anger was a new form of misery, a sense that she was betraying her eldest son by resenting what he had brought on her family, how he had disrupted her orderly world. It had been hard rebuilding her life after her husband—Robert, Senior—had died from a sudden heart attack when he was sixty-five and she fifty-eight. She'd managed, though.

When her husband had died, Samantha had been working part-time for the state, putting aside just a bit more money for their retirement. Then that dream had vanished into the ground along with her husband. Somehow her department managed to combine two positions to bring her on full-time. She played bridge twice a week with some friends, visited the kids when she could. They were her stability, her pride and joy, and now Rob had ruined that last precious illusion of permanence.

As from a great distance, Samantha heard the chimes on the anniversary clock in the dining room sing out the hour. Sweet and light, they reminded her of church bells. She grasped at a strand of hope.

Rising on legs stiff from inaction, she found her purse and car keys. She'd been a practicing Catholic all her life, never very devout, most of the time quite passive. Right now, however, the dark quiet of a church seemed the perfect sanctuary for her troubled soul.

Samantha fought down a sense of anticipation as she drove, feeling as if she was heading toward some important appointment. Hope, as fragile as the sound of the bells, took hold in her heart.

FROM WHERE HE STOOD before the presence, the archangel Phanuel became aware of Samantha Dunning—her grief, her anger, her shame, and her hope.

Theologians have spent much time and covered reams of paper speculating on the nature of angels.

Do angels share in any aspect of divine omniscience? As creatures of pure spirit, can they manifest as matter? Are they merely messengers, or do they possess will to act for themselves?

Phanuel knew those answers or perhaps he did not. What he did know was that a voice was calling out in desperation, a voice filled with pain and yet not without hope.

Among other honors—including being one of the four angels of the presence and the angel of penance—Phanuel is the angel of hope. Most theologians would agree that this means that Phanuel is a messenger of God, one who is responsible for sustaining hope, that most fragile and elusive of emotions.

Some would say that this interpretation is mere nonsense, that neither God nor angels are in any way so concrete or understandable. They could be right, but Phanuel didn't trouble himself with such abstract notions.

Hearing Samantha Dunning cry out for some reason to hope Phanuel reached out, anchoring himself to her barely formed hope and seeking to strengthen it. He drifted so that he might share her time and place, taking on to himself a form she needed to see.

AT THE BRISK SOUND of hard-soled shoes on the tile floor, Samantha looked up from her folded hands. When she had arrived she had found the church open but empty. Now a strange man stood alongside the back pew where she was kneeling.

He was dressed all in black, shirt and trousers vaguely ecclesiastical in cut, though he lacked the little white dog collar. His hair was a sandy brown, neatly cut, a touch long around the ears. She guessed he might be Father Bucknell's summer substitute, though she thought she remembered Father saying he was going away later in the month.

The stranger looked at her with an expression so distant and serious that for a moment Samantha thought he was going to tell her she needed to leave. Then he smiled.

It wasn't a very big smile, but it warmed her through.

"May I help you?" the stranger asked.

Samantha shook her head, starting to reject his offered aid. Then she shrugged away her own complex emotions and sat back on the bench, patting the seat next to her. The stranger slid in beside her.

"It's a long story," she began, "about my son, Rob. I don't know if anyone can help him."

In a rush of breath, she started telling the stranger all about Rob, about his current troubles. By the time she finished, she'd told everything, even about her own nebulous anger.

"The situation is driving my family crazy," she finished, "this not being able to do anything, not even knowing where Rob is. I'm worried, too. I'd hoped . . ."

She trailed off, suddenly feeling shy.

"You'd hoped," the stranger prompted.

"I'd hoped that if I prayed that God would find Rob for us. I heard the bells and remembered that bit about not a sparrow falling without God knowing where it is. I'd hoped . . ."

The stranger touched the back of her hand lightly, not so much a caress as an assurance that someone was listening.

"You were right to hope. God does know where your missing son is, even if Rob himself does not."

Samantha looked at him, reaching for some profound concept she half-sensed beneath those simple words.

"Rob is lost," she said slowly, "even to himself. Then the first step toward getting him back to us is to hope that he finds himself—or that God finds him for us."

She bent her head in prayer and she thought the stranger bent his beside her, but when she looked up again, he was gone.

PHANUEL REFLECTED UPON WHAT Samantha Dunning had said.

The difficulty was that though God may see where every sparrow falls, he doesn't stop them from falling. If they're going to stop, they must spread their own wings and fly.

The archangel reached and found Rob Dunning crawling out of a drunken sleep, a hangover battering all sense from inside his head. He seemed a poor candidate for life, much less flight.

Still, even a hangover could be a start. At least with a hangover, Rob would need to fight harder to maintain the comfortable tissue of illusions he used to justify the course of his life. It remained to be seen whether he could face the reality of what he had become.

PHANUEL BECAME A BREEZE and blew aside the curtain.

Brilliant Arizona daylight poured into the hotel room making Rob shrink into the pillow, his arm curled across his eyes to protect his aching head from the light.

After a few minutes, he lowered his arm just slightly, trying to see just how far he'd have to move to pull the curtains shut again. Through the clear glass of the window, he saw blue light reflected from water and a man walking in the sunshine.

He blinked, lowering his arm even more, not believing what he had seen. Outside his room was a small, outdoor pool—one of those kidney-shaped affairs just large enough for lounging. Walking along the rim of the pool was a man Rob had never forgotten—a man he hated for ruining his life.

Coach Wilson.

Adrenaline washed the hangover from Rob's head. Sitting up, he patted himself, realizing he'd slept in his clothes, that he reeked of cheap whiskey, that his mouth felt like something fat and very furry had crawled inside and shed every hair off its body before rotting away into slime.

Rob downed a tumbler of flat-tasting warm water from a glass he didn't remember setting on the nightstand. He didn't bother to change into the clean clothes in his gym bag. Why should he improve himself? Shouldn't Coach Wilson see what he had made of his once-prize student?

Rob staggered out into the light, intercepting Coach Wilson half-way around the aquamarine kidney. They were the only people outdoors—not surprising given the rising heat of an Arizona summer day. Rob was almost sorry. He'd like an audience to watch him get his own at last.

"Hey, Coach!" he called and he heard the angry whine in his voice.

Coach Wilson turned slowly. The passage of twenty-some years had aged him, but Coach must have kept swimming because for a man of at least sixty, he was in very good shape. His shoulders remained powerful, his posture upright. His skin looked good, but then he'd always been a stickler about moisturizers, long before they were fashionable.

His hair, always bleached fair by chlorine and other pool chemicals, was a silvery white now. With a flash of anger, Rob realized that it was probably thicker than his own.

"Hey, Coach!" he called again. "Remember me?"

"Rob Dunning," came the well-remembered voice, "the swimmer with perhaps the most raw potential I ever trained. What happened to you after we lost touch? Did you ever go back to swimming?"

Rob felt a surge of anger that Coach had apparently never heard of his success as a model, in Hollywood society, of his wealth and prominence.

"No," he jeered, "I never went back to swimming. How could I, after you ruined my chance at the Olympics with your push, push, push?"

"Quite easily," Coach said unperturbed. "The torn muscles were painful, but the injury wouldn't have set you back forever. You were young, if you'd worked hard, you could have qualified for the next Olympic tryouts."

"How could I have worked any harder?" Rob asked angrily. "You were already working me to death! That's how I tore the damn muscle."

"You tore the muscle in one of the accidents that happens to athletes," Coach replied levelly. "I wasn't surprised by the accident, but I must admit, I was surprised by how you took it. I'd never figured you for lazy."

"Lazy!"

"Lazy." The single word was repeated uncompromisingly. "I'd recognized you as a natural swimmer from the day I met you. I had boys on the team who worked twice as hard as you who never came close to your times and style. If you'd worked as hard as they did, you'd have been back in form by the end of the term, but you were lazy."

Rob remembered how day after day he'd risen when it was still dark to go to the pool, how his afternoons had been spent in dank, echoing concrete caverns, the grueling practice sessions. How could this man dare call him lazy?

As if in answer, Rob found himself remembering events he'd never called up in his carefully scripted memories. He remembered his teammates, remembered their admiration when he'd completed some complex routine, heard his own voice, younger, touched with ringing teenage arrogance:

"Work hard? Oh, I practice, but I've been swimming since I was five. I guess it comes naturally."

How many times had he made that statement—superficially so modest, actually such a brag? A hundred times, a thousand?

How many teammates had gone home tasting despair because for all their hard work they could never be as good as the golden-haired youth with the natural affinity for water?

Rob felt sick—and not from any return of his hangover—but he wasn't ready to admit that he might have been somewhat at fault, not at least until Coach admitted that he, too, was to blame.

"I wasn't lazy," Rob protested. "You were a slave driver. You just wanted to brag that you'd coached someone right up to the Olympics. I was a tool you used in your private quest for glory."

Coach smiled at him. "Of course I would have been proud if you'd made the team."

"If?" Rob heard his voice crack. "If? I had what it takes!"

"You and many other young swimmers. Why do you think they have tryouts? You might have made the team that year; but face it, you were young, your body hadn't reached its peak. I'm not certain you had the endurance."

Rob glowered at the silver-haired man standing so tall in the sun. What an arrogant jerk! And he wasn't even sweating! For some reason, that seemed the final insult.

"So you're not sorry for what you did," he said angrily.

"Are you?" the voice echoed. The words hung in the air, vibrating with strange resonances.

PHANUEL STOOD IN THE sun, looking on as the fallen sparrow beat his broken wings against the cage he had built for himself.

Had Phanuel not been more than the angel of hope he might have turned away, for the cause seemed hopeless.

However, Phanuel was not only the angel of hope; he was also the angel of penance. Deep within his spirit he could sense that penance—true regret and the desire to make amends for past failings—held the key to the cage Rob Dunning had been knotting about himself for over two decades.

The archangel extended this slim hope.

"ARE YOU?" COACH WILSON asked again. "Are you sorry for what you've done?"

"What do you know about what I've done?" Rob replied angrily.

"I have the evidence of my eyes," Coach Wilson said levelly. "I see you standing before me in rumpled clothing, reeking of bad whiskey, residing in a flea-bag hotel in the middle of a barren desert. That doesn't seem to indicate that you've done much with your life."

"You're here," Rob retorted, grasping at straws. "If this place is so bad, why are you here?"

"I'm just passing through," Coach replied, "on my way to Tucson to visit my granddaughter. She's a student at U. of A."

"My mother lives in Phoenix," Rob said impulsively and instantly he felt guilty. Had she started worrying about him? Did she even know he was gone? How could he ever face having his whole family learn about the mess he'd made of his life?

He must have spoken aloud, because Coach asked, "What mess?"

Briefly, curtly, Rob told Coach Wilson about the shambles he had made of his finances, about the ruin of his business. He left out his private suspicions that he also drank too much and might have what was politely called a "substance abuse" problem.

Coach seemed to guess what Rob didn't say. He listened, steering Rob to a chair in the shade and offering him water from a bottle he'd been carrying. When Rob had finished his tale of woe, Coach asked as simply as he had before:

"Are you sorry for what you've done?"

Rob looked at him, started to mouth one of his automatic excuses about other people's problems, bad luck, fluctuations in the market. Somehow the truth slid out.

"I am sorry, Coach. I'm damn sorry, but I guess it's too late for me to be sorry, isn't it?"

Coach shook his silver-haired head and smiled as he had back when Rob completed a race in record time.

"You know, Rob, there's a lot said about how the road to hell is paved with good intentions. What you don't hear so often is that it can also be paved with no intentions at all. From what you've told me, that's how you've lived your life since the accident—with no intentions except getting by and having the best time you could while doing so."

Rob felt a flash of anger. He certainly hadn't expected a sermon in response to his heartfelt confession—sympathy, perhaps, but not a lecture.

"Was that wrong?"

"Maybe. Tell me. Did you enjoy that road?"

Rob broke then, tears filling his eyes and flooding his voice.

"No, the best times I ever had were when I was swimming—trying hard to be something. I'm sorry, but I guess it's too late for me to do anything about it, isn't it?"

Coach grinned at him. "It's never too late to be sorry, not if you really mean it and if you mean to make amends."

"Like go to prison?"

"If you must. You might find some other way of making restitution to your clients. They might drop their suits and leave you free."

"And then? I've blown every chance I ever had."

"Then it's time you gave up on chance," Coach Wilson said firmly, "and tried working toward a goal. You yourself said you've been happiest when you were doing just that, and I can think of worse goals than repaying the debt you owe to your clients. While you're at it, why not apologize to yourself as well?"

"To me?" Rob was frankly astonished.

"That's right. Apologize to yourself for all the potential you wasted. Try and find a way to make restitution for that crime as well. It's just as important as paying the monetary debt you owe to your clients."

Rob nodded, a pristine understanding temporarily freeing him from the last twenty years. For the first time he understood how that first excuse had trapped him, had forced him to maintain it by slipping further and further from the person he wanted to be.

"I see," he said, trying to voice this fragile revelation aloud. "From the moment I decided that I didn't want to take responsibility for recovering from the accident, I had to make more excuses to justify that first choice. I chose to be less than I could be. What an idiot!"

"Maybe," Coach Wilson agreed. "Now, go call your mother. I'm sure she's worrying about you."

Obeying the authority in Coach's voice, Rob turned automatically. When he spun back to thank the man, Coach Wilson was gone.

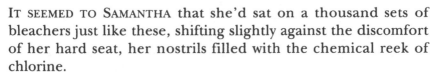

IT SEEMED TO SAMANTHA that she'd sat on a thousand sets of bleachers just like these, shifting slightly against the discomfort of her hard seat, her nostrils filled with the chemical reek of chlorine.

Today was unique, though, for she was certain that never before had she been so happy, never before so proud.

Down at pool-side was her eldest son, her Rob. This time he wasn't one of those tucked into the unforgiving sleekness of a racing suit; instead he wore loose, comfortable trunks and a whistle strung from a lanyard around his neck.

He had crouched down to talk seriously to a group of little boys—the eldest something like twelve—giving them their pep-talk before the day's race began. They looked up at him with trust and adoration, just as she had seen Rob himself look up to coach after coach.

That trust might be enough to keep him straight, she thought. *I hope so. I hope and pray.*

She felt a vibration on the bleachers and glanced over, recognizing with some surprise the stranger who had listened to Rob's story the year before.

"So he came home again," the stranger said without preamble, "and he seems to be doing well. I expect it hasn't been easy."

"It hasn't," Samantha replied honestly. "And sometimes it isn't. Rob finds working in the business office of his father's old construction firm unglamorous and boring at times, especially after Hollywood."

"I expect he might," the stranger agreed, "but he's sticking to it and giving back something of himself. It's more than I might have expected."

Samantha smiled, then said impulsively, "You were my good angel that day, showing up just when I needed someone to listen. If you hadn't been there, I wouldn't have worked through what I felt, might not have been ready to deal with my own mixed emotions. Instead, when Rob called that afternoon, I felt as if my prayer had been answered."

"Who's saying that your prayer *wasn't* answered?"

Samantha expected to find that the man was teasing her, but the smile that twitched his lips wasn't playful or the least bit irreverent. It was simply quietly pleased.

"The race is starting," the stranger commented with slight motion of his hand toward the pool.

Following his gesture, Samantha turned in time to see the swimmers launch. She heard a cascading splash as a covey of young bodies sliced into the water, sleek as seals—or like sparrows freed for flight.

The Big Sky

Charles de Lint

*"We need Death to be a friend. It is best to have
a friend as a traveling companion when you
have so far to go together."*
—attributed to Jean Cocteau

She was sitting in John's living room when he got home from the recording studio that night, comfortably ensconced on the sofa, legs stretched out, ankles crossed, a book propped open on her lap that she was pretending to read. The fact that all the lights in the house had been off until he turned them on didn't seem to faze her in the least. She continued her pretense, as though she could see equally well in the light or dark and it made no difference to her whether the lights were on or off. At least she had the book turned right-side up, John noted.

"How did you get in?" he asked her.

She didn't seem to present any sort of a threat—beyond having gotten into his locked house, of course—so he was more concerned with how she'd been able to enter than for his own personal safety. At the sound of his voice, she looked up in surprise. She laid the book down on her lap, finger inserted between the pages to hold her place.

143

"You can see me?" she said.

"Jesus."

John shook his head. She certainly wasn't shy. He set his fiddlecase down by the door. Dropping his jacket on top of the case, he went into the living room and sat down in the chair across the coffee table from her.

"What do you think?" he went on. "Of course I can see you."

"But you're not supposed to be able to see me—unless it's time and that doesn't seem right. I mean, really. I'd know, if anybody, whether or not it was time."

She frowned, gaze fixed on him, but she didn't really appear to be studying him. It was more as though she were looking into some unimaginably far and unseen distance. Her eyes focused suddenly and he shifted uncomfortably under the weight of her attention.

"Oh, I see what happened," she said. "I'm so sorry."

John leaned forward, resting his hands on his knees. "Let's try this again. Who are you?"

"I'm your watcher. Everybody has one."

"My watcher."

She nodded. "We watch over you until your time has come, then if you can't find your own way, we take you on. They call us the little deaths, but I've never much cared for the sound of that, do you?"

John sighed. He settled back in his chair to study his unwanted guest. She was no one he knew, though she could easily have fit in with his crowd. He put her at about twenty-something, a slender five-two, with pixy features made more fey by the crop of short blonde hair that stuck up from her head with all the unruliness of a badly mowed lawn. She wore black combat boots; khaki trousers, baggy, with two or three pockets running up either leg; a white T-shirt that hugged her thin chest like a second skin. She had little in the way of jewelry—a small silver ring in her left nostril and another in the lobe of her left ear—and no makeup.

"Do you have a name?" he tried.

"Everybody's got a name."

John waited a few heartbeats. "And yours is?" he asked when no reply was forthcoming.

"I don't think I should tell you."

"Why not?"

"Well, once you give someone your name, it's like opening the door to all sorts of possibilities, isn't it? Any sort of relationship could develop from that, and it's just not a good idea for us to have an intimate relationship with our charges."

"I can assure you," John told her, "we're in no danger of having a relationship—intimate or otherwise."

"Oh," she said. She didn't look disappointed so much as annoyed. "Dakota," she added.

"I'm sorry?"

"You wanted to know my name."

John nodded. "That's right. I—oh, I get it. Your name's Dakota?"

"Bingo."

"And you've been . . . watching me?"

"Well, not just you. Except for when we're starting out, we look out after any number of people."

"I see," John said. "And how many people do you watch?"

She shrugged. "Oh, dozens."

That figured, John thought. It was the story of his life. He couldn't even get the undivided attention of a loonie.

She swung her boots to the floor and set the book she was holding on the coffee table between them.

"Well, I guess we should get going," she said.

She stood up and gave him an expectant look, but John remained where he was sitting.

"It's a long way to the gates," she told him.

He didn't have a clue as to what she was talking about, but he was sure of one thing.

"I'm not going anywhere with you," he said.

"But you have to."

"Says who?"

She frowned at him. "You just do. It's obvious that you won't be able to find your way by yourself, and if you stay here you're just going to start feeling more and more alienated and confused."

"Let me worry about that," John said.

"Look," she said. "We've gotten off on the wrong foot—my fault, I'm sure. I had no idea it was time for you to go already. I'd just come by to check on you before heading off to another appointment."

"Somebody else that you're *watching*?"

"Exactly," she replied, missing, or more probably, ignoring the sarcastic tone of his voice. "There's no way around this, you know. You need my help to get to the gates."

"What gates?"

She sighed. "You're really in denial about all of this, aren't you?"

"You were right about one thing," John told her. "I am feeling confused—but it's only about what you're doing here and how you got in."

"I don't have time for this."

"Me, neither. So maybe you should go."

That earned him another frown.

"Fine," she said. "But don't wait too long to call me. If you change too much, I won't be able to find you and nobody else can help you."

"Because you're my personal watcher."

"No wonder you don't have many friends," she said. "You're really not a very nice person, are you?"

"I'm only like this with people who break into my house."

"But I didn't—oh, never mind. Just remember my name and don't wait too long to call me."

"Not that I'd want to," John said, "but I don't even have your number."

"Just call my name and I'll come," she said. "If it's not too late. Like I said, I might not be able to recognize you if you wait too long."

Though he was trying to take this all in stride, John couldn't help but start to feel a little creeped out at the way she was going on. He'd never realized that crazy people could seem so normal—except for what they were saying, of course.

"Good-bye," he said.

She bit back whatever it was that she was going to say and gave him a brusque nod. For one moment, he half-expected her to walk through a wall—the evening had taken that strange a turn—but she merely crossed the living room and let herself out the front door. John waited for a few moments, then rose and set the deadbolt. He walked through the house, checking the windows and back door, before finally going upstairs to his bedroom.

He thought he might have trouble getting to sleep—the woman's presence had raised far more questions than it had answered—but he was so tired from twelve straight hours in the studio that it was more a question of could he get all his clothes off and crawl under the blankets before he faded right out? He had one strange moment: when he turned off the light, he made the mistake of looking directly at the bulb. His uninvited guest's features hung in the darkness along with a hundred dancing spots of light before he was able to blink them away. But the moment didn't last long, and he was soon asleep.

HE DIDN'T REALIZE THAT he'd forgotten to set his alarm last night until he woke up and gave the clock a bleary look. Eleven-fifteen. Christ, he was late.

He got up, shaved, and took a quick shower. You'd think someone would have called him from the studio, he thought as he started to get dressed. He was doing session work on Darlene Flatt's first album, and the recording had turned into a race to get the album finished before her money ran out. He had two solos up first thing this morning, and he couldn't understand why no one had called to see where he was.

There was no time for breakfast—he didn't have much of an appetite at the moment anyway. He'd grab some coffee and a bagel at the deli around the corner from the studio. Tugging on his jeans, he carried his boots out into the living room and phoned the studio while he put them on. All he got was ringing at the other end.

"Come on," he muttered. "Somebody pick it up."

How could there be nobody there to answer?

It was as he was cradling the receiver that he saw the book lying on the coffee table, reminding him of last night's strange encounter. He picked the book up and looked at it, turning it over in his hands. There was something different about it this morning. Something wrong. And then he realized what it was. The color dust wrapper had gone monochrome. The book and . . . His gaze settled on his hand and he dropped the book in shock. He stared at his hand, turning it front to back, then looked wildly around the living room.

Oh, Jesus. Everything was black and white.

He'd been so bleary when he woke up that he hadn't noticed that the world had gone monochrome on him overnight. He'd had a vague impression of gloominess when he got up, but he hadn't really thought about it. He'd simply put it down to it being a particularly overcast day. But this . . . this . . .

It was impossible.

His gaze was drawn to the window. The light coming in was devoid of color where it touched his furniture and walls, but outside . . . He walked slowly to the window and stared at his lawn, the street beyond it, the houses across the way. Everything was the way it was supposed to be. The day was cloudless, the colors so vivid, the sunlight so bright it hurt his eyes. The richness of all that color and light burned his retinas.

He stood there until tears formed in his eyes and he had to turn away. He covered his eyes with his hands until the pain faded. When he took his palms away, his hands were still leached of color. The living room was a thousand monochrome shades of black and white. Numbly, he walked to his front door and flung it open. The blast of color overloaded the sensory membranes of his eyes. He knelt down where he'd tossed his jacket last night and scrabbled about in its pockets until he found a pair of shades.

The sunglasses helped when he turned back to the open door. It still hurt to look at all that color, but the pain was much less than it had been. He shuffled out onto his porch, down the steps. He looked at what he could see of himself. Hands and arms. His legs. All monochrome. He was like a black and white cutout that someone had stuck onto a colored background.

I'm dreaming, he thought.

He could feel the start of a panic attack. It was like the slight nervousness that sometimes came when he stepped onto stage— the kind that came when he was backing up someone he's never played with before, only increased a hundredfold. Sweat beaded on his temples and under his arms. It made his shirt clammy and stick to his back. His hands began to shake so much that he had to hug himself to make them stop.

He was dreaming, or he'd gone insane.

Movement caught his eye down the street and he recognized one of his neighbors. He stumbled in the man's direction.

"Bob!" he called. "Bob, you've got to help me."

The man never even looked in his direction. John stepped directly in front of him on the sidewalk and Bob walked right into him, knocking him down. But Bob hadn't felt a thing, John realized. Hadn't seen him, hadn't felt the impact, was just walking on down the street as if John had simply ceased to exist for him.

John fled back into the house. He slammed the door, locked it. He pulled the curtains in the living room and started to pace, from the fireplace to the hallway, back again, back and forth, back and forth. At one point he caught sight of the book he'd dropped earlier. Slowly, he walked over to where it lay and picked it up. He remembered last night's visitor again. Her voice returned to him.

If you change too much . . .

This was all her fault, he thought.

He threw the book down and shouted her name.

"Yes?"

Her voice came from directly behind him and he started violently.

"Jesus," he said. "You could've given me a heart attack."

"It's a little late for that."

She was wearing the same clothes she'd worn last night except today there was a leather bomber jacket on over her T-shirt and she wore a hat that was something like a derby except the brim was wider. There was one other difference. Like himself, like the rest of his house, she'd been leached of all color.

"What did you do to me?" he demanded.

She reached out and took his hand to lead him over to the sofa. He tried to pull free from her grip, but she was stronger than she looked.

"Sit down," she said. "And I'll try to explain."

Her voice was soothing and calm, the way one would talk to an upset child—or a madman. John was feeling a little bit like both at the moment, helpless as a child and out of his mind. But the lulling quality of her voice and the gentle manner of her touch helped still the wild drumming of his pulse.

"Look," he said. "I don't know what you've done to me—I don't know how you've done this to me or why—but I just want to get back to normal, okay? If I made you mad last night, I'm sorry, but you've got to understand. It was pretty weird to find you in my house the way I did."

"I know," she said. "I didn't realize you could see me, or I would have handled it differently myself. But you took me by surprise."

"I took *you* by surprise?"

"What do you remember about last night?" she asked.

"I came home and found you in my living room."

"No, before that."

"I was at High Lonesome Sounds—working on Darlene's album."

She nodded. "And what happened between when you left the studio and came home?"

"I . . . I don't remember."

"You were hit by a car," she said. "A drunk driver."

"No way," John said, shaking his head. "I'd remember something like that."

She took his hand. "You died instantly, John Narraway."

He didn't want to believe her, but her words settled inside him with a finality that could only be the truth.

"It's not something that anyone could have foreseen," she went on. "You were supposed to live a lot longer—that's why I was so surprised that you could see me. It's never happened to me like that before."

John had stopped listening to her after she'd said, "You were supposed to live a lot longer." He clung to that phrase, hope rushing through him.

"So it was a mistake," he said.

Dakota nodded.

"So what happens now?" he asked.

"I'll take you to the gates."

"No, wait a minute. You just said it was a mistake. Can't you go back to whoever's in charge and explain that?"

"If there's anyone in charge," she said, "I've never met or heard of them."

"But—"

"I understand your confusion and your fear. Really I do. It comes from the suddenness of your death and my not being there to help you adjust. That's the whole reason I exist—to help people like you who are unwilling or too confused to go on by themselves. I wasn't ready to go myself when my time came."

"Well, I'm not ready, either."

Dakota shook her head. "It's not the same thing. I wasn't ready to go because when I saw how much some people need help to reach the gates, I knew I had to stay and help them. It was like a calling. You just aren't willing to accept what happened to you."

"Well, Christ. Who would?"

"Most people. I've seen how their faces light up when they step through the gates. You can't imagine the joy in their eyes."

"Have you been through yourself?" John asked.

"No. But I've had glimpses of what lies beyond. You know how sometimes the sky just seems to be so big it goes on forever?"

John nodded.

"You stand there and look up," she went on, "and the stars seem so close you feel as though you could just reach up and touch them, but at the same time the sky itself is enormous and has no end. It's like that, except that you can feel your heart swelling inside you, big enough to fill the whole of that sky."

"If what's waiting beyond these gates is so wonderful," John wanted to know, "why haven't you gone through?"

"One day I will. I think about it more and more all the time. But what I'm doing now is important and I'm needed. There are never enough of us."

"Maybe I'll become a watcher instead—like you."

"It's not something one takes on lightly," Dakota said. "You can't just stop when you get tired of doing it. You have to see through all of your responsibilities first, make sure that all of your charges have gone on, that none are left behind to fend for themselves. You share the joys of your charges, but you share their sorrows, too. And the whole time you know them, you're aware of their death. You watch them plan, you watch their lives and the tangle of their relationships grow more complex as they grow older, but the whole time you're aware of their end."

"I could do that," John said.

Dakota shook her head. "You have always been sparing with your kindnesses. It's why your circle of friends is so small. You're not a bad person, John Narraway, but I don't think you have the generosity of spirit it requires to be a watcher."

The calm certainty with which she delivered her judgment irritated John.

"How would you know?" he said.

She gave him a sad smile. "Because I've been watching you ever since you were born."

"What? Every second of my life?"

"No. That comes only at first. It takes time to read a soul, to unravel the tangle of possibilities and learn when the time of death is due. After that it's a matter of checking in from time to time to make sure that the assessment one made still holds true."

John thought about the minutes that made up the greater portion of everyone's life and slowly shook his head. And what if you picked a person who was really dull? Everybody had slow periods in their lives, but some people's whole lives were one numbed shuffle from birth to death. And since you knew the whole time when the person was going to die . . . God, it'd be like spending your whole life in a doctor's waiting room. Boring and depressing.

"You don't get tired of it?" he asked.

"Not tired. A little sad, sometimes."

"Because everybody's got to die."

She shook her head. "No, because I see so much unhappiness and there's nothing I can do about it. Most of my charges never see me—they make their own way to the gates and beyond. I'm just there as a kind of insurance for those who can't do it by themselves, and I'm only with them for such a little while. I miss talking to people on a regular basis. Sometimes I see some of the other watchers, but we're all so busy."

"It sounds horrible."

She shrugged. "I never think of it that way. I just think of those who need help and the looks on their faces when they step through the gates." She fell silent for a moment, then gave him a smile. "We should go now. I've got other commitments."

"What if I refuse to go? What happens then?"

"No one can force you, if that's what you mean."

John held up his hand. He looked around himself. Okay, it was weird, but he could live with it, couldn't he? Anything'd be better than to be dead—even a half life.

"I know what you're thinking," she said. "And no, it's not because I'm reading your mind, because I can't."

"So what's going to happen to me?"

"I take it you're already experiencing some discomfort?"

John nodded. "I see everything in black and white—but only in the house. Outside, nothing's changed."

"That will grow more pronounced," she told him. "Eventually, you won't be able to see color at all. You might lose the clarity of your vision as well so that everything will seem to be a blur. Your other senses will become less effective as well."

"But—"

"And you won't be able to interact with the world you've left behind. In time, the only people you'll be able to see are others like yourself—those too willful or disturbed to have gone on. They don't exactly make the best of companions, John Narraway, but then, by that point, you'll be so much like them, I don't suppose it will matter."

"But what about all the stories of ghosts and hauntings and the like?"

"Do you have a particularly strong bond with a certain place or person?" she asked. "Someone or something you couldn't possibly live without?"

John had to admit that he didn't, but he could tell that she already knew that.

"But I'll still be alive," he said, knowing even as he said the words that they made no real sense.

"If you want to call it that."

"Don't you miss life?"

Dakota shook her head. "I only miss happiness. Or maybe I should say, I miss the idea of happiness because I never had it when I was alive."

"What happened to you?" John wanted to know.

She gave him a long sad look. "I'm sorry, John Narraway, but I have to go. I will listen for you. Call me when you change your mind. Just don't wait too long—"

"Or you won't be able to recognize me. I know. You already told me that."

"Yes," she said, "I did."

This time she didn't use the door. One moment she was sitting with him on the sofa and the next she had faded away like Carroll's Cheshire cat except with her it was her eyes that lingered the longest, those sad dark eyes that told him he was making a mistake, those eyes to which he refused to listen.

HE DIDN'T MOVE FROM the sofa after Dakota left. While the sunlight drifted across the living room, turning his surroundings into a series of shifting chiaroscuro images, he simply sat there, his mind empty more often than it was chasing thoughts. He was sure he hadn't been immobile for more than a few hours, but when he finally stood up and walked to the window, it was early morning, the sun just rising. He'd lost a whole night and a day. Maybe more. He still had no appetite, but now he doubted that he ever would again. He didn't seem to need sleep, either. But it scared him that he could lose such a big chunk of time like that.

He turned back to the living room and switched on the television set to make sure that all he'd lost had been the one day. All he got on the screen was snow. White noise hissed from the speaker grill. Fine, he thought, remembering how he'd been unable to put a call through to the recording studio yesterday morning. So now the TV wouldn't work for him. So he couldn't interact with the everyday mechanics of the world anymore. Well, there were other ways to find out what he needed to know.

He picked up his fiddlecase out of habit, put on his jacket, and left the house. He didn't need his shades once he got outside, but that was only because his whole street was now delineated in shades of black and white. He could see the color start up at the far ends of the block on either side. The sky was overcast above him, but it blued the farther away, from his house it got.

This sucked, he thought. But not so much that he was ready to call Dakota back.

He started downtown, putting on his sunglasses once he left the monochromic zone immediately surrounding his house. Walking proved to be more of a chore than he'd anticipated. He couldn't relax his attention for a moment or someone would walk into him. He always felt the impact while they continued on their way, as unaware of the encounter as his neighbor Bob had been.

He stopped at the first newsstand he came upon and found the day's date. Wednesday, he read on the masthead of the *Newford Star.* November tenth. He'd only lost a day. A day of what, though? He could remember nothing of the experience. Maybe that was what sleep would be like for him in this state—simply turning himself off the way fiction described vampires at their rest.

He had to laugh at the thought. The undead. *He* was one of the undead now, though—he certainly had no craving for blood.

He stopped laughing abruptly, suddenly aware of the hysterical quality that had crept into the sound. It wasn't that funny. He pressed up close against a building to keep out of the way of passing pedestrians and tried to quell the panic he could feel welling up inside his chest. Christ, it wasn't funny at all.

After a while he felt calm enough to go on. He had no particular destination in mind, but when he realized he was in the general vicinity of High Lonesome Sounds, he decided to stop by the studio. He kept waiting for some shock of recognition at every corner he came to, something that would whisper, this is where you died. This is where the one part of your life ended and the new part began. But the street corners all looked the same, and he arrived at the recording studio without sensing that one had ever had more importance in his life than the next.

He had no difficulty gaining entrance to the studio. At least doors still worked for him. He wondered what his use of them looked like to others, doors opening and closing, seemingly of their own accord. He climbed the stairs to the second-floor loft where the recording studio was situated and slipped into the control booth where he found Darlene and Tom Norton listening to a rough mix of one of the cuts from Darlene's album. Norton owned the studio and often served as both producer and sound engineer to the artists using his facilities. He turned as John quietly closed the door behind him, but he looked right through John.

"It still needs a lead break," Norton said, returning his attention to Darlene.

"I know it does. But I don't want another fiddle. I want to leave John's backing tracks just as they are. It doesn't seem right to have somebody else play his break."

Thank you, Darlene, John thought.

He'd known Darlene Flatt for years, played backup with her on and off through the past decade and a half as she sang out her heart in far too many honky-tonks and bars. Her real name was Darlene Johnston, but by this point in her career everyone knew her by her stage name. Dolly Parton had always been her idol and when Darlene stepped on stage with her platinum wig and over-the-top rhinestone outfits, the resemblance between the two was uncanny. But Darlene had a deeper voice, and now that she'd finally lost the wigs and stage gear, John thought she had a better shot at the big time. There was a long tradition of covering other people's material in country music, but as far as John was concerned, nothing got tired more quickly than a tribute act.

She didn't look great today. There was a gaunt look about her features, hollows under her eyes. Someone mourned him, John realized.

"Why don't we have Greg play the break on his dobro?" Darlene said. She sounded so tired, as though all she wanted to do was get through this.

"That could work," Norton said.

John stopped listening to them, his attention taken by the rough mix that was still playing in the control booth. It was terrible. All the instruments sounded tinny and flat, there was no bass to speak of, and Darlene's voice seemed to be mixed so far back you felt you had to lean forward to be able to hear it. He winced, listening to his own fiddle playing.

"You've got a lot more problems here than what instrument to use on the break," he said.

But of course they couldn't hear him. As far as he could tell, they liked what they were hearing, which seemed particularly odd, considering how long they'd both been in the business. What did they hear that he couldn't? But then he remembered what his mysterious visitor had told him. How his sight would continue to deteriorate. How . . .

Your other senses will become less effective as well.

John thought back to the walk from his house to the studio. He hadn't really been thinking of it at the time, but now that he did he realized that the normal sounds of the city had been muted. Everything. The traffic, the voices of passersby, the construction site he'd passed a couple of blocks away from the studio. When he concentrated on Darlene and Norton's conversation again, listening to the tonal quality of their voices rather than what they were saying, he heard a hollow echo that hadn't registered before.

He backed away from them and fumbled his way out into the sitting room on the other side of the door. There he took his fiddle out of his case. Tuning the instrument was horrible. Playing it was worse. There was nothing there anymore. No resonance. No depth. Only the same hollow echoing quality that he'd heard in Darlene and Norton's voices.

Slowly he laid his fiddle back into its case, loosened the frog on his bow and set it down on top of the instrument. When he finally made his way back down the stairs and out into the street, he left the fiddle behind. Outside, the street seemed overcast, its colors not yet leached away, but definitely faded. He looked up into a cloudless sky. He crossed the street and plucked a pretzel from the cart of a street vendor, took a bite even though he had no appetite. It tasted like sawdust and ashes. A bus pulled up at the curb where he was standing, let out a clutch of passengers, then pulled away again, leaving behind a cloud of noxious fumes. He could barely smell them.

It's just a phase, he told himself. He was simply adjusting to his new existence. All he had to do was get through it and things would get back to normal. They couldn't stay like this.

He kept telling himself that as he made his way back home, but he wasn't sure he believed it. He was dead, after all—that was the part of the equation that was impossible to ignore. Dakota had warned him that this was going to happen. But he wasn't ready to believe her, either. He just couldn't accept that the way things were for him now would be permanent.

HE WAS RIGHT. THINGS didn't stay the same. They got worse. His senses continued to deteriorate. The familiar world faded away from around him until he found himself in a gray-toned city that he didn't always recognize. He stepped out of his house one day and couldn't find his way back. The air was oppressive, the sky seemed to press down on him. And there were no people. No living people. Only the other undead. They huddled in doorways and alleys, drifted through the empty buildings. They wouldn't look at him, and he found himself turning his face away as well. They had nothing they could share with each other, only their despair, and of that they each had enough of their own.

He took to wandering aimlessly through the deserted streets, the high points of his day coming when he recognized the corner of a building, a stretch of street, that gargoyle peering down from an utterly unfamiliar building. He wasn't sure if he was in a different city, or if he was losing his memory of the one he knew. After a while, it didn't seem to matter.

The blank periods came more and more often. Like the other undead, he would suddenly open his eyes to find himself curled up in a nest of newspapers and trash in some doorway, or huddled in the rotting hulk of a sofa in an abandoned building. And finally he couldn't take it anymore.

He stood in the middle of an empty street and lifted his face to gray skies that only seemed to be kept aloft by the roofs of the buildings.

"Dakota!" he cried. "Dakota!"

But he was far too late, and she didn't come.

Don't wait too long to call me, she'd told him. *If you change too much, I won't be able to find you and nobody else can help you.*

He had no one to blame but himself. It was as she'd said. He'd changed too much and now, even if she could hear him, she wouldn't recognize him. He wasn't sure he'd even recognize himself. Still, he called her name again, called for her until the hollow echo that was his voice grew raw and weak. Finally he slumped there in the middle of the road, shoulders sagging, chin on his chest, and stared at the pavement.

"The name you were calling," a voice said. "Did it belong to one of those watchers?"

John looked up at the man who'd approached him so silently. He was a nondescript individual, the kind of man he'd have passed by on the street when he was alive and never looked at twice. Medium height, medium build. His only really distinguishing feature was the fervent glitter in his eyes.

"A watcher," John repeated, nodding in response to the man's question. "That's what she called herself."

"Damn 'em all to hell, I say," the man told him. He spat on the pavement. "'Cept that'd put 'em on these same streets and Franklin T. Clark don't ever want to look into one of their stinkin' faces again—not unless I've got my hands around one of their necks. I'd teach 'em what it's like to be dead."

"I think they're dead, too," John said.

"That's what they'd like you to believe. But tell me this: If they're dead, how come they're not here like us? How come they get to hold onto a piece of life like we can't?"

"Because . . . because they're helping people."

Clark spat again. "Interferin's more like it." The dark light in his eyes seemed to deepen as he fixed his gaze on John. "Why were you calling her name?"

"I can't take this anymore."

"An' you think it's gonna be better where they want to take us?"

"How can it be worse?"

"They can take away who you are," Clark said. "They can *try*, but they'll never get Franklin T. Clark, I'll tell you that. They can kill me, they can dump me in this stinkin' place, but I'd rather rot here in hell than let 'em change me."

"Change you how?" John wanted to know.

"You go through those gates of theirs an' you end up part of a stew. Everythin' that makes you who you are, it gets stole away, mixed up with everybody else. You become a kind of fuel—that's all. Just fuel."

"Fuel for what?"

"For 'em to make more of us. There's no goddamn sense to it. It's just what they do."

"How do you know this?" John asked.

Clark shook his head. "You got to ask, you're not worth the time I'm wastin' on you."

He gave John a withering took, as though John was something he'd stepped on that got stuck to the bottom of his shoe. And then he walked away.

John tracked the man's progress as he shuffled off down the street. When Clark was finally out of sight, he lifted his head again to stare up into the oppressive sky that hung so close his face.

"Dakota," he whispered.

But she still didn't come.

THE DAY HE FOUND the infant wailing in a heap of trash behind what had once been a restaurant made John wonder if there wasn't some merit in Clark's anger toward the watchers. The baby was a girl and she was no more than a few days old. She couldn't possibly have made the decision that had left her in this place—not by any stretch of the imagination. A swelling echo of Clark's rage rose up in him as he lifted the infant from the trash. He swaddled her in rags and cradled the tiny form in his arms.

"What am I going to do with you?" he asked.

The baby stopped crying, but she made no reply. How could she? She was so small, so helpless. Looking down at her, John knew what he had to do. Maybe Clark was right and the watchers were monsters, although he found that hard to reconcile with his memories of Dakota's empathy and sadness. But Clark was wrong about what lay beyond the gates. He had to be. It couldn't be worse than this place.

He set off then, still wandering aimlessly, but now he had a destination in mind, now he had something to look for. He wasn't doing it for himself, though he knew he'd step through those gates when they stood in front of him. He was doing it for the baby.

"I'm going to call you Dolly," he told the infant. "Darlene would've liked that. What do you think?"

He chucked the infant under her chin. Her only response was to stare up at him.

JOHN FIGURED HE HAD it easier than most people who suddenly had an infant come into their lives. Dolly didn't need to eat and she didn't cry unless he set her down. She was only happy in his arms. She didn't soil the rags he'd wrapped her in. Sometimes she slept, but there was nothing restful about it. She'd be lying in his arms one minute, the next it was as though someone had thrown a switch and she'd been turned off. He'd been frantic the first time it happened, panicking until he realized that she was only experiencing what passed for sleep in this place.

He didn't let himself enter that blank state. The idea had crept into his mind as he wandered the streets with Dolly that to do so, to let himself turn off the way he and all the other undead did would make it all that much more difficult for him to complete his task. The longer he denied himself, the more seductive the lure of that strange sleep became, but he stuck to his resolve. After a time, he was rewarded for maintaining his purposefulness. His vision sharpened; the world still appeared monochromatic, but at least it was all back in focus. He grew more clear-headed.

He began to recognize more and more parts of the city. But the gates remained as elusive as Dakota had proved to be since the last time he'd seen her.

One day he came upon Clark again. He wasn't sure how long it had been since the last time he'd seen the man—a few weeks? A few months? It was difficult to tell time in the city as it had become because the light never changed. There was no day, no night, no comforting progression from one into the other. There was only the city, held in eternal twilight.

Clark was furious when he saw the infant in John's arms. He ranted and swore at John, threatened to beat him for interfering in what he saw as the child's right of choice. John stood his ground, holding Dolly.

"What are you so afraid of?" he asked when Clark paused to take a breath.

Clark stared at him, a look of growing horror spreading across his features until he turned and fled without replying. He hadn't needed to reply. John knew what Clark was afraid of. It was the same fear that kept them all in this desolate city: Death. Dying. They were all afraid. They were all trapped here by that fear. Except for John. He was still trapped like the others; the difference was that he was no longer afraid.

But if a fear of death was no longer to be found in his personal lexicon, despair remained. Time passed. Weeks, months. But he was no closer to finding those fabled gates than he'd been when he first found Dolly and took up the search. He walked through a city that grew more and more familiar. He recognized his own borough, his own street, his own house. He walked slowly up his walk and looked in through the window, but he didn't go in. He was too afraid of succumbing to the growing need to sit somewhere and close his eyes. It would be so easy to go inside, to stretch out on the couch, to let himself fall into the welcoming dark.

Instead he turned away, his path now leading toward the building that housed High Lonesome Sounds. He found it without any trouble, walked up its eerily silent stairwell, boots echoing with a hollow sound, a sound full of dust and broken hopes. At the top of the stairs, he turned to his right and stepped into the recording studio's lounge. The room was empty, except for an open fiddlecase in the middle of the floor, an instrument lying in it, a bow lying across the fiddle, horsehairs loose.

He shifted Dolly from the one arm to the crook of the other. Kneeling down, he slipped the bow into its holder in the lid of the case and shut the lid. He stared at the closed case for a long moment. He had no words to describe how much he'd missed it, how incomplete he'd felt without it. Sitting more comfortably on the floor, he fashioned a sling out of his jacket so that he could carry Dolly snuggled up against his chest and leave his arms free.

When he left the studio, he carried the fiddlecase with him. He went down the stairs, out onto the street. There were no cars, no pedestrians. Nothing had changed. He was still trapped in that reflection of the city he'd known when he was alive, the deserted streets and abandoned buildings peopled only by the undead. But something felt different. It wasn't just that he seemed more himself, more the way he'd been when he was still alive, carrying his fiddle once more. It was as though retrieving the instrument had put a sense of expectation in the air. The dismal gray streets, overhung by a brooding sky, were suddenly pregnant with possibilities.

He heard the footsteps before he saw the man: a tall, rangy individual, arriving from a side street at a brisk walk. Faded blue jeans, black sweatshirt with matching baseball cap. Flat-heeled cowboy boots. What set him apart from the undead was the purposeful set to his features. His gaze was turned outward, rather than inward.

"Hello!" John called after the stranger as the man began to cross the street. "Have you got a minute?"

The stranger paused in mid-step. He regarded John with surprise but waited for him to cross the street and join him. John introduced himself and put out his hand. The man hesitated for a moment, then took John's hand.

"Bernard Gair," the man said in response. "Pleased, I'm sure." His look of surprise had shifted into one of vague puzzlement. "Have we met before . . . ?"

John shook his head. "No, but I do know one of your colleagues. She calls herself Dakota."

"The name doesn't ring a bell. But then there are so many of us—though never enough to do the job."

"That's what she told me. Look, I know how busy you must be so I won't keep you any longer. I just wanted to ask you if you could direct me to . . ."

John's voice trailed off as he realized he wasn't being listened to. Gair peered more closely at him.

"You're one of the lost, aren't you?" Gair said. "I'm surprised I can even see you. You're usually so . . . insubstantial. But there's something different about you."

"I'm looking for the gates," John told him.

"The gates."

Something in the way he repeated the words made John afraid that Gair wouldn't help him.

"It's not for me," he said quickly. "It's for her." He drew back a fold of the sling's cloth to show Gair the sleeping infant nestled against his chest.

"I see," Gair said. "But does she want to go on?"

"I think she's a little young to be making that kind of decision for herself."

Gair shook his head. "Age makes no difference to a spirit's ability to decide such a thing. Infants can cling as tenaciously to life as do the elderly—often more so, since they have had so little time to experience it."

"I'm not asking you to make a judgment," John said. "I'm just asking for some directions. Let the kid decide for herself once she's at the gates and can look through."

Gair needed time to consider that before he finally gave a slow nod.

"That could be arranged," he allowed.

"If you could just give me directions," John said.

Gair pulled up the left sleeve of his sweatshirt so that he could check the time on his wristwatch.

"Let me take you instead," he said.

EVEN WITH DIRECTIONS, JOHN couldn't have found the gates on his own. "The journey," Gair explained, "doesn't exercise distance so much as a state of mind." That was as good a description as any, John realized as he fell in step with his new companion, for it took them no time at all to circumvent familiar territory and step out onto a long boulevard. John felt a tugging in that part of his chest where his heart had once beaten as he looked down to the far end of the avenue. An immense archway stood there.

Between its pillars the air shimmered like a heat mirage and called to him.

When Gair paused, John came to a reluctant halt beside him. Gair looked at his watch again.

"I'm sorry," he said, "but I have to leave you now. I have another appointment."

John found it hard to look at the man. His gaze kept being drawn back to the shimmering air inside the arch.

"I think I can find my way from here," he said.

Gair smiled. "I should think you could." He shook John's hand. "Godspeed," he murmured, then he faded away just as Dakota had faded from his living room what seemed like a thousand lifetimes ago.

Dolly stirred against John's chest as he continued on toward the gates. He rearranged her in the sling so that she, too, could look at the approaching gates, but she turned her face away and for the first time his holding her wasn't enough. She began to wail at the sight of the gates, her distress growing in volume the closer they got.

John slowed his pace, uncertain now. He thought of Clark's cursing at him, of Gair telling him that Dolly, for all her infancy, was old enough to make this decision on her own. He realized that they were both right. He couldn't force her to go through, to travel on. But what would he do if she refused? He couldn't simply leave her behind, either.

The archway of the gates loomed over him now. The heat shimmer had changed into a warm golden light that washed out from between the pillars, dispelling all the shadows that had ever taken root in John's soul. But the infant in his arms wept more pitifully, howled until he covered her head with part of the cloth and let her burrow her face against his chest. She whimpered softly there until John thought his heart would break. With each step he took, the sounds she made grew more piteous.

He stood directly before the archway, bathed in its golden light. Through the pulsing glow, he could see the big sky Dakota had described. It went on forever. He could feel his heart swell to fill it. All he wanted to do was step through, to be done with the lies of the flesh, the lies that had told him this one life was all, the lies that had tricked him into being trapped in the city of the undead.

But there was the infant to consider, and he couldn't abandon her. Couldn't abandon her, but he couldn't explain it to her, that there was nothing to fear, that it was only light and an enormous sky. And peace. There were no words to capture the wonder that pulsed through his veins, that blossomed in his heart, swelled until his chest was full and he knew the light must be pouring out of his eyes and mouth.

Now he understood Dakota's sorrow. It would be heartbreaking to know what waited for those who turned their backs on this glory. It had nothing to do with gods or religions. There was no hierarchy of belief entailed. No one was denied admittance. It was simply the place one stepped through so that the journey could continue.

John cradled the sobbing infant, jigging her gently against his chest. He stared into the light. He stared into the endless sky.

"Dakota," he called softly.

"Hello, John Narraway."

He turned to find her standing beside him, her own solemn gaze drinking in the light that pulsed in the big sky between the gates and flowed over them. She smiled at him.

"I didn't think I'd see you again," she said. "And certainly not in this place. You did well to find it."

"I had help. One of your colleagues showed me the way."

"There's nothing wrong with accepting help sometimes."

"I know that now," John said. "I also understand how hard it is to offer help and have it refused."

Dakota stepped closer and drew the infant from the sling at John's chest.

"It is hard," she agreed, cradling Dolly. Her eyes still held the reflected light that came from between the gates, but they were sad once more as she studied the weeping infant. She sighed, adding, "But it's not something that can be forced."

John nodded. There was something about Dakota's voice, about the way she looked that distracted him, but he couldn't quite put his finger on it.

"I will take care of the little one," Dakota said. "There's no need for you to remain here."

"What will you do with her?"

"Whatever she wants."

"But she's so young."

The sadness deepened in Dakota's eyes. "I know."

There was so much empathy in the voice, in the way she held the infant, in the gaze. And then John realized what was different about her. Her voice wasn't hollow, it held resonance. She wasn't monochrome, but touched with color. There was only a hint, at first, like an old tinted photograph, but it was like looking at a rainbow for John. As it grew stronger, he drank in the wonder of it. He wished she would speak again, just so that he could cherish the texture of her voice, but she remained silent, solemn gaze held by the infant in her arms.

"I find it hardest when they're so young," she finally said, looking up at him. "They don't communicate in words, so it's impossible to ease their fears."

But words weren't the only way to communicate, John thought. He crouched down to lay his fiddlecase on the ground, took out his bow, and tightened the hair. He ran his thumb across the fiddle's strings to check the tuning, marveling anew at the richness of sound. He thought perhaps he'd missed that the most.

"What are you doing?" Dakota asked him.

John shook his head. It wasn't that he didn't want to explain it to her, but that he couldn't. Instead he slipped the fiddle under his chin, drew the bow across the strings, and used music to express what words couldn't. He turned to the gates, drank in the light and the immense wonder of the sky, and distilled it into a simple melody, an air of grace and beauty. Warm generous notes spilled from the sound holes of his instrument, grew stronger and more resonant in the light of the gates, gained such presence that they could almost be seen, touched, and held with more than the ear.

The infant in Dakota's arms fell silent and listened. She turned innocent eyes toward the gates and reached out for them. John slowly brought the melody to an end. He laid down his fiddle and bow and took the infant from Dakota, walked with her toward the light. When he was directly under the arch, the light seemed to flare and suddenly the weight was gone from his arms. He heard a joyous cry, but could see nothing for the light. His felt a beating in his chest as though he were alive once more, pulse drumming. He wanted to follow Dolly into the light more than he'd ever wanted anything before in his life, but he slowly turned his back on the light and stepped back onto the boulevard.

"John Narraway," Dakota said. "What are you doing?"

"I can't go through," he said. "Not yet. I have to help the others—like you do."

"But—"

"It's not because I don't want to go through anymore," John said. "It's . . ."

He didn't know how to explain it and not even fiddle music would help him now. All he could think of was the despair that had clung to him in the city of the undead, the same despair that possessed all those lost souls he'd left there, wandering forever through its deserted streets, huddling in its abandoned buildings, denying themselves the light. He knew that, like Dakota and Gair, he had to try to prevent others from making the same mistake. He knew it wouldn't be easy, he knew there would be times when it would be heartbreaking, but he could see no other course.

"I just want to help," he said. "I have to help. You told me before that there aren't enough of you and the fellow that brought me here said the same thing."

Dakota gave him a long considering look before she finally smiled. "You know," she said, "I think you do have the generosity of heart now."

John put away the fiddle. When he stood up, Dakota took his hand and they began to walk back down the boulevard, away from the gates.

"I'm going to miss that light," John said.

Dakota squeezed his hand. "Don't be silly," she said, "The light has always been inside us."

John glanced back. From this distance, the light was like a heat mirage again, shimmering between the pillars of the gates, but he could still feel its glow, see the flare of its wonder and the sky beyond it that went on forever. Something of it echoed in his chest, and he knew Dakota was right.

"We carry it with us wherever we go," he said.

"Learn to play that on your fiddle, John Narraway," she said.

John returned her smile. "I will," he promised. "I surely will."

Guardian of the Peace

Laura Hayden

Dying in the line of duty sounded better in theory than in practice. Officer Reed Wilson had learned that the hard way.

In the light of Columbine and other school tragedies, Reed had always approached in-school calls with heightened caution, but never thought he'd be in danger at the show-and-tell session at a third-grade class. The theme was police and protection.

Who would've guessed that one of the kids would bring his dad's purloined gun?

Reed had no idea until the bullet hit him in the chest.

After the fact, he could be a bit more pragmatic about it. Sure, the kid didn't mean to pull the trigger, but then again, no matter the kid's intent, Reed was just as dead . . .

But what really irked him was being forced back on duty at the same school where he'd died. "Guardian Angel of the Peace." What a stupid title. Whoever thought of that title—much less the program—had a sick sense of humor.

Reed knew what he was. A ghost.

God knew he didn't have the qualifications to become an angel, much less a Guardian Angel for that matter.

But you don't argue with God . . . and expect to win.

Reed didn't know what to expect the first time he stepped into the room where he died.

Would he relive the pain?

Remember the screams of the children as he bled to death in front of them?

Recall the look of horror on the face of the little boy with the gun?

But only one thought circulated through his mind as he stood in the same spot where died: *I hate kids.* And even worse, he hated object lessons, and this one was going to be a real beaut. Make the man who died at the hands of a child be the guardian angel for not just one child, but a whole freakin' room full of them.

The school district in its infinite wisdom had reassigned the portable schoolroom to a new class. Instead of hosting third-graders, the room-trailer now housed a load of kindergarteners— drippy-nosed, whiny, and best of all, possessing no memories of the day a kid splattered cop parts all over the windowless south wall. Said wall was now painted a cheery sky blue with smiling clouds.

Heaven?

Hardly.

Try hell on earth.

Okay, maybe Reed didn't exactly hate kids. While he was alive, he could take them or leave them. But was it fair that his entire life . . . er . . . death now revolved around a whole gaggle of them, spending four long hours a day, watching them learn such monumental lessons as their colors, the alphabet, and that the paste-eaters of the old days still existed and had switched to ingesting a modern, cool-looking gel glue that came in a convenient squeeze bottle?

Remembering his own early school years, he recalled having the hots for his kindergarten teacher, Mrs. Sutton. What a babe . . . Then the next year in first grade, the teacher was the grandmother-soft and highly huggable Mrs. Kingsbury who always smelled like April Violets.

But this kindergarten teacher, Ms. Shaw, was neither; she was a pale, thin woman with an equally pale, thin personality. Reed couldn't imagine any child warming to her . . . until he heard her read a book to the kids.

Animation filled her face and her voice as she did more than just read; she acted out the stories demonstrating a surprising range of voices so that each character sounded different. It was as if the joy of fiction filled a void in her, providing the natural spark and drive that she lacked otherwise in her very plain life. And when she said those magic words, "Story time!" every student immediately found his or her place in the circle of carpet squares and sat mesmerized as she read.

It was while they were quiet and behaving, that Reed realized he couldn't tell them apart. With their personalities temporarily suspended by their enormous interest in the pending entertainment, they all looked the same with nondescript light brown hair, wide eyes, and gaping mouths. No cultural diversity here.

But whenever Ms. Shaw finished, and they reverted to their predominant traits, then they became distinguishable by personality alone.

After careful observations, Reed decided that all classes, even kindergarten classes had specific positions to be filled by specific students. It was true in his day and evidently true now. Although his interest in a bunch of snot-nosed brats was scant at best, he couldn't help but start categorizing them by their personality traits. It was sure a lot easier than learning all their names.

There was Princess—who came to school in designer clothes and with her hair in perfect curls. She lived for superlatives— wanting to be constantly told she was the prettiest, the smartest, the best . . .

And she wasn't.

Tomboy had her beat by a mile. Tomboy came to school in jeans with holes in the knees, not artful ones frayed by Kathie Lee's Guatemala work crew, but ones worn away by a different sort of child labor: honest play. Without even trying, Tomboy managed to make the clothing choices look like the latest fashion and started an inadvertent trend within her class. Everyone started wearing jeans with hole-y knees and pocket T-shirts in primary colors.

And Tomboy naturally won the accolades that Princess so desperately wanted. Tomboy could out-throw all of the other kids and, when dared, managed to recite the alphabet backwards without missing a beat. Worst of all for Princess, Tomboy already had classic looks that would eventually mature into great beauty.

As luck would have it, Princess wasn't quite bright enough to realize that Tomboy was her true competition for Homecoming Queen 2013, so Princess spent all her time believing she sat at the top of the kindergarten hierarchy when, in reality, she hovered somewhere around the middle of the pyramid.

There were other classic roles filled by various kids—Class Clown—the one who most often dined on the gel glue; Sports Guy who had more natural sports ability in his little finger than the rest of the class put together—with the exception of Tomboy who could go toe-to-toe to him. There was Barf who had the world's worst gag reflex and his antithesis Mr. Clean who shrieked whenever he saw that look of impending explosion in Barf's eyes.

Prez was the class's natural leader and had future Student Government President stamped on his forehead. Earth Mother spent her time playing at the sand table, making organically pure mud pies. Melody was one of the few of them who could sing and when her clear, sweet voice warbled "Jose can you see . . ." Reed allowed himself to contemplate the existence of heaven.

Angel, whose name turned out to actually be Angel, was the class peacemaker, trying to mediate between disputes and casting oil on troubled watercolors whenever possible. Her opposite was Bully, who delighted in knotting up the situations that Angel tried to unravel.

But when Ms. Shaw started reading, they became as one, all in rapt attention for the furthering adventures of the book in progress. There they sat, cross-legged, eyes bugged, and mouths hanging open.

Every child but one.

There was no convenient personality-archetype title for Travis, more frequently known as Poor Travis. Poor as in pity, not lack of wealth.

Travis was . . . different. The child had nondescript brown hair and a permanent hunch in his thin shoulders. He spent all of his time crouching at a table, arms in a protective circle around what appeared to be his most valuable possessions—his crayons and his paper. But he wasn't Mr. Greedy because his sole interest was one box of crayons and one stack of paper. He had no interest in hogging anybody else's colors or possessing every sheet of paper in the room. He didn't care anything about the other toys or objects in the room. Just his.

When Poor Travis wasn't warding off the other kids from his paper, he was drawing. And judging by the quality of his art work, his name wasn't Artist, either. The kid drew all the time, methodically using every crayon in the box of sixty-four in order. If anyone dared touch much less rearrange his crayons, the brat howled like a banshee in heat. But other than his wailing, he said nothing.

Not a single word.

Silent Travis, maybe.

At first, Reed thought Trav might be deaf because the child summarily ignored all the other children. He also paid no attention to school bells, morning announcements on the speaker, songs, the teacher or the sometimes hideous racket the children created. (Reed figured the noise level alone was why the kindergarten class had been relegated to the trailer in the parking lot rather than inside like the other classes.)

Instead of responding to any outside stimulus, Travis continued to draw pictures, sometimes trying to use them to communicate with his teacher when he needed something.

At first, Ms. Shaw would stare at the different-colored blobs—most of which looked like mutant butterflies—and try to figure out what they looked like. Travis would becoming increasingly annoyed at her inability to interpret the design and end up stomping back to his sacred table, snatching what he evidently needed from another child or returning to his chair and wetting his pants.

To her credit, she learned to go through a laundry list of things, making big gestures with her hands as if she wasn't sure he could hear her.

"Is someone bothering you, Travis?" She'd point to Bully, the chief instigator of most class problems.

She'd tap a pile of paper on the corner of her desk. "Do you need more paper?"

"Are you hungry?" She'd make the universal sign of taking a bite from an invisible sandwich.

And the all important: "Travis, do you need to go to the bathroom?" To her credit, she had no gesture for toilet needs other than pointing out the door to the bathroom one trailer over.

Every once in a while, she'd slip up and try to compliment his handiwork with an over-enunciated, too-loud version of "What a lovely *fill-in-the-blank-color* butterfly, Travis," to which the kid would throw his hands up, wad the picture into a ball, and kick it back silently to the table.

So maybe the kid wasn't deaf.

One day, Reed decided to test his hypothesis. After the children had gotten settled for a rare nap with the exception of Travis who continued drawing, Reed managed to summon all his ghostly concentration and push a stack of books from the table. When the books banged to the floor, every child jumped, including Travis who drew an inadvertent line on his latest mess-terpiece.

So much for the deaf theory.

But Reed made another startling discovery. Travis turned, stared straight at him and scowled, picked up his paper, wadded it into a ball and then tossed it straight at Reed.

The wad passed through him and continued its trajectory to the trash can directly behind Reed.

Rim shot. He sighed. *Trav wasn't aiming at me.*

But a little while later, Reed glanced at Travis's current art project and saw that today's blue-green mutant butterfly had either crapped blue-green or was standing over a pile of . . . books on the floor?

Couldn't be . . .

Now Reed had a new hypothesis to test. After all, wasn't literature—and movies even—full of stories about people who communicated with ghosts?

Then reality hit him.

Great, here I am, stuck, maybe for all eternity, haunting the place where I died and the only person who can see me is some kid who doesn't talk.

Reed glanced at the sky-blue wall, spotting the nearly invisible repair patch in the drywall. It was the place where the bullet had struck after passing through him . . .

To his amazement, Travis stood up, took his crayon-du-jour and walked over to the sky-blue wall. With great deliberation, he inscribed a small *X* in the exact center of the repaired dry wall.

Reed stared at the *X* and said words that no kindergartner should hear, much less repeat.

Travis stared straight at him, raised his eyebrow in obvious dis-
taste at such language, then sat back down and began to draw his
mutant butterflies again.

Great, Reed thought to himself. Not only was his life on earth
a royal waste of time, his afterlife on earth wasn't going to be
much better.

Haunting a classroom.

What a job.

REED STAYED AWAY FROM Travis as best as he could for almost three
weeks, which wasn't easy, considering the trailer's size and the fact
that Reed couldn't leave. Whenever he stepped toward the door,
an invisible hand pulled him back. He supposed it made sense
that ghosts would have boundaries. So Reed tried to interest himself in the other children and step around, avoid, and generally
ignore Travis whenever possible.

And Travis seemed quite content to be ignored. On the rare
occasions that their gazes met, Travis would merely shrug or sigh,
then turn away.

Peaceful co-nonexistence, Reed figured.

Reed did manage to stay clear of Travis until a cold day in
November when Bully decided a kid who never spoke made an
easy mark. Travis withstood Bully's snide taunts and underhanded
threats. But the moment Ms. Shaw's attention was diverted by Barf
and his impending mess, Bully reached for Travis's latest art project, motioning as if he was about to shred it. Sensing a too-easy
victory, Bully went one step further, suggesting that his next act
would be to shred Travis.

Travis just sat there, doing nothing, and it irked Reed. Hadn't
anyone taught the kid how to protect himself?

"Stand up to him," Reed ordered.

Travis looked at him.

"He's nothing but a bully. They're all mouth. No follow-
through. You stand up to him and he'll back down."

Travis watched as Bully tore the picture into long strips, giggling at the sound of tearing paper.

"If you let him win the first time, he'll win every time. Stand up to him."

Travis's gaze hardened. Then he stood and glanced pointedly over Bully's shoulder, as if Ms. Shaw was standing behind him, watching the whole exchange. Bully instinctively turned, anticipating an inevitable reprimand.

Travis took advantage of Bully's misdirection and resulting unbalance to push his tormentor, snatch his paper back and leave a jagged red crayon streak across Bully's favorite T-shirt. To add insult to injury, Travis deftly slipped the offending red crayon in Bully's T-shirt pocket.

Reed watched in amazement and a small sense of pride.

Ms. Shaw spotted the commotion and trotted over, intercepting Bully's arm as he cocked it back to throw a punch in Travis's direction.

Caught in the act, Bully exploded in accusations. "I wasn't doing nuffin'. He pushed me!" He rubbed an imaginary injury on the wrong arm, then noticed the red zigzag that decorated his shirt. His voice wavered. "And he ruined my shirt. My mom's going to kill me!"

Ms. Shaw spotted the offending crayon in Bully's pocket. Pulling it out, she held it up for general inspection. "Travis, is this your crayon?"

He nodded.

"Did you draw on his shirt on purpose?"

He said nothing. As always.

She turned to Bully. "And I suppose you're going to say you weren't bothering him or his pictures." She glanced down at the telltale paper curls Bully was trying to nudge out of sight with his foot.

The teacher released a sigh. "You go sit in the red quiet chair for fifteen minutes and think about our rules about respecting other people's properties." Bully stomped off toward the red chair, a place where he spent more time than his own desk. She turned to Travis. "You could have told me he was bothering you. I would have done something about it."

Travis shot her a stony look in reply, and Reed could hear the unspoken words forming in the child's mind. "*I don't talk, remember?*"

"I think you need to go sit in the blue chair and think about a better way to deal with bullies."

Travis reached for his crayons and a fresh piece of paper.

"And don't take that with you. You sit and think, instead."

A look of absolute shock crossed Travis's face, then the look shattered to dismay and resignation. He abandoned his art supplies on his desk and trudged to the blue chair of discipline, collapsing in it as if his whole world had been destroyed.

Once seated, Travis looked up and met Reed's concerned gaze with one of complete and total hatred.

That's what I get for interfering.

THE NEXT COUPLE OF weeks, Reed managed to not involve himself an any aspect of Travis's life. Instead, Reed tried to distract himself by spending most of his time attempting to reach the other children—to see if any of them could see him, much less be influenced by him.

No such luck.

Just Travis.

Although Reed avoided the kid as best as possible, he couldn't help but be concerned. Travis didn't seem to be learning anything. He wasn't talking or interacting with either the teacher or the other kids. And over the course of a couple of weeks, even Bully showed signed of having absorbed some of the lessons Ms. Shaw repeated with irritating frequency.

Reed's concern deepened the day the office called for Travis for an appointment. Reed wasn't sure what sort of appointment it was, but he hoped it was either a date with a shrink or at least a speech therapist. It became a regular thing with Travis disappearing every Thursday morning for an hour. When he came back, he seemed agitated and his resulting pictures were more jagged in style, but still monochrome.

Unfortunately, Bully saw the mysterious appointment as fodder for loud speculation, suggesting to the class that Travis was a nutcase and getting his head shrunk. Reed, having learned his lesson about encouraging Travis, instead began a program whereby he attempted to distract Bully every time he started his diatribe against Travis. It involved knocking over books, misplacing papers, untying Bully's shoes—anything to divert him from his verbal assaults.

But one Thursday morning, curiosity got the best of Reed and he decided to try a different experiment. When the door opened and the student escort came for Travis, Reed tried to tag along. To his amazement, he made it out of the door and got a few steps into the parking lot before being pulled back into the trailer by whatever unseen force that kept him there.

The next week, he managed to accompany Travis a few more steps closer to the regular school building. The next week, Travis took pity on him and when the forces began to pull Reed back, Travis held out his hand.

Reed took it and suddenly the forces stopped. Together, they walked hand in hand into the school. Once inside, Travis broke contact but no new force struck Reed. He remained with Travis, walking along with him to a counselor's office.

There was no head-shrinking, but the counselor, a Mr. Green, had a manner about him that would have been highly conducive to conversation with anyone else but Travis. Heck, Reed wouldn't have minded sitting down with the guy, knocking back a couple of beers, and discussing life, liberty, and the pursuit of whatever. The guy would have made a helluva bartender, but he was making no headway with Travis.

The man was smart enough to give Travis a box of crayons— albeit only sixteen colors—and some paper and let him express himself with pictures. To Travis's credit, he drew something other than mutant butterflies, but Reed had no idea what the various color blobs were.

Evidently, neither did Mr. Green. At the end of their hour, Travis left a stack of drawings and accepted a hug from his counselor. The student escort led Travis back to the door leading to the parking lot.

"I'm not going out there. Didn't bring my coat. You go on and I'll watch you from here."

Travis sighed, rolled his eyes and opened the door to let himself out. He paused, then held out his hand to Reed.

For a split second, Reed considered not going. Thanks to Travis, he'd escaped the trailer, escaped that part of fate that suggested he had to haunt the place where he died. Maybe this was the first step to going to some sort of real afterlife.

But Reed looked into the child's eyes and changed his mind instantly. After all, Travis had proved that together they could leave the trailer. Who's to say they won't be able to do it again? Another time . . . the right time would come some day when Reed could leave. Right now, it was enough to know that he could leave that made returning not that bad.

He slipped his hand in Travis's and they headed back to the trailer. When they entered, the children were taking a nap, which was unusual this time of day. Even Ms. Shaw had placed her head on the desk and was taking a snooze.

Something was wrong.

Travis realized it too. He pointed to Bully who had been sitting in the red chair, but was now sprawled on the floor as if he'd fallen from the chair and not gotten up.

Reed sniffed the air, belatedly realizing that smell was a sense he no longer had. As far as that went, he didn't really breathe any more, either. "Travis, does it smell funny in here?"

Travis drew in a deep breath then shook his head.

No odor. Although he felt neither cold nor hot, a shiver coursed up Reed's spine. Carbon monoxide. That would explain why they were all asleep.

"Open the door, Travis and leave it open." The child obeyed instantly. "And stay out there." Travis nodded and stepped out. He needed to open the windows but there was no way he could do it himself and he wasn't going to let Travis back into the room.

"Go to the office. Get help!" he ordered. Then Reed turned to the windows, discovering that his total strength wasn't enough to finesse the lock or lift the sash. He looked around for a weapon, anything he could use to break the glass and let good air into the room. He spotted Bully's show and tell rock collection.

Sorry, kid, he said, picking up a nondescript rock and hurling it through the window. It would be lost forever among the gravel scattered across the parking lot.

It took only a few precious seconds before every window has been broken and healthy air poured into the room. But would it be too little too late?

Reed looked through the broken panes and was stunned to see Travis still standing in shock in the parking lot. "Go, Trav. Get someone!"

The child shook his head and held out his hand. Reed pushed his way past the boundaries that usually held him to the room and reached Travis. The moment they touched, the forces that held him disappeared. Hand in hand, they ran into the school and toward the office.

The school secretary looked startled by Travis who skidded into the room, making wild gestures, but saying nothing. She stepped around the counter and into the waiting area, knelt and tried to get him to calm down and talk. That made Travis even more agitated.

Reed knelt beside the woman so that he too was at face-level with Travis. "Buddy, you have to calm down. You can do this. Ms. Shaw and the others need you to bring help and save them."

Travis nodded and made a visible effort to calm down. He made a scribbling motion which the secretary understood. She reached over the counter and snagged a piece of paper and a pencil. "Here, honey."

Travis quickly sketched a recognizable drawing of the trailer which the secretary recognized as well. "Do you need someone to take you to your class?" She smiled. "That's a good boy. You know you're not supposed to cross the parking lot by yourself."

He shook his head furiously, his agitation growing again.

Reed shifted so that he was between Travis and the woman. "Listen buddy, this is a matter of life and death. I know you don't want to talk, but if you don't say something, Ms. Shaw and the others might die."

Travis reached out and with one shaky hand, pointed his forefinger at Reed, a gesture that Reed intrinsically knew. "Yeah, Trav. They'll be dead. Just like me."

Travis closed his eyes, clenched his hands into small fists and his tremors stopped. In a rusty voice, he spoke.

"They're asleep and I can't wake them up."

The woman looked puzzled by his comment, not realizing that one, she should be amazed and elated that he spoke at all and, two, she should be responding instantly to his message.

"What do you mean, honey?"

Travis turned to Reed in frustration and Reed pronounced the words one syllable at a time which Travis dutifully repeated.

"Car-bon mo-no-xide."

REED LOST TRACK OF Travis in all the hoopla with ambulances, fire trucks, paramedics, safety inspectors, heating and air conditioning folks and the like. Reed remained at his station, supervising the repairs, watching the school district engineers repair the blocked heater intake vent as well as replace all the broken windows.

Everyone was amazed that a mere kindergarten student not only recognized the danger his teacher and fellow schoolmates were in, but took such suitable actions to save them. He was truly a hero.

And when class resumed in the newly inspected trailer, Ms. Shaw showed a rare burst of animation in her open thanks to Travis. Even Bully managed to grit out a half-hearted thanks. Both Princess and Tomboy gave him a kiss, but he scrubbed away the sensation from his cheeks in typical school kid fashion.

"You just wait. Someday, you'll appreciate girls like that."

Travis offered him a secret grin, which suggested that perhaps he already held some hidden appreciation for girls or their kisses. He bent over his art paper.

"Can I ask you a question?"

Travis nodded slightly. They'd already realized that it wasn't smart for the Class Hero to be seen talking to the Class Ghost.

Reed glanced at the drawing Travis had just started which consisted of the body of what would likely become another mutant butterfly, drawn this time in a navy blue. He pointed to the paper. "What's that?"

Travis shrugged as if adults asked the stupidest questions. "You."

"Me?" Reed stared at the misshapen lump. It did look somewhat like a person. There were legs, arms, and a head wearing a hat. And in navy blue, it bore an eerie resemblance to him in his police uniform.

Travis consulted his box of crayons, turned to give Reed a critical once-over, then returned to his box, selecting a gold crayon.

He began to sketch a delicate curve stretching beyond the

figure's right shoulder. Then he arched the line back down to the body and started on a matching set of curves on the left shoulder.

"Why aren't you use the blue crayon? Up to now, everything's always been the same color."

Travis sighed. "'Cause now I can see them. Before, I was only guessing they were there."

Reed stared in amazement as Travis began coloring between the lines, creating what appeared to be a magnificent pair of gold wings.

"Wings?" Reed said in a strangled voice.

"Uh huh . . ." Travis continued coloring.

"But I'm a ghost," Reed offered.

Travis stopped coloring, glared at his paper and then at Reed. "Nope." He tapped the paper with his forefinger. "You look like this." He studied the picture, adding a gold splotch at the chest, right at police badge level.

"I do?"

Travis nodded without bothering to look up.

"I do . . ." Reed tasted the words. They began to build momentum in his mind. "I do . . ."

He stood up, straightened. Something opened inside of him as if it had been held in a tight grasp and now had been released. Shivers crossed his back and then wings unfolded from the places on his shoulders where the shivers stayed to dance.

"See?" Travis said with all the certainty of the very young and the very faithful.

Reed grinned. "I see." He rose into the air, now wearing his navy blue police uniform and sporting his badge in its usual place on his chest.

"I see so much more, now."

And Officer Reed Wilson spread his wings and took his place as the Christopher Columbus Elementary School Guardian Angel of the Peace.

Paul Dellinger

S o you want to know my life story, do you? Okay, sonny, you asked for it. But I may as well tell you now, you'll never get your editor to publish it. Unless he does it as fiction.

I guess the best place to start is back when I got killed.

I had to be dead, you see. I'd taken three bullets, two in the chest, and then the coup de grace of a shotgun blast directly in the face. That was the last thing I remembered after seeing Jim Stacey and Sam Cooper, the two in our band of Texas Rangers who had been riding in front of me, fall from their horses, and then being slammed to the ground myself. The sound of the gunshots registered only after I lay helpless, unable to defend myself against the ambushers who emerged to walk among the bodies and make sure we were finished.

So I had to be dead. The strong arm I felt supporting me and the cool, refreshing water trickling down my parched throat might be some sort of welcome to the afterlife, I decided. Was I in heaven? I'd always figured I was headed for the other place.

I opened my eyes. It was dark, but I could make out the wrinkled features of the form bending over me. If I'd had a scream in me, I'd have let it rip then. The ancient-looking Indian with the buffalo horns headdress and beaded robe should have been dead, too.

It had been a few years back, on one of our forays against a marauding band of Comanches. Those clashes were usually pretty one-sided; bows and arrows or even single-shot rifles could hardly stand up to our six-shooters. Sam Colt may have developed the revolving pistol up in New England, but it took one of us to make it into a weapon for the frontier. Its original version didn't even have a trigger guard, and you had to pull off the whole barrel to reload it, which wasn't much fun from the back of a galloping horse. Ranger Sam Walker fixed those things, improved the trigger, lengthened the cylinder, which made loading easier, and improved the grip so the pistol could be used as a club if it did come up empty. That was the single piece of technology that spelled the end of Indian dominance in Texas.

But this old guy, who looked to me like a medicine man or a shaman, hadn't been fighting. He'd stood out in front of the village as we rode down on it, empty hands held up as though to ward us off, or maybe just to show that he was unarmed. I pulled my gunsight off him, but riders on either side of me fired a volley before I could yell at them to hold up. We rode right over where he'd been standing. I had time for a quick glance over my shoulder. I couldn't spot his body, but he couldn't have survived all the bullets and horses' hooves.

Except—here he was. The same man whose features had been etched into my memory all these years.

I must've lost consciousness again, but it seemed I could hear him speaking to me—which was strange in itself, since I knew no Indian languages. "You are the one I have sought," I thought I heard. "You have committed your share of sins against my people, and your own—but you have it within you to make amends for your acts, by helping to eradicate the new and growing evils among your own kind . . ."

The words still echoed in my mind when I awoke in daylight, the bodies of the rest of our group sprawled around me. I staggered to my feet, my fingers probing beneath the holes in my shirt for some idea of how badly I was hurt.

I could find no wounds. It didn't make sense. I knew I'd been hit—knew it beyond any possibility of doubt—but I couldn't even find a bruise.

My own horse must have run off but, after walking maybe a mile, I found the tough little mustang that had belonged to another ranger, calmly chomping grass in a small wooded area. He'd found a small pond of water, too. I pulled off his saddle and bridle and checked him over. Then I went to the pond to splash some water on my face, and recoiled at what I saw reflected back at me.

The upper part of my face was blackened, from the powder of the shotgun charge, I supposed. I wondered how my eyes had escaped damage. No matter how I scrubbed with my soaked bandanna, the blackness remained. Somehow I'd survived the gunfire, but it had left me marked forever.

The disfigurement was less noticeable beneath the shadow of my broad-brimmed hat. But it was enough to change my plan to report back to the nearest ranger station—not forever branded the way I was. I didn't see how I could face anyone in what passed for civilization out here.

Even as I re-saddled the bay, I wasn't sure where I would go, but something seemed to pull me north. As good a direction as any, I supposed. In the weeks and months ahead, I camped out on the prairie most nights, not wanting to show my face to townspeople. But occasionally, I had to. I would take jobs swamping out saloons, cleaning stables, even reverting to my former occupation of telegrapher when I could find an operator who could use an assistant and could stand looking at me, until I'd made enough money to buy provisions and move on.

I traveled in that fashion through Colorado and into the Dakota Territory. That was where I encountered my silent Indian shadow once more, just outside the town of Deadwood.

Sweating from the summer heat, I had just rounded a curve in the trail I'd been following when I saw him standing in my path. I jerked the horse to a stop, more forcefully than I'd intended. The animal had seemed about to walk over him, as though not even seeing him.

"Who are you?" I demanded hoarsely.

The old Indian simply held out a piece of paper to me. I reached down and took it. It was a map of some kind, showing streams and foot trails that meant nothing to me at the time. When I turned back to ask what I was supposed to do with it, the trail before me was empty. For all his apparent age, I decided, that Indian could sure move fast.

I shook my head, befuddled. Pocketing the paper in my vest, I walked the bay on into the muddy street of Deadwood, flanked by

log buildings of various kinds. I stopped in front of Nuttall &
Mann's saloon, such places always being good sources of information on what trails were open, where there might be hostiles, and
other news.

I heard the gunshot before I got to the door.

"Wild Bill is shot! Wild Bill is shot!" I heard someone yelling.
Before I could move, a disheveled and slightly crossed-eyed man
came backing out of the place holding a pistol. Forgetting that I
no longer carried a ranger's authority, my hand dropped to my
own Colt. Before I could draw, I felt a hand on my wrist. I turned
and saw it was the old Indian.

His lips didn't seem to move, but I was sure I heard the word,
"No."

The armed man had spotted me by then, and triggered his
revolver at me. I cringed automatically but, instead of the blast I
expected, there was a hollow click. The gun had misfired. The
man turned and ran. Moments later, others from the saloon
came running out in pursuit.

I turned angrily toward the Indian, about to complain that
he'd nearly gotten me killed. Again, he was nowhere to be seen. I
rubbed my knuckles in my eyes, thinking maybe they had been
affected months ago by that shotgun, after all.

THEY TRIED JACK MCCALL in a miners' court for shooting James
Butler Hickok in the back. Even I'd read about Hickok, starting
about eight years ago in a piece by Henry Stanley—the same
gentleman who would later track down a missing Dr. Living-
stone—in the *Weekly Missouri Democrat*, painting "Wild Bill" as a
near-superman who had killed perhaps a hundred villains. Of
course, I knew a tall story when I saw it, even if Mr. Stanley
didn't, but I'd seen other tracts on Hickok since then, even dime
novels. The man had been a legend—and now he had been cut
down while playing a game of cards.

I didn't attend the trial. I was busy putting that strange little
map to use, the one that Indian had handed me. I panned for
gold in a stream that had been marked with an arrow and got
lucky. All of a sudden, I was rich enough so people didn't even

care that my face was disfigured—or at least they didn't say so—while enjoying the drinks I was buying them.

Then one night, while I was actually sleeping in a hotel with a roof over my head, that old Indian came to me yet again. This time, I wasn't sure whether I was dreaming or he was actually there. My spirit guide, he called himself, and he told me I needed to travel east this time, and in a hurry.

After the luck his map had brought me, I wasn't about to ignore him, dream or not. I traveled by horseback, coach and rail, never real sure where I was going although Minnesota seemed to stand out in my mind.

So I missed McCall's trial, and his inexplicable acquittal after he claimed he shot Hickok because Hickok had killed his brother. From what I heard later, the residents of Deadwood had become distracted from the sensation of Hickok's murder by news about Custer and his Seventh Cavalry getting wiped out at the Little Big Horn. They were afraid Deadwood might be next in line for a raid by the victorious Sioux.

Meanwhile, I was leaning back in a chair on a wooden porch in a place called Northfield, wondering why my so-called spirit guide had led me to this little town. Surely there was no gold to be found here. I sat there, half-dozing, my hat pulled low enough to conceal the blackness across my upper face, waiting for some kind of a sign from my Indian mentor, when I noticed the first three riders covered by linen dusters ambling into town with a kind of studied aimlessness—the kind that told me they were up to something.

Looking around, I spotted several other horsemen, similarly attired, and saw where they were converging—the First National Bank. I'd been a ranger long enough to realize what was about to happen, but also long enough to know better than to take on eight bank robbers by myself.

I got up, stretched, and strolled just as casually as they were trying to be into a hardware store. "Howdy," the man behind the counter said with a smile. "Can I help you?"

I pointed to a Remington repeating rifle on the wall behind him. "You might want to grab that," I said, "and get over by your door. Your bank across the street is about to be hit by bandits."

He started to laugh, then looked more closely at me beneath my hat. "Hey, who are you, anyway?" he demanded. But I was moving on to the next store along the street by then.

I'd alerted half a dozen of the townspeople, and some of them had spread the word to others, when five of the horsemen began firing into the air and riding up and down the street. I ducked around the side of a building, but saw the other three running into the bank, no doubt thinking the distraction of all the shooting would make them safe.

I drew my Colt and started to fire back, but felt a hand on my wrist. I turned, and found the old Indian standing next to me in the building's shadow. He didn't speak, but I seemed to pick up the thought from him that it would never again be necessary for me to kill anyone.

Luckily, the rest of the town didn't seem to feel that way. Rifles and shotguns began returning the bandits' fire. I saw one of the bank employees run from the building and fall in the middle of the street, gripping his shoulder. Foolishly, I broke cover to help him to safety. I could almost feel two more bullets from the bank whiz by us, but we made it.

Three of the bandits were down in the street, and others were reeling in their saddles, obviously hit one or more times. "We're beat!" I heard one of them yell. "Let's go!"

One of the downed robbers called out for help, and a rider swung back to pick him up. Riding double, they joined in the general retreat out of town.

A posse tracked most of them down in a couple weeks, killing another and bringing back three badly wounded prisoners—the three Younger brothers, it turned out, holdup artists who had become famous since the Civil War. Two others escaped and were identified as Frank and Jesse James, one of whom had gunned down a bank teller who'd refused to open the safe for them. It would be another six years before one of Jesse's own gang killed him for the reward and Frank gave himself up. But the power of their legend as train, bank, and stagecoach robbers had been broken at Northfield.

Me, I was headed west again. I'd gotten another summons from my spirit guide.

"SO I WALKED UP behind him and let him have it," McCall was telling onlookers in the saloon who were buying him drinks. "He never knew what hit him. One shot, and the great Wild Bill Hickok was history."

He'd been putting on this show practically every night, in saloons from Cheyenne to Laramie. But on this night, I'd found another man to join me as part of his audience. I looked over at the man now, and he gave me a nod.

The next day, the U. S. marshal I'd found arrested McCall who was surprised to find that the miners' court had no standing because it was convened on Indian land. He was tried this time before a jury in Yankton in the Dakota Territory and convicted of murder. He would hang the following year.

The gold I'd panned in the Dakota Territory had finally run out, but I found a new source of income—one where my employers never had to see my face to pay me. If Henry Stanley could create magazine articles about the legends of the west, and Ned Buntline could put them in dime novels and even script live-action shows for "Buffalo Bill" Cody to entertain people back east, so could I. That was when my telegrapher experience came in handy. I could transmit the copy myself.

But even that idea I have to attribute to my spirit guide. Gradually, whether in dreams or in person, he conveyed to me that the west was going to become the mythological underpinning of this new nation. It could glamorize outlaws, or law enforcers, and which way it went could affect how the country turned out.

Six months after Jack McCall was hanged as a killer instead of honored as a hero, I was on board a train in Florida, heading for Alabama. A nice thing about my new occupation was that I could do it from anywhere, and the mark that still remained across my face made me reluctant to take up roots. I'd thought my travel route had been my own idea. Once more, however, my spirit guide apparently had his hand in it.

I reclined in the train seat with my hat pulled low, as usual, but I was watching the two men seated across from me. There seemed something furtive about them. I found myself wishing I'd worn my gunbelt, instead of packing it in my carpetbag. But the old Indian whose advice had proved so good for me up to now opposed my involvement in any killing.

I was conscious of several other men coming into the train car, and I recognized one of them. Seaton, his name was; I remembered him from a few years ago when we were both rangers.

All at once, one of the men across from me leaped up and ran from the car. The other reached for a pistol that had been concealed under his coat. Without even thinking, I lunged across the intervening space and wrapped my arms around him, pinning his gun-arm in place. Then Seaton and three other men had him handcuffed.

"Thanks, friend," Seaton said to me as the other men led the prisoner away. "You just helped us catch John Wesley Hardin. He's killed more than thirty men in his time . . ."

He broke off as he got a look at my face under my hat. Then, half-questioningly, he spoke my name.

"We figured you'd been killed with the others," he said later, as we sat in a restaurant over coffee. "But we never found your body."

It had been so long since I'd been able to be myself with anybody that I couldn't seem to stop talking. I told Seaton everything I've told you and, somewhat to my surprise, he didn't laugh it off.

"I've heard stories of Indian spirit guides," he mused, leaning back in his chair. "Can't say I ever knew anyone that'd met one himself, though. Can't say I ever met one of those dime novel writers, either. I wonder if I've ever read any of your stuff?"

I told him that he might be reading about how he and Captain Armstrong and the other rangers captured Hardin, if he kept his eye on the periodicals. I planned to telegraph an account of that to at least half a dozen papers and maybe do something more elaborate for the magazines. I might even fictionalize it into one of those dime novels he'd mentioned, I said.

"You know," he said, regarding me across the table, "I think you're becoming one of those legends you write about yourself. I've heard stories about a masked man who's brought warnings to towns or to lawmen." My hand jerked to my face, where the blackness across my eyes and forehead could well be mistaken for a mask. "Some of those stories say the man was accompanied by an old Indian . . ."

I found myself wondering if I might rejoin the rangers, defaced as I was, and again be part of the camaraderie of others. But Seaton and myself ended up saying our farewells that evening, and going our separate ways.

My way took me all over the west, always prompted by my half-phantom companion—to New Mexico where I warned a sheriff that an outlaw known as Billy the Kid was hiding out at a friend's ranch; to Tombstone where I actually fired a few shots to break up an ambush of three Earp brothers who were lawmen about to arrest some rustlers at the O.K. Corral; to Coffeyville, Kansas, where the Daltons tried to rob two banks and got what the James and Younger gangs had gotten at Northfield fourteen years earlier . . .

The shots I fired? That was at some gunmen hiding in a photo gallery during the Tombstone thing, where they were going to plug the Earps and Doc Holliday from behind. My Indian friend gave me some special bullets just before, bullets that splintered rifles and shattered six-guns rather than killing any of the men who held them. I've never seen their like before or since.

You know, I haven't seen him in years, either. Maybe he figures I don't need him, anymore. Or maybe he's gone on to whatever happy hunting ground Indians go to and is waiting for me to join him.

Nowadays, as you know, I've been doing scripts for films, still trying to de-glamorize the outlaws and promote the law bringers. It hasn't been that easy, considering that Frank James and Cole Younger and Emmett Dalton are all out of prison and going around selling their takes on their histories. At least old Wyatt Earp is still out here in Hollywood, too . . .

THE OLD MAN HAD been right, the reporter reflected. His editor wouldn't approve the story. Too fantastic, he'd said. Something you'd expect to read in one of those lurid pulp magazines, not a respectable newspaper.

Actually, the reporter had considered turning it into a yarn for one of the pulps. But he didn't know what the old man would have thought of that, so he never tried it.

Now, it didn't matter anymore, he thought, as he watched the casket being lowered into the ground. He wondered how old the man had been. Wyatt Earp had been eighty when he'd passed on early in 1929. This man must have been at least that . . .

A misty rain had enveloped the little cemetery on the outskirts of Los Angeles. Besides the minister, there were only a couple of others present besides the reporter—probably from one of the studios where the old man had helped generate so many movie scripts. Maybe the old man had had the right idea, at that, the reporter reflected. He just might take that job in Detroit at that new radio station, where they planned to launch their own network with a new western program. The old man's tales had given the reporter all kinds of ideas that might be part of a radio series.

The rain grew heavier, and the minister wound up the burial service quickly. The other mourners standing on the opposite side of the grave from the reporter became blurred in the sudden downpour . . .

The reporter's eyes widened as he spotted yet another figure standing just behind them. He couldn't be sure, but it looked like someone wearing a head-piece with horns protruding from it. Buffalo horns? The reporter rubbed his eyes and stared, trying to see the man's features.

Then the funeral was over, the two men in raincoats were departing, and the figure behind them was gone, if it had ever been there. The reporter turned to leave, too. His second stop might be that radio station in Detroit, but his first one was going to be in the nearest bar.

Random Acts of Kindness

Von Jocks

What was it about pick-up trucks, anyway?

Fingers tight on her worn steering-wheel cover, Wendy split her attention between the red taillights in front of her and the blank headlights looming in her rearview mirror. As small as her old Datsun hatchback was, all she could see of the pick-up, other than its headlights, was a toothy grill, complete with the horned head of a silver Dodge ram.

Objects in the mirror may be closer than they appear . . .

The red truck had zoomed up to her rear bumper as if she, unlike the rest of the three-lane, rush-hour-crowded highway, could go faster than thirty-five miles per hour. Now it danced behind her, dropping back about a foot, then zooming forward as if to knock her off the highway, stopping with what looked like mere centimeters to spare. It was playing with her, like a big cat might play with a bunny. Its engine snarled each time, choosing intimidation over gas conservation. A heavy bass rift shook her hatchback's frame, shuddered through her. She considered rolling up her windows, but unlike most of the cars on the Texas highway, the demonic pick-up truck included, she had no air-conditioning. Besides, she wasn't

193

hearing the music past the oldies station on her own radio so much as she was feeling it. Her pulse sped to match . . . or was that her blood-pressure?

Wendy tried the usual stress-management techniques. She deep-breathed several summer-hot lungfuls of gasoline fumes. She counted backwards. She tried to go to her Happy Place—

VRRRROOOOOOMMMMM!!!

"*Screw you!*" she yelled, as if the pick-up's driver could hear her past his closed, anonymously tinted windows; over his blast-o-testosterone stereo; past the power of who-knew how many horses.

Just in case that wasn't cause enough for deafness, he laid on his horn.

The hell with that! His truck must've cost ten times what her used hatchback had. Her insurance rates were probably lower. Frankly, she no longer gave a flying flip about safety, much less goodwill.

When the headlights bobbed back again, Wendy tapped her brakes.

She heard the satisfying squeal of tires as, with a jolt, the pick-up driver compensated. Then, since he'd slowed, she used that opportunity to tap her brakes again. He wanted to ride her bumper? *Fine.* Let him ride it at thirty mph.

Twenty-five.

Twenty!

He laid on his horn again, longer and angrier, and his impatience shuddered through her as surely as his bass.

"*You want fifteen?*" Wendy yelled, even if he *couldn't* hear her.

Cars behind him began to honk, too. Dizzy with anger, Wendy felt beyond caring. When she saw the truck's turn-indicator blink on in her mirror, orange bursts of impatience, she laughed what came out as an ugly laugh. "Oh, yeah. Good luck finding a lane, you . . ."

She didn't finish that sentence, since her windows were open.

But the blood-red truck started nosing its way left, into the next lane anyway, as if the white station wagon beside and slightly behind Wendy would just make room for him. *Who the hell did he think he was?*

"Don't let him in," she muttered, more to herself than the

wagon . . . unless maybe the station-wagon driver could receive her desperate, telepathic sending. "Do not let him in!"

But the station wagon slowed down anyway.

With a triumphant blare of horn, the truck darted into that lane so suddenly that the wagon had to screech onto *its* brakes, too—so much for gratitude. As the truck roared past Wendy, its driver's hand raised out of the window, a gold watch on his wrist and one finger significantly raised.

The back window displayed the boast, "No Fear!"

Cold with fury against the summer heat, she watched as the truck rushed up onto another car's bumper, intimidated *them* out of the way, then continued its reign of terror up the highway. He certainly thought he was someone special. And the worst part was, *he was getting away with it!*

Resuming her own speed in deference to the cars behind her, Wendy fumbled at the cola in her cracked-plastic cup-holder, hoping to wash the bitterness out of her mouth. The can was empty and warm, both. She tossed it into the back seat where it clunked hollowly against others.

Pick-up trucks. Did the dealers waft pheromones into the air to attract only the most obnoxious of drivers? Why the hell couldn't they just go their thirty-five miles per hour until the highway opened up again, like the rest of the mere mortals?

She glanced with disgust at the station wagon that had let the pick-up truck by. If it weren't for *him*, the truck driver would still be stuck, learning a needed lesson about bullying other vehicles. But instead, the only lesson the driver had learned was that intimidation *worked.*

The white wagon was an old Subaru Legacy. Not as old as her Datsun, but she was willing to bet the driver wasn't so vain about *his* vehicle as the driver of the Dodge Ram had been.

Keeping an eye on the traffic in front of her, Wendy glanced quickly sideways several times, wondering what kind of driver would wimp out like this one had. When she saw the old man, she thought maybe she understood. He looked *very* old, short as a child behind the wheel, with hunched shoulders and thick glasses and a bald head ringed by white wisps. His windows, like hers, were open. Here in the South, that meant he couldn't afford to get his air-conditioning fixed either.

He waved at her.

Normally, Wendy would wave back. She was usually a nice person; *really* she was. But her defeat, her anger at seeing the pick-up driver rewarded, still clung to her. She pretended not to have noticed the wave.

As the Legacy drew gently ahead, she did notice its bumper sticker:

Never Drive Faster than Your Angel Can Fly.

SHE WAS STILL THINKING of the pick-up truck, the station wagon, and the bumper sticker over dinner that night, on a date with her friend Gabe. "What?" she asked, missing his question.

"I said, let's go see that new World War II movie," he repeated.

Wendy dragged her mind back from *Never Drive Faster* . . . "But we're seeing the romantic comedy."

"That's a chick flick!"

She took a sip of iced tea, well aware of how the movement pursed her lips around the straw, and glared at him.

"You can see that one with your girlfriends," Gabe wheedled. "I read a review of the war film in the paper today, and it looks really good. It got a B+."

"My movie got a B."

"Yeah, but does a single tank explode?" he teased. "Anybody die in a bloody mess? Now *that's* filmmaking." But his charming, one-dimple grin didn't have its usual effect.

"Look, I don't need any more testosterone today," announced Wendy. "I had enough of that on the drive home from work. If you want to see the war movie, take me home first and go alone."

He back-peddled. "Okay! Geez. If it means that much to you, we'll see the chick flick."

"Good," she said. Then, stymied, she took another sip of tea. Victory didn't feel good. It felt like being stuck in traffic, with someone's bass booming through her whole body.

Then Gabe said, "If you don't mind me sitting through a movie I don't even want to see . . ."

She slammed her glass down onto the table. "Never mind."

He actually brightened. "You'll see the war movie?"

"I'm not seeing *any* movies with you. I want to go home."

"Oh come on, Wendy. I *said* I'd see the chick flick."

Screw you. She almost said it, whether it kissed their relationship good-bye or not. But something, someone, over Gabe's shoulder caught her attention. A little old man, slightly hunched, was leaving through the restaurant's double doors. The parking-lot lights from outside lit up the halo of white hair around his bald head.

"'Scuse me a minute," said Wendy, chair legs scraping as she pushed back from the table.

"Sure," said Gabe. But when she didn't head toward the restrooms, he called, "Wait, where are you going?"

She barely heard him. Instead, she shouldered her way out the restaurant doors—just in time to catch sight of a white station wagon leaving the parking lot. It couldn't be the same car. This was a big city . . .

But when he paused before turning onto the road, the red of his brake lights illuminated his bumper sticker.

Never Drive Faster than Your Angel Can Fly.

She was still standing on the sidewalk when Gabe came out, pocketing his wallet. "What's up, anyway? You're acting sort of weird."

Weird, as in standing up for herself? Refusing to be bullied? *That* kind of weird?

She took a deep breath, a lungful of good food smells. Unlike in the traffic this afternoon, it helped. But not completely.

"Look, it was a good dinner, but you probably *should* just take me home."

"I *said* I'd go to the stupid—"

She cut him off with a glare and one raised hand. *Yield.*

He took her home.

UNLESS THE TRAFFIC GODS sympathized with Gabe, Wendy didn't know what she'd done to anger them. But the very next night's drive home from work found her facing more obnoxious drivers, this time sitting dead still.

Left Lane Closed, orange signs had warned, starting over a mile back. Like a good driver, an obedient citizen, Wendy had graciously merged right. But did that keep other idiots from shooting ahead in the almost-empty lane, all the way to where it ended in a flashing arrow? Did it keep them from stopping her lane—the good people's lane—for the privilege of cutting in front of everyone they'd just zipped past?

Noooooo.

Elbow propped through her open window, Wendy tried to distract herself by admiring the roadside wildflowers. Most of the bluebonnets were gone, but Indian paintbrush and a mist of goldenrod mixed with purple thistle-puffs. The early evening sun cast lumpy, turtle-like shadows off the row of waiting cars. Far too often, another car bolted through them, rabbit-like, in a hurry to make trouble farther ahead.

Never Drive Faster, her Aunt Fanny! If guardian angels monitored traffic, they were surely loitering today.

Starting and stopping, Wendy finally crept her Datsun to the front of the line, a full half hour after she would normally get home. Sure enough, a silver Caddy—a DeVille, proclaimed its silver script—came flying up the cleared left lane to try nosing its way in front of her.

"Not today, you don't," Wendy muttered.

It quickly became a game of road chicken—who was more willing to risk a fender bender? Wendy snuggled her Datsun up as close to the bumper in front of her as she dared. Every time the car in front of her moved, Wendy and the DeVille raced to edge their own bumper into the resulting inches.

Wendy's right foot felt downright twitchy.

The big DeVille slithered centimeters closer.

As soon as the red glare of brake-lights in front of her dimmed, Wendy caressed the gas-pedal with her foot, just enough to ease forward. The DeVille's driver—big hair and sunglasses vaguely visible through tinted windows—honked angrily, the vehicular equivalent of stomping a foot.

But Wendy was driving an older car, an uglier car—a steel car. The Caddy probably wasn't mere fiberglass-and-aluminum either, but its insurance payments were probably higher. With another angry wail of the horn, the DeVille gave up and Wendy rolled triumphant feet ahead, past the arrow of blinking lights that ended the far left lane.

Poor sportsmanship or not, she reached out the window and flipped off the Caddy's driver. Take *that*! In fact, she half wished the woman *had* hit her. She would *gladly* wait, stopped in this heat, for a chance to tell the authorities about the rich bitch who thought she owned the highway.

But the driver behind her, whoever he was, let the DeVille into the center lane. The good people's lane. Great.

Like yesterday, revisited.

"What are you doing to me?" Wendy demanded upward through her windshield at the pale, cloudless summer sky.

Then she saw the skittering strobe of turn indicators ahead and realized, with a sinking sensation, that her lane was ending too.

Great! Just freaking dandy . . .

She flicked on her own turn indicator, then girded herself for a long, metronomic wait—except that a car honked at her. It had a gentle, abridged honk, more to catch her attention than to lodge complaints.

When she checked her side mirror, a small white sedan flashed headlight encouragement at her, inviting her to pull in front of it.

Wow! No need to ask *her* twice . . . or, well, three times! As soon as space opened, Wendy gratefully pulled into the right-hand lane, then waved her thanks so that the car behind her could see it. For a moment, the hunched figure in the driver's seat, raising a hand in acknowledgment, looked familiar . . .

Surely not!

Wendy nearly sprained her neck, between watching the road and her rearview mirror, then laughed at her mistake. This was not her old man, the one who maintained angel-speed, but an elderly *woman*. She resembled the Legacy's driver, but her thick glasses were *sun*glasses, and her halo of white hair surrounded a baseball cap. Angel though she'd been to Wendy, this was clearly *not* the same person as before.

Wendy sank back into the fake-fleece of her seat cover and relaxed. Slow traffic or not, the battle was over. An unexpected breeze slipped through her open windows at the same time that the commercials on the radio ended and a sweet oldie started to play. She claimed her going-home cola from the cup-holder and, despite the long drive, it was hardly tepid. Ahhhhh.

Then someone laid on their horn beside her, where the middle lane had all but closed, and she looked over at the same silver DeVille.

The Caddy actually started pulling into her lane! *With Wendy's Datsun still in it!*

"*What is it with you?*" Wendy yelled, whether or not the driver could hear from her haven of air-conditioned comfort. Well, Wendy had won this battle of wills once; with the same road-chicken tactics, she managed to beat out the more expensive car a second time.

But . . . when she did, it somehow didn't feel as good as it had before. Especially not when she heard the familiar, friendly chirp of a beep and saw the white sedan making room for the DeVille, just as she'd done for Wendy.

In her rearview mirror, Wendy saw the rich bitch's silhouette waving a gracious thank-you to the old lady, just as Wendy had done. And she felt . . . dissatisfied.

Not angry, really. Nowhere near the cardiac-arrest fury she'd felt the day before, or even a few minutes earlier. But . . .

She felt almost as if she should have passed on the favor that the white sedan had paid her, and let the silver DeVille in herself. Which didn't make sense. If the DeVille's driver had played fair, she would easily be a mile behind all of them. She'd taken cuts, damn it! People shouldn't be rewarded for taking cuts!

When she saw that the middle lane had closed because of a fender-bender—both cars sitting still with their hazards on, both drivers yelling and gesturing while they awaited the police— Wendy wondered if they'd been playing road chicken, and she felt even more dissatisfied.

Yards farther, the road opened up again. The DeVille shot around her and down the highway with one last wail of her horn. The white Sedan pulled more politely past Wendy in the middle lane, and she saw that it was an AMC Spirit. The short, hunch-shouldered driver *did* look familiar, baseball cap and sunglasses aside. But she didn't wave, so neither did Wendy.

She did find herself loitering in the right-hand lane, though, long enough to see if the Spirit had a bumper sticker.

It did.

Practice Senseless Beauty and Random Acts of Kindness.

Its design included stars, hearts . . . and simplified angel figures.

"ALL I'M SAYING IS, two angel bumper stickers in two days," she told her friend Cynthia on the phone that night. "It's weird."

"It's not that weird," reassured Cynthia. "Angels are very popular nowadays. There are movies, TV shows, and those little guardian-angel tie-tacks people wear on their collars . . ."

"Yes," said Wendy, vaguely watching the muted television news. "But—"

". . . those little Raphael cupids—which are cupids, by the way, not even angels—and angel encyclopedias, and greeting cards . . ."

"I get it," said Wendy. "But—"

". . . I even saw an Angel Board at the new-age store the other day, and I *swear* it was nothing but a Ouija board with a lot of angels drawn onto it, and there are angel tarot cards . . ."

Wendy changed channels to a muted talk show. "I *get* it."

Cynthia said, "I'm just saying—"

"That angels are very popular." Shifting on the couch, Wendy moved the phone receiver from her left ear to her right ear. "You made the point."

"Then why are you obsessing over a couple of bumper stickers?"

"I guess . . ." She considered it, framing her ideas even as she spoke. "Maybe I'm wondering if I should've let the DeVille into the lane myself."

"After she took cuts? No way!"

"Well, the bumper sticker didn't say to practice random acts of kindness only toward good drivers."

"And you're going to—hold on a second." Cynthia yelled something very muffled, presumably toward her husband, presumably with the mouthpiece covered. Then Wendy heard the raspy sound of a hand leaving a mouthpiece. "You're going to model your life after bumper stickers now? Why not choose, *51 percent Lady, 49 percent Bitch, Don't Push Me?*"

"Cyn . . ." But Wendy knew her grin sounded in her voice.

"Or, *Where Am I Going, and What Am I Doing in this Handbasket?*"

Wendy laughed.

"That's how silly you sound."

And yet . . . "I don't really know why she was even *in* such a hurry. What if she was on the way to the hospital? Or her wedding?"

"What if she was on the way to her appointment at the spa?"

"Good point," admitted Wendy, starting to feel better. If the lady in the DeVille wanted fair treatment, then she should play fair herself!

"I always make good points," agreed Cynthia. Then she added a whole different element of stress to the conversation by asking, "So how was the movie with Gabe?"

"I haven't even *talked* to him since yesterday," admitted Wendy.

She felt dissatisfied about that, too . . .

WENDY TOOK OFF A half-day the next afternoon to avoid the rush-hour traffic completely. It was Friday of a very long week. She had a date planned with Gabe—or she'd *had* a date planned, as of Wednesday. She didn't need to get herself worked up about traffic for a third day in a row.

But it wasn't easy.

At least the cars were moving. Wow, were they moving. The *slow* lane—where Wendy stayed, pacing the flow of traffic—was clocking ten miles over the speed limit! But some drivers seemed to be enjoying the excitement of block-jockeying more than she would like.

"Maybe I should move somewhere with really good mass transit," Wendy muttered to herself, prying the fingers of her right hand off the worn steering wheel cover long enough to turn up the radio. She did *not* pry her eyes off the road. As fast as things were moving, heaven-knew what could happen during one mistimed glance at the radio dial.

Then she saw the van climbing the entrance ramp, hesitating to make merging speed. The way Wendy calculated it, the white van would—at best—reach the end of the merge lane right beside *her*, forcing *one* of them to slow down.

Her first reaction was familiar annoyance—yes, city traffic was scary, but if you wanted to drive on the highways you had to keep up with everyone else! Even if the van *couldn't* accelerate fast enough, shouldn't they keep their car running well enough to make the speed requirements?

Then it occurred to her that she sounded like a rich bitch herself. And in a *Datsun*, for mercy's sake!

She began to slow down.

The van—a Honda Odyssey—dared go a little faster, but not fast enough. Wendy slowed more.

Down to sixty.

Down to fifty-five.

The car behind her laid on its horn and pulled into the center lane. Ignoring it, Wendy tapped lightly on her horn—a gentle, abridged honk, more to catch attention than to lodge complaints—and waved the van's driver into her lane.

A dark, withered old hand came out the driver's window, fingers spread to acknowledge her favor, and he merged in front of her.

Wendy stared, unbelieving. His bumper sticker read, *This Car Is Protected by a Guardian Angel.*

As they both sped up, slowly beginning to match the rest of the traffic, she tried to see the driver through the van's back windows. She couldn't. His headrest was too high. She wondered if it could possibly, by any stretch of the imagination, be the same old man she'd seen before—or the old woman—but that would be too weird. It would be as if . . . as if there were angels roaming the highways, being nice to other drivers.

If angels even existed, surely they had better things to do than—

But she didn't get a chance to finish that thought, because a red sports car in the far left lane started cutting diagonally across traffic, trying to make the right-hand exit. Misjudging the speed of the other cars, it clipped the van—at over seventy miles per hour.

Cliché or not, everything *did* happen in slow motion.

The metallic crash of impact exploded through Wendy's open windows. Tires, forced in ways they weren't meant to go, screamed into a stench of burning rubber as the red car skidded sideways against the Odyssey's front bumper. Other car's horns wailed as they swerved around the disaster. The van angled toward the guardrail, as if to lessen its damage to the sports car, just before Wendy heard more smashing of metal against concrete.

During it all, Wendy stood on her brake—stood as high as her suddenly tight seatbelt allowed her—and, with her own screech, slid the Datsun to a controlled stop just behind the wreck. Then all she could hear was her own breath, and the oldies station blasting from her radio, and the *whoosh* of highway traffic still rushing by.

Then she began to shake.

"Oh no," she breathed. Through some instinct, or the benefit of Driver's Ed, she thought to snap on her hazard lights, then to climb over her stick shift and parking brake and out the passenger door, instead of on the traffic side. "Oh no. Let them be all right. *Please . . .*"

The summer air smelled rank with gas fumes and burnt rubber and . . . metal? She'd never realized that torn metal gave out its own scent.

Even as she edged beside the van, Wendy could hear the driver of the red sports car, clearly alive and with her priorities as skewed as ever. "My *car*! Look at my *car*! Daddy's going to *freak*!"

It was, she realized peripherally, a Lamborghini Diablo. But she cared more about making sure the driver of the van was okay.

Whoosh! went the highway traffic, louder than ever now that she stood unprotected on the shoulder. *Whoosh!* She felt like a squirrel with a death wish.

"Mister!" she called, edging up to the driver's door. "Are you all right? *Mister?*"

And then, with a satisfying *ka-chunk*, the door opened.

"Thank you, ma'am," said the elderly gentleman, climbing with aching slowness out of his seat. He was hunched and balding, complete with thick glasses and a halo of white hair. But . . . this time he was a black man.

This time?

"I was wearing my belt," he informed her. "You know, them seatbelts aren't just the law. They're a *good idea.*"

Then his head came up at the other young woman's voice. "Someone get this damned thing . . ." But the younger driver managed to extricate herself from the Lamborghini's belt and airbag by herself. She tottered to a standstill beside the open door, staring in horror. "My dad's *car*!"

Wendy would have liked the girl to seem less vulnerable but, despite looking as wealthy as her car, she also radiated the uncertainty of youth like some kind of aura. Maybe her bad driving wasn't just her fault. Maybe some adult should've been more thorough before giving her a sports car and a driver's license. Maybe.

"Cars can be fixed or replaced, little lady," assured the van's driver. "Harder with folks; best you remember that. Now, how about you set down, here, and make sure you didn't get banged up yourself?"

Which seemed an awfully nice attitude considering that, inexperienced or not, she could have gotten him killed. Wendy said, "Good advice. Maybe you should take it yourself."

"Oh, I'm fine," insisted the elderly driver, as the young lady settled unsteadily onto the cement guardrail. "Didn't you see the bumper sticker?"

For a moment, Wendy could barely breath. It seemed a significant moment for the shoulder of a sunny eight-lane highway. "You mean . . . your car really *is* protected by a guardian angel?"

"And the other one," he added knowingly, as he shuffled slowly to where the younger driver had taken his advice.

Wendy glanced back at the crumpled remains of his van and saw, unmarred on the front bumper, his other sticker. *Choose Love.*

"LUCKILY, SHE HAD A cell phone," Wendy finished that night, as she and Gabe hiked across the parking lot toward the multiplex movie theater. "I left my name and number with both of them, in case they need it for insurance or something. But I didn't get *their* names."

"You didn't think to ask?" he challenged.

She really hadn't, and now she wondered why. "Uhn-uh."

He squeezed her hand and said, "You were probably in shock from the near-miss."

But she wondered.

"What *really* has me thinking," she admitted, "is that if I hadn't slowed down and let the van in front of me, the Lamborghini might have hit *me*."

When she glanced toward him, he was frowning in thought, showing no sign of his one dimple.

This might prove too weird for him, but . . . "It's as if the whole rest of this week was training me to be a nicer driver at the very moment I really needed to."

They reached the line for tickets, serpentining slowly along a simple maze of cording and metal posts. When she couldn't stand not knowing further, Wendy glanced at her date again. "Do you think that's possible?"

He shrugged. "Anything's possible."

"And it's not even just about driving, if you think about it. It's bigger than that. Being nice. Giving people the right of way." *Choosing love.*

When she glanced at him again, the one dimple was starting to shadow his cheek. "Does that mean we can see the World War II film?"

She narrowed her eyes playfully. "Only if you're up to a double feature with the romantic comedy."

He considered it and nodded. "That's doable."

"Good," said Wendy.

"Good," said Gabe.

A screech of tires, then shouts, caught their attention. A pick-up truck with a double-cab full of teenagers tore out of the parking lot with a louder roar of engines than was even *remotely* necessary.

What *was* it about pick-up trucks?

Wendy sighed, shook her head, and hoped they made it home safely—them and everyone they came across! Then she noticed that Gabe was still watching her.

"What are you looking at?" she challenged, uncertain. But he just grinned, dimple and all.

"Senseless beauty?" he suggested.

She squeezed his hand. She liked not being angry. She liked him better . . . and she liked *herself* better.

This Woman Protected by a Guardian Angel.

Maybe more than one.

The Scent of an Angel

Nancy Springer

I am a couple hundred years old now, but I was just a nameless he-puppy in my first fur when I chose for myself an oddling's path. A long, weathersome road it's been and sore paw pads. It happened because—there is no telling why it happened, really. But on the surface of it, it happened because I bespoke the haughty, braggart cat from the neighboring cottage.

A fat black cat, larger than I was, with her tail in the air. "My mistress is a witch," she told me with a glare of her copper eyes, "and I am her familiar. Why should I hold converse with you, dog?"

Having experienced little more than cuffs and harsh words in my young life, I was not offended. My mother was dead, her head crushed in the jagged jaws of a bear trap, so there was no one to teach me that cats were meant to be chased. In my puppy mind I accepted the tales the cat told me as simply as I had accepted my mother's death. "Is the old woman truly a witch?" I asked humbly. I had heard the humans say that the bent old crone in the next cottage was a witch. They said they could tell because she lived all alone and talked to herself. They said her mumbling made hens lay bloody eggs and milk cows go dry, and she could do worse than that with her evil eye. They said that when the evil fit was upon her she could fly. No one spoke to her. She limped, she stared into the air, she gave no one greeting, but she cosseted her cat like an infant. Folk said she suckled it at her sagging teat.

The proud cat did not answer my question, only repeated, "I am her familiar." The cat declared, "She gives me milk and juicy bits of chicken to eat." Hearing this, I drooled with envy, having known only crusts and hunger, myself. "She gives me a velvet cushion on which to sleep." Whereas I had the hard clay floor of the cowshed. "She anoints me with fragrant oils and strokes me and calls me Precious." I could believe it, for the cat smelled like bacon fat and her fur shone glossier than a crow's wing. Around her smug, fluffy neck she wore a silver bell on a striped ribbon of silk.

"I want to be a witch's familiar," I said.

The cat sat on her fat haunches and purred in merriment. "You can't," she said with utmost scorn. "You're *white*."

So I was, although the dirt on which I lay had yellowed my fur. White, a color easily made foul. Not like the cat's rich, shining black. Now that she had made me yearn for some softness in my life, something more than a kick from the farmer's booted foot, she would deny me because my fur was white? She angered me. Witch's familiar, indeed. If a witch's familiar had to be black, then—

"I'll be an angel's familiar, then," I said, and I turned tail and trotted away. The black cat's purring laughter followed me.

I kept trotting, for there was nothing to hold me to that place. Still with my milk teeth in my mouth, I trotted off, any way the wind blew, to find an angel.

I KNEW OF ANGELS only that an angel was the opposite of a witch. Where witches flew foul, angels flew fair. Where witches smoldered, angels blazed. Where witches cursed, angels blessed. Where witches glared the evil eye, angels—I was not sure how an angel looked. I had never seen one.

This did not matter greatly, because seeing is for humans. For a dog, the way of knowing is through the nose. I would not just search; I would track. Surely I could do this. I knew how to track a rabbit or a deer or even an old leather shoe once I found the right scent—

But what was the scent of an angel?

The witch smelled like soot and lavender. Ghosts smelled like gunpowder—this I knew, for ghosts were plentiful, spirits of slain Indians and fever-killed babies and all the witches the Pilgrims had hung. The smell of ghosts hung everywhere over the wood lots and cornfields, especially at dusk or on nights of the full moon—but ghosts were not the same as angels. What did an angel smell like?

I had no idea.

Angels had to be scarce.

I trotted along a rutted wagon road with my stubby snout uplifted and my pink nostrils whiffing the damp air. I smelled mice and shrews and voles in the hay. I smelled worms and robins, bugs and bluebirds. I smelled beech trees and red squirrels and rabbits. I smelled springwater and moss and a distillery midden. I smelled deer turds. I smelled something dead enough to roll in somewhere. Or maybe *that* was the scent of an angel?

It wasn't, but I rolled anyway, then trotted on.

Three days later my paw pads were cracked and raw, I was starving hungry, I no longer cared to roll no matter how ripe the carrion; I was so weak I could barely walk. When I whiffed a good smell of potatoes and mutton simmering, I turned toward it, staggered to a farmhouse, and sat whining by the kitchen door.

"Where did you come from, puppy?" exclaimed a woman's voice. She came out, picked me up in gentle hands, patted me. She said softly, "I believe the angels sent you."

She fed me, then filled a washtub and bathed me—I did not like that part, but bore it without biting because she had given me soft cooked meat to eat. After she had soaped me clean, she rubbed me with a feed sack and made me lie on the warm hearth to dry. I dozed, and when I awoke she was brushing my fur with her own hairbrush. She brushed me all over until I lustered like white velvet. "Good puppy," she whispered, her eyes red and weary and intent on me, her hands taut and intent.

Finally she took me upstairs to her daughter, who lay sick in bed. The little girl hugged me in her arms.

That was long ago. Although I slept on the child's bed and licked away her tears if she cried and lay close by when she was too weak to hold me, I do not remember her name or how long I stayed with her—a week, a month? But I do remember the night she died. Snuggled against her side, I lay dozing when her shallow breathing stopped. My head jerked up and I nuzzled her face, but she did not move, and in the room I whiffed—something, a fragrance that made me tremble, scent of sunfire, white wild roses, lightning—I could not say what was that shiversome aroma. Scent of glory incarnate—but just as I sampled it, in a breath it was gone. I lay yearning and whimpering until morning.

"The angels took her," the woman said.

When she put me outside, I trotted away. I trotted on to track my own angel.

I HEADED ANY DIRECTION whence the breeze blew, so that every breath of air carried to me the scents of carrots and newborn calves, mud and marshes, birchbark and timothy grass, lamb slaughter and wood smoke, horse manure and pig manure and sheep manure and cow manure and a dead woodchuck baking in the sun—all the scents of the world, but never that otherworldly scent for which I searched.

I traveled far. I was larger than a cat now, and instead of my puppy fuzz I had grown fur that hung in white feathers from my belly and legs. I had learned to kill rats and rabbits to eat, I had learned to lift my leg when I peed, and sometimes I turned aside from my road when I whiffed the sweet aroma of a she-dog in heat. Sometimes, but sometimes not. The memory of that other warm, fierce, ethereal scent abided strong in me, sweeter even than the scent of lust.

That was long ago, and I am no longer sure of my memories. Things happened; perhaps then, perhaps some other time.

It may have been then—yes, I am almost sure that it was during those days that I saw a wagoner lashing his patient draft horses up a steep hill, roaring and laying on with the whip as they strained and stumbled and dripped sweat. I leaped into the wagon and bit him in the leg as hard as I could. He screamed and dropped his whip, then turned his wrath on me, and I led him a lively chase as his horses rested, baiting him out of the wagon and down the road and across some old woman's turnip patch before I left him in a thorny bog and trotted on my way.

It may have been during those days that I saw the freckle-faced boy with the bamboo fishing pole. Grubbing in the loam of a creek bank for worms, he turned up a nest of baby vipers instead, and thought he had found himself a lucky, rare sort of squirmy bait for his hook. I tugged with my teeth on his shirt tail before he could touch his own death, distracted him with play and led him romping away. All that day I stayed with him, until the serpents had slithered away and nightfall saw him safely home.

It may have been during that time that I saw the raccoon lurching along a footpath in stark daylight, teeth bared, red eyes glaring, drool dripping from his jaws. Rabid. Mad. I fled, running ahead of the raccoon, and encountered a barefoot young woman ambling along with her eyes on the sky, daydreaming of her lover perhaps. I jumped on her, whining, entreating her to turn back. She shrieked and struck at me because I had muddied her long white apron with my paws. In looking down at me, she looked down the path ahead of her also, and then she saw her danger, screamed anew, and fled without thanking me.

And it may have been during that time that I saw the scrawny old man sitting on his porch long after dark, sitting in his shirt sleeves in the cold and just staring. I went to him and whined, and still he stared into nothingness. I laid my forepaw on his knee, and his slow gaze shifted to me. "Puppy," he murmured as if from another world. He stared at me now, and I gazed back. After minutes had gone by, he said, "Puppy, are you hungry?" and he rose stiffly and tottered into his house. "Nothing in here to eat," he murmured. "I ain't been eating." But he found me some stale bread, then lay down on the davenport to sleep, and I slept on the rag rug beside him. The next day, because he had to feed me, he hobbled to the neighbors and got food, and he ate with me. I stayed with him until I made sure the neighbor woman was looking after him, then trotted on my way.

And so it went. I followed the breeze, searching it for the scent of an angel, and it led me where I was needed. Why I gave aid to the folk and creatures in my way, I do not know. I felt as if I could not do otherwise, even though sometimes I had to stay with some lonely, suffering soul for weeks or even months, interrupting my search—I could not help it, perhaps because I myself knew what it was to suffer, or perhaps—perhaps it was simply my nature. I am, after all, a dog. I give of myself without stint or reckoning. Such is my being.

It seems to me that this went on for a long time, and I considered that I was getting nowhere. I despaired of finding my angel. I trotted on, when no one needed me, following where the wind led, simply from habit. Perhaps in our lives we all make shining choices that turn into shadowy habits. I trotted on, but I felt no hope any longer.

It is odd the way things turn out. Without my knowing it, the wind led me back to where I had begun.

TO MY EYES AT first it was just another village where I might beg a scrap of bread to eat—but then, I did not yet know why, my heart trembled and began to howl. And then I saw—that cowshed, it was —yes, it was where I had suckled at my mother's belly before she had stuck her hungry head into the bear trap after the bait. Before she was killed. And that was the very farmhouse where the fat woman had given me many curses and a few scraps. And that cottage . . .

That was the cottage where the witch lived. On the breeze I smelled soot and lavender. On the breeze also, I heard the sound of weeping.

I wanted to trot on to the cowshed, for it was home of a sort. I knew I would never see my mother again, but my heart yearned for . . . something. Perhaps I might find some of my litter mates still there?

But—that soft, weary, sobbing—who was weeping?

That tired, muted sound would not let me pass the cottage by. My heart would not let me. Limping with soreness from the stony road, I turned and trotted that way.

On the grassy hill behind the cottage, under a huge oak tree with its limp leaves hanging, I found the bent old woman on her knees, hunched over something that lay on the ground, black.

I whined, and she looked at me. "'They—killed—my Precious," she sobbed.

The black cat lay there, looking not nearly so smug in death, its fur no longer sleek, now a bloody mess from a blast of buckshot.

"They killed her. Now I have nothing."

Still crying wanly, like a baby crying itself to sleep, the crone wrenched at the sod with a hand trowel, trying to dig the cat a grave.

"They hate me," she said, talking to herself, the grass, the oak, me.

She wrested from the ground a teacup's worth of sod and a thimble's worth of earth.

"They killed my sweet Precious just because they hate me."

I whined, sat with my plumy tail wrapped around my hind paws, and cocked my head to show her I was listening. Taking no notice, she scratched away at the heartless earth and mumbled her plaint.

"They say I put the evil eye on Goody Flowers. Goody Flowers? I don't even know Goody Flowers."

Day drew on toward evening as she nattered and wept, slowly ceasing to weep, and grubbed at the hard ground with her trowel and her bent, scaly old fingers and her thick, ridged fingernails. Dozing as I listened, I lay down nearby.

"Flowers," she said, streaks of dirt on her wrinkle-shirred face where the tears had dried. "I'll show them flowers. Flowers growing over my Precious. Hollyhocks, larkspur, lady's slippers, foxglove, forget-me-not." Day darkened into twilight, and still she dug. "'Flowers for my Precious, and a white marble marker. I'll—"

In back of the old woman's babbling I heard a darker muttering, and I whiffed human sweat, fury, fear. Jolted alert, I stood up and peered into the dusk. In the deepening darkness at the base of the hill, village folk were gathering, men and women and youths, some of them carrying grim-reaper scythes or butcher knives or clubs of wood, some hefting stones, a few lifting flaring torches. I recognized the farmer whose booted foot I had suffered when I was a pup, and his fat wife who had cursed me as she threw a few miserable scraps my way, and the wagoner who had whipped his horses, and others. Some scowling, some grimacing, a few women weeping with wrath and terror. "Are you digging your grave, witch?" the farmer roared.

"Witch!" others yelled.

"Your turn, witch!" bellowed the wagoner, lashing the air with his whip, lowering his head like a charging bull as he stepped toward her.

"Are you ready to go to hell, witch?" shrilled the farmer's fat wife, brandishing a butcher knife. "Are you ready to meet your master the Devil?"

"She's met him already," growled another man, taking two steps up the hill. Given a miserable sort of mob courage by their own shouting, the crowd surged forward. I snarled at them, baring my teeth to try to warn them back, but they took no notice of me. I was, after all, just a little white dog. Just one little dog, and they were many; they were not frightened of me.

Behind me I heard the old woman whimpering like a puppy. *Run*, I willed her, although I knew she could barely totter. *I can hold them back for a little while. Run, run away!*

But she did not. Instead, she startled me utterly: grabbing me from behind, she lifted me by the belly and heaved me up into her bent old arms. She hugged me to her ribby chest above her sagging breasts, cradling me like a baby.

Torches flared in my eyes, nightfall thundered with threatening voices, knives and clubs loomed like a forest in my sky, I felt my jowls freeze into a snarl of fear, and clutching me as if she were drowning the old woman babbled in a frenzy of terror, "God help me! Angels help me! God help me! Angels help me! God help me! Angels help—"

Everyone screamed, including, I suppose, me.

I did not know what happened, other than a blaze of glory that whitened the night. I could not see it happening, for it was in me, of me, throughout me, a great holy heat and a fireball of comfort and a huge fierce peace beyond understanding and that scent, that scent, the very scent of light—for a moment it was my own, the scent of an angel, and white flame enough to encompass the world. Awash in that glory all around me, clubs dropped, knives dropped; I saw the folk of the mob swaying like trees in a high wind, their faces flat white ovals punctured by cavernous eyes and mouths as their screaming formed a muddle of words.

"Fire! The dog's on fire—"

"That's not a dog! It's a—"

"Wings! Those are wings, idiot!"

"It's a golden wheel!"

"You're crazy! It's a man in a furnace!"

"What furnace?"

"Watch out! He's got a sword!"

"Back! I'm burning!"

"Those are wings, I tell you!"

They screamed, and shouted nonsense, and ran, and within a moment it was all over as if it had never been. They fled, every mother's son of them, leaving darkness and silence behind. The old woman had dropped me, naturally enough, and the stars winked down just as always, and I lay panting on the ground, a tired little white dog again.

But someone was patting me. Patting my head, stroking my back, caressing me with a warm, sure hand.

And it wasn't the old woman. She tottered nearby, gasping for breath. I could hear her.

It wasn't anyone human.

It was—a heavenly scent in the air, aroma of sunfire, wild white roses, lightning. It was love and peace beyond understanding. It was a holy presence that spoke no words—yet with my whole comforted body I heard words. *Well done, my good and faithful servant,* that touch said to me.

But I saw nothing. There was no one there.

Stay with her a while, my master told me, *until I find her another companion.* An otherworldly hand rumpled my ears. Then my angel was gone.

I DO NOT REMEMBER precisely how long I stayed with her—a month, a year? That was long ago. I do recall that she talked a great deal and fed me milk and bits of juicy chicken and gave me a velvet cushion to sleep upon. And I recall that the scattered weapons disappeared from the hillside, and the dead cat was buried by someone or other, and from time to time gifts appeared on the doorstep: fresh-baked bread, a poke of apples, a basket of brown eggs.

Then, one day, in another basket, there appeared a peace offering of a different sort: a mewling kitten, calico and white.

It was time for me to go.

So I sniffed the kitten, licked the old woman's dried-up hand, and trotted on my way.

As I have said, that was a couple hundred years ago. I suppose I really am an angel's familiar, for something has made me an exception to death. Horse and wagon have given way to automobiles and airplanes, but I am still here. I trot through culverts and factory lots now instead of lanes and fields, but I am still here. I follow the wind wherever it leads me, and sometimes I starve and sometimes I am kicked and sometimes I am able to be of help and comfort to someone for a while before I wander on my way.

Always I have to go, to move on, because I yearn always for my master. Only three more times in my long life have I sensed that presence, but I must keep searching, for what else can I do? A waft of wild roses on a June breeze, a hint of lightning in the night air, and my head lifts, and longing takes hold of my heart, and there can be no dozing by a warm fire for me any longer; I have to set off again on my search. I am, after all, a dog, with a dog's heart, love beyond comprehension. Even though I know it is all but hopeless, I must trot off, seeking the scent of an angel.

It is very possible that you have encountered me. That dirty little dog trotting along the interstate yesterday, the one who stopped to lick the oil from the asphalt—that might have been me. That mutt you chased out of your yard because you thought it might damage your zinnias—that might have been me. The homeless guy's pooch, the one that crawled inside the cardboard box on the sidewalk when it started to rain—that might have been me. The stray rooting in the Dumpster behind the convenience store, its fur matted with burrs, the one you thought somebody ought to take to the SPCA—that might have been me. Hey, were you the one who gave me a whole Taco Bell burrito yesterday? A hamburger would have been better, but still, thank you. And listen—you humans, I know your sense of smell is duller than a cobblestone, but—did you by any chance catch the scent of an angel?

Hailey's Angel

Mickey Zucker Reichert

Paula Heberden swayed gently back and forth in the softly contoured rocking chair, two-month-old Hailey clutched in her arms. The infant blinked, sleepy blue eyes striped by long lashes, scalp sporting a fine layer of nearly invisible hair, nose baby-flat and tiny. She little resembled her black-haired, dark-eyed mother who still carried twenty extra pounds of pregnancy weight on a frame that had already supported a spare ten. It did not bother Paula Heberden; she ate the prescribed healthy foods the articles stated nursing mothers needed. To Paula, Hailey's needs offset any social or personal concerns, even her own health. During her two-year sabbatical from social work, she would see to it her baby had everything her single mother could provide.

Hailey's lids drifted closed. Paula continued to rock, ignoring the untended breakfast dishes, the layers of dust on the piano and mantel. The stand that had once held a television and VCR now provided the resting place for *Pat the Bunny*, *Goodnight Moon*, *The Very Hungry Caterpillar*, and a host of other award-winning books for infants and young children. Television, she knew, could warp the minds of babies and would not leave

217

the closet until Hailey reached her twentieth month. Corner protectors hugged every jutting surface; plastic locks sealed every cupboard, the oven, and the toilet; every outlet clutched a safety plug. Sturdy gates spanned the staircase to the bedroom, one at the top and another at the bottom. Paula had seen the aftermath of infants who crawled up steps protected only by an upper gate, then tumbled down from the secondmost stair. In Paula's mind, allowing such a disaster constituted child abuse as surely as a physical attack. The consequences could be equally dire.

Certain Hailey slept, Paula hefted the child and set her, still wrapped in blankets, in the hollow of two plush chairs pushed together. The high arms and backs would protect her if she suddenly learned to roll. Paula placed the baby on her back, the best position for preventing sudden infant death syndrome during sleep. Hailey heaved a tiny sigh and smacked her lips. A milk bubble appeared, and Paula wiped it away with the edge of the blanket. For several moments, she studied her sleeping daughter, a smile etched onto her features. Images haunted her, of some of the homes of women who called themselves mothers: dirty, sometimes with feces and animal hair; televisions blaring talk shows all day long; infants in walkers. She shuddered, recalling the statistics. *Children who use walkers have a serious accident rate of 85 percent. More dangerous than motorcycles, and no one's stupid enough to place a helpless baby on one of those. Also, their hips can get damaged, and they walk much later than those allowed only to crawl.* So many of the women Paula served reeked of alcohol and cigarettes, and they shouted at or slapped their children without any clear realization that they had done anything wrong.

Paula cursed the system that forced her to return innocent children to these conditions day after day. One supervisor had even told her that a house full of shit could only be considered a hazard if the children were not old enough to step over it. The thought infuriated Paula. Reports of spanking went nowhere unless the "assault," as Paula referred to physical discipline, caused a mark. Verbal abuse did not even raise an eyebrow. In the short time she had practiced her career before the pregnancy, she had yet to see a woman on assistance nurse her infant. *Cheapest food in the world and the best for the infant and bonding. Not breastfeeding should be considered a crime, and the programs that give away inferior formula should be shut down, not financed and celebrated.*

Paula set to cleaning, trying to force her thoughts from the things that never failed to irritate her. She had gone into social work to help people, she reminded herself. Yet the world she had found differed crucially from the one she had anticipated. The hungry she planned to feed did not exist; she discovered that, in the United States, low socioeconomic status was actually the primary risk factor for obesity. For every appreciative client for whom she found money, a home, complimentary medical care, two more cursed her for not finding them enough. She grew tired of clients begging unabashedly for free utilities on internet computers and cellular phones, complete with call waiting. *Things I can't even afford.* She watched in horror as her youthful exuberance ebbed, replaced by the cold facts of a human reality she had never imagined.

Paula was determined to raise her daughter right.

Paula set down the can of "natural" polish, containing no chemicals that might pollute the air and harm her baby. It had an organic antibacterial agent, to protect them both from germs. *Get off your high horse, Paula.* Sleepless nights always brought out the worst in her, and the pediatrician appointment scheduled for that afternoon had her spooked and irritable. *Some people just need education. If we teach them how to properly care for their kids, instead of throwing money at the problem, we could fix it.* It would require time, time that her overworked self and colleagues did not have. She tried her best to coach as well as serve, but her efforts often met hostility from those who preferred to do things "their way." *The wrong way. The dangerous, hurtful way.* And her supervisor chastised her daily for spending too much time with clients and not enough on her paperwork.

Paula tiptoed to the chairs to check on Hailey, who slumbered peacefully, belly rising and falling with every breath. The thought of bringing Hailey into a waiting room filled with germs, sick children, and unwashed adults, of stabbing needles into her little angel, brought tears to Paula's eyes. Intellectually, she knew the importance of immunizations, that the risk of contracting the diseases, of dying from them, far outweighed the chance of any significant reaction to the vaccine. She knew the so-called "studies" that shots could cause everything from autism to seizure disorders to death came from the same biased sources that made wild, therapeutic claims for vitamins, plant stems, spinal manipulation, and other scientifically groundless alternative therapies. But, even the minor, proven side effects terrified her: fever, crying, swelling at the site. Hailey deserved a perfect life: attention to every distress, love, the trust that her mother would always protect her from pain.

Hailey took a shuddering breath. Instantly, Paula dashed to her side, giving her a light shake to make certain she had not stopped breathing. The baby smacked her lips. Paula's heart seemed to stop. She had rushed Hailey to the Emergency Room twice before, worried the movements might constitute seizures. *What did Dr. Harris say to do?* As Paula's heartbeat resumed, quickening in frantic increments, she tried to remember. Her thoughts muddled, overcome by a force that scattered her wits. *He said to time it. Don't estimate; use a watch. If it lasts longer than two minutes, call.* By the time Paula glanced at her watch, the lip smacking had stopped. *It felt like five minutes, at least.* She reached for the phone, then stopped. Dr. Harris had said it was not an emergency. She would talk about the problem at the visit that afternoon and suggest postponing the shots.

SIXTEEN-MONTH-OLD HAILEY Heberden toddled around the living room, her mother dogging every broad-based step. She placed her right foot, angled too far outward, lost her balance, and started to fall. Paula caught her daughter, swinging her into her arms. "Ooopsy."

Hailey laughed. Wispy blonde hair now dangled around her face, and her eyes had darkened to hazel. She met her mother's brown, love-filled eyes and full-lipped smile. Paula's sabbatical had nearly ended, but she had already decided not to return. She did not believe any baby-sitter could give Hailey the full extent of love and attention she needed. Day-care centers, packed with snot-nosed, sneezing children, could never keep her daughter safe. Though it meant accepting the very charity Paula had spent two years distributing to others, she would remain with her daughter. She could think of no one more deserving than her precious Hailey.

The toddler snuggled into her mother's arms.

"Nappy time, Sweetie?" Paula crooned to her daughter in the lispy, high-pitched speech adults use around young children. "Nappy time?"

Hailey closed her eyes.

Paula carried her daughter to the bedroom they shared, tucking her carefully beneath the blankets. A light spring breeze, carrying the scent of freshly mown grass, funneled through the screens, flicking the curtains into a lazy dance. Paula locked the siderails in place, ran her hand through the girl's fine hair, and sang a soft lullaby. Seized by the urge to urinate, she cut the last note of the song short and tiptoed to the bathroom. There, she started a new song, humming just loudly enough for Hailey to hear.

Paula finished her business, flushed, and scrubbed her hands and nails. So far, her aggressive hand-washing policy had kept Hailey from contracting a single illness. Beginning a new song, she emerged from the bathroom back into the bedroom and glanced at the bed. Hailey was not there.

Paula's heart stilled in her chest. She sucked in a sudden sharp breath and a mouthful of saliva. She choked and sputtered, frantic gaze sweeping the room. "Hailey," she managed to gasp out, though it sent her into a spasm of coughing. "Hailey!" Her voice emerged desperately hoarse. Paula's thoughts exploded, flying through a thousand impossible, horrible scenarios. *I was only gone a second. A second too long.* She whirled into a terrified dance, eyes desperately unfocused. Something thumped behind her, followed by a wild spray of pencils, pens, and markers. Paula jerked her glance to the dresser top where the empty plastic holder lay on its side. Perched on top, Hailey leaned against the window screen.

"No!"

Paula lunged for the baby.

Startled, Hailey jumped. The screen tore soundlessly from the frame, funneling the child through it.

"No!" Paula shrieked again. "No! No! NO!"

She sobbed, charging the window, knowing she had come too late. She could only watch her beloved tumble toward the ground in impotent horror.

Hailey wailed.

"Hailey! Hailey!" It all seemed to happen in slow motion while mindless terror froze Paula. She could not even cringe as the baby sailed past the lilac bush. *God help us.*

Then, something streaked beneath Hailey's diving form, bringing a strange sense of peace that lulled Paula's panic into the grim certainty that everything would turn out all right. It looked fuzzy and gray, formless, like dust-filled wind. Paula blinked. The moment her eyes opened, she discovered a winged, androgynous human as beautiful as prayer clutching Hailey. The child looked as peaceful as Paula felt, eyes calmly studying her savior, hands clutching arms like unblemished cream. A mane of black hair swirled in the breeze, liquid silk. The dark eyes held a soft wisdom and a supernatural twinkle. It smiled, its lips full and shimmering pink. Every feather stood out against the emerald background of lawn, as white as milk.

Before Paula could think to speak, the angel flew to the torn window and dumped the toddler into her arms. Hailey's eyes had drifted closed, and her breaths came in an easy, comfortable rhythm. "Thank you," Paula stammered, looking up. But the angel had disappeared as swiftly and mysteriously as it had come. Only the shredded screen fluttering from its frame remained as a record of tragedy averted. Otherwise, Paula might have believed it the worst of nightmares followed by the most wondrous of dreams.

OVER THE ENSUING MONTHS, Paula Heberden further upped her safety measures. The windows stayed permanently closed and locked. She missed the sweet aroma of summer flowers carried on a cool, fresh breeze; but air conditioning seemed a small price to pay for her daughter's security. The floor held nothing but soft, sterile infant toys and furniture too solid for a toddler to move. She refused all visitors and the germs they might bring. No one held Hailey unless they scrubbed or gloved first, including Dr. Harris and his nurses. Some of her friends objected enough to stop calling as well. Though much higher, Paula did not object to that sacrifice either. She was determined to be an exemplary mother. Always, Hailey came first.

Then, one day, Paula paused to sweep a new spider web from the bedroom wall. A soft click echoed through her hearing, bringing a strangled, nameless dread. She jerked her head up as the security gate separated from the wall, tearing free a jagged chunk of plaster, then crashed down the stairs, Hailey toppling after it.

Paula screamed. "Oh my God, oh my God, oh my God . . ." She dashed for the steps, the words a wild mantra she could not stop.

Hailey bounced off the second stair. "Mama!"

Then, the angel came again, scooping Hailey from the carnage and setting her gently on the landing. This time, Paula tried not to blink as relief flooded her, but the angel still disappeared an instant later, leaving nothing to indicate it had ever come except an oddly unbruised Hailey and a broken gate.

Paula enfolded Hailey into her arms, the girl's body warm and solid against her, and wept tears of joy.

HAILEY CELEBRATED HER SECOND birthday with only her mother. Securely strapped into her perfectly balanced highchair, she shoveled handfuls of applesauce/carrot cake and frozen yogurt into her mouth with hands scoured clean only moments before she started. Seated beside her grinning daughter, Paula Heberden ate her portion with a fork, studying Hailey with a love so vast it pained. She mashed the crumbs onto her fork. "So, Hailey-bailey. What do want to do for your birthday?"

"Birfday," Hailey repeated.

"Right." Paula licked her fork clean, then set it on her plate. "Your birthday, Hailey. You get to chose what we do." She suggested the youngster's favorite video. "Bambi?"

"No Bambi," Hailey said.

"Pooh bear game?" Paula tried. "Dolls? Animals? Farm?"

Hailey looked at her mother, face smeared with cake. "Park," she said.

"Yes. We saw a park on *Sesame Street*, didn't we?" Now that Paula allowed the television, she kept it always set to PBS. "A big park."

"Go park." Hailey smeared cake across the arms of her high chair. "Park. Go park."

Paula winced. So far, she had managed to limit their time on public playgrounds to off-hours, when they would not run into other children who might bully Hailey, shove her, or share some loathsome virus. Paula had carefully wiped down the equipment with disinfectant, steering Hailey away from the ones with chipped paint or rough edges. Now, on a breezy summer Saturday, all the playgrounds and parks would have hordes of kids and animals. She had also deliberately kept Hailey from fur, cow's milk, peanuts, and strawberries, just in case she developed an allergy. "How about Bambi?" she tried again, taking the dirty dishes to the sink and snatching up a washcloth for Hailey's face.

"No Bambi. No, no, no Bambi. Park," Hailey said insistently. "Want park. Go park. Please, Mommy?"

Sighing, Paula nodded. She found it difficult to deny Hailey, and she would have to come in contact with others eventually. Every article and physician mentioned the need for socialization. Paula looked over her daughter, from the neatly braided sand-colored hair to the slender body wrapped in short coveralls swarmed with multicolored butterflies and a matching white shirt with embroidered flowers now hidden beneath a cake-covered bib. She seemed so small and frail, no match for the three-and-older crowd she would likely run into on the playground. "All right, Hailey. The park it is."

Hailey grinned as her mother peeled off the bib, wiped her face and hands, and set her on the floor. Hailey ran straight to the door. Paula opened it, guiding Hailey to the left rear door of the Volvo, then strapping her securely into the car seat. The girl squirmed and wriggled throughout the seven-minute trip, talking incessantly about swings and slides and "mewwygwounds."

Hyperalert, Paula pulled into the parking lot, her gaze skipping over the scene. Children of every age scurried through the tunnels and over rickety bridges. Slides of various sizes and curves jutted from a towering wooden structure, and girls squealed as they swung from metal bars. Paula took a deep breath, then forced herself out of the car. She opened the door behind hers. Hailey jerked back and forth, this way and that, trying to see everything at once.

"Be still," Paula cautioned as she unfastened the five-point restraints and they fell away. Hailey jumped to the gravel. Paula shut the door, losing sight of her daughter for less than an instant. As she turned, she saw Hailey charging through the parking lot, directly into the path of a red sport utility vehicle.

Before Paula could scream, before Hailey even realized the danger, the angel swooped in, nudging the child to safety. Hailey continued running to the playground, heedless or uncaring. Paula smiled as her rising heart rate returned to normal. She did not know why the angel had chosen Hailey nor why bad luck seemed to follow the girl, but she appreciated the safety net and wished she could properly thank whoever was responsible for it. *As if I didn't know.* Rolling her eyes to the heavens, she said a short, but heartfelt, prayer.

Hailey rushed to the twisting assortment of openings, ropes, nets, slides, and towers, already swarmed with children. A leggy boy with tight, brown curls clambered up a covered, plastic slide, shoes slipping, fingers curled under the rails. Shortly, he eased to the bottom and ran off. The moment he left, Hailey leaped in to take his place. She wrapped her hands around the undercurled siding, planted her feet on the incline, and attempted to climb. A girl a couple of years older hopped around a corner to the top of the slide and started down.

Foreseeing a collision, Paula darted in, hefting Hailey from harm's way. The sliding girl glided to the bottom and tensed to rise. Before she could, Paula caught her arm, her touch eliciting a startling static shock. Sternly, she looked into huge green eyes framed by white-blond bangs. "You need to be careful of smaller kids, OK?"

The strange girl pulled free of Paula's grip. "OK," she said in a tearful whisper, then ran for a nearby net rope.

Paula turned her attention to Hailey. "Honey sweet, slides are for coming down, not up. You could have gotten hurt."

Tears blurred Hailey's dark eyes to pools. "Sorry, Mommy."

Paula smiled, pulling a tissue from her pocket. She dabbed Hailey's eyes. "That's all right, Sweetie. Go play."

Hailey ran for a ladder, Paula watching, hawklike. She found herself intervening constantly while the other parents watched casually from the sidelines or talked amongst themselves. They seemed so calm, so utterly unconcerned. Paula tried to condemn them for laissez-faire parenting but found herself incapable of summoning the same holier-than-thou attitude that rose naturally when she worked with broken, dysfunctional families. These came from every walk of life, most middle-classed, well-versed and well-read, intimately familiar with *Parenting, Family Life,*"and other resources so valuable to competent parenting. No child got hurt, even without the interference of mothers and angels. Except Hailey.

The girl seemed fearless. She would leap boldly from the tops of platforms so high most of the three- and four-year-olds climbed only with trepidatious, white-knuckled grips. She attempted to dance across railings, like an Olympic gymnast on a balance beam. She clambered onto the outside of the slides. Each time, either Paula or the angel rescued Hailey, who skipped happily away, utterly undaunted by admonishments or near-death experiences. No one else seemed to notice Hailey's supernatural guardian, though they nudged one another and whispered about her behavior. Paula found herself on the defensive, smiling a crooked "kids will be kids" smile and wishing Hailey's antics did not put her parenting abilities so far into question.

After Hailey took a header over a high wooden safety railing, rescued, as always, by the angel, Paula called the play to a halt and took Hailey home for a nap.

THE PEDIATRICIAN HAD A name for Hailey's behavior: the terrible twos. Paula accepted that, even as the terrible twos became the terrible threes and fours. It was not that Hailey was an unlikable child: soft-spoken, loving, mostly obedient, and never cruel. She simply required constant attention to keep her safe. Soon, it became too much for Paula, but never for the angel. Always, it appeared when needed, bringing a gale of inescapable tranquillity and scooping Hailey from whatever horrible danger she had placed herself in at the moment. Near-drownings, falls, close encounters with sharp implements, mastery of childproof caps, Hailey seemed to find a new disaster daily.

The Sunday before the start of kindergarten was sunny and cool, perfect for a last full day of summer fun. Paula Heberden took her rambunctious five-year-old to the small zoo about a mile from their home. Hailey skipped through the gate and into the souvenir store while Paula displayed their family pass to the attendant. Sandy braids adorned with two blue ribbons bounced with every movement. She wore her favorite jeans shorts, now frayed and faded, and a shirt with kittens sitting in a basket. Lean legs slathered in sun screen moved in a jerky rhythm, ending in navy socks and aqua sport shoes with rainbow stripes. Paula smiled after Hailey, thinking how lucky she was to have such a sweet and beautiful daughter. *Blessed.* She smiled at the realization. *Truly and literally blessed, the charge of an angel.*

"How many?" the attendant said, with a slight edge that suggested he had asked previously and not received an answer.

Paula reluctantly pulled her attention from Hailey to place it on the man behind the counter. Red-faced and heavy-set, he twitched his lips into a grin.

"Tigger," Hailey said.

Paula responded without looking up. "Yes, honey. There's a lot of stuffed tigers in there." She turned her attention to the attendant. "Two."

Dutifully, the attendant added "Heberden" to his list, followed by the number "2."

"Tigger," Hailey repeated, voice more muffled and distant. "Tigger!"

"Go on in." He pushed the card toward her.

Paula scooped up the card and placed it back in her wallet, then dropped the wallet into her purse. She gathered her things.

A scream pierced the birdsong.

Paula froze. Conversation died, replaced by shouts and more screaming.

Hailey. Paula tore into the souvenir store. A woman paid for purchases while her three children continued to browse the rubber animals, polished stones, and T-shirts, seemingly oblivious to the ruckus outside.

No Hailey.

Paula shoved through the door into the zoo proper. A crowd had gathered in front of the tiger pit, people shouting, pointing, screaming.

"Hailey!" Paula paddled through strangers, insides clutching in icy terror. "Hailey!" She slammed into the bars, "Hailey!" Panic warred with certainty. *She's all right. The angel—always there for her. Always there.*

Snippets of conversation pierced Paula's desperation: . . . climbed the fence . . . fell through the razor wire . . . bloody mess, no wonder the tigers . . . some parents can't control . . ."

Denial slogged through Paula's blurred senses, and she tried to think through ideas that felt thick as Jell-O. "Hailey?"

The tigers feasted, their jaws covered with blood. An aqua sneaker, striped scarlet, rolled awkwardly toward the bars. "Hailey," Paula moaned. Her gaze found the angel beside her. Even with wings tucked beneath a bulky shirt, it could not quite pass for human: the eyes seemed to radiate light, the skin glistening white, the hair like ink. Paula seized it by the collar, glaring into a face that had once symbolized everything good. "Why?" she demanded, sobbing. "Why? Why? Why?"

"One of my other charges needed me." The angel spoke in a honeyed voice, out-of-place amid the screams. "Needed me for the *first* time." Without apology, it turned, melting into the crowd.

Other charges? Paula sank to the ground, awash in a grief too strong to fight. She surrendered to oblivion.

PAULA HEBERDEN AWAKENED IN her own bed, heart pounding, a scream balled in her throat. "Hailey," she whispered in agony. She opened her lids, surprised to find her vision clear. Her eyes did not feel puffy or stinging. She sat up. "A dream?" For a moment she dared to hope, but the events seemed far too clear for nightmare.

An unfamiliar crib stood near the foot of the bed. She had always slept with Hailey, ignoring the studies that found unhealthy sleep patterns and a much higher risk of death by suffocation in co-sleeping children for articles that encouraged bonding in this manner. A firm mattress, siderails, and shedding all pillows and blankets had mitigated the risk. Now, Paula lay on a pillow, snugged beneath a blanket, without the ever-present siderails. Confused, she blinked, glancing around the room. The calendar on the wall no longer held pictures of Pooh bear and his companions, but the Audubon scenes that had graced the walls the year of Hailey's birth.

Paula threw back the covers and ran to the crib. Two-month-old Hailey lay quietly slumbering in a pink sleeper on a Sesame Street sheet. Paula sank to the bed, still staring at the baby. *This can't be. Now, I must be dreaming.* The events of the last five years remained too detailed, too vivid. *How?* Then, suddenly, she understood. The angel had rescued Hailey the only way it could, by turning back time and giving Hailey, and Paula, a second chance.

A million thoughts churned through Paula's mind, relief and confusion, desperate worry and boundless hope. Though five years younger than yesterday, she felt decades older, world-weary but also wiser. The things that had once seemed so obvious and certain now became great, puzzling mysteries; and issues that never existed moved to the forefront of understanding. She had rescued Hailey from every tiny pain at the expense of learning, had coddled her beyond recognition of any danger.

Bruises and bumps are a child's badges of honor, their introduction to the real world. The thought crept into Paula's head, wholly foreign yet filled with undeniable logic. *This time, let the child live.*

"Thank you," Paula said to no one in particular. She, too, had learned the hardest of lessons. "Thank you so much. With all my heart. And I will."

Sunlight streamed through the windows, and Paula dressed methodically, still stunned, her attention fully focused on the sleeping baby. In addition to insight, that lesson brought appreciation for all she had, for all she knew. *Every parent, every child, every experience is different. Normal, right, and proper encompass a wider definition than I've given it in the past.*

Paula pulled on her shoes, then hefted the baby. Hailey snuggled into her arms, a warm miracle nearly lost because of her mother's obsession. "Come on, Hailey," Paula whispered. "Let's get dressed." She smiled. "We need to buy some Band-Aids."

Desperation Gulch

Jody Lynn Nye

The sneaky little brat!" Dan Harkness exclaimed furiously, watching his grandson's car disappear down the dusty road. "How dare he duck out on me like that? He belongs right here, where I want him!"

The rangy old man swayed slightly on his feet. The only shade for miles was thrown by a saguaro cactus and a cluster of stunted scrub trees. He straightened his cap, shouldered his oxygen tank and hobbled off the edge of the road toward a boulder on the far side.

"Don't go back there," said his companion, a compact, round-faced Asian woman whose gray hair was braided into a bun on the top of her head. "He won't be able to see you when he comes back."

With difficulty, Dan heaved himself up onto the big rock and dusted his hands. He squinted at her out of a tanned, creased face with clear blue eyes. "He's not coming back, Ko. No, he's leaving the old man to do the decent thing and die. I wouldn't have thought he'd had the guts." His breath caught, and he wheezed. He checked the gauge on the oxygen bottle

231

slung over his shoulder. "Not too long now. Maybe an hour. Maybe two."

"You can't mean that," Ko said in horror. "Matt's a good boy."

"If he was such a good boy he'd be right here where he belongs, doing what I tell him!" Dan barked. "He's supposed to be here, taking care of me."

"He's only sixteen," Ko said. "It's been a lot for him to absorb, coming to care for you after his losing his parents. It hasn't been that long."

Dan's head jerked away from her. He stared out over the countryside. Faded countryside. Faded terra cotta and beige spread out under a sky of endless blue so pure it almost broke his heart. Ko watched with sympathy as a tear rolled down Dan's creased cheek. "My little girl . . . but that's what I mean! He doesn't know how to think for himself yet. I remember when he was six he didn't know the difference between ground ivy and poison ivy. Hasn't developed any better judgment . . ."

"Have you given him half a chance?" Ko interrupting him briskly but kindly. She came around to press his hands in between hers. "You and Matt need one another."

"I don't need anyone. I'll be with God soon."

Ko gave his hands an impatient shake. "I'm going to go get him."

Dan didn't bother to say she couldn't have known where the boy had gone, or that he was miles away and she had no means of transportation. Those things didn't matter to angels. But, "He's never been able to see you."

"He'll see me," she promised him. The blaze of glory as she disappeared was as brilliant as the sunlight.

THE ENGINE SPUTTERED AND died. Matt Tyler yanked the aging yellow Buick off the road and let it coast to a halt beside the faded adobe building. The needle in the gauge pointed to E. Out of gas. What a laugh. He couldn't do anything right, could he? Not even run away from an angry, tiresome old man without stranding himself in the middle of the desert, too.

Tears blurred his sight so much he almost rolled into the swinging sign that said "Desperation Gulch Café." When the car stopped he let his head drop forward onto his forearms. How could he do something so horrible? The impulse came all of a sudden, while he was listening to yet another one of the old man's interminable, rambling stories, ones he'd heard a thousand times since he was little. He couldn't stand for one more minute hearing how Matt didn't have a right to complain about the heat in the Mojave. It had been hotter in the Pacific Theater—moist heat, not like here. Real men didn't gripe about little things like weather. He, Dan, liked the heat!

Well, he'd gotten it. All at once, Matt had had an impulse. Just like a game. Nip down a side road. *Let's stop here in the Mojave, Grandpa, and look at the dinosaur footprints.* Then, when the old man's back was turned—whoosh. Out of there. Vamoose. Away. Later, dude. He hated baby-sitting, especially when it had turned unexpectedly into a full-time gig with an ungrateful old man who never had a good word for him or listened when he wanted to talk.

But Matt loved his grandfather.

He didn't know what to do.

Spots were dancing in front of his eyes when a tapping sound interrupted his thoughts. He looked up.

"Do you need help?" asked the motherly-looking, silver-haired woman in the apron. He wound down the window. "Are you all right?"

Matt swallowed hard. "I'm okay."

She beckoned him out of the car with a friendly grin. "Come in and have some coffee. I didn't burn this batch too bad."

She stood at least a foot shorter than he did, but she had authority. He was out of the car before he realized it. He loped along behind as she trotted along the flagstones that marked the path to the door.

"Have you got a pay phone?" Matt asked. "I need to call for help. My car's out of gas."

"We'll take care of you, son. Come on in."

In contrast to the dusty adobe of the exterior, the inside of the café was spotless and welcoming. Cheerful paintings of desert flowers hung on the turquoise walls. Somewhere a radio was playing low. A snatch of music drifted out, and an announcer's voice said, "Well, it's 105 degrees, folks, tonight dropping down to . . ."

Four polished wooden tables with four chairs apiece sat underneath the peach curtained windows, but all of the patrons, five men and two women, were seated at the aluminum-rimmed counter. Matt was surprised to see so many people. There had been no other cars in the lot and no houses within sight. Maybe the bus came down this road.

"Hey, son," said the oldest man, an African American with a monk's tonsure of grizzled hair. "We thought you were never coming in."

"H'lo," Matt said, uncomfortably. The others all smiled at him.

"Coffee?" the small woman asked. "I hope you're not going to ask for one of those cappuccino things. Here it's drip brew or instant."

"Regular's fine, thanks," Matt said, finding his voice and his manners. He sat down in the one empty seat at the melamine counter. She plunked down a cup and filled it, pushing it toward him with a crinkly eyed smile. He was surprised to note that she was Asian. He'd automatically assumed that with her golden skin and graying dark hair she was Hispanic. Since she was the only one he'd seen on this miserable, forlorn highway, he wondered how she'd come to be there. He took a sip of the coffee. It tasted wonderful. No double caramel latte cappuccino had ever had the perfume of this plain stoneware cup in a seedy little diner in the middle of the desert. Matt breathed in the smooth essence, feeling it touch the corners of his being.

"First one's free."

Matt fumbled in a pocket for his thin billfold. "I can pay."

"Save it. I've got some equally awful doughnuts. You want one?" A plate joined the saucer. Pink-iced rings with sprinkles, smelling fresh and sweet. Grandpa used to take him and his folks out for frosted doughnuts at the place on the corner. Before the accident. Matt's throat tightened, and tears pushed at his eyes. Even a harmless indulgence like this had associations Matt couldn't deal with. Pink doughnuts had been his mother's favorite. Or maybe it was because his grandfather insisted they were. He might have decided about that when Matt's mother, Sophia, was a child, and she'd just gone along with it to keep peace in the household. No one ever argued with Daniel Harkness. In any case, that was the only kind Matt had ever been allowed to order in the old man's presence. He pushed the plate away.

"No, thank you."

"Eat them anyway," the woman said. "They'll only get stale." But Matt couldn't look at them. The very sight brought back too many memories.

"Looked like you had some car trouble," said the old African American man at the end of the bar.

Matt dropped his head, abashed. "I'm out of gas. I guess I wasn't paying attention. Where's the nearest station?"

The old man raised his eyebrows. "Oh, about thirty miles from here, son. Didn't you see the signs driving into the Mojave? They warn you enough."

Matt suddenly felt resentful. "No. I missed 'em." He'd been listening to his grandfather gassing on, something about Sophia, when she was a teenager, and grateful to have a roof over her head, unlike Matt. All Matt could do not to cry was to concentrate on the line that ran up the middle of the highway and pretend he was alone. It was true, anyway. His mother and father, and his fifteen-year-old sister, all dead and gone. If he hadn't had a soccer game that evening, he'd have been in the car when the semi rolled over on it.

"It happens a lot," the old man said, interrupting the boy's thoughts. "That's why they call this Desperation Gulch. Used to be called Hooperville, except there's no town here any more. Not even a spot on the map. A lot of people who aren't paying attention end up here. Some of 'em never leave." He laughed, a creaky, engaging sound that made Matt grin a little in spite of his misery. "And some of 'em come back." He nodded at the waitress. "Like Coco, here."

"That's not my name, you old bully," the woman said, in a fussy little voice. The two of them bantered together like close friends. "So, Matt, where do you live?"

"Charlotte," he said.

"You're a long way from home. Visiting family?"

"No. A reunion on the West Coast. My grandfather's army unit from World War II." That seemed safe to admit. The others all nodded. He realized that everyone in the café was old. They'd probably remember the war.

"Dropped him off?" the old man asked. Matt started, wondering if the other man could read his mind.

"Uh, yeah."

"Your whole family there?"

"Just me and Granddad," Matt said. He grabbed for the cup, just to have something in his hands.

"Where's your folks?"

"Dead," Matt said, shortly, wanting desperately to change the subject. "If there's nothing here in Hooperville, then why do you stay?"

"I didn't say there was *nothing*," the old man corrected him. "I just said there's no town. The others are here. We enjoy each other's company. And we've all got a lot in common. We all lost someone important to us. It's good to have someone else around who understands. Each of us is a comfort to others. And there's always God, even in the remote places."

Matt looked away. He couldn't talk about God as easily or as comfortably as they did, especially not when he felt God had let him down. Life couldn't be lower.

"So, what's it like with just the two of you?" asked the thin little woman at the end of the counter. She was birdlike in build, with curly white hair and very bright black eyes.

"Oh, you know," Matt said, uncomfortably.

"Not really," the little woman said, cheerfully. "I never had grandchildren."

"It's been hard," Matt admitted. "He doesn't understand what I'm like."

"Do you tell him?" asked the old man.

Matt didn't want to say anything that might sound disloyal, but he realized none of them had ever met Grandpa. They were all interested in him. "He doesn't listen to me," he blurted out. "*He's* always talking."

"Uh-huh. And do you listen to him?"

"I've done nothing but listen to him all my life! And now I have to listen to him every day until . . ."

Matt's throat tightened up. He didn't want to think about when his grandfather might die. It could be happening right that very moment. He ought to go. The car didn't have any gas, but he could walk back there. He glanced out the window at the sun-baked landscape. It must be miles back. He'd have to ask Coco

for water. Grandpa would read him out when he got there. He'd
have to put up with a lecture every single minute for the rest of
his life. He started to get up.

"No, don't leave," Coco said, catching his arm. "You haven't
finished your coffee."

"I . . ." But she pointed to the cup, and he sat down. They said
they'd take care of him. Maybe they had a gas can behind the
café. He'd drink his coffee, then ask.

"So, what's he like, then?" inquired the man on Matt's other
side. He had a shock of crisp white hair and had sharp, dark eyes
behind thick-rimmed glasses. His skin was smooth and beardless.
He might be a Native American. Was it Navajos who lived around
here? "Your grandfather?"

"I don't know," Matt said, sulkily.

"The two of you do things together?" the old black man
asked.

"Can't. He's got pulmonary insufficiency. He can't go far on
his own. He's got to have an oxygen tank with him all the time."

"Got gassed during the war, did he?"

"Shot," Matt said, recalling with ease the story his grandfather
told. "In the jungle, he and his men overran a Japanese gun
emplacement, but they got hit. Grandpa took three bullets, but
he kept going until they overran the gunners. He managed to
walk all the way back to camp. He never collapsed."

He recited the details as they'd been related to him since he
was a child. His listeners looked impressed. Matt was a little surprised, but he thought back to what he'd been saying. After all
those years of hearing it told, he'd ceased to realize what the tale
had meant.

"Your granddad was a hero," the old man said, nodding.

"Yeah," Matt said, a little surprised to realize it. "I guess so."

"What'd he do after the war?"

Easily, without thinking about it, Matt started to recite the
stories his grandfather used to tell him. How he'd met
Grandma at a USO dance. How he'd worked for a man for ten
years, then started his own business. About his hobbies. About
his favorite foods. Why he hated fishing, after being yanked out
of a speedboat by a marlin he had on the hook. They laughed
at that one. Matt paid attention to the way the others listened
to his stories and started to think about the words he was

saying. His grandpa was an interesting man who'd led an interesting life.

"You have a picture of him?" the man in glasses asked. Matt nodded. He took out his wallet and showed them the last photo his family had taken all together. He felt his mouth quivering as he passed the picture around. "Except for your hair being dark, you look just like him. He must be proud."

"I don't know," Matt said. He took back the photo, trying not to look at the smiling images of his lost father, mother, and sister.

Coco poured out a tall glass of water. "Excuse me a moment." She stepped through the door toward the kitchen.

DAN WAS SQUINTING UNDER his cap brim at the horizon when Ko appeared beside him, holding out a glass of water.

"Drink," she said.

"I'm not thirsty."

She ignored his protestation, continuing to offer the glass until he sighed and took it.

"How's the boy?"

"Hasn't opened up yet," Ko said.

"He needs to. His family's been gone four months already. I've been priming the pump, but nothing comes out."

Ko grinned at him, her eyes crinkling. "Did you ever stop priming and let him pump on his own?"

Dan looked at her, pretending outrage. "Now what makes you say something like that?"

"He doesn't do anything for himself because he's too busy following your orders. He hasn't got a whit of self-esteem, Daniel Harkness. He thinks you don't care about him."

"That's not true," Dan growled.

"Do you think he loves you?"

"Of course he loves me!"

"Do you think it's a normal act to abandon someone you love in the desert?"

"No, of course not!"

"Then why do you think he did it?"

"He's an unnatural child," Dan spat. "An evil spawn."

Ko glared at him impatiently. "He's nothing of the kind. He's a normal teenage boy, who has been struck by tragedy and given responsibilities far greater than he ought to handle."

"Nonsense."

Ko held out her hand. "Come and see for yourself."

Dan took a step forward. He felt light all of a sudden. Glancing back, he saw himself sitting on a rock, his slack hands holding the empty glass.

"Am I dead?" he demanded. "I want to know when I die, confound it."

"You're still alive and kicking," Ko assured him. "This is just a way for you to watch Matt without his being able to see you. That way you'll know what he really thinks."

THE DOOR FLAPPED. MATT glanced up. No one entered, but a gust of dry, hot air whistled in, startling against the air-conditioned cool. He swallowed.

"Senior year, eh?" asked the woman beside him, a plump lady with iron-gray hair and startlingly black eyebrows. "Where do you plan to go to college?"

"I'm not going," Matt said, and all the resentment he felt about that subject poured into his voice.

"Why not?" asked a bald man sitting nearest the door. "These days you can't get far without a diploma. It's not like when we were young."

A chorus of agreement rose. Matt stared into his coffee cup, trying not to let the hot tears pressing against his eyes flood out.

"I've got to take care of Grandpa. There's no one else."

That's right, Dan said, firmly, pounding the counter with his fist. It made no sound. *Your first obligation is to family, and that's me.*

Quiet, Ko said. *He can't hear you. Listen, for a change. You need to see what you've done to him.*

The plump woman smiled. "You're a generous young man, taking the years of your youth to care for your elders."

"I'm doing it," Matt said, feeling desperate. "I just don't know if I'm doing it right. You don't know what it's like. Grandpa's got a schedule you wouldn't believe. You have to pound on his back six times a day to loosen things up in his lungs. I can tell it hurts him, but if I don't hit hard enough, nothing happens. He never eats enough. Then he gets light-headed. I've got to watch him all the time to make sure he does-n't fall over. He's got to be turned over in the night. Sometimes he doesn't wake up and I have to push. I'm afraid of hurting him. And I get so tired. I want to take care of him, but I don't know anything about nursing. I'm afraid I'm going to mess something up." Matt's shoulders quivered as the plump woman put an arm around him. "Grandpa's always hammering into me that you should *shoulder your burdens willingly.* I'm trying, but I hate it. I can't do intramural sports. I can't be in the band. I have to get home right after school to look after him. I've got no life. I can't stand it any more."

Dan stared at him. *I've never heard him say a single thing like this. Not a single thing.*

It's time you did, Ko said.

Matt stared into the inky depths of his coffee, feeling as though he was the most evil creature to walk the earth. He waited for the others to condemn him for the monster he was.

"Well," said the old black man, slowly, breaking into Matt's thoughts. "Sounds like you're a tad overwhelmed."

"What?" Matt's head flew up. He realized everyone was staring at him. He felt his cheeks burn, but there was no judgment in their eyes, only kindness. That was even harder to bear than con-demnation.

"Don't you know there's caregiver groups out there?" the birdlike woman asked, with a sweet smile. "You can get help caring for him. His doctor can probably give you some numbers to call. I'm sure you're not meant to take all this on yourself. How old are you? Nineteen?"

"Sixteen."

"Have you thought of hiring some help?"

"With what?" Matt asked. "I haven't got any money."

"Well," said the old man, "how much does your granddad have?"

"I don't know," Matt admitted.

Ko turned to Dan accusingly. *Why doesn't he know? Don't you ever discuss finances with him?*

It's none of his business, dammit! He's only a boy.

He's almost an adult and it is his business. Look at the decisions you're forcing him to make. He ought to be allowed to feel secure.

He knows we have enough to get by.

Well, what does that mean? Ko asked.

Dan glared at her, but she wasn't accusing him. She was asking an honest question. *I was raised never to talk about politics, religion, or money.* She continued to look at him in that searching way that she had.

You didn't tell him because you want him dependent on you, so he can't leave.

If he really loved me, he wouldn't leave.

So you order him to stay? Ko asked. *Being tethered out of fear and need is captivity, not family. He'll stay even if it kills him, but there'd be no joy in it. Give the child some peace of mind, Dan.*

Dan was silent a long time, watching the boy staring down at his coffee. Did the boy really care so much about him that he was sacrificing his future for him? How much more proof of love did he need? *I sold my business three years ago,* he said. *There's over a million and a half, invested in bonds. Happy?*

Ecstatic, Ko said. "You said he started his own company," she asked, as Coco. "What kind of company was it?"

"Tool and die."

"And what happened to it? He doesn't work there any more, does he?"

Matt frowned, thinking back to anything his grandfather might have said. "He's been too weak to work. I guess he sold it."

"It was all his?" the spectacled man asked. Matt nodded. "Good lord, son, he could have made a few million dollars on it. You could hire him a full-time nurse."

"A full-time nurse?" Matt echoed.

"Sure," said Coco. "Someone to be with him while you're at school. You don't have to do it all for him."

"My mom did," Matt said, feeling foolish.

"Was your mother a doctor or nurse?"

"Uh . . . yes. A nurse."

"Then she knew what she was doing. No one expects you to, right off the top of your head, no matter how much you love your granddad. You're just a baby. You don't have to muddle along alone, son. You should go to college. A man needs an education these days. You can't just wait until after he's gone. How old is he?"

"Eighty next birthday," Matt said. He'd been so miserable he hadn't thought about getting outside help. It seemed so obvious when they said it.

"Eighty? He could live a long time yet."

"Yeah, you're right. He could," Matt said, cheerful at the thought of a professional helping him.

No, he couldn't. Matt felt a horrible drop in the pit of his stomach as he remembered what he'd done, and how he came to be sitting there with all those people. His grandfather might not live another day. He clutched his empty cup.

I'm sorry, boy, Dan said, seeing him hurting. *I pushed you to it. I didn't want to hold you against your will. I just don't want you to go away. I love you. You're all I've got left.*

He can't hear you, Ko said, a gentle hand on his shoulder. *Time to go back, now. Let him work out his problems.*

It'd better be soon, then, Dan said, his mouth set in a grim line.

It's his choice. Let him make it. Have faith in him.

I do, Dan said, sadly. *I just wish I'd let him know that.*

You can tell him later. Ko shooed him out the kitchen door and shut it on him.

"So, where'd you drop your granddad off?" the old black man asked. Matt flinched as though the old man could read his mind and was accusing him. How could the guy know? "His army buddies meeting around here?"

"N . . . no."

"You need to go back there," the motherly waitress said suddenly, taking the coffee cup out of Matt's nerveless fingers. "His air's going to run out in a little bit. Then he'll be in real trouble. The nearest trauma hospital's over sixty miles away." She took his arm and guided him toward the door. He stared at her.

"How do you know that?" he demanded. She smiled.

"I know your grandfather, Matt. Go. It'll be all right."

"How do you know?" Matt asked. "Who are you?"

"A friend. It's time to go."

Matt looked at his watch. Shocked, he realized more than an hour had passed. He'd nearly done murder, leaving his grandfather out in the middle of nowhere with a nearly depleted tank. He was horrified with himself, sitting here in the air-conditioned café while Dan sat alone in the blazing sun. The heat smacked him in the face like a rebuke as he ran out of the café. He hoped Grandpa could forgive him.

"Forgive yourself," the motherly woman said, as she slammed his car door for him. "He loves you, and God loves you. You're young, that's all." The other customers looked out the plate-glass window at him. The old man held out his fist, encouraging him with a thumb's up. "Don't try to do too much. And you can ask for help. It's out there."

"But what about gas?" Matt asked.

Coco smiled. "There's plenty. Go on. Go to him. The two of you have a lot to say to each other."

Unbelieving, Matt turned the key. The indicator needle on the gas gauge climbed from *E* to *F* at once. He looked up. Coco was gone. She must have gone back inside. Leaving the car running, he went to the door and threw it open.

"Thank—"

The café was empty. None of the eight people he'd been talking to were there. He walked around the counter and into the back room. No one.

"Hello?" he called. No answer. Not a single sound, not even a whistle from the percolator.

Dee dee doo doo, dee dee doo doo, Matt thought, backing out quickly. *Twilight Zone* time. He ran out of the café, back to his car.

Grandpa was waiting. Please, God, he would be all right.

Matt looked in the rear-view mirror toward the café just before he crested the rise heading east. All he could see of it was the sign creaking in the wind. He bet himself that if he turned back again that would be gone, too. A real ghost town, full of benevolent spirits. He was grateful to them. Of course, he wondered if he'd really ever been out of gas.

He believed in God's love, but occasionally it was nice to get some kind of confirmation that it was really there for him. He put his foot down hard on the accelerator.

AT THAT TIME OF year, twilight would be a long time off. Dan was a little sorry about that. He'd always hoped to pass away at sunset, when the day was saying its colorful farewell. Seemed properly symbolic. The day was still bright, but God couldn't be too far away now.

He took out his billfold to look at the pictures he kept of his family. All of them were gone except Matt. Dan had nothing to berate himself for, no, indeed. He'd served his country, worked hard, raised a family, lived to see his grandchildren. Nothing much to regret. Well, maybe one thing. He turned the old wallet inside out, opening a secret compartment. One last photo lay hidden within it. Dan extracted the faded black-and-white snapshot of a tiny Japanese woman with the Golden Gate Bridge behind her.

"If I'd only had the brains to go back and look you up, darling." He'd trusted her as he had never trusted anyone else on God's green earth, no matter what foolish people said at the time. She was the only person he'd ever known who had never let him intimidate her or push her around. He respected her for that. It was kind of God to give him a guardian angel to light his last days who looked like his lost love. He never had found out what became of Kimiko after he left the service. He hoped she was living a long, happy life and found someone to love her as much as Dan had loved her.

He took a deep breath. It didn't sustain him as well as it should. He fiddled with the tubes running into his nostrils. Clear. The tank must just be running out of air. The valve squeaked as he opened it up, but he heard only a faint hiss. The canister was just about empty. Not long now. It was time for the last prayers. Did it make sense to pray to a God he hoped he'd be seeing in a few minutes?

The dazzle of the sunlight dimmed for a moment as a face leaned over his. "Hold on, Dan. He's coming."

"I welcome Him," Dan said, mustering all the dignity an old coot could while lying on his back in the dust.

"Not God yet, you foolish man," said Ko, looking down into his face with tears in her eyes. "Matt."

"Matt. He's a good boy. Wish I'd told him so." Dan's attention wandered for a moment. When he looked up again, the tearstained face was his grandson's. The boy knelt beside him.

"I'm sorry, I'm sorry," Matt kept saying. "Can you forgive me?"

Dan parted his dry lips and licked them. "The good thing

about the slough of despond," he said, drawing a long, hard breath, "is that if you keep going, you'll come out the other side. I need forgiveness, too. Do you have some for an stubborn old ass like me?"

In spite of himself, Matt started to cry as he helped the old man to sit up. He yanked the tube from the hot, empty tank and jammed it onto the top of the fresh one. The valve turned and he heard the blessed rush of air. "I did, Grandpa. I do. I'm so sorry. I almost killed you."

"No harm done, boy," Dan said, reviving at once. He took a deep breath. "I like the heat, remember? That was the one thing I never minded about the war." Dan noticed a sly grin quirking the corners of the teen's mouth as he helped the old man into the car. "What's wrong? I know: you've heard it about a hundred times. Should I stop?"

"No, Grandpa," Matt said, thankful he could say the words. He swung the steering wheel, guiding the big car out onto the road. "Please. Tell me the story. I want to hear it."

Dan opened his mouth, then shut it. "No, son. You tell me one. You talk for a while."

Kimiko, invisible in the rear seat, smiled.

Unworthy of the Angel

Stephen R. Donaldson

• • •

And stumbled when my feet seemed to come down on the sidewalk out of nowhere. The heat was like walking into a wall; for a moment, I couldn't find my balance. Then I bumped into somebody. That kept me from falling. But he was a tall man in an expensive suit, certain and pitiless, and as he recoiled his expression said plainly that people like me shouldn't be allowed out on the streets.

I retreated until I could brace my back against the hard glass of a display window and tried to take hold of myself. It was always like this; I was completely disoriented—a piece of cork carried down the river. Everything seemed to be melting from one place to another. Back and forth in front of me, people with bitten expressions hurried, chasing disaster. In the street, too many cars snarled and blared at each other, blaming everything except themselves. The buildings seemed to go up for miles into a sky as heavy as a lid. They looked elaborate and hollow, like crypts.

And the heat—I couldn't see the sun, but it was up there somewhere, in the first half of the morning, hidden by humidity

247

and filth. Breathing was like inhaling hot oil. I had no idea where I was; but wherever it was, it needed rain.

Maybe I didn't belong here. I prayed for that. The people who flicked glances at me didn't want what they saw. I was wearing a gray overcoat streaked with dust, spotted and stained. Except for a pair of ratty shoes, splitting at the seams, and my clammy pants, the coat was all I had on. My face felt like I'd spent the night in a pile of trash. But if I had, I couldn't remember. Without hope, I put my hands in all my pockets, but they were empty. I didn't have a scrap of identification or money to make things easier. My only chance was that everything still seemed to be melting. Maybe it would melt into something else, and I would be saved.

But while I fought the air and the heat and prayed, Please, God, not again, the entire street sprang into focus without warning. The sensation snatched my weight off the glass, and I turned in time to see a young woman emerge from the massive building that hulked beside the storefront where I stood.

She was dressed with the plainness of somebody who didn't have any choice—the white blouse gone dingy with use, the skirt fraying at the hem. Her fine hair, which deserved better, was efficiently tied at the back of her neck. Slim and pale, too pale, blinking at the heat, she moved along the sidewalk in front of the store. Her steps were faintly unsteady, as if she were worn out by the burden she carried.

She held a handkerchief to her face like a woman who wanted to disguise the fact that she was still crying.

She made my heart clench with panic. While she passed in front of me, too absorbed in her distress to notice me or anyone else, I thought she was the reason I was here.

But after that first spasm of panic, I followed her. She seemed to leave waves of urgency on either side, and I was pulled along in her wake.

The crowd slowed me down. I didn't catch up with her until she reached the corner of the block and stopped to wait for the light to change. Some people pushed out into the street anyway; cars screamed at them until they squeezed back onto the sidewalk. Everybody was in a hurry, but not for joy. The tension and the heat daunted me. I wanted to hold back—wanted to wait until she found her way to a more private place. But she was as distinct as an appeal in front of me, a figure etched in need. And I was only afraid.

Carefully, almost timidly, I reached out and put my hand on her arm.

Startled, she turned toward me; her eyes were wide and white, flinching. For an instant, her protective hand with the handkerchief dropped from the center of her face, and I caught a glimpse of what she was hiding.

It wasn't grief. It was blood.

It was vivid and fatal, stark with implications. But I was still too confused to recognize what it meant.

As she saw what I looked like, her fright receded. Under other circumstances, her face might have been soft with pity. I could tell right away that she wasn't accustomed to being so lost in her own needs. But now they drove her, and she didn't know what to do with me.

Trying to smile through my dirty whiskers, I said as steadily as I could, "Let me help you."

But as soon as I said it, I knew I was lying. She wasn't the reason I was here.

The realization paralyzed me for a moment. If she'd brushed me off right then, there would have been nothing I could do about it, She wasn't the reason—? Then why had I felt such a shock of importance when she came out to the street? Why did her nosebleed—which really didn't look very serious—seem so fatal to me? While I fumbled with questions, she could have simply walked away from me.

But she was near the limit of her courage. She was practically frantic for any kind of assistance or comfort. But my appearance was against me. As she clutched her handkerchief to her nose again, she murmured in surprise and hopelessness, "What're you talking about?"

That was all the grace I needed. She was too vulnerable to turn her back on any offer, even from a man who looked like me. But I could see that she was so fragile now because she had been so brave for so long. And she was the kind of woman who didn't turn her back. That gave me something to go on.

"Help is the circumference of need," I said. "You wouldn't be feeling like this if there was nothing anybody could do about it.

Otherwise the human race would have committed suicide two days after Adam and Eve left the Garden."

I had her attention now, but she didn't know what to make of me. She wasn't really listening to herself as she murmured, "You're wrong." She was just groping. "I mean your quote. Not help. Reason. 'Reason is the circumference of energy.' Blake said that."

I didn't know who Blake was, but that didn't matter. She'd given me permission—enough permission, anyway, to get me started. I was still holding her arm, and I didn't intend to let her go until I knew why I was here—what I had to do with her.

Looking around for inspiration, I saw we were standing in front of a coffee shop. Through its long glass window, I saw that it was nearly empty; most of its patrons had gone looking for whatever they called salvation. I turned back to the woman and gestured toward the shop. "I'll let you buy me some coffee if you'll tell me what's going on."

She was in so much trouble that she understood me. Instead of asking me to explain myself, she protested, "I can't. I've got to go to work. I'm already late."

Sometimes it didn't pay to be too careful. Bluntly, I said, "You can't do that, either. You're still bleeding."

At that, her eyes widened; she was like an animal in a trap. She hadn't thought as far ahead as work. She had come out onto the sidewalk without one idea of what she was going to do. "Reese—" she began, then stopped to explain, "My brother." She looked miserable. "He doesn't like me to come home when he's working. It's too important. I didn't even tell him I was going to the doctor." Abruptly, she bit herself still, distrusting the impulse or instinct that drove her to say such things to a total stranger.

Knots of people continued to thrust past us, but now their vehemence didn't touch me. I hardly felt the heat. I was locked to this woman who needed me, even though I was almost sure she wasn't the one I was meant to help. Still smiling, I asked, "What did the doctor say?"

She was too baffled to refuse the question. "He didn't understand it. He said I shouldn't be bleeding. He wanted to put me in the hospital. For observation."

"But you won't go," I said at once.

"I can't." Her whisper was nearly a cry. "Reese's show is tomorrow. His first big show. He's been living for this all his life. And he has so much to do. To get ready. If I went to the hospital, I'd have to call him. Interrupt—he'd have to come to the hospital."

Now I had her. When the need is strong enough—and when I've been given enough permission—I can make myself obeyed. I let go of her arm and held out my hand. "Let me see that hand-kerchief."

Dumbly, as if she were astonished at herself, she lowered her hand and gave me the damp cloth.

It wasn't heavily soaked; the flow from her nose was slow. That was why she was able to even consider the possibility of going to work. But her red pain was as explicit as a wail in my hand. I watched a new bead of blood gather in one of her nostrils, and it told me a host of things I was not going to be able to explain to her. The depth of her peril and innocence sent a jolt through me that nearly made me fold at the knees. I knew now that she was not the person I had been sent here to help. But she was the reason. Oh, she was the reason, the victim whose blood cried out for interven-tion. Sweet Christ, how had she let this be done to her?

But then I saw the way she held her head up while her blood trickled to her upper lip. In her eyes, I caught a flash of the kind of courage and love that got people into trouble because it didn't count the cost. And I saw something else, too—a hint that on some level, intuitively, perhaps even unconsciously, she under-stood what was happening to her. Naturally she refused to go to the hospital. No hospital could help her.

I gave the handkerchief back to her gently, though inside I was trembling with anger. The sun beat down on us. "You don't need a doctor," I said as calmly as I could. "You need to buy me some coffee and tell me what's going on."

She still hesitated. I could hardly blame her. Why should she want to sit around in a public place with a handkerchief held to her nose? But something about me had reached her, and it wasn't my brief burst of authority. Her eyes went down my coat to my shoes; when they came back up, they were softer. Behind her hand, she smiled faintly. "You look like you could use it."

She was referring to the coffee; but it was her story I intended to use.

She led the way into the coffee shop and toward one of the booths; she even told the petulant waiter what we wanted. I appre-ciated that. I really had no idea where I was. In fact, I didn't even

know what coffee was. But sometimes knowledge comes to me
when I need it. I didn't even blink as the waiter dropped heavy
cups in front of us, sloshing hot, black liquid onto the table.
Instead, I concentrated everything I had on my companion.

When I asked her, she said her name was Kristen Dona. Following a hint I hadn't heard anybody give me, I looked at her left
hand and made sure she wasn't wearing a wedding ring. Then I
said to get her started, "Your brother's name is Reese. This has
something to do with him."

"Oh, no," she said quickly. Too quickly. "How could it?" She
wasn't lying: she was just telling me what she wanted to believe.

I shrugged. There was no need to argue with her. Instead, I
let the hints lead me. "He's a big part of your life," I said, as if we
were talking about the weather. "Tell me about him."

"Well—" She didn't know where to begin. "He's a sculptor.
He has a show tomorrow—I told you that. His first big show. After
all these years."

I studied her closely. "But you're not happy about it."

"Of course I am" She was righteously indignant. And under
that, she was afraid. "He's worked so hard—! He's a good sculptor. Maybe even a great one. But it isn't exactly easy. It's not like
being a writer—he can't just go to a publisher and have them
print a hundred thousand copies of his work for two ninety-five.
He has to have a place where people who want to spend money
on art can come and see what he does. And he has to charge a lot
because each piece costs him so much time and effort. So a lot of
people have to see each piece before he can sell one. That means
he has to have shows. In a gallery. This is his first real chance."

For a moment, she was talking so hotly that she forgot to
cover her nose. A drop of blood left a mark like a welt across
her lip.

Then she felt the drop and scrubbed at it with her handkerchief. "Oh, damn!" she muttered. The cloth was slowly becoming
sodden. Suddenly her mouth twisted and her eyes were full of
tears. She put her other hand over her face. "His first *real* chance.
I'm so scared."

I didn't ask her *why*. I didn't want to hurry her. Instead, I
asked, "What changed?"

Her shoulders knotted. But my question must have sounded safe
to her. Gradually, some of her tension eased. "What do you mean?"

"He's been a sculptor for a long time." I did my best to sound reasonable, like a friend of her brother's. "But this is his first big show. What's different now? What's changed?"

The waiter ignored us, too bored to bother with customers who only wanted coffee. Numbly, Kristen took another handkerchief out of her purse, raised the fresh cloth to her nose; the other one went back into her purse. I already knew I was no friend of her brother's.

"He met a gallery owner." She sounded tired and sad. "Mortice Root. He calls his gallery The Root Cellar, but it's really an old brownstone mansion over on Forty-ninth. Reese went there to see him when the gallery first opened, two weeks ago. He said he was going to beg—He's become so bitter. Most of the time, the people who run galleries won't even look at his work. I think he's been begging for years."

The idea made her defensive. "Failure does that to people. You work your heart out, but nothing in heaven or hell can force the people who control *access* to care about you. Gallery owners and agents can make or break you because they determine whether you get to show your work or not. You never even get to find out whether there's anything in your work that can touch or move or inspire people, no matter how hard you try, unless you can convince some owner he'll make a lot of money out of you."

She was defending Reese from an accusation I hadn't made. Begging was easy to understand; anybody who was hurt badly enough could do it. She was doing it herself—but she didn't realize it.

Or maybe she did. She drank some of her coffee and changed her tone. "But Mr. Root took him on," she said almost brightly. "He saw Reese's talent right away. He gave Reese a good contract and an advance. Reese has been working like a demon, getting ready, making new pieces. He's finally getting the chance he deserves."

The chance he deserves. I heard echoes in that—suggestions she hadn't intended. And she hadn't really answered my question. But now I had another one that was more important to me.

"Two weeks ago," I said. "Kristen, how long has your nose been bleeding?"

She stared at me while the forced animation drained out of her face.

"Two weeks now, wouldn't you say?" I held her frightened eyes. "Off and on at first, so you didn't take it seriously? But now it's constant? If it weren't so slow, you'd choke yourself when you went to sleep at night?"

I'd gone too far. All at once, she stopped looking at me. She dropped her handkerchief, opened her purse, took out money, and scattered it on the table. Then she covered her face again. "I've got to go," she said into her hand. "Reese hates being interrupted, but maybe there's something I can do to help him get ready for tomorrow."

She started to leave. And I stopped her. Just like that. Suddenly, she couldn't take herself away from me. A servant can sometimes wield the strength of his Lord.

I wanted to tell her she'd already given Reese more help than she could afford. But I didn't. I wasn't here to pronounce judgment. I didn't have that right. When I had her sitting in front of me again, I said, "You still haven't told me what changed."

Now she couldn't evade me, couldn't pretend she didn't understand. Slowly, she told me what had happened.

Mortice Root had liked Reese's talent—had praised it effusively—but he hadn't actually liked Reese's work. Too polite, he said. Too reasonable. Aesthetically perfect, emotionally boring. He urged Reese to "open up"—dig down into the energy of his fears and dreams, apply his great skill and talent to darker, more "honest" work. And he supplied Reese with new materials. Until then, Reese had worked in ordinary clay or wax, making castings of his figures only when he and Kristen were able to afford the caster's price. But Root had given Reese a special, black clay that gleamed like a river under a swollen moon. An ideal material, easy to work when it was damp, but finished when it dried, without need for firing or sealer or glaze—as hard and heavy as stone.

And as her brother's hands had worked that clay, Kristen's fear had grown out of it. His new pieces were indeed darker, images that chilled her heart. She used to love his work. Now she hated it.

I could have stopped then. I had enough to go on. And she wasn't the one I'd been sent to help; that was obvious. Maybe I should have stopped.

But I wanted to know more. That was my fault: I was forever trying to swim against the current. After all, the impulse to "open up"—to do darker, more "honest" work—was hardly evil. But the truth was, I was more interested in Kristen than Reese. Her eyes were full of supplication and abashment. She felt she had betrayed her brother, not so much by talking about him as by the simple fact that her attitude toward his work had changed. And she was still in such need.

Instead of stopping, I took up another of the hints she hadn't given me. Quietly, I asked, "How long have you been supporting him?"

She was past being surprised now, but her eyes didn't leave my face. "Close to ten years," she answered obediently.

"That must have been hard on you."

"Oh, no," she said at once. "Not at all. I've been happy to do it." She was too loyal to say anything else. Here she was, with her life escaping from her—and she insisted she hadn't suffered. Her bravery made the backs of my eyes burn.

But I required honesty. After a while, the way I was looking at her made her say, "I don't really love my job. I work over in the garment district. I put in hems. After a few years"—she tried to sound self-deprecating and humorous—"it gets a little boring. And there's nobody I can talk to." Her tone suggested a deep gulf of loneliness. "But it's been worth it," she insisted. "I don't have any talent of my own. Supporting Reese gives me something to believe in. I make what he does possible."

I couldn't argue with that. She had made the whole situation possible. Grimly, I kept my mouth shut and waited for her to go on.

"The hard part," she admitted finally, "was watching him grow bitter." Tears started up in her eyes again, but she blinked them back. "All that failure—year after year—" She dropped her gaze; she couldn't bear to look at me and say such things. "He didn't have anybody else to take it out on."

That thought made me want to grind my teeth. She believed in him—and he took it out on her. She could have left him in any number of ways—gotten married, simply packed her bags, anything. But he probably wasn't even aware of the depth of her refusal to abandon him. He simply went on using her.

My own fear was gone now; I was too angry to be afraid. But I held it down. No matter how I felt, she wasn't the person I was here to defend. So I forced myself to sound positively casual as I said, "I'd like to meet him."

In spite of everything, she was still capable of being taken aback. "You want me to—?" She stared at me. "I couldn't!" She wasn't appalled; she was trying not to give in to a hope that must have seemed insane to her. "He hates being interrupted. He'd be furious." She scanned the table, hunting for excuses. "You haven't finished your coffee."

I nearly laughed out loud. I wasn't here for her—and yet she did wonderful things for me. Suddenly, I decided that it was all worth what it cost. Smiling broadly, I said, "I didn't say I needed coffee. I said you needed to buy it for me."

Involuntarily, the corners of her mouth quirked upward. Even with the handkerchief clutched to her face, she looked like a different person. After all she had endured, she was still a long way from being beaten. "Be serious," she said, trying to sound serious. "I can't take you home with me. I don't even know what to call you."

"If you take me with you," I responded, "you won't have to call me."

This time, I didn't need help to reach her. I just needed to go on smiling.

But what I was doing made sweat run down my spine. I didn't want to see her hurt any more. And there was nothing I could do to protect her.

THE WALK TO THE place where she and her brother lived seemed long and cruel in the heat. There were fewer cars and crowds around us now—most of the city's people had reached their destinations for the day—and thick, hot light glared at us from long aisles of pale concrete. At the same time, the buildings impacted on either side of us grew older, shabbier, became the homes of ordinary men and women rather than of money. Children played in the street, shrieking and running as if their souls were on fire. Derelicts shambled here and there, not so much lost to grace as inured by alcohol and ruin, benumbed by their own particular innocence. Several of the structures we passed had had their eyes blown out.

Then we arrived in front of a high, flat edifice indistinguishable from its surroundings except by the fact that most of its windows were intact. Kristen grimaced at it apologetically. "Actually," she said, "we could live better than this. But we save as much money as we can for Reese's work." She seemed to have forgotten that I looked worse than her apartment building did. Almost defiantly, she added, "Now we'll be able to do better."

That depended on what she called *better*, I was sure Mortice Root had no end of money. But I didn't say so.

However, she was still worried about how Reese would react to us. "Are you sure you want to do this?" she asked. "He isn't going to be on his good behavior."

I nodded and smiled; I didn't want her to see how scared and angry I was. "Don't worry about me. If he's rude, I can always offer him some constructive criticism."

"Oh, terrific," she responded, at once sarcastic and relieved, sourly amused. "He just *loves* constructive criticism."

She was hardly aware of her own bravery as she led me into the building.

The hall with the mail slots and the manager's apartment was dimly lit by one naked bulb; it should have felt cooler. But the heat inside was fierce. The stairs up to the fourth floor felt like a climb in a steambath. Maybe it was a blessing after all that I didn't have a shirt on under my coat. I was sweating so hard that my shoes felt slick and unreliable against my soles, as if every step I took were somehow untrustworthy.

When Kristen stopped at the door of her apartment, she needed both hands to fumble in her purse for the key. With her face uncovered, I saw that her nosebleed was getting worse.

Despite the way her hands shook, she got the door open. After finding a clean handkerchief, she ushered me inside, calling as she did so, "Reese! I'm home!"

The first room—it would've been the living room in anybody else's apartment—was larger than I'd expected; and it implied other rooms I couldn't see—bedrooms, a kitchen, a studio. The look of dinginess and unlove was part of the ancient wallpaper and warped baseboards, the sagging ceiling, not the result of carelessness; the place was scrupulously kempt. And the entire space was organized to display Reese's sculptures.

Set on packing crates and endtables, stacks of bricks, makeshift pedestals, old steamer trunks, they nearly filled the room. A fair number of them were cast; but most were clay, some fired, some not. And without exception they looked starkly out of place in that room. They were everything the apartment wasn't— finely done, idealistic, painless. It was as if Reese had left all his failure and bitterness and capacity for rage in the walls, sloughing it away from his work so that his art was kind and clean.

And static. It would have looked inert if he'd had less talent. Busts and madonnas stared with eyes that held neither fear nor hope. Children that never laughed or cried were hugged in the arms of blind women. A horse in one corner should have been prancing, but it was simply frozen. His bitterness he took out on his sister. His failures reduced him to begging. But his sculptures held no emotion at all.

They gave me an unexpected lift of hope. Not because they were static, but because he was capable of so much restraint. If reason was the circumference of energy, then he was already halfway to being a great artist. He had reason down pat.

Which was all the more surprising because he was obviously not a reasonable man. He came bristling into the room in answer to Kristen's call, and he'd already started to shout at her before he saw I was there.

At once, he stopped; he stared at me. "Who the hell is *this*?" he rasped without looking at Kristen. I could feel the force of his intensity from where I stood. His face was as acute as a hawk's, whetted by the hunger and energy of a predator. But the dark stains of weariness and strain under his eyes made him look more feverish than fierce. All of a sudden I thought, Only two weeks to get a show ready. An entire show's worth of new pieces in only two weeks. Because of course he wasn't going to display any of the work I could see here. He was only going to show what he'd made out of the new, black clay Mortice Root had given him. And he'd worn himself ragged. In a sense, his intensity wasn't directed at me personally; it was just a fact of his personality. He did everything extremely. In his own way, he was as desperate as his sister. Maybe I should have felt sorry for him.

But he didn't give me much chance. Before I could say anything, he wheeled on Kristen. "It isn't bad enough you have to keep interrupting me," he snarled. "You have to bring trash in here, too. Where did you find him—the Salvation Army? Haven't you figured out yet that I'm *busy*?"

I wanted to intervene; but she didn't need that kind of protection. Over her handkerchief, her eyes echoed a hint of her brother's fire. He took his bitterness out on her because she allowed him to, not because she was defenseless. Her voice held a bite of anger as she said, "He offered to help me."

If I hadn't been there, he might have listened to her; but his fever made him rash. "*Help* you?" he snapped. "This bum?" He looked at me again. "He couldn't help himself to another drink. And what do you need help—?"

"*Reese.*" This time, she got his attention. "I went to the doctor this morning."

"What?" For an instant, he blinked at her as if he couldn't understand. "The doctor?" The idea that something was wrong with her hit him hard. I could see his knees trying to fold under him. "You aren't sick. What do you need a doctor for?"

Deliberately, she lowered her hand, exposing the red sheen darkening to crust on her upper lip, the blood swelling in her nostrils. He gaped as if the sight nauseated him. Then he shook his head in denial. Abruptly, he sagged to the edge of a trunk that held two of his sculptures. "Damn it to hell," he breathed weakly. "Don't scare me like that. It's just a nosebleed. You've had it for weeks."

Kristen gave me a look of vindication; she seemed to think Reese had just showed how much he cared about her. But I wasn't so sure. I could think of plenty of selfish reasons for his reaction.

Either way, it was my turn to say something. I could have used some inspiration right then—just a little grace to help me find my way. My emotions were tangled up with Kristen; my attitude toward Reese was all wrong. I didn't know how to reach him. But no inspiration was provided.

Swallowing bile, I made an effort to sound confident. "Actually," I said, "I can be more help than you realize. That's the one advantage life has over art. There's more to it than meets the eye."

I was on the wrong track already; a half-wit could have done better. Reese raised his head to look at me, and the outrage in his eyes was as plain as a chisel. "That's wonderful," he said straight at me. "A bum *and* a critic."

Kristen's face was tight with dismay. She knew exactly what would happen if I kept going.

So did I. I wasn't stupid. But I was already sure I didn't really want to help Reese. I wanted somebody a little more worthy.

Anyway, I couldn't stop. His eyes were absolutely daring me to go on.

"Root's right," I said. Now I didn't have any trouble sounding as calm as a saint. "You know that. What you've been doing"—I gestured around the room—"is too controlled. Impersonal. You've got all the skill in the world, but you haven't put your heart into it.

"But I don't think he's been giving you very good advice. He's got you going to the opposite extreme. That's just another dead end. You need a balance. Control and passion. Control alone has been destroying you. Passion alone—"

Right there, I almost said it: passion alone will destroy your sister. That's the kind of bargain you're making. All it costs you is your soul.

But I didn't get the chance. Reese slapped his hand down on the trunk with a sound like a shot. One of his pieces tilted; it would have fallen if Kristen hadn't caught it. But he didn't see that. He jerked to his feet. Over his shoulder, he said to her, "You've been talking to this tramp about me." The words came out like lead.

She didn't answer. There was no defense against his accusation. To catch the sculpture, she'd had to use both hands, and her touch left a red smudge on the clay.

But he didn't seem to expect an answer. He was facing me with fever bright in his eyes. In the same heavy tone, he said, "It's your fault, isn't it. She wouldn't do that to me—tell a total stranger what a failure I've been—if you hadn't pried it out of her.

"Well, let me tell *you* something. Root owns a gallery. He has *power*." He spat the word as if he loathed it. "I have to listen to him. From you I don't have to take this kind of manure."

Which was true, of course. I was a fool, as well as being useless. In simple chagrin I tried to stop or at least deflect what was coming.

"You're right," I said. "I've got no business trying to tell you what to do. But I can still help you. Just listen to me. I—"

"No," he retorted. "You listen. I've spent ten years of my life feeling the way you look. Now I've got a chance to do better. You don't know anything I could possibly want to hear. I've *been* there."

Still without looking at his sister, he said, "Kristen, tell him to leave."

She didn't have any choice. I'd botched everything past the point where there was anything she could do to save it. Reese would just rage at her if she refused—and what would that accomplish? I watched all the anger and hope drain out of her, and I wanted to fight back; but I didn't have any choice either. She said in a beaten voice, "I think you'd better leave now," and I had to leave. I was no use to anybody without permission; I could not stay when she told me to go.

I didn't have the heart to squeeze in a last appeal on my way out. I didn't have any more hope than she did. I studied her face as I moved to the door, not because I thought she might change her mind, but because I wanted to memorize her, so that if she went on down this road and was lost in the end there would be at least one man left who remembered. But she didn't meet my eyes. And when I stepped out of the apartment, Reese slammed the door behind me so hard the floor shook.

The force of his rejection almost made me fall to my knees.

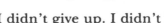

IN SPITE OF THAT, I didn't give up. I didn't know where I was or how I got here; I was lucky to know why I was here at all. And I would never remember. Where I was before I was here was as blank as a wall across the past. When the river took me someplace else, I wasn't going to be able to give Kristen Dona the bare courtesy of remembering her.

That was a blessing, of a sort. But it was also the reason I didn't give up. Since I didn't have any past or future, the present was my only chance.

When I was sure the world wasn't going to melt around me and change into something else, I went down the stairs, walked out into the pressure of the sun, and tried to think of some other way to fight for Kristen's life and Reese's soul.

After all, I had no right to give up hope on Reese. He'd been a failure for ten years. And I'd seen the way the people of this city looked at me. Even the derelicts had contempt in their eyes, including me in the way they despised themselves. I ought to be able to understand what humiliation could do to someone who tried harder than he knew how and still failed.

But I couldn't think of any way to fight it. Not without permission. Without permission, I couldn't even tell him his sister was in mortal danger.

The sun stayed nearly hidden behind its haze of humidity and dirt, but its brutality was increasing. Noon wasn't far away; the walk here had used up the middle of the morning. Heatwaves shimmered off the pavement. An abandoned car with no wheels leaned against the curb like a cripple. Somebody had gone down the street and knocked over all the trashcans, scattering garbage like wasted lives. Somewhere there had to be something I could do to redeem myself. But when I prayed for help, I didn't get it.

After a while, I found myself staring as if I were about to go blind at a street sign at the corner of the block. A long time seemed to pass before I registered that the sign said, "Twenty-first Street."

Kristen had said that Root's gallery, the Root Cellar, was "over on Forty-ninth."

I didn't know the city; but I could at least count. I went around the block and located Twentieth. Then I changed directions and started working my way up through the numbers.

It was a long hike. I passed through sections that were worse than where Kristen and Reese lived and ones that were better. I had a small scare when the numbers were interrupted, but after several blocks they took up where they'd left off. The sun kept leaning on me, trying to grind me into the pavement, and the air made my chest hurt.

And when I reached Forty-ninth, I didn't know which way to turn. Sweating, I stopped at the intersection and looked around. Forty-ninth seemed to stretch to the ends of the world in both directions. Anything was possible; the Root Cellar might be anywhere. I was in some kind of business district—Forty-ninth was lined with prosperity—and the sidewalks were crowded again. But all the people moved as if nothing except fatigue or stubbornness and the heat kept them from running for their lives. I tried several times to stop one of them to ask directions; but it was like trying to change the course of the river. I got glares and muttered curses, but no help.

That was hard to forgive. But forgiveness wasn't my job. My job was to find some way to help Reese Dona. So I tried some outright begging. And when begging failed, I simply let the press of the crowds start me moving the same way they were going.

With my luck, this was exactly the wrong direction. But I couldn't think of any good reason to turn around, so I kept walking, studying the buildings for any sign of a brownstone mansion and muttering darkly against all those myths about how God answers prayer.

Ten blocks later, I recanted. I came to a store that filled the entire block and went up into the sky for at least thirty floors; and in front of it stood my answer. He was a scrawny old man in a dingy gray uniform with red epaulets and red stitching on his cap; boredom or patience glazed his eyes. He was tending an iron pot that hung from a rickety tripod. With the studious intention of a half-wit, he rang a handbell to attract people's attention.

The stitching on his cap said, "Salvation Army."

I went right up to him and asked where the Root Cellar was.

He blinked at me as if I were part of the heat and the haze. "Mission's that way." He nodded in the direction I was going. "Forty-ninth and Grand."

"Thanks, anyway," I said. I was glad to be able to give the old man a genuine smile. "That isn't what I need. I need to find the Root Cellar. It's an art gallery. Supposed to be somewhere on Forty-ninth."

He went on blinking at me until I started to think maybe he was deaf. Then, abruptly, he seemed to arrive at some kind of recognition. Abandoning his post, he turned and entered the store. Through the glass, I watched him go to a box like half a booth that hung on one wall. He found a large yellow book under the box, opened it, and flipped the pages back and forth for a while.

Nodding at whatever he found, he came back out to me.

"Down that way," he said, indicating the direction I'd come from. "About thirty blocks. Number 840."

Suddenly, my heart lifted. I closed my eyes for a moment to give thanks. Then I looked again at the man who'd rescued me. "If I had any money," I said, "I'd give it to you."

"If you had any money," he replied as if he knew who I was, "I wouldn't take it. Go with God."

I said, "I will," and started retracing my way up Forty-ninth.

I felt a world better. But I also had a growing sense of urgency. The longer I walked, the worse it got. The day was getting away from me—and this day was the only one I had. Reese's show was tomorrow. Then Mortice Root would've fulfilled his part of the bargain. And the price would have to be paid. I was sweating so hard my filthy old coat stuck to my back; but I forced myself to walk as fast as the fleeing crowds.

After a while, the people began to disappear from the sidewalks again, and the traffic thinned. Then the business district came to an end, and I found myself in a slum so ruined and hopeless I had to grit my teeth to keep up my courage. I felt hostile eyes watching me from behind broken windows and gaping entrances. But I was protected, either by daylight or by the way I looked.

Then the neighborhood began to improve. The slum became closebuilt houses, clinging to dignity. The houses moved apart from each other, giving themselves more room to breathe. Trees appeared in the yards, even in the sidewalk. Lawns pushed the houses back from the street, and each house seemed to be more ornate than the one beside it. I would have thought they were homes, but most of them had discreet signs indicating they were places of business. Several of them were shops that sold antiques. One held a law firm. A stockbroker occupied a place the size of a temple. I decided that this was where people came to do their shopping and business when they were too rich to associate with their fellow human beings.

And there it was—a brownstone mansion as elaborate as any I'd seen. It was large and square, three stories tall, with a colonnaded entryway and a glass-domed structure that might have been a greenhouse down the length of one side. The mailbox on the front porch was neatly numbered, 840. And when I went up the walk to the porch, I saw a brass plaque on the door with words engraved on it. It said:

THE ROOT CELLAR
a private gallery
Mortice Root

AT THE SIGHT, MY chest constricted as if I'd never done this before. But I'd already lost too much time; I didn't waste any more of it hesitating. I pressed a small button beside the door and listened to chimes ringing faintly inside the house as if Mortice Root had a cathedral in his basement.

For a while, nothing happened. Then the door opened, and I felt a flow of cold air from inside, followed by a man in a guard's uniform, with a gun holstered on his hip and a badge that said, "Nationwide Security," on his chest. As he looked out at me, what he saw astonished him; not many of Root's patrons looked like I did. Then his face closed like a shutter. "Are you out of your mind?" he growled. "We don't give handouts here. Get lost."

In response, I produced my sweetest smile. "Fortunately, I don't want a handout. I want to talk to Mortice Root."

He stared at me. "What in hell makes you think Mr. Root wants to talk to you?"

"Ask him and find out," I replied. "Tell him I'm here to argue about Reese Dona."

He would have slammed the door in my face; but a hint of authority came back to me, and he couldn't do it. For a few moments, he gaped at me as if he were choking. Then he muttered, "Wait here," and escaped back into the house. As he closed the door, the cool air breathing outward was cut off.

"Well, naturally," I murmured to the sodden heat, trying to keep myself on the bold side of dread. "The people who come here to spend their money can't be expected to just stand around and sweat."

The sound of voices came dimly through the door. But I hadn't heard the guard walk away, and I didn't hear anybody coming toward me. So I still wasn't quite ready when the door swung open again and Mortice Root stood in front of me with a cold breeze washing unnaturally past his shoulders.

We recognized each other right away; and he grinned like a wolf. But I couldn't match him. I was staggered. I hadn't expected him to be so *powerful.*

He didn't look powerful. He looked as rich as Solomon— smooth, substantial, glib—as if he could buy and sell the people who came here to give him their money. From the tips of his gleaming shoes past the expanse of his distinctively styled suit to the clean confidence of his shaven jowls, he was everything I wasn't. But those things only gave him worldly significance; they didn't make him powerful. His true strength was hidden behind the bland unction of his demeanor. It showed only in his grin, in the slight, avid bulging of his eyes, in the wisps of hair that stood out like hints of energy on either side of his bald crown.

His gaze made me feel grimy and rather pathetic.

He studied me for a moment. Then, with perfectly cruel kindness, he said, "Come in, come in. You must be sweltering out there. It's much nicer in here."

He was that sure of himself.

But I was willing to accept permission, even from him. Before he could reconsider, I stepped past him into the hallway.

As I looked around, cold came swirling up my back, turning my sweat chill. At the end of this short, deeply carpeted hall, Root's mansion opened into an immense foyer nearly as high as the building itself. Two mezzanines joined by broad stairways of carved wood circled the walls; daylight shone downward from a skylight in the center of the ceiling. A glance showed me that paintings were displayed around the mezzanines, while the foyer itself held sculptures and carvings decorously set on white pedestals. I couldn't see anything that looked like Reese Dona's work.

At my elbow, Root said, "I believe you came to argue with me?" He was as smooth as oil.

I felt foolish and awkward beside him, but I faced him as squarely as I could. "Maybe 'contend' would be a better word."

"As you say." He chuckled in a way that somehow suggested both good humor and malice. "I look forward to it." Then he touched my arm, gestured me toward one side of the foyer. "But let me show you what he's doing these days. Perhaps you'll change your mind."

For no good reason, I said, "You know better than that." But I went with him.

A long, wide passage took us to the glass-domed structure I'd taken to be a greenhouse. Maybe it was originally built for that; but Root had converted it, and I had to admit it made an effective gallery—well-lit, spacious, and comfortable. In spite of all that glass, the air stayed cool, almost chill.

Here I saw Reese's new work for the first time.

"Impressive, aren't they," Root purred. He was mocking me.

But what he was doing to Reese was worse.

There were at least twenty of them, with room for a handful more—attractively set in niches along one wall, proudly positioned on special pediments, cunningly juxtaposed in corners so that they showed each other off. It was clear that any artist would find an opportunity like this hard to resist.

But all the pieces were black.

Reese had completely changed his subject matter. Madonnas and children had been replaced by gargoyles and twisted visions of the damned. Glimpses of nightmare leered from their niches. Pain writhed on display, as if it had become an object of ridicule. In a corner of the room, a ghoul devoured one infant while another strove urgently to scream and failed.

And each of these new images was alive with precisely the kind of vitality his earlier work lacked. He had captured his visceral terrors in the act of pouncing at him.

As sculptures, they were admirable; maybe even more than that. He had achieved some kind of breakthrough here, tapped into sources of energy he'd always been unable or unwilling to touch. All he needed now was balance.

But there was more to these pieces than just skill and energy. There was also blackness.

Root's clay.

Kristen was right. This clay looked like dark water under the light of an evil moon. It looked like marl mixed with blood until the mud congealed. And the more I studied what I saw, the more these grotesque and brutal images gave the impression of growing from the clay itself rather than from the independent mind of the artist. They were not Reese's fears and dreams refined by art; they were horrors he found in the clay when his hands touched it. The real strength, the passion of these pieces, came from the material Root supplied, not from Reese. No wonder he had become so hollow-eyed and ragged. He was struggling desperately to control the consequences of his bargain. Trying to prove to himself he wasn't doing the wrong thing.

For a moment, I felt a touch of genuine pity for him.

But it didn't last. Maybe deep down in his soul he was afraid of what he was doing and what it meant. But he was still doing it. And he was paying for the chance to do such strong work with his sister's life.

Softly, my opponent said, "It appears you don't approve. I'm so sorry. But I'm afraid there's really nothing you can do about it. The artists of this world are uniquely vulnerable. They wish to create beauty, and the world cares for nothing but money. Even the cattle who will buy these"—he gave the room a dismissive flick of the hand—"trivial pieces hold the artist in contempt." He turned his wolf-grin toward me again. "Failure makes fertile ground."

I couldn't pretend that wasn't true; so I asked bitterly, "Are you really going to keep your end of the bargain? Are you really going to sell this stuff?"

"Oh, assuredly," he replied. "At least until the sister dies. Tomorrow. Perhaps the day after." He chuckled happily. "Then I suspect I'll find myself too busy with other, more promising artists to spend time on Reese Dona."

I felt him glance at me, gauging my helplessness. Then he went on unctuously, "Come, now, my friend. Why glare so thunderously? Surely you realize that he has been using her in precisely this manner for years. I've merely actualized the true state of their relationship. But perhaps you're too innocent to grasp how deeply he resents her. It is the nature of beggars to resent those who give them gifts. He resents *me*." At that, Root laughed outright. He was not a man who gave gifts to anybody. "I assure you that her present plight is of his own choice and making."

"No," I said, more out of stubbornness than conviction. "He just doesn't understand what's happening."

Root shrugged. "Do you think so? No matter. The point, as you must recognize, is that we have nothing to contend *for*. The issue has already been decided."

I didn't say anything. I wasn't as glib as he was. And anyway I was afraid he was right.

While I stood there and chewed over all the things I wasn't able to do, I heard doors opening and closing somewhere in the distance. The heavy carpeting absorbed footsteps; but it wasn't long before Reese came striding into the greenhouse, He was so tight with eagerness or suppressed fear he looked like he was about to snap. As usual, he didn't even see me when he first came into the room.

"I've got the rest of the pieces," he said to Root. "They're in a truck out back. I think you'll like—"

Then my presence registered on him. He stopped with a jerk, stared at me as if I'd come back from the dead. "What're *you* doing here?" he demanded. At once, he turned back to Root. "What is *he* doing here?"

Root's confidence was a complete insult. "Reese," he sighed, "I'm afraid that this—gentleman?—believes that I should not show your work tomorrow."

For a moment, Reese was too astonished to be angry. His mouth actually hung open while he looked at me. But I was furious enough for both of us. With one sentence, Root had made my position impossible. I couldn't think of a single thing to say now that would change the outcome.

Still, I had to try. While Reese's surprise built up into outrage, I said as if I weren't swearing like a madman inside, "There are two sides to everything. You've heard his. You really ought to listen to mine."

He closed his mouth, locked his teeth together. His glare was wild enough to hurt.

"Mortice Root owes you a little honesty," I said while I had the chance. "He should have told you long ago that he's planning to drop you after tomorrow."

But the sheer pettiness of what I was saying made me cringe. And Root simply laughed. I should have known better than to try to fight him on his own level. Now he didn't need to answer me at all.

In any case, my jibe made no impression on Reese. He gritted, "I don't care about that," like a man who couldn't or wouldn't understand. "This is what I care about." He gestured frantically around the room. "*This*. My work."

He took a couple of steps toward me, and his voice shook with the effort he made to keep from shouting. "I don't know who you are—or why you think I'm any of your business. I don't care about that, either. You've heard Kristen's side. Now you're going to hear mine."

In a small way, I was grateful he didn't accuse me of turning his sister against him.

"She doesn't like the work I'm doing now. No, worse than that. She doesn't mind the work. She doesn't like the *clay*." He gave a laugh like an echo of Root's. But he didn't have Root's confidence and power; he only sounded bitter, sarcastic, and afraid. "She tries to tell me she approves of me, but I can read her face like a book.

"Well, let me tell you something." He poked a trembling finger at my chest. "With my show tomorrow, I'm alive for the first time in ten years. I'm alive *here*. Art exists to communicate. It isn't worth manure if it doesn't communicate, and it can't communicate if somebody doesn't look at it. It's that simple. The only time an artist is alive is when somebody looks at his work. And if enough people look, he can live forever.

"I've been sterile for ten years because I haven't had one other soul to look at my work." He was so wrapped up in what he was saying, I don't think he even noticed how completely he dismissed his sister. "Now I am alive. If it only lasts for one more day, it'll still be something nobody can take away from me. If I have to work in black clay to get that, who cares? That's just something I didn't know about myself—about how my imagination works. I never had the chance to try black clay before.

"But now—" He couldn't keep his voice from rising like a cry. "Now I'm alive. *Here*. If you want to take that away from me, you're worse than trash. You're evil."

Mortice Root was smiling like a saint.

For a moment, I had to look away. The fear behind the passion in Reese's eyes was more than I could stand. "I'm sorry," I murmured. What else could I say? I regretted everything. He needed me desperately, and I kept failing him. And he placed so little value on his sister. With a private groan, I forced myself to face him again.

"I thought it was work that brought artists to life. Not shows. I thought the work was worth doing whether anybody looked at it or not. Why else did you keep at it for ten years?"

But I was still making the same mistake, still trying to reach him through his art. And now I'd definitely said something he couldn't afford to hear or understand. With a jerky movement like a puppet, he threw up his hands. "I don't have time for this," he snapped. "I've got five more pieces to set up." Then, suddenly, he was yelling at me. "And I don't give one lousy damn what you think!" Somehow, I'd hit a nerve. "I want you to go away. I want you to leave me alone! *Get out of here and leave me alone!*"

I didn't have any choice. As soon as he told me to go, I turned toward the door. But I was desperate myself now. Knotting my fists, I held myself where I was. Urgently—so urgently that I could hardly separate the words—I breathed at him, "Have you looked at Kristen recently? Really looked? Haven't you seen what's happening to her? You—"

Root stopped me. He had that power. Reese had told me to go. Root simply raised his hand, and his strength hit me in the chest like a fist. My tongue was clamped to the roof of my mouth. My voice choked in my throat. For one moment while I staggered, the greenhouse turned in a complete circle, and I thought I was going to be thrown out of the world.

But I wasn't. A couple of heartbeats later, I got my balance back.

Helpless to do anything else, I left the greenhouse.

As I crossed the foyer toward the front door, Reese shouted after me, "And stay away from my sister!"

Until I closed the door, I could hear Mortice Root chuckling with pleasure.

Dear God! I prayed. Let me decide. Just this once. He isn't worth it.

But I didn't have the right.

On the other hand, I didn't have to stay away from Kristen. That was up to her; Reese didn't have any say in the matter.

I made myself walk slowly until I was out of sight of the Root Cellar, just in case someone was watching. Then I started to run.

It was the middle of the afternoon, and the heat just kept getting worse. After the cool of Root's mansion, the outside air felt like glue against my face. Sweat oozed into my eyes, stuck my coat to my back, itched maliciously in my dirty whiskers. The sunlight looked liked it was congealing on the walks and streets. Grimly, I thought, If this city doesn't get some rain soon it will start to burn.

And yet I wanted the day to last, despite the heat. I would happily have caused the sun to stand still. I did not want to have to face Mortice Root and Reese Dona again after dark.

But I would have to deal with that possibility when it came up. First I had to get Kristen's help. And to do that, I had to reach her.

The city did its best to hinder me. I left Root's neighborhood easily enough; but when I entered the slums, I started having problems. I guess a running man dressed in nothing but an over-coat, a pair of pants, and sidesplit shoes looked like too much fun to miss. Gangs of kids seemed to materialize out of the ruined buildings to get in my way.

They should have known better. They were predators them-selves, and I was on a hunt of my own; when they saw the danger in my eyes, they backed down. Some of them threw bottles and trash at my back, but that didn't matter.

Then the sidewalks became more and more crowded as the slum faded behind me. People stepped in front of me, jostled me off my stride, swore angrily at me as I tried to run past. I had to slow down just to keep myself out of trouble. And all the lights were against me. At every corner, I had to wait and wait while mobs hemmed me in, instinctively blocking the path of anyone who wanted to get ahead of them. I felt like I was up against an active enemy. The city was rising to defend its own.

By the time I reached the street I needed to take me over to Twenty-first, I felt so ragged and wild I wanted to shake my fists at the sky and demand some kind of assistance or relief. But if God couldn't see how much trouble I was in, He didn't deserve what I was trying to do in His name. So I did the best I could—running in spurts, walking when I had to, risking the streets whenever I saw a break in the traffic, And finally I made it. Trembling, I reached the building where Reese and Kristen had their apartment.

Inside, it was as hot as an oven, baking its inhabitants to death. But here at least there was nobody in my way, and I took the stairs two and three at a time to the fourth floor. The light-bulb over the landing was out, but I didn't have any trouble find-ing the door I needed.

I pounded on it with my fist. Pounded again. Didn't hear any-thing. Hammered at the wood a third time.

"Kristen!" I shouted. I didn't care how frantic I sounded. "Let me in! I've got to talk to you!"

Then I heard a small, faint noise through the panels. She must have been right on the other side of the door. Weakly, she said, "Go away."

"Kristen!" Her dismissal left a welt of panic across my heart. I put my mouth to the crack of the door to make her hear me. "Reese needs help. If he doesn't get it, you're not going to sur-vive. He doesn't even realize he's sacrificing you."

After a moment, the lock clicked, and the door opened.

I went in.

The apartment was dark. She'd turned off all the lights. When she closed the door behind me, I couldn't see a thing. I had to stand still so I wouldn't bump into Reese's sculptures.

"Kristen," I said, half pleading, half commanding. "Turn on a light."

Her reply was a whisper of misery. "You don't want to see me."

She sounded so beaten I almost gave up hope. Quietly, I said, "Please." She couldn't refuse. She needed me too badly. I felt her move past me in the dark. Then the overhead lights clicked on, and I saw her.

I shouldn't have been shocked—I knew what to expect—but that didn't help. The sight of her went into me like a knife.

She was wearing only a terry cloth bathrobe. That made sense; she'd been poor for a long time and didn't want to ruin her good clothes. The collar of her robe was soaked with blood.

Her nosebleed was worse.

And delicate red streams ran steadily from both her ears.

Sticky trails marked her lips and chin, the front of her throat, the sides of her neck. She'd given up trying to keep herself clean. Why should she bother? She was bleeding to death, and she knew it.

Involuntarily, I went to her and put my arms around her.

She leaned against me. I was all she had left. Into my shoulder, she said as if she were on the verge of tears, "I can't help him anymore. I've tried and tried, I don't know what else to do."

She stood there quivering; and I held her and stroked her hair and let her blood soak into my coat. I didn't have any other way to comfort her.

But her time was running out, just like Reese's. The longer I waited, the weaker she would be. As soon as she became a little steadier, I lowered my arms and stepped back. In spite of the way I looked, I wanted her to be able to see what I was.

"He doesn't need that kind of help now," I said softly, willing her to believe me. Not the kind you've been giving him for ten years. "Not anymore. He needs me. That's why I'm here.

"But I have to have permission." I wanted to cry at her, You've been letting him do this to you for ten years! None of this would've happened to you if you hadn't allowed it! But I kept that protest to myself. "He keeps sending me away, and I have to go. I don't have any choice. I can't do anything without permission.

"It's really that simple." God, make her believe me! "I need somebody with me who wants me to be there. I need you to go back to the Root Cellar with me. Even Root won't be able to get rid of me if you want me to stay.

"Kristen." I moved closer to her again, put my hands in the blood on her cheek, on the side of her neck. "I'll find some way to save him. If you're there to give me permission."

She didn't look at me, she didn't seem to have the courage to raise her eyes. But after a moment I felt the clear touch of grace. She believed me—when I didn't have any particular reason to believe myself. Softly, she said, "I can't go like this. Give me a minute to change my clothes."

She still didn't look at me. But when she turned to leave the room, I saw determination mustering in the corners of her eyes.

I breathed a prayer of long-overdue thanks. She intended to fight. I waited for her with fear beating in my bones. And when she returned—dressed in her dingy blouse and fraying skirt, with a towel wrapped around her neck to catch the blood—and announced that she was ready to go, I faltered. She looked so wan and frail—already weak and unnaturally pale from loss of blood. I felt sure she wasn't going to be able to walk all the way to the Root Cellar.

Carefully, I asked her if there was any other way we could get where we were going. But she shrugged the question aside. She and Reese had never owned a car. And he'd taken what little money was available in order to rent a truck to take his last pieces to the gallery.

Groaning a silent appeal for help, I held her arm to give her what support I could. Together, we left the apartment, went down the old stairs and out to the street.

I felt a new sting of dread when I saw that the sun was setting. For all my efforts to hurry, I'd taken too much time. Now I would have to contend with Mortice Root at night.

Twilight and darkness brought no relief from the heat. The city had spent all day absorbing the pressure of the sun; now the walks and buildings, every stretch of cement seemed to emit fire like the sides of a furnace. The air felt thick and ominous—as charged with intention as a thunderstorm, but trapped somehow, prevented from release, tense with suffering.

It sucked the strength out of Kristen with every breath. Before we'd gone five blocks, she was leaning most of her weight on me. That was frightening, not because she was more than I could bear, but because she seemed to weigh so little. Her substance was bleeding away. In the garish and unreliable light of the street-lamps, shop windows, and signs, only the dark marks on her face and neck appeared real.

But we were given one blessing: the city itself left us alone. It had done its part by delaying me earlier. We passed through crowds and traffic, past gutted tenements and stalking gangs, as if we didn't deserve to be noticed anymore.

Kristen didn't complain, and I didn't let her stumble. One by one, we covered the blocks. When she wanted to rest, we put our backs to the hot walls and leaned against them until she was ready to go on.

During that whole long, slow creep through the pitiless dark, she only spoke to me once. While we were resting again, some-time after we turned on Forty-ninth, she said quietly, "I still don't know your name."

We were committed to each other; I owed her the truth. "I don't either," I said. Behind the wall of the past, any number of things were hidden from me.

She seemed to accept that. Or maybe she just didn't have enough strength left to worry about both Reese and me. She rested a little while longer. Then we started walking again.

And at last we left the last slum behind and made our slow, frail approach to the Root Cellar. Between streetlights I looked for the moon, but it wasn't able to show through the clenched haze. I was sweating like a frightened animal. But Kristen might have been immune to the heat. All she did was lean on me and walk and bleed.

I didn't know what to expect at Root's mansion. Trouble of some kind. An entire squadron of security guards. Minor demons lurking in the bushes around the front porch. Or an empty build-ing, deserted for the night. But the place wasn't deserted. All the rest of the mansion was dark; the greenhouse burned with light. Reese wasn't able to leave his pieces alone before his show. And none of the agents that Root might have used against us appeared. He was that sure of himself.

On the other hand, the front door was locked with a variety of bolts and wires.

But Kristen was breathing sharply, urgently. Fear and desire and determination made her as feverish as her brother; she wanted me to take her inside, to Reese's defense. And she'd lost a dangerous amount of blood. She wasn't going to be able to stay on her feet much longer. I took hold of the door, and it opened without a sound. Cool air poured out at us, as concentrated as a moan of anguish.

We went in.

The foyer was dark. But a wash of light from the cracks of the greenhouse doors showed us our way. The carpet muffled our feet. Except for her ragged breathing and my frightened heart, we were as silent as spirits.

But as we got near the greenhouse, I couldn't keep quiet anymore. I was too scared.

I caused the doors to burst open with a crash that shook the walls. At the same time, I tried to charge forward.

The brilliance of the gallery seemed to explode in my face. For an instant, I was dazzled.

And I was stopped. The light felt as solid as the wall that cut me off from the past.

Almost at once, my vision cleared, and I saw Mortice Root and Reese Dona. They were alone in the room, standing in front of a sculpture I hadn't seen earlier—the biggest piece here. Reese must have brought it in his rented truck. It was a wild, swept-winged, malignant bird of prey, its beak wide in a cry of fury. One of its clawed feet was curled like a fist. The other was gripped deep into a man's chest. Agony stretched the man's face.

At least Reese had the decency to be surprised. Root wasn't. He faced us and grinned.

Reese gaped dismay at Kristen and me for one moment. Then, with a wrench like an act of violence, he turned his back. His shoulders hunched; his arms clamped over his stomach. "I told you to go away." His voice sounded like he was strangling. "I told you to leave her alone."

The light seemed to blow against me like a wind. Like the current of the river that carried me away, taking me from place to place without past and without future, hope. And it was rising. It held me in the doorway; I couldn't move through it.

"You are a fool," Root said to me. His voice rode the light as if he were shouting. "You have been denied. You cannot enter here."

He was so strong that I was already half turned to leave when Kristen saved me.

As pale as ash, she stood beside me. Fresh blood from her nose and ears marked her skin. The towel around her neck was sodden and terrible. She looked too weak to keep standing. Yet she matched her capacity for desperation against Reese's need.

"No," she said in the teeth of the light and Root's grin. "He can stay. I want him here."

I jerked myself toward Reese again.

Ferocity came at me like a cataract; but I stood against it. I had Kristen's permission. That had to be enough.

"Look at her!" I croaked at his back. "She's your sister! *Look* at her!"

He didn't seem to hear me at all. He was hunched over himself in front of his work. "Go away," he breathed weakly, as if he were talking to himself. "I can't stand it. Just go away."

Gritting prayers between my teeth like curses, I lowered my head, called up every ache and fragment of strength I had left, and took one step into the greenhouse.

Reese fell to his knees as if I'd broken the only string that held him upright.

At the same time, the bird of prey poised above him moved. Its wings beat downward. Its talons clenched. The heart of its victim burst in his chest. From his clay throat came a brief, hoarse wail of pain.

Driven by urgency, I took two more steps through the intense pressure walled against me. And all the pieces displayed in the greenhouse started to move.

Tormented statuettes fell from their niches, cracked open, and cried out. Gargoyles mewed hideously. The mouths of victims gaped open and whined. In a few swift moments, the air was full of muffled shrieks and screams.

Through the pain, and the fierce current forcing me away from Reese, and the horror, I heard Mortice Root start to laugh.

If Kristen had failed me then, I would have been finished. But in some way she had made herself blind and deaf to what was happening. Her entire soul was focused on one object—help for her brother—and she willed me forward with all the passion she had learned in ten years of self-sacrifice. She was prepared to spend the last of her life here for Reese's sake.

She made it possible for me to keep going.

Black anguish rose like a current at me. And the force of the light mounted. I felt it ripping my skin. It was as hot as the hunger ravening for Reese's heart.

Yet I took two more steps.

And two more.

And reached him.

He still knelt under the wingspread of the nightmare bird he had created. The light didn't hurt him; he didn't feel it at all. He was on his knees because he simply couldn't stand. He gripped his arms over his heart to keep himself from howling.

There I noticed something I should have recognized earlier. He had sculpted a man for his bird of prey to attack, not a woman. I could see the figure clearly enough now to realize that Reese had given the man his own features. Here, at least, he had shaped one of his own terrors rather than merely bringing out the darkness of Mortice Root's clay.

After that, nothing else mattered. I didn't feel the pain or the pressure; ferocity and dismay lost their power.

I knelt in front of Reese, took hold of his shoulder, and hugged him like a child. "Just look at her," I breathed into his ear. "She's your sister. You don't have to do this to her."

She stood across the room from me with her eyes closed and her determination gripped in her small fists.

From under her eyelids, stark blood streamed down her cheeks.

"Look at her!" I pleaded. "I can help you. Just *look*."

In the end, he didn't look at her. He didn't need to. He knew what was happening.

Suddenly, he wrenched out of my embrace. His arms flung me aside. He raised his head, and one lorn wail corded his throat:

"*Kristen!*"

Root's laughter stopped as if it'd been cut down with an axe.

That cry was all I needed. It came right from Reese's heart, too pure to be denied. It was permission, and I took it.

I rose to my feet, easily now, easily. All the things that stood in my way made no difference. Transformed, I faced Mortice Root across the swelling force of his malice. All his confidence was gone to panic.

Slowly, I raised my arms.

Beams of white sprouted from my palms, clean white almost silver. It wasn't fire or light in any worldly sense; but it blazed over my head like light, ran down my arms like fire. It took my coat and pants, even my shoes, away from me in flames. Then it wrapped me in robes of God until all my body burned.

Root tried to scream, but his voice didn't make any sound.

Towering white-silver, I reached up into the storm-dammed sky and brought down a blast that staggered the entire mansion to its foundations.

Crashing past glass and frame and light fixtures, a bolt that might have been lightning took hold of Root from head to foot. For an instant, the gallery's lights failed. Everything turned black except for Root's horror etched against darkness and the blast that bore him away.

When the lights came back on, the danger was gone from the greenhouse. All the crying and the pain and the pressure were gone. Only the sculptures themselves remained.

They were slumped and ruined, like melted wax.

Outside, rain began to rattle against the glass of the greenhouse.

Later, I went looking for some clothes; I couldn't very well go around naked. After a while, I located a suite of private rooms at the back of the building. But everything I found there belonged to Root. His personal stink had soaked right into the fabric. I hated the idea of putting his things on my skin when I'd just been burned clean. But I had to wear something. In disgust, I took one of his rich shirts and a pair of pants. That was my punishment for having been so eager to judge Reese Dona.

Back in the greenhouse, I found him sitting on the floor with Kristen's head cradled in his lap. He was stroking the soft hair at her temples and grieving to himself. For the time being, at least, I was sure his grief had nothing to do with his ruined work.

Kristen was fast asleep, exhausted by exertion and loss of blood. But I could see that she was going to be all right. Her bleeding had stopped completely. And Reese had already cleaned some of the stains from her face and neck.

Rain thundered against the ceiling of the greenhouse; jagged lilies of lightning scrawled the heavens. But all the glass was intact, and the storm stayed outside, where it belonged. From the safety of shelter, the downpour felt comforting.

And the manufactured cool of the building had wiped out most of Root's unnatural heat. That was comforting, too.

It was time for me to go.

But I didn't want to leave Reese like this. I couldn't do anything about the regret that was going to dog him for the rest of his life. But I wanted to try.

The river was calling for me. Abruptly, as if I thought he was in any shape to hear me, I said, "What you did here—the work you did for Root—wasn't wrong. Don't blame yourself for that. You just went too far. You need to find the balance. Reason and energy." Need and help. "There's no limit to what you can do, if you just keep your balance."

He didn't answer. Maybe he wasn't listening to me at all. But after a moment he bent over Kristen and kissed her forehead.

That was enough. I had to go. Some of the details of the greenhouse were already starting to melt.

My bare feet didn't make any sound as I left the room, crossed the foyer, and went out into . . .

Guilt

Gary A. Braunbeck

"What art can wash guilt away?"
—Oliver Goldsmith

Ken Willis, feature writer for the Cedar Hill *Ally*, sat at his desk thinking about his dead parents and how he had helped kill them and, despite what the psychiatrist had told him, realized that, on some level, he *had* realized what was going to happen and chosen not to stop it.

He became aware of himself then in a way that always unnerved him, of the stillness in his center and the thrumming pain behind his right eye and the ultimately comical fragility of the fibrous shell that was his body and, thinking this, turned toward one of the office windows as a snippet of an old poem crept into his mind:

I am moved by fancies that are curled/Around these images, and cling: The notion of some infinitely gentle/Infinitely suffering thing . . .

Outside, it was a gray night, chiseled from gray stone, shadowed by gray mist. It was more than a night of freezing rain, it was a tone—the kind that is part of the province of loss and cannot be vicariously conveyed to anyone who has not lived with the physical tension, stilled violence, and protracted anguish of grief. It was a dismal night following a string of dateless, nameless, empty dismal days. Grieving had long ago crippled Ken's anger, dividing his life into moments of cheerless survival, the passage of time going unheeded except to note that he was still alive and his parents were still dead and the guilt was still very much present in his heart.

A large shadow loomed over his desk. The sickly-sweet aroma of pipe tobacco and spicy cologne betrayed the presence of Jim Dardis, editor of the *Ally*.

"Didn't the EPA ban the use of that cologne last year?" said Ken.

"This coming from a man who thinks aftershave with a ship on its bottle is Class City." Jim Dardis stood well over six feet tall and reminded Ken of Boris Karloff; same deep-set, left-out-in-the-rain-too-long puppy eyes, same everlastingly arched brow, same silvery hair, even the same timbre to his sing-song voice. "What are your views on art?"

"Never met the man," replied Ken.

"That's very funny," said Dardis, assuming a stringent, inspiring, Listen-Up pose. "I just had a interesting chat with the wife of our beloved publisher. Seems the new owner of the Altman Gallery called her a little while ago. Construction of the new addition's about finished and there's a big exhibit scheduled to open soon. They've offered us an exclusive preview."

"They called us instead of a Columbus paper?"

"Yes, they did—and here's the interesting part: They specifically requested you."

"Not interested, but thanks."

"You don't have a choice. I already promised you'd be there around eight."

"Then you'll just have to call them back and un-promise. It's almost seven o'clock and I am going home."

"I gave them my word, Ken."

"That was silly of you."

"Save us both a headache and go to the damn preview. An hour of your time and I'll make sure you get the front page of the

Arts and Entertainment section this week. Whatta you say? Please?" Ken was caught off-guard by that last word: Jim Dardis never said *please*.

He suddenly remembered that Dardis's wife—a middle-aged debutante wannabe whose type was all-too typical in central Ohio—had recently and without explanation walked out on him and their four-year-old autistic daughter. The man had enough frustration without Ken's adding to it.

Still . . .

"Look, Jim, I'm just a feature writer. This is out of my territory. Courteney should be the one to cover it. I understand the position you're in but I—"

"—want to go home and mope. Don't look at me like that. I know the anniversary's coming up, but I'm not going to walk on eggshells with you. In case you've forgotten, I'm your friggin' boss. I sympathize, but it's not my problem; this stinking 'exclusive preview' is. *Dammit*, I wish you wouldn't glare at me like that! You got the angriest eyes I've ever seen—or haven't you ever noticed how people can't keep eye contact with you during a conversation?"

"Sort of like you're doing now?"

Dardis looked up. "Touché. That's one wicked stare you've got. Goes right through a person."

Ken smiled. "Before the divorce, Janice used to say that I smiled as if someone had just stuck a gun in my back and told me to act natural."

"Smart girl."

"Nice of you to say so, but I'm still not going." He continued staring, good and hard and unblinkingly.

Dardis turned away. "Hell," he whispered. "Some days it just doesn't seem worth . . ." His words trailed off as he shook his head and stepped a little to the right, directly in line with a window that looked out over the downtown square. Rain spattered against the glass in dreary blurred slashes and for a moment it looked to Ken as if Dardis was standing on the other side of the window, head lowered, hands balled into fists, getting soaked to the marrow and listening as the staccato rhythm of the downpour against the sidewalk underscored the constricting chaos of his life. Dardis lifted a slightly trembling hand to massage his temple and in that moment, because of that simple, lonely-looking gesture, try as he did not to, Ken Willis saw the

whole of his editor's existence: The silent house where the only
things awaiting his return were bitter memories, a still, voiceless
child who sat unnoticing of him, a refrigerator that was full of
microwave dinners because he couldn't cook worth shit, and a
television set that was probably constantly on because he couldn't
stand the quiet. Did the scent of his wife's perfume still linger on
some of the pillows and sheets because he couldn't bring himself
to wash her fragrance out of them? Were some of her clothes still
hanging next to his own in the closet? Did he sometimes touch
them to remind himself that she'd been real, maybe pinch the
sleeve of an abandoned dress and try to remember the last time
she'd worn it?

(. . . *some infinitely gentle/Infinitely suffering thing* . . .)

Ken apologized for his unprofessional behavior and agreed to
go to the Altman. Dardis thanked him (something else the man
was not famous for) said good-night, then left for his house that
once was called home.

Thirty minutes later Ken found himself standing at the
entrance to the Altman Museum. The wind had changed direction, throwing the sleet directly into his face, soaking through his
coat and skin seemingly down to his marrow—but he was already
shuddering from more than the cold.

There was a security speaker next to the door. Ken pressed
the button.

"Yes?" said a soft voice through layers of static.

"Ken Willis from the Cedar Hill *Ally*."

"Ah. You're a bit early, aren't you?"

"I'm also cold, wet, and grumpy, but we're not here to discuss
my dreadful personality problems." He was too rattled to be cour-
teous. Unable to stop his hands from shaking, he jammed them
deep into his pockets and looked out toward the street, momen-
tarily losing himself in the slick, cold sheen given the asphalt by
the sleet. He wanted to be somewhere dark and warm and lonely
and safe where he could think about his parents and how much
he wanted to hold their hands one last time and talk to them
about all the things left unspoken and unresolved between them.

(*Just to help your mother's nerves, Ken, that's all. She's all worried
about the crime in the area lately, and what with her not being able to
move around like she used to . . . well, the gun would make her feel
better.*)

The voice from the speaker said, "I'll need a few more minutes, Mr. Willis."

"Look, I apologize for being early, but are you going to let me in or not? If not, then you can find the number of the Columbus *Dispatch* in the business pages. G'night."

The doors buzzed open and he quickly stepped inside. Dark silence enfolded him as he slipped through the foyer and into a long corridor. A door opened at the far end, creating a glowing archway of light that silhouetted a robed scarecrow.

"I'm pleased you could make it, Mr. Willis. I would apologize for the inconvenience but as a newspaper reporter I'm sure you understand that timeliness is everything."

"Second lesson of Journalism 101. It comes right after 'Never Scratch Your Ass With the Sharp End of the Pencil.'"

The figure chuckled softly. "I'm glad to see you haven't lost that sarcastic edge. I—whoa! Hello."

Something pushed past the figure, moving low and stealthily. Light spilling from the opened door made broken glissandos over its form.

The roll of powerful shoulders.

The arch of an ebony back.

The swish of a tail.

And glittering jade pinpoints that soon resolved into a pair of large green eyes.

With an almost inaudible *click!* of its claws against the marble floor, the sleek black leopard stopped less than a foot away from Ken, glaring.

His mouth went desert-dry. The tissue connecting his muscles turned instantaneously into bone. He had walked right into the middle of something really awfully seriously damn scary.

The leopard snarled, curling back its upper lip.

Everything faded away; all Ken could see were those powerful jaws and gleaming teeth.

"Scheherazade!" called the scarecrow. The leopard closed its mouth, then leaned forward, pressed its nose against Ken's hand, and sniffed twice.

"Remain still, Mr. Willis."

"No kidding."

The leopard pulled back and cocked its head to the side as if trying to decide which limb to sample first.

"He's okay," said the scarecrow. Scheherazade sauntered forward and began rubbing her face against Ken's leg, purring contentedly.

"She likes you. She doesn't usually give rubbies to strangers." The scarecrow reached for a light switch, then paused. "I want you to know that I am deeply sorry for your recent loss, Mr. Willis."

Ken swallowed. Once. Very hard. Odd, how a year's distance could still deem a death *recent.* "Thank you."

The scarecrow moved forward into the light that spilled from the doorway of an adjacent room. He wore a long, heavy robe and walked with a pair of metal arm crutches.

Ken felt his breath catch in his throat.

At first he had thought the man to be gaunt, but *lithe* was actually more precise. There was an almost ancient grace to him, despite the way he shuffled along with the crutches. Long, brilliant white hair hung about his shoulders like layers of silk. It was impossible to tell the man's age from his face—his strange, *lovely* (that was the only word Ken could think of) face.

The black leopard raised its head and licked Ken's left hand a few times.

"I need to ask you a question, Mr. Willis."

"If I give the right answer, will you call her off?" asked Ken, nodding down toward Scheherazade.

"Of course. Here is my question: Have you been drinking tonight?"

"No."

"Are you on any prescription medications that might impair your mental faculties?"

"You said one question."

"Please answer me."

"No, no drinking, no medication, no grass, no ecstasy, nothing. I'm about as stone-cold sober as I've ever been."

The figure smiled. "Good."

"Why do you ask?"

"Because it's important that you believe what your eyes are going to see." The man locked his gaze with the leopard's, and Scheherazade turned away and began slowly walking through the slashes of light coming from the other room.

"Watch her closely, Mr. Willis."

Ken watched as the leopard passed through the alternating light- and shadow-slashes: in the light, the same sleek black leopard that had scared him half to death; in the shadow, darker movement; in the light, she pushed off on her front paws and rose up, walking on her back legs; in the shadow, her darker movements became more awkward; in the light again she became something part leopard, part something else, more graceful than before, on ballerina's legs; in the shadow, that grace became liquid; and finally, in the last slash of light, a staggeringly beautiful woman, wrapped in translucent veils, her bronze skin shimmering as she turned to face the man gawking at her in the corridor. She smiled, blew him a kiss, then glided through another doorway to someplace unseen.

"Do you have any doubt about what you've just seen?" asked the scarecrow.

". . . wh-what . . . what the hell is going on here?" Ken's legs felt as if they were going to dissolve into cotton.

"Curious that you'd use that particular word—'hell,' I mean. I've always thought that—oh, my, you look like you need to sit down."

"Before I pass out, please, yes."

The man guided Ken into a different room off the corridor, this one containing two wing-backed chairs that sat facing a fireplace where warm flames beckoned. Between the two chairs was an antique table. The figure helped Ken into one of the chairs, then seated himself in the other. A few moments later Scheherazade entered, carrying a silver tray. She was beyond stunning—and undeniably human. She once again smiled at Ken, then set the tray onto the table and proceeded to pour Ken a steaming cup of hot chocolate. He was too numb to refuse. He sipped at it for a moment, found it to be not too hot, then took a good swallow before setting the cup and saucer onto the tray.

"Who are you?"

The figure stared at him for a moment. "Actually, 'what' would be more precise in this case, Mr. Willis."

Ken rubbed his eyes. "Fine—*what* are you?"

"I am an angel, sir."

Ken looked at the man, nodded his head once, then rose to his feet and said, "Have a nice evening."

He picked up his bag and turned to leave.

He was no longer in the same room; in fact, he was no longer in the museum.

He was standing in the living room of his parents' home as it had been almost a year ago to the day; there was his father's favorite chair, his mother's collection of knickknacks, what-nots, and thingamajigs that cluttered the mantel above the fireplace, and, of course, the hospital bed that Dad had rented for Mom, since she was no longer able to go up the stairs. This was one of her good days because she was up and in the kitchen, fixing some fruit salad. On days like this, she could go without having to use the oxygen for a couple of hours at a time, and it was easy for them to pretend that she was going to be All Right, that she'd be Up and At 'Em in no time . . . but her emphysema was now so advanced that it was only a matter of time, and on days like this Ken could see that knowledge in her eyes, so sad and frightened and—more often than not—betraying the pain of her every breath, which she did her best to hide from her son and husband. And here he stood, the gun in its box along with a fully loaded clip, handing it to his father and suspecting somewhere in the back of his mind that this was not, repeat *not* a good idea, but Dad had said that it would make Mom feel safer, and there *was* a lot of trouble in the area lately but they'd refused to move despite how much Ken had begged them to, and now Dad was taking the gun from him and Ken suddenly realized that this wasn't happening, not really, no, because he was in a room at the Altman Museum in downtown Cedar Hill, talking to some nut-case who thought he was—

—he turned around again, blinking, and found himself back in the room.

The man in the chair simply stared at him. "Did that do the trick for you, or do I need to show you more?"

Ken rubbed his face to make sure his flesh was still real. "You're telling me you did that?"

"Yes."

"I don't believe you."

The man laughed softly, without humor. "Somehow, I didn't think you would."

Then came another voice, familiar: "Kenny?"

Mom?

Ken turned slowly around this time to see both his parents standing behind him, looking as they had when he'd found them three days after giving Dad the gun; the huge holes in the sides of their heads from where the bullets had exited still seeped with exploded tissue and blood so black it looked almost like oil.

"*Kenny*. . ." whispered his mother, reaching for his hand.

Ken cried out and stumbled backward, tripping over the leg of a chair and spinning as he fell, landing on hands and knees and feeling a scream pulling itself to life from somewhere deep in his core, but then the man in the chair was kneeling beside him, placing a cool, strong hand against the back of Ken's head, and the fear and horror and revulsion and confusion were gone.

Just like *that*.

Ken tried to stand, couldn't, and so simply plopped down on his ass right in front of the fire.

The man in the robe stood over him for a moment, then returned to his chair. "*Please* tell me that was enough to do it for you. I loathe these types of parlor tricks, but sometimes one has to do what one has to do in order to make one's point." He leaned forward. "Do you believe me now?"

". . . yes . . ."

"You're not just saying that?"

". . . no . . ."

"You believe everything you've seen? You believe now that I am what I say I am?"

". . . *yes* . . ."

"Good. That's one obstacle."

Ken wiped his eyes and blew his nose, swallowing painfully. "You mean this gets better?"

"You've not asked my name."

"Yes I did."

"No—you asked me, 'Who are you?' Close, yes, but not a direct inquiry. Before we go any further, you must ask me my name."

"Why?"

The man exhaled impatiently. "Because it's one of the terms of my sentence. I cannot offer my name, you have to ask."

"Fine, fine, whatever: What's your name?"

The man smiled widely, radiantly, and held out his hand. "My name is Lucifer. Pleased to meet you."

Ken stared at the offered hand but did not take it.

"I really do wish you'd shake my hand," said Lucifer.

"Deal with the Devil time, is it?"

Lucifer threw his hands up in the air and said, "Oh, shit! Not you, too! Look, pal, let's get something straight right now—I am not 'the Devil,' nor am I 'Satan' nor 'Beelzebub' nor any one of a million different names that have been assigned to me over the eons. Those names and the figures with whom they are associated are . . . what to call them? *Variations* of me, given a sad form of truth by people simply believing that's the way it is. Look at me! Do you see a forked tail? Cloven hooves? Am I trying to shove a red-hot pitchfork up your ying-yang? *No!* I am simply Lucifer, and I *am* an angel—a little fact that people continuously overlook." He thrust out his hand again. "I am not trying to buy your soul, pal, I am, believe it or not, trying to save it."

"*Huh?*"

"You heard me."

Ken shook his head. "I don't get it. I mean . . . you *do* come from Hell, right?"

Lucifer sighed and sat down in the chair. "Yes, I come from Hell—but not Hell as you've come to believe in it. There are two aspects to Hell, my friend: one is *where* it is, the other is *what* it is. Where it is, is the north side of the Third Heaven."

"Hell is part of heaven?"

Lucifer nodded. "And ain't that a kick in the parts? Yet people continue to believe a bunch of tall tales written thousands of years ago by a bunch of half-assed zealots who were only interested in promoting their own brand of spirituality. The mind boggles."

Then: "Of course, that's all my fault, so I don't have a lot of room to complain."

Ken managed to get himself back in his chair. "Please make me understand all of this. Please."

Lucifer looked at him, then once more offered his hand. "Please shake my hand. It's been so long since I've felt a friendly handshake I've forgotten what it feels like. You're not sealing your fate by doing it, you're not striking any sort of black bargain with the Prince of Darkness, you're simply shaking my hand, that's all."

Ken considered everything for a moment, and then, a bit hesitantly at first, reached out and took his hand.

As handshakes went, it was a good one, strong and friendly.

Lucifer smiled as he pulled his hand away, and wiped a tear from his eye. "Thank you, Ken. Thank you very much."

Ken poured himself another cup of hot chocolate, took a couple of sips, then sat back and said, "You said there were two aspects to Hell. You've told me where it is; how about telling me what it is?"

Lucifer rubbed his eyes and sighed. "The whole story, in specific detail, would take about five years to tell, so I hope you won't be offended by the Cliff's Notes version."

"Not at all," Ken replied, removing his micro-cassette recorder from the bag and firing it up.

Lucifer pointed to it and said, "That's a joke, right?"

"Uh, no, not really."

"Save yourself the trouble, Ken. Despite what William Peter Blatty portrayed in *The Exorcist*—good movie, but the book's better—my voice cannot be recorded. Nor can I be photographed. So sit back and have yourself a little listen.

"Okay. The part about me gathering up an army and trying to overthrow God, that's pretty much true. Except I wasn't trying to stage a *coup*, so much as I was trying to get God's attention. He and many of the angels had a strong disagreement about the Book of Forbidden Knowledge. Understand this: everyone in heaven was 100 percent behind God's creating humankind. Overall, a winner, that. So much potential there. But God has great patience; many of the angels did not. We wanted to sort of give humankind a little edge, so to speak, by gifting them with the Forbidden Knowledge."

"What exactly *is* this Forbidden Knowledge?"

"The casting and resolving of enchantments—what has come to be known as Modern Medicine, the knowledge of the clouds, the science of the constellations, how to make knives and swords and devise ornaments, tinctures for the beautifying of women, the course of the moon, the signs of the sun, the ability to express ideas through Art, how to fashion the weapons of war, the craft of writing—which, when you come to think of it, is sort of ironic, because without the Knowledge of Writing, there never would have been a Bible, and without the Bible there would have been no tome upon which to base Christianity, but I digress.

"You see, the idea was that, as humankind moved toward realizing its potential, bits and pieces of the Forbidden Knowledge—that which would best serve humankind's purpose—would be doled out as it was needed, until your race had reached a point where it could obtain and use the rest of this knowledge on its own. You were designed to be a clever people, so it would only be a matter of time before you figured most of this out for yourselves. And before you ask: the reason it was Forbidden was because to have gifted humankind with all this Knowledge right out of the gate would create a great spiritual chaos that would leave God with only one of two choices: un-make humankind and the universe and start over from scratch, or let it be and see what happens.

"Okay, so then, I round up my army and we steal the Forbidden Knowledge and give it to humankind and God gets really pissed and gives us a swift kick in our celestial asses and sends us all to Hell, and because the whole thing was my idea, I get to rule the place. I also get all the blame . . . which, as the eons go by, I have less of a problem with."

Ken lifted his hand. "Can I ask you something?"

"Go ahead."

"Where does evil come from, then?"

"From my actions that day in heaven. I did not create Evil, but I damn sure *caused* it."

"I'm not sure I—"

Lucifer waved his hand, silencing Ken. "Do you remember when you were a kid and you went out to your uncle's farm to stay one summer?"

Ken smiled. "Yeah! That was one of the best summers of my life."

"Except for killing that bird."

Ken froze. His eyes grew wide. "Oh, my God . . . I'd forgotten all about that."

Lucifer nodded. "Your cousin had gotten a set of boomerangs for his birthday, and the two of you were out in the field tossing them. Remember how the thing would soar up and away from you, spinning and spinning so fast and powerfully?"

". . . yes . . ."

"And remember how, after you got really good at it, you gave yours a really good throw and it sliced up into the air—"

"—and then this big, beautiful bird flew right into its path and the damn boomerang took its head off. God—I cried for hours afterward."

Lucifer nodded in sympathy. "Well, Evil works the same way. Follow me on this: My giving all of the Forbidden Knowledge to humankind was the equivalent of your throwing that boomerang. Once it was out of your hands and in the air, you could not control what happened because of the action. It's the same with me and the Forbidden Knowledge; once I gave it to humankind, I couldn't control what happened with it. Your boomerang only killed a bird—quickly and painlessly, you should know, it never felt a thing; mine, on the other hand, birthed spiritual chaos and resulted in the Knowledge being used in ways it was never intended to be used: in short, my spinning boomerang caused— and still causes—Evil. I know this is all a bit simplistic, but it's the best I can do in the time I'm allotted here."

"You on some sort of schedule?"

"Yes, as a matter of fact. I need to answer your second question now: *What* is Hell?

"Hell, my dear Ken, is complete, focused, crystal-clear knowledge of the wrongs you have committed, and total realization of the consequences of your actions upon others. And it *never goes away*. Not for one second. You have a conscience unlike any you've ever known before, you are agonizingly aware of the hurt you've caused, of the misery and pain and suffering, and you know how terrible it is, and you are alone with this wisdom, and you are powerless to do anything to change it. Do you have any idea how many times I've begged God to at least let me *experience* some of this pain and misery? To share it along with those who suffer? But that's also part of what Hell is—Knowledge, Realization, Isolation—and no way in which to punish yourself so you might feel that you're paying some form of penance."

Tears of rage and sorrow glistened in Lucifer's eyes. "And that is why I am the guardian angel of Pain and Misery and Suffering. The boomerang is out there, spinning through the universe, causing Evil, and I am responsible, and there is nothing I can do to take it back. He wiped his eyes.

"But God is not completely without sympathy for me, which only goes to prove what an OK guy He really is. I miss His company every day. But you pays your money, you takes your chances. Anyway, every so often I am allowed to walk among humankind for a limited amount of time and do what I can to ease some of the suffering that my actions have caused. I can't

do anything big, mind you—cure diseases, stop natural disas-
ters—but I *can* help people on an individual basis. How many
individuals I can help depends on the method I choose and
whether or not I can find people who are willing to help me."

"What do you mean by 'help'?"

"I cannot bring back those who have died or been murdered, I
can't take away cancer or make a missing limb grow back, but what
I can do is give them a certain measure of inner peace. It does
nothing to ease my own conscience, just so you know—only God
can lift that particular sadness from me, and that's not going to
happen anytime soon. But I can help. I want to help. I *have* to,
Ken; this whole damned mess is my fault." He leaned forward
again. "The method I have chosen this time is Art, and the person
I'm asking to help me is you. I'm sorry about your mother's sick-
ness and your father's depression and what happened after you
gave them that gun. That was all my fault, and I do not expect you
to forgive me—it wouldn't do any good, anyway. Forgiveness
lessens one's burden, and mine shall never be so."

Ken thought about it for a moment, then asked: "Why me?"

"Because you can reach people with your words. You use the
Forbidden Knowledge of Writing the way in which it was
intended to be used. But you also suffer from one of the most
obscene after-effects of my actions: Guilt. I can take it away, if
you'll let me."

Ken shook his head. "No, you can't. Look, I *knew*, on some
level, why Dad wanted me to buy that gun. They were running out
of money, Mom was in constant pain and was going to die soon,
anyway, and God knows he was useless without her—'She's my
heart and my life,' he used to say—and I . . . I just *knew*, that's all.
And I helped. As a kid I threw a boomerang; as an adult I handed
him that box with the gun and bullets in it. It's all the same."

Lucifer rose from his chair and gestured for Ken to follow him.

Lucifer led him to a set of large oak doors and placed his
hands on the door handles. "I would advise you to take a deep
breath and let it out very slowly, Ken."

Scheherazade came by and took Ken's bag from him, then
kissed his cheek and went away.

Ken pointed in her direction. "Is she—?"

"One of the Fallen Angels who joined me that day, yes.
'Scheherazade' is not her real name, though."

"What is it?"

Lucifer grinned. "To quote Leonard Nimoy as Mr. Spock on *Star Trek*: 'You wouldn't be able to pronounce it.'"

Lucifer threw open the doors and they stepped into the room.

What lay on the other side was beyond astonishing.

Unable to absorb all of it at once (and, *God*, there was so much here, so many sculptures and paintings and things he could never hope to describe), Ken closed his eyes, swallowed, took a deep breath, and looked to his right.

He saw alternating rows of books and video monitors that reached from floor to ceiling, just as they did on the other side of the room. The books were old, leather-bound tomes, twice the size of an encyclopedia; stamped on their spines in gold were words and sygils he couldn't understand. The ancient smell wafting from them filled the air.

The banks of video monitors were all turned on, each screen displaying different images and scenarios: Spring-greened fields; animals giving birth; scenes of war that shook and jerked from side to side because whoever was filming them was unable to hold the camera still; an empty playground; a pair of gloves lying on a sand dune; silently screaming faces, some streaked with blood; children playing; old folks dying; homeless ones begging for money from passing strangers who would not look at them; couples making love; people in uniforms torturing prisoners; babies being murdered by their parents; priests celebrating Mass; bright fireworks over rivers; political assassinations; roses in bloom; wedding photographs; mangled bodies littering bomb-blasted streets—

—Ken had to look away.

The next thing he saw was a series of sharply defined beams of moonlight that bled down into the room from the far side. Looking toward their source, he saw that the upper half of the back wall and a large section of the ceiling had been replaced with greenhouse windows. The cold, incandescent moon was centered above these windows as if it were part of the display. Ken focused on one of the moonbeams and followed its path with his gaze to a pair of tubercular torsos encased in bulky lucite squares sitting atop large, ersatz-Roman columns. Looking past them he saw gigantic tumors that squatted in fossilized silence, syphilitic skulls staring out from glass cases, infected eyes and rows of malformed infants floating in chemical-filled glass coffins, the corpse of a man whose tissue connecting his muscles had turned to bone, a woman whose mouth was open as if in her last moments she had been calling out the name of some long-lost love.

He moved past these sculptures (if indeed they *were* sculptures) and stopped in front of a piece depicting a baby born with no cranium. It lay nestled on a bed of cotton in a large glass case filled to the brim with a clear, thick liquid. The baby's skin was ghostly white. It sat in a semi-upright position, legs bent at the knees, feet horizontal, arms thrust straight out from the elbows as if resting on the arms of a chair or throne; a wise old sage waiting for truth-seekers to approach. Extra cotton packed behind its ears and around its neck kept its head from lolling too far forward or to either side; only the closest scrutiny could detect the thin, clear wire that ran down from the center of the lid into the case, snaking through the layers of cotton, emerging with small metal hooks on its end that was attached to a catch protruding from the back of the baby's skull.

"What is this?" he asked, barely getting the words out.

"Ken Willis," replied Lucifer, "say hello to Guilt, in the flesh, so to speak."

Ken reached out and placed a hand atop the case—

—and Guilt opened its eyes and looked at him.

It was as if its gaze seeped down into his core and spread through him like the first cool drink on a hot summer's day: an ice-bird spreading chill wings that pressed against his lungs and bones until Ken was flung wide open, dizzy and disoriented, seized by a whirling vortex and spun around, around, around in a whirl, spiraling higher, thrust into the heart of all Creation's whirling invisibilities, a creature whose puny carbon atoms and other transient substances were suddenly freed, unbound, scattered amidst the universe—yet each particle still held strong to the immeasurable, unseen thread that linked it inexorably to his soul and consciousness and, most importantly, his conscience; twirling fibers of light wound themselves around impossibly fragile, molecule-thin membranes of memory and moments that swam toward him like proud children coming back to shore after their very first time in the water alone, and when they reached him, when these memories and moments emerged from the sea and reached out for him, they wore the faces of his parents, finally at peace, not condemned, happy and healthy at last in the place they had found waiting on the other side of this life, and Ken ran toward them, arms open wide, meeting them on windswept beaches of thought, embracing them, accepting them, absorbing them, becoming Many, becoming Few, becoming One, knowing, learning, feeling; his blood mingled with their blood, his thoughts with their thoughts, dreams with dreams, hopes with hopes, frustrations with frustrations, and in this mingling, in this unity, in this actualization, he felt their peace and their love for him, and when they kissed him and whispered, "Shhh, there, there, it's all right, it wasn't your fault, not at all, God didn't condemn us, He knows that there's only so much pain people can endure before they can't take any more, we love you, Kenny, we love you, it's all right . . ." Ken felt the sadness and guilt being lifted from his eyes and soul, and he felt more alive and complete and purposeful than he had in years, and then—

—then he felt himself being wrenched backward, down through the ages, through the infinite allness of want and desire and isolation and dreams, raw with pain yet drenched in wonder, and he stretched himself under the weight of this knowing, this peace, his eyes staring toward the truth that was his cleansed soul, his whole body becoming involved in drawing it back into himself in one breath, and in the moment before he came away whole, clean, and filled with glory, in the millisecond before he found himself once again standing before the strange baby who was Guilt made flesh, in that brief instant of eternity that revealed itself to him just this once before his final metamorphosis took place, he told his parents how much he loved and missed them and they, in turn, told him they would always be there, watching over him, they were just fine now, and they were waiting for him to join them.

Someday.

A long time coming.

For he had a life ahead of him.

Ken fell on hands and knees and the last of it coursed through him, feeling whole and clean and forgiven.

"Now how's *that* for a parlor trick?' said Lucifer.

Ken looked up to see that Lucifer had removed his robe and was working on the elaborate brace that covered his entire torso.

"They . . . they *thanked* me," Ken choked out.

"Of course they did. You didn't help kill them, Ken; you enabled them to escape their suffering."

". . . th-thank you . . . thank you . . ."

Lucifer shook his head as he worked free another set of straps. "Thank yourself. You were a good and true and a loving son. Now you can mourn them without guilt and live a happy life without feeling you don't deserve to." A surge of light rippled behind him as the brace fell away, rising higher and becoming brighter on both sides of his body, a rainbow of pastel colors that shimmered and gleamed. These light-growths grew wider and brighter still, the colors all fusing into one as Lucifer flexed the muscles in shoulders and the brace fell away and his wings spread out from wall to wall.

"That's much better," he sighed, then moved his wings and began to rise.

Lucifer's wings were the most beautiful things Ken had ever seen, thick with layers upon layers of rich, tawny, curving golden feathers that rustled ever so slightly as they moved, lifting the Guardian Angel of Misery and Pain higher.

It was only as Lucifer soared far above his head that Ken saw the configuration of the feathers formed faces.

Faces filled with sorrow, pain, misery, loneliness.

"It will happen like this," called Lucifer as he hovered above the massive work of art that took up the entire room. "You will write of this place, and people will read it. And, one by one, they'll find their way here. People who thought they had no interest in ever going to a museum will read your words and feel compelled to come here for reasons they won't be able to articulate. And they will enter this room and they, like you, will see what they need to see in order to lighten their burdens. They will come here, and they will see, and in the seeing, the sadness will be lifted from their eyes and they will leave here feeling renewed, peaceful, forgiven.

"Whole and healthy and alive.

"I *have* to do this, Ken, and I need your help." Lucifer then descended, folded his majestic wings behind him, and offered his hand to Ken.

"Will you help me, Ken Willis?"

Ken took hold of Lucifer's hand. "It would be an honor, sir."

"Congratulations: You've just made a deal with the Devil."

Ken blanched.

"I'm kidding," said Lucifer, smiling. "Remind me to help you work on your sense of humor. Come on, then; we should get started."

String of Pearls

Bonnie Jeanne Perry

*C*leary McDonald *loved to dance.*

And she wished she were dancing right now instead of looking up at the Celtic cross on top of the brown shingle church.

Whoever said "Confession is good for the soul" couldn't have been raised in an Irish household, Cleary thought as she counted off the front steps leading to Saint Lawrence O'Toole's Church.

One step for God the Father . . .

One step for God the Son . . .

And the third step for God the Holy Spirit.

Cleary squinted at the Northern California sun, enjoying the warmth on her neck and wishing that she were anywhere but about to enter a dark confessional. But Saturday in the McDonald family meant 3:00 confession just as Sunday meant 10:00 Mass and Holy Communion.

The McDonalds were praying for victory in Europe and the South Pacific. *World War II changed everything,* she thought. *Nothing's ever going to be the same again.*

299

The war effort came first on the homefront. Everywhere she went Cleary was reminded of that. Gasoline and tires were rationed. So were shoes.

No need looking down at the ugly brown oxfords she wore. There'd be no new shoes for her *again* this year. The McDonalds pooled their shoe rationing stamps. They had to. Harry, her nine-year-old brother, seemed to outgrow *his* shoes every three months.

And poor Daddy's cigarettes were rationed, too. Mama had to stand in a long line for one carton. Grandma stood in line at Hanrahan's Butcher Shop.

There were lines for everything. Coffee. Sugar. Even stockings . . . when they were available. Mama had resorted to leg makeup. Rationing had become a way of life in Oakland, California, since Pearl Harbor. The "make do with what you have" motto was heard everywhere from the grocery store to the Sunday pulpit. And the McDonalds, like the rest of the nation, were standing with President Roosevelt supporting the war effort.

Prayer was an important part of that effort. The family asked the angels, especially the guardian angels, to watch over *all* of the service men and women.

A collective prayer of *Deo gratias* echoed from the McDonald house when Victory Mail arrived from Cleary's older brother, Ian, who was a sailor aboard a flat top somewhere in the South Pacific. And another prayer of thanks filled the house when V-Mail came from Mama's brother, Uncle Jack, who was aboard a heavy cruiser in the South Pacific, too. But all mention of their exact location was never mentioned. Even comments about the weather aboard ship were actually cut from their letters.

The rosary was recited every Friday evening in the McDonald parlor. Three generations lived in the white, clapboard house on Quigley Street. Grandma and Grandpa McDonald were usually the first to take their places opposite the trio of Victorian windows. Young Harry would be the last to arrive. Mama would kneel beside her chair, head bowed, fingering her beads until Harry squeezed between Grandma and Grandpa. Daddy would be there, too, although his curly head never seemed to bow quite as deeply as Mama's. Michael "Harp" McDonald always looked uncomfortable on his bony knees. Grandma would say Uncle Jack's name. Then Ian's. After each name, Cleary would say, "Protect him, O Lord."

Then Grandma recited each name of the neighborhood boys fighting overseas.

"Good afternoon, Cleary Catherine."

Cleary recognized the lilt of Father Duggan's Kilkenny brogue and turned toward the sound. "Good afternoon, Father." She gave a slight dip of her knee to the youngest of the three parish priests. And the handsomest.

She bit her lip.

There's another sin to add to your confession, she thought, and quickly dipped her hand into the holy water fount for an added blessing.

"Here for confession, are you?" Father Duggan held open the tall church door for her.

"Yes, Father. Thank you, Father," she stammered before stepping into the darkness of the church. She was relieved to see the young priest heading to the rectory next door.

"Thank you, Lord," she whispered. "I just couldn't confess to Father Duggan today."

Ten years of parochial school had taught Cleary the value of prayer. She prayed hard every day for the war effort. She'd been praying a lot lately, especially now that May had arrived. May, the month dedicated to the Blessed Virgin. The month of roses and sweet peas. The scent of May roses filled the church.

But May roses weren't on Cleary's mind. May was the month of Saint Mary's College High School's Senior Prom. Cleary just had to go to the prom. Since January first, she'd prayed that her prom date would be Tony Bischeri.

Closing her eyes, Cleary prayed: "Angel of God, my guardian dear. To whom His love commits me here. Ever this day be at my side. To light and guard, to rule and guide. Amen."

The leather heels of her oxfords clicked as she turned toward the dim alcove to the right. A stained glass window, ringed with green shamrocks and Celtic knots, glowed with natural sunlight. Round as the silver guardian angel's medal she always wore around her neck, the window depicted a willowy, winged angel with arms outstretched, hovering behind a small boy and girl crossing a narrow stone bridge.

The inscription below the window was printed in Gallic script: *In loving memory of Ellen Cleary McDonald from her children, grandchildren, and great-grandchildren.*

"My McDonald," Cleary spoke the name she'd given her great-grandmother. She knelt before the window remembering how they'd sing "Old McDonald had a farm . . ."

The serene face of the window's Guardian Angel took on the look of the feisty woman with the knot of alabaster hair. A woman who had been dead these last five years, but remained alive in Cleary's heart. She searched the pocket of her cotton dress for the pennies she'd saved for the votive candle.

"You are my Guardian Angel, aren't you, My McDonald?"

A wisp of air brushed Cleary's cheek.

And who else might be taking the job? My McDonald whispered.

"No one but you," Cleary mused. "I've been writing in my angel journal even though I'm no angel."

And myself will vouch for that. Such thoughts about Father Duggan.

"I'm sorry. But I've managed to list five things to be thankful for in my journal every night before I go to bed."

And 'tis a splendid job you've done with the paste, too. Putting all those angel faces on the cover of your journal.

"I cut the pictures from the church bulletins," Cleary bragged.

If the only prayer you ever say is thank you . . . it will be enough.

Clink, clink, clink, clink went the copper pennies into the donation slot. Cleary took a wooden match from the brass box and struck it. The match blazed blue and orange before she touched it to the waxed wick. The votive candle glowed in its red glass cup while she blew out the match and buried it in the sand beneath the bank of candles.

"It's not such a big sin to pray for a prom date, is it, My McDonald?" Cleary closed her eyes and imagined swaying to her favorite song—"String of Pearls."

'Tis no great sin. But 'tis nothing to be bragging about in church either, I'm thinking.

"Oh, My McDonald, could you . . . just this once . . . ?"

And do you think I have nothing better to do than see to your dancing, girl?

Sweetly chastised, Cleary bowed her head. But she was still thinking about dancing. Dancing to the haunting melody of Glenn Miller's music. To dance with Tony. To feel his arms about her. To see his smile shining down at her. Tony with his black curly hair and teddy bear brown eyes.

She'd seen him emerging from the boys' locker room after a basketball game, his black hair still damp from a shower. He'd waved to her. She'd said something real stupid like "Nice game."

He'd walked along behind her carrying the zipper bag containing his basketball uniform and towel. He shortened his strides when he caught up with her and walked step-for-step beside her.

They walked together out of the gym; his hand brushed hers. Her heart raced in double time until she knew Tony must've heard it.

The touch of his hand against hers happened too many times to be accidental. And yet, Tony never seemed to notice the touching. Out of the corner of her eye, she looked at him, straining to catch her breath. She had to concentrate on the simplest things.

Like walking.

And talking.

And breathing.

"The prom. With Tony. Please, My McDonald. I know you're watching out for Ian and Uncle Jack. But this is the last dance of the school year. And Tony is turning eighteen next month. . ." She slammed her eyes closed, trying not to think of where he might be next year at this time.

The half door to the confessional opened and a gray-haired lady, wearing a black hat stepped out. It was Mrs. Haban. Her twin sons, Marvin and Mellon, were overseas. Marines. But Mrs. Haban didn't notice Cleary. With her palms pressed together, Mrs. Haban marched her way to the altar to say her penance.

Cleary checked the black and white framed name on the middle confessional door. "Father Hennessey. Whew. Thank you, My McDonald."

So, still selecting the right priest, are you?

"He's handy."

And why aren't you lining up on the other side? It would seem Pastor O'Connell has not a soul waiting.

Cleary never went to confession with Pastor O'Connell. None of the kids did, especially if your sin was an "impure" one. She took Mrs. Haban's place inside the confessional. The sliding "speakeasy" door opened. In the filtered light, she could make out the profile of the assistant pastor. Father Hennessey was known for his light penances. In fact, by this time of day, he'd usually be nodding off.

Cleary made the Sign of the Cross. "Bless me, Father, for I have sinned. It has been one week since my last confession. Now I tell my sins: I fought with my little brother three times; and argued with my mother." She speeded up, "had impure thoughts and talked back to my grandfather."

"For your penance, say three Our Fathers and two Hail Marys."

Whew. That was close, she thought. She'd managed to slide the "impure thoughts" part by Father Hennessey. Cleary began her Act of Contrition as Father cleared his throat.

"About those 'impure thoughts,'" Father said. "Perhaps we should explore them for a moment so we can take measures to avoid them."

If Cleary didn't know better she'd have thought Father Hennessey's cheeks were puffed in a grin. A Cheshire cat grin. "What? I mean. I thought I was finished, Father."

"How old are you, child?"

"Sixteen."

"And do you have a special young man?"

"Kind of," she answered, sheepishly.

"How old is he?"

"He'll be eighteen next month, Father."

"And he'll be off to the war soon, then won't he?"

"Yes, Father. The Marines. It's a family tradition. His father was a Marine. And his older brothers are . . ."

"Are what, child?"

Even in the murky shadows, Cleary could see Father Hennessey lean closer to the partition separating them. "His family isn't sure where one brother is."

"Then I'd say you'd best serve your young man by not including him in any 'impure thoughts' that might be crossing your mind." Father leaned closer still. "You have not acted on these—" He cleared his throat. "These thoughts of yours, have you?"

"No, Father."

"But you did take pleasure in them?"

"Sometimes."

"Most of the times?"

Cleary bowed her head. "Yes."

"Sometimes it's very difficult to keep such thoughts out of your head when you care a lot for someone. Isn't it?"

"Yes, Father."

"Do not allow yourself to dwell on these thoughts. Go in peace and sin no more. Now continue your Act of Contrition." Father made the Sign of the Cross while saying the Latin words absolving Cleary of her sins.

"I am heartily sorry for all my sins. I firmly resolve to say my penance and amend my life. Amen." Cleary breathed a relieved sigh when the screen panel went black and she knew Father had closed the door.

Mrs. Haban was still kneeling at the altar rail, praying when Cleary took her place at the rail. She said her penance and left by the side door. Mrs. Haban was still praying.

A small alley, one car wide, ran between the church and rectory. Strips of concrete bordered a narrow line of gravel running all the way to the front sidewalk. Usually, the driveway was empty. Not today. A white truck stood parked close to the hedge.

Cleary froze. The sign on the cab door read: *Bischeri & Sons Plumbing.*

The crunch of gravel behind her made her gasp.

"Cleary? Confessing some deep dark sin?"

She didn't bother to turn. She knew the voice. "And I bet *you* haven't been on your knees confessing, Tony Bischeri."

Tony stepped to the pickup and hoisted a tool box onto the flatbed and slammed the tailgate. He mopped his brow with a swipe of his forearm.

"The rectory's kitchen sink stopped up again. Dad is helping my uncle rip out some pipes for the sisters at Providence Hospital. So . . ." He spread his arms wide apart. "Here I am."

"And Pastor O'Connell's sink?"

Tony wiped his palms on the sides of his overalls. "Another satisfied customer of Bischeri and Sons." He opened the passenger door. "Can I give you a lift?"

She nodded, remembering the votive candle. She imagined the flickering red and gold candle and My McDonald's face. "Thank you."

"You're welcome. Wait," he said. "Let me get that." He reached in front of her to retrieve a faded Oakland Oaks baseball cap from the front seat.

He slapped on the cap before closing the truck door behind her. In an instant, he was sitting beside her, gunning the engine and backing the truck out of the rectory's driveway.

They made a left turn off High Street onto Quigley Street.

The drive home to 4018 was a short one. Only a block and a half. Today it seemed even shorter. Cleary wished she lived miles and miles away so there'd be an excuse for her and Tony to be together longer.

The truck passed house after house displaying a satin and gold fringed flag. The number of blue stars on the flag represented the number of loved ones serving in the war. And there were four flags with gold stars for loved ones who had died.

When the truck passed the Haban house, Tony took his foot off the accelerator.

The thirties bungalow with its patches of green grass looked exactly as it had the day Marvin and Mellon shipped out. They'd been so proud. So broad-shouldered in their Marine uniforms. Handsome, identical twins. They'd been All City on the Fremont High School Baseball Team. Saint Mary's College had talked to Mr. and Mrs. Haban about scholarships. Twin scholarships.

"I saw Mrs. Haban go into church," Tony said.

"I saw her, too. Praying," Cleary added.

"Have they heard anymore about Marvin and Mellon?"

Cleary shook her head. "Nothing. Not yet anyway."

"Always the hopeful one. You were praying for them, weren't you?"

A wave of guilt flashed over Cleary. She had said a small prayer for the Haban twins, but the bulk of her prayers were self-ish ones. Prayers for herself. For what *she* wanted.

Guardian Angel. My McDonald. Please bring Marvin and Mellon home safely so they can play baseball. Forget about that darned prom anyway. And take special care of Ian and Uncle Jack. Let there be a letter today, for Mama's sake. And Grandma's. And Daddy's, too. And if I don't get to go to the prom, I promise I won't be too jealous of Dolores DeTata and Tommy Dolan.

Amen! My McDonald whispered.

Tony turned the truck into the driveway next to the two-story Victorian house. Grandma and Grandpa's house towered over the bungalows lining Quigley Street. The house and the vacant lot next door were all that remained of the Quigley Farm.

Grandma's rose garden filled the square next to the front stairs and a Japanese Kadota Fig towered over the walk and lawn. Everyone enjoyed the figs except Grandpa. Since Pearl Harbor, he refused to eat anything Japanese even though figs had once been his favorite. Only Grandma's pleading stopped him from chopping down the ancient tree.

Tony turned off the engine. They sat silently. Not daring to look at one another. Minutes ticked by until Jeep, Grandpa's black and white Springer Spaniel, jumped up on Cleary's door and peered into the truck.

Jeep barked a welcome and wagged her stubby tail.

Cleary patted Jeep's head and quieted the barking. "I guess I should be going."

"Yeah. Me, too. I've got to swing by and get my dad. We're down to one truck, you know." His knuckles whitened as he gripped the steering wheel. He kept his eyes straight ahead, then suddenly jumped out of the truck to open her door.

"Thanks for the ride, Tony."

"Sure. Anytime. I was wondering. Are you going to be home later?"

"Yeah. I've got oodles of homework."

"On a weekend?"

"But I can finish it on Sunday night." As an after thought, she added: "Would you like to come for dinner? I can't say what we're having, but Grandma always seems to perform 'the miracle of the loaves and fishes' somehow."

"Are you sure your folks won't mind?" Tony asked.

"Daddy and Mama are working overtime at the shipyard. So I'm not certain who'll be home. Harry of course. He *never* misses a meal."

"That's what Mom says about me."

"Bring your appetite. And your sense of humor. We Irish can be a rowdy bunch."

"You should see the Italians!"

Cleary watched until Tony's truck disappeared. It was then she saw her grandmother hunched over a white rose bush. "Grandma? I didn't see you."

"I wonder why? Is it safe to move now? My back is killing me." She put a hand on her hip and groaned. "I didn't want to embarrass you."

"You'll never embarrass me." Cleary walked carefully between Grandma's prize roses so she could kiss Grandma's cheek.

"I'm not exactly dressed for company." She hoisted her slacks. Grandma only wore slacks when she was working in her roses or tending the victory garden growing in the vacant lot.

"I've been spreading manure," Grandma continued. "I'm not presentable. Your brother, Harry is going to catch it tonight. He rode off on his bike before gathering all the eggs this morning."

"Harry is scared of Beulah. She pecks him when he tries to snatch her eggs. I'll check the chickens."

"And did you ask Tony to dinner?"

Grandma never missed much. "I did. Are we having chicken?" Cleary really hoped there might be something else for dinner.

Grandma grinned. "I went to Hanrahan's today."

"And? Did you find a surprise in the sack when you came home?" Cleary's voice rose an octave.

"A pork roast. It's not big. But it's the prettiest thing. You get the applesauce from the basement."

"And could we have some of the apple slices you canned? The cinnamon ones?"

"We're having company, aren't we? Let's show him how we Irish do a pork roast. I'll make my raisin stuffing. And I just happened to make bread pudding this morning." Grandma picked up her shovel.

"I just love you, Grandma." Cleary gave her another big kiss.

"Well, get on with you, girl. We've got company coming."

GRANDMA SET OUT THE Sunday china. The blue and white Meissen plates had belonged to Cleary's My McDonald. They'd eat in the kitchen, as usual. There'd be only five. Cleary set the table herself. She even arranged yellow roses for the center of the table. The table cloth was a plain white everyday one.

"No need for linen tonight, is there, Cleary? After all, the Pope isn't coming," Grandma teased.

"No use scaring the lad," Grandpa added from behind his newspaper. He sat rocking in the corner of the country kitchen beside his radio.

"EVERYTHING WAS GREAT, MRS. McDonald," Tony said, drying the last of the dinner plates.

Grandpa rocked back in his chair. "Sure you got enough to eat?"

"Yes, sir." Tony stacked the last of the blue and white plates and folded the dish towel.

"President Roosevelt is speaking in thirty minutes," Grandpa said. "I'll be turning on the console radio in the parlor."

"Coming," Grandma said. Then to Cleary and Tony, "Grandpa never misses the president's fireside chats."

Minutes later, Tony and Cleary sat cross-legged on the carpet opposite the tall radio. Grandma and Grandpa sat in their chairs. Harry wiggled on the sofa, playing with a wooden airplane Grandpa had made. Harry twirled the propeller, making a roaring sound until Grandpa frowned.

Cleary imagined the president sitting in the oval office with his Scottish terrier, Fala, at his feet. She knew if she walked down Quigley Street tonight, the street would be deserted. And from behind the screened doors she would hear President Roosevelt's distinctive voice. As one, the forty-eight states listened.

"I ask you to join me in prayer," the president said. "Our sons, pride of our nation . . ."

Cleary thought of Tony sitting beside her. He'd be joining the fight soon. She thought of Ian. Her ruddy-cheeked, handsome brother. Full of teasing. And laughter. And Uncle Jack. The dark Irish, leggy one in the family.

"Their road will be long and hard," the president prayed. "Success may not come with rushing speed, but we shall return again and again; and we know that by Thy grace, and by the righteousness of our cause, our sons will triumph. They will be sore tried, by night and by day, without rest—until victory is won."

Cleary cringed. There hadn't been any word from Ian or Uncle Jack. Only an empty mailbox. And a house full of empty hearts.

No one sitting around the radio spoke. Even Harry stopped fiddling with his airplane. And when the president finished, Cleary and Tony stood up. Tony nodded to Grandma and Grandpa, mouthing a last "thank you."

"You're welcome, son. Anytime," Grandpa said. "It's a fine thing to have a pair of long legs under our kitchen table again."

Grandma mustered a weak smile. Cleary knew she was thinking about Uncle Jack and Ian.

They *all were*.

"Will you walk me to the truck, Cleary?"

The street was deserted. Not a dog barked. Not a child played anywhere on the block. They walked across the lawn before Tony stopped and took her hand. The evening breeze ruffled the fingered leaves of the giant fig tree. Tony squeezed her hand. His expression graver than before. His eyes dark. Serious.

"I've done something dumb, Cleary. Real dumb."

The pressure on her hand increased. "I don't understand. Is it one of your brothers?"

"No. No. They're fine as far as we know. You know I'm enlisting in the Marines, too. Right after graduation." He kicked a dirt clump at the base of the fig tree. "I'll be off to boot camp this summer. So that's why . . . why . . . I . . . I didn't think it was fair to date you now, Cleary."

"Date me?"

"But Sonny's wife. You remember Sonny. My big brother. Well, Helen, his wife, told me to tell you."

"What?"

"Didn't you ever wonder why I never asked you to a movie? Or out for an ice cream? Why I never stopped by your house before?"

She shrugged. "I didn't think you thought of me as a girl you'd want to—"

"I think of you *all* the time. Not just when we're together on the social committee at school. Or collecting for war bonds. When we work on the paper drives." The clump of dirt crashed into the tree trunk. "I even think of you in church when I should be praying for my brothers."

A puff of his breath smacked her cheek. He smelled like cinnamon apples and sunshine. And for the first time in her life, Cleary Catherine McDonald couldn't think of a single thing to say.

"Cleary, Saint Lawrence O'Tooles isn't even my parish. Why do you think I always come to your 10:00 mass?"

"I thought you wanted to see Dolores. All the boys—"

"DeTata? Tommy Dolan asked her to go steady last night." He raised Cleary's hand and, closing his eyes, he slowly rubbed her finger tips back and forth against his chin.

She felt the sparse whiskers beneath the cleft in his chin. She could smell the Old Spice he'd splashed on his face. "You mean it was me you wanted to see?"

His smile brightened like a thousand suns, when there was only a faint glimmer of stars in the sky. "It's always been *you*, Cleary. Ever since I saw you praying at the guardian angel window. The green stained glass is almost the color of your eyes." He worked his jaw. "Time's short for us now. Since Pearl Harbor. No telling what might happen. And hearing the president tonight. Being here with you."

"I know. Everything's changed. We have to grow up fast."

He swallowed and his Adam's apple went up and down twice. "Did I ever tell you I like your green eyes?"

She suddenly lost her ability to speak again and could only shake her head.

"I meant to tell you. So many times. But it's hard for a guy to say mushy things to a girl."

"It's hard for girls, too."

"And your smile. It's lopsided. I like lopsided smiles. The way you dip your chin and giggle when you're nervous. And when you look at me like you are right now . . . I'm a puddle."

He leaned down. And for an instant, she thought he was going to kiss her. His lips were so close. Almost touching hers.

"I'm not going to kiss you. Oh, I want to. But I want our first kiss to be on the night of the prom. You will go to the prom with me, won't you, Cleary?"

You made me wait, didn't you, My McDonald, she thought. You were right. The good things in life are worth the wait. Springing into the air, Cleary threw both arms around his neck. "Yes. Yes. Oh, yes! I'll go to the prom with you, Tony."

He swung her around and around until they were both kneeling on the grass. Laughing. Looking at one another with innocent eyes that seemed, for an instant, much wiser. And older beyond their years.

"I never want you to feel you have to wait for me. That isn't fair. But I was thinking, maybe . . . maybe you'd be my girl for a little while. Until I ship out."

His girl? She hesitated. Could she be as honest as he was? She wanted to.

You can. Speak from your heart, My McDonald whispered, *before this moment passes, child.*

Cleary let My McDonald guide her. In her mind, Cleary saw her guardian angel nodding, encouraging her. "I've always been your girl, Tony. You just never knew it. Those times you saw me praying. What do you think I was asking my guardian angel for?" She dipped her chin and giggled.

This time on purpose.

⌒

"DO YOU BELIEVE IT, Mama?" Cleary asked. "I'm going to the prom. And with Tony."

"Grandma told me. This overtime is killing me." Cleary's mother sat on the edge of the twin bed, wiping off Pond's cold cream with a damp face cloth. "I don't know, Cleary. You'll need a dress."

"I'll take care of that," Grandma spoke from the bedroom door. "You've got enough on your hands at the shipyard. Don't give Cleary's prom another thought. We've all got our jobs to do. Yours is to sleep."

That evening Cleary sat on the edge of her bed, writing in her angel journal. She glanced back at the last few pages. There were so many things to be grateful for. She clutched the dog-eared tablet and said a special thank-you prayer. But would it be enough?

It is enough, My McDonald whispered.

Cleary drifted off with a smile and complete joy in her heart.

⌒

THE NEXT MORNING, RIGHT after Sunday mass, Grandma began. She had more ideas for the prom dress than their chickens had feathers. She whipped her yellow tape measure out and started measuring Cleary. "You're taller than the last time we put a notch in the door. I thought Harry was the only McDonald still growing."

She opened the cedar chest at the foot of her double bed with a flourish. "Fold back the bedspread."

Cleary loved the old sleigh bed with its yellow and white chenille spread. "Grandma, I can wear my blue dress."

Grandma knelt before the chest. "We might not be buying a new dress, but we certainly can make one of these look like new."

Cleary recognized a long dress Grandma had worn years ago. Her shoulders drooped.

Straighten up there, My McDonald scolded.

Cleary felt a sharp elbow nudge her ribs.

Do you want a long dress or not?

Nodding, Cleary shook out the yellow dress.

"There's bound to be lots of things in here we can use." Grandma sounded ten years younger. "Let's see. I've always liked you in pink."

"Pink is nice," Cleary said.

"We're getting ahead of ourselves." Grandma's smile poked around the side of the cedar lid. "Let's consider the kind of fabrics we've got here. Lace. The beige lace still has some wear left in it."

Cleary held up the lace and satin dress.

"That's the most expensive dress I ever bought. Tuck it under your chin." Grandma dropped a small stack of other dresses onto the bed. "And stop fidgeting."

Cleary did as she was told.

My McDonald screwed up her face, studying the dress. *A tad old for you, I'm thinking.*

With relief, Cleary saw Grandma's frown mirrored My McDonald's opinion.

"Perhaps we should look at the yellow one, " Grandma suggested. "We need something fresh."

Cleary buried the lace dress at the bottom of the pile, hoping never to see it again. Grandma tossed a blue dress and an assortment of flowered ones back into the chest. Cleary silently said a thank-you. She tucked the yellow dress under her chin and looked over Grandma's shoulder, checking her reflection in the dressing table mirror. "I like the color. But I wish it were longer."

"The dotted Swiss underskirt is like new." Grandma took her sewing basket from under the bed. Sunlight flashed on the blades of her sewing scissors. Grandma looked like a surgeon about to operate on a dying patient.

Before Cleary could speak, both sleeves of the yellow dress were snipped off. "What about the skirt? And the neckline, Grandma?"

"I've got an idea. You start dinner. I'll crank up the old Singer."

Cleary protested. But Grandma shushed her away with a wave of her hand. Cleary knew better than to argue with an Irish woman holding a pair of very sharp scissors.

Days passed. Grandma was mum about the yellow dress. Cleary kept writing faithfully in her angel journal each night listing five things to be thankful for. And praying. Praying for a miracle.

The Tuesday before the prom, the miracle happened. She got home from school right on time. The house was quiet except for some music. Irish music. One of Grandma's favorite songs—"Danny Boy." Cleary heard Grandma singing along with the radio:

"And I'll be here, in sunshine . . ."

Then she heard a choked sob. "Grandma?" She walked by the open bedroom door. The chenille bedspread lay smooth on the cherry sleigh bed. Sunshine shone in through the trio of windows like a keylight. The yellow roses in the ironstone pitcher looked freshly picked. But it was what was on the bed that made Cleary gasp.

"Grandma. You finished my dress."

"Not quite." The song on the radio died. Then, Grandma peeked into the bedroom. Her eyes looked red.

"Are you okay?" Cleary asked.

"That song always did make me tear up. Try on the dress. Careful, mind you. The skirt is pinned. I want to make certain the length is exactly to your liking."

Cleary was out of her navy blue school jumper in a heartbeat. Her white blouse floated to the hardwood floor. She stood in her white slip while Grandma lifted the dress.

"I reversed the skirts. The dotted Swiss is on top, now." Grandma zipped up the back. "Dropped the waist on the under-skirt. And—"

"Grandma, the double ruffles are perfect around the neck."

"And do you like the scooped neckline? More to the point, I hope your father doesn't think we're showing too much shoulders."

"Daddy will love it. *I* love it!"

Grandma was kneeling, fluffing the skirt.

Cleary hadn't really noticed the skirt before. The hem was scalloped and lay perfectly above the solid yellow underskirt. She bent over to take a better look when a pin at the waist found its mark. "Ouch." She rubbed her right side.

"I told you to watch those straight pins. Now, take a few twirls in front of the mirror so we can see if we like it, Cleary."

"Grandma, you're an angel."

And what am I? Kadota figs? Who was it that suggested you take another look at the yellow dress? Me. Your My McDonald.

"Sorry. This is for you." Cleary blew a kiss.

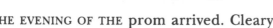

THE EVENING OF THE prom arrived. Cleary had spent an hour soaking in a pink bubble bath, much to the chagrin of Harry, who couldn't understand why any girl would spend so much time washing.

Grandma and Mama helped her dress. Mama kept tugging at the neckline of the dress. "I don't know, Mother McDonald. There's a lot of shoulder showing."

"And such pretty shoulders. It does look a might bare though." Grandma opened the cedar chest and produced a blue velvet box.

Cleary and her mother knew what was in the box.

"Mother McDonald. No," Mama protested. "Not the pearls."

Grandma opened the box and took out a strand of creamy pearls. "I know the tradition. Cleary is suppose to wear the McDonald pearls for the first time on her wedding day. But times have changed. There's no guarantees about our tomorrow. The pearls are mine. Until I die. Then, they'll pass to Cleary. I want to see her wear them. Tonight."

"But—" Mama said.

"There's the end to it. Come here, Cleary. Let me put these on you. I want to see how beautiful they look against your fair skin. Your great-grandmother wore these on her wedding day."

"My McDonald," Cleary whispered.

Right here. It's been a long spell since I saw my pearls. They look as fine as they did the day I first wore them.

"They were a wedding gift from her groom," Grandma continued. "You favor her, Cleary. She had a few more freckles, though."

I did not. My skin was as fair as a baby's cheek.

Cleary felt the string of pearls against her skin. She touched the pearls, feeling their smoothness. But it was only when she opened her eyes and caught her reflection in the mirror that her breath caught in her throat.

My pearls never looked lovelier.

"*Beautiful*," Grandma whispered. "Now do one more twirl."

Cleary did as she was told.

The doorbell rang.

"That'll be your Tony." Grandma made one final fluff of the skirt. "Run and show your father and grandpa how you look."

"Grandma, how can I ever—"

"You and I . . . we don't need words, child. Go on. Give us a kiss. Then, do the same to the McDonald men. Even Harry. If you can catch him."

Cleary enjoyed seeing the expression on Daddy and Grandpa's faces. Moments later, she stood behind the kitchen door ready to make her grand entrance to the parlor where Tony waited. She turned the knob slowly, taking one last moment to touch the string of pearls. Then, she felt for the silver angel medal she'd pinned to her slip.

"I'm wearing the medal you gave me, My McDonald."

And I'm proud you remembered. Off with ya. Tony's awaiting.

A kiss brushed Cleary's cheek.

Have a wonderful time, Cinderella.

Cleary opened the door. She paused, framed in the doorway.

Dressed in his best Sunday suit, Tony sat opposite her in Grandpa's easy chair. He jumped to his feet. His jaw dropped open. The silent tribute was more eloquent than anything he could have said.

"Gee, Cleary, you sure look different," Harry said. "I guess you should take a bubble bath more often."

Everyone laughed.

"Maybe you should try one once in a while, Son," Daddy teased.

Harry shook his head.

Everyone laughed again.

"Is that for me?" Cleary asked, looking at the corsage box Tony gripped in his hands.

"Yeah." He held out the box labeled "Rossi & Sons."

Cleary untied the yellow satin ribbon. "Gardenias. My favorite."

Tony's grin broadened. "I know. Your grandmother told me."

CLEARY HAD NEVER SEEN the Bischeri truck so clean. Tony must have spent the afternoon washing and polishing it. He'd even spread a plaid blanket over the front seat to protect her prom dress.

"Did you hear about the music tonight?" he asked, backing the truck out of the driveway. "Live."

"A band?"

"Well, kind of. Dolan and a few of the marching band guys have been practicing. Lots of brass, like Glenn Miller."

"He's my favorite."

"I know. Da. Da, da, da, da-da da-da," he sang.

Even though he sang slightly off key, she recognized "String of Pearls." She hummed along as the truck pulled up in front of the school gym. Tonight the gray building was bright with lights.

Red, yellow, blue, and green balloons hung above the open double doors. As Tony parked the truck, an unmistakable rendition of Glenn Miller's "Pennsylvania Six Five Thousand" echoed from inside the gym.

Tony and Cleary sang along. "Pennsylvania six five."

"Oh."

"Oh."

"Oh!"

Her shoulders moved to the beat of the music. Her feet refused to stay still.

Tony took her hand and led her inside. A giant glitterball hung from the ceiling. Balloons were everywhere. It looked like a combination birthday party and nightclub. The kind of a celebration Cleary had only seen in movies.

It was magic time.

Tony introduced her to the chaperones. Then he steered her toward one of the long tables. "Punch?"

"I'm fine."

"Want to dance?" He opened his arms and stepped closer.

Her hand was still in his when his arm encircled her waist. The embrace felt so wonderful. So natural. So right.

In seconds, he swept her onto the dance floor. Her yellow dress flared about her like Cinderella's ball gown. And she felt as if she had glass slippers on her feet instead of the borrowed pair of ballerina slippers.

Tony smelled of Old Spice and warm skin. His eyes were dancing, too. And he hadn't stopped smiling since he first saw her. His shoulder muscles strained against the woolen fabric of his blue suit. The pressure of his hand on her back, coaxed her closer until her breasts touched his hard chest.

With every breath she took, Cleary was more and more in heaven.

His cheek brushed hers, nudging back the curls framing her temple. "You're wearing earrings."

"They're my great-grandmother's. I'm wearing her string of pearls, too."

"They're beautiful. Like you."

THE EVENING FLEW BY. And, like Cinderella, Cleary found herself wishing there were more than twenty-four hours in a day. After the prom they stopped by Fenton's Ice Cream Shoppe with a group of other kids and filled up on black and white sundaes and chocolate malts. Cleary was still bursting from the double malt she and Tony shared when they pulled into the driveway of her house.

"I had a wonderful time, Tony."

"The prom's not over yet," Tony said, opening her side of the truck. "I'm walking you to the door like a gentleman."

Hand in hand, they stepped beneath the fig tree.

He pulled her to a stop. "Sweet sixteen. And never been kissed?" He stepped closer.

"Never."

The tip of his shoe bumped hers.

"Until now."

"Until *you*." She tilted her face up to his. His lips warmed hers.

It was everything she imagined a first kiss would be. And for the rest of her life, Cleary Catherine McDonald would remember the prom.

The music.

        The yellow dress.

                And her first kiss.

But most of all. She'd remember *Tony*!

IT WASN'T UNTIL SHE stepped into the house that Cleary realized something was wrong. Perhaps it was the song playing on the phonograph. "Danny Boy."

"Oh, Danny boy. Oh, Danny boy. I love you so."

Grandma and Grandpa were still up. Mama and Daddy were there, too. Only Harry was missing. Daddy switched off the phonograph. "How was the prom?"

The smile on his face seemed strained. Not quite the usual broad grin of the man named after an Irish harp.

"I bet you had a wonderful time," Grandpa added.

"I can smell the gardenia clear over here." Grandma patted her knee. "Come over here, Cleary. There's something you must be knowing. And now is the time for the telling."

All thoughts of the prom vanished from Cleary's head. She was suddenly alarmed. Frightened. Of what she knew not.

"We've word. About your brother. Ian." Grandma's face paled. Mama burst into tears.

Cleary knelt beside Grandma's chair. Grandma took her hand. "It's bad. Isn't it?"

"Kamikaze bombers sunk Ian's ship." Grandma's hand lay very still. "And there's no word of him."

"At least he hasn't been spotted yet," Grandpa said.

Cleary held on tight to Grandma's hand. "But he might be."

CLEARY COULDN'T SLEEP THAT night. And when she took her angel journal from beneath her pillow, it was difficult to think of five things to be thankful for. There was the prom, of course. Even when she looked at My McDonald's pearls, all Cleary could think about, pray about, was Ian.

He might be floating in the ocean out there in the darkness so far from home. "Please, God. Let Ian be alive. Let a ship find him. She squeezed her eyes tight. Tears tumbled down her cheeks.

"Please, Lord. I'll never ask you for another thing. Not another prom. Not a dress. Nothing. Only bring my brother back to us safely. And soon"

Yes, Lord, echoed My McDonald. *Soon.*

IAN MCDONALD WAS RESCUED at sea. Both he and Uncle Jack returned home after the peace treaty was signed. So did Marvin and Mellon Haban, although Mellon's shrapnel wounds and Marvin's loss of his right leg ended their baseball dreams. Marvin attended the University of California at Berkeley on the G.I. Bill and is a veteran's advocate. Mellon went to UC Berkeley on the G.I. Bill, too. He's an architect and owns his own firm.

Tony Bischeri was mortally wounded taking a then-unknown island named Iwo Jima. He lived long enough to see the Marines raise the American flag. When he died, Tony was still wearing a sterling medal with the profile of a Guardian Angel next to his dog tag. A medal Cleary had placed around his neck just before she kissed him good-bye on the day he shipped overseas.

Cleary McDonald Thomas still lives in Northern California with her husband, grown daughters and grandchildren. Her daughters wore My McDonald's pearls on their wedding day. So did her granddaughters.

Cleary writes in her angel journal every night.

And talks to My McDonald.

And she *still* loves to dance.

Contributors

Neesa Hart writes contemporary romance under her own name and historical romance as Mandalyn Kaye. Her latest release, *You Made Me Love You*, is a contemporary single title romance from Avon Books. Neesa lives in Washington, D.C., where she writes full time. Sometimes, she lives other places around the country where she manages and produces theatrical presentations for churches large and small. Neesa's work has been honored with multiple awards by readers and her peers. She's a three time HOLT Medal winner, a Romantic Times Reviewer's Choice Winner, and a Gold Congressional Medal winner. This story is dedicated to "Reverend Ken Nuss, a very wise man who helped me find my way."

Stobie Piel has published thirteen novels and seven novellas since her first book was published by DLP/Pinnacle Books in 1995. She has written in a variety of sub-genres for Leisure/Dorchester, including historical, time travel, fantasy, and futuristic romance, winning Affaire de Coeur's Best Futuristic of the Year for *The Midnight Moon*. Her recent time travel, *Blue-Eyed Bandit*, was a Romantic Times Top Pick for August 2000. She has been invited to contribute a novella, "Wizard's Brew," to an illustrated anthology put together by Lynn Sanders and Cherif Fortin, which will also feature Connie Brockway, Marsha Canham, and Heather Graham. Her next novel is *Renegade*, a lead Love Spell release in February 2001. She lives in Maine with her three children and numerous pets.

Ken Wisman's fiction has appeared in a number of anthologies and other venues, including the collection Heaven Sent. He lives in Boxborough, Massachusetts.

Susan Sizemore lives in the Midwest and spends most of her time writing. Some of her other favorite things are coffee, dogs, travel, movies, hiking, history, farmers markets, art glass, and basketball—you'll find mention of quite a few of these things inside the pages of her stories. She works in many genres, from contemporary romance to epic fantasy and horror. She's the winner of the Romance Writers of America's Golden Heart award and a nominee for the 2000 Rita Award in historical romance. Her available books include historical romance novels from Avon, a dark fantasy series, *The Laws of the Blood*, from Ace Science Fiction, science fiction from Speculation Press, and several electronically published books and short stories. One of her electronic books, the epic fantasy *Moons' Dreaming*, written with Marguerite Krause, is a nominee for the Eppie, the e-publishing industries writing award. Susan's e-mail address is Ssizemore@aol.com, and her webpage address is: HYPERLINK http://members.aol.com/Ssizemore/storm/home.htm

Tim Waggoner has published more than fifty stories of fantasy and horror. His most current stories can be found in the anthologies *Civil War Fantastic, Single White Vampire Seeks Same*, and *Bruce Coville's UFOs*. His first novel, *The Harmony Society*, is forthcoming from DarkTales Publications. He teaches creative writing at Sinclair Community College in Dayton, Ohio.

Michelle West is the author of several novels, including *The Sacred Hunter* duology and *The Broken Crown*, both published by DAW Books. She reviews books for the on-line column "First Contacts" and less frequently for *The Magazine of Fantasy & Science Fiction*. Other short fiction by her appears in *Black Cats and Broken Mirrors, Elf Magic, Olympus*, and *Alien Abductions*.

Charles de Lint is a full-time writer and musician who presently makes his home in Ottawa, Canada, with his wife MaryAnn Harris, an artist and musician. His latest novel is *Forests of the Heart* (Tor Books, 2000). He has a new collection called *Triskell Tales* due from Subterranean Press in the fall of 2000, and Orb/Tor will be reprinting his classic novel *Svaha* later in the year. Other recent publications include mass market editions of *Moonlight* and *Vines*, a third collection of Newford stories (Tor Books, 2000) and his novel *Someplace to Be Flying* (Tor Books, 1999). For more information about his work, visit his website at <http://www.cyberus.ca/~cdl>.

Jody Lynn Nye lists her main career activity as "spoiling cats." She lives northwest of Chicago with two of the above and her husband, author and packager Bill Fawcett. She has written twenty-two books, including four contemporary fantasies (the Mythology 101 series), three SF novels, four novels in collaboration with Anne McCaffrey, including *The Ship Who Won*, a humorous anthology about mothers, *Don't Forget Your Spacesuit, Dear!*, and more than fifty short stories. Her latest book (coming in August) is *The Grand Tour*, third in her new fantasy epic series, "The Dreamland."

Nancy Springer is a lifelong fiction writer, author of thirty-one volumes of mythic fantasy, children's literature, mystery, suspense, short stories, and poetry. Her latest novel is *I Am Mordred*, a young-adult Arthurian fantasy from the point of view of Mordred's unacknowledged son. Also published are the novels *Sky Rider* and *Plumage*. A longtime Pennsylvania resident, she teaches creative writing at York College of Pennsylvania. In her spare time she is an enthusiastic, although not expert, horseback rider, and a volunteer for the Wind Ridge Farm Equine Sanctuary, a home for horses that have been rescued from neglect or abuse. She lives in Dallastown with a phlegmatic guinea pig and a psychotic cat.

Mickey Zucker Reichert is a pediatrician whose science fiction and fantasy novels include *The Legend of Nightfall*, *The Unknown Soldier*, and several books and trilogies about the Renshai. Her most recent release from DAW Books is *Spirit Fox*, with Jennifer Wingert, and *The Flightless Falcon*. Her short fiction has appeared in numerous anthologies, including *Battle Magic*, *Zodiac Fantastic*, and *Wizard Fantastic*. Her claims to fame: she has performed brain surgery, and her parents really are rocket scientists.

Paul Dellinger, a long-time newspaper reporter, has published stories in *Amazing Stories* and *Fantasy & Science Fiction* magazines, and a number of paperback anthologies, including *The Williamson Effect*, *First Contact*, *Lord of the Fantastic*, and *Guardsmen of Tomorrow*. He and his wife Maxine, who serves as his guardian angel, live in Virginia.

Laura Hayden never lacks for a change of pace or venue in her life. The wife of an active duty Air Force officer, she has written and traveled all across the country. Her next book, *Stolen Hearts*, a time-travel romance, will be available fall 2001. It's part of the "Hope Chest" series from Zebra Ballad, a five-book continuity series being written by members of her critique group, the Wyrd Sisters. She's also embarking on a new writing adventure—working as a ghostwriter on a big mystery series for a major publishing house. And as much as she'd love to tell you all about the project, her lips are sealed! Laura credits her close ties to the Wyrd Sisters and the wonders of e-mail for keeping her focused on her career, despite all her moves. She enjoys hearing from her fans and welcomes them to e-mail her at suspense@suspense.net.

Von Jocks believes in the magic of stories. She has written since she was five, publishing her first short story at the age of twelve in a local paper. Under the name Evelyn Vaughn she sold her first romantic suspense novel, *Waiting for the Wolf Moon*, to Silhouette Shadows in 1992. Three more books completed her "Circle Series" before the Shadows line closed. Her most recent project is a series of historical romance novels— *The Rancher's Daughters, Behaving Herself,* and *Forgetting Herself*—for Leisure Books. Yvonne also enjoys writing short stories and novellas in the science fiction/fantasy and mystery genres. Her short fiction most recently appeared in *Dangerous Magic,* from DAW Books. The book was selected as one of the top 100 of the year by the New York City Public Library, and her story was nominated for a Sapphire Award. Yvonne received her master's degree at the University of Texas in Arlington, writing her thesis on the history of the romance novel. An unapologetic TV addict, she resides in Texas with her cats and her imaginary friends and teaches junior-college English to support her writing habit, or vice versa. All sentence fragments in her stories are for effect. Really.

Lucy A. Snyder has co-authored several stories with Gary A. Braunbeck. The first appears in IFD Publishing's anthology *Bedtime Stories to Darken Your Dreams*, and the second appears in the anthology *Civil War Fantastic.* (in case you were wondering: no, they don't have the same middle name). By day, Lucy builds Web pages. By night, she writes fiction, publishes *Dark Planet Webzine* [http://www.sfsite.com/darkplanet/] and writes the occasional interview or book review for SF Site. Lucy was born in South Carolina, grew up in Texas, and currently lives in Columbus, Ohio.

Jane Lindskold is a full-time writer whose recent novels include *Changer* and *Legends Walking*, and *Through Wolf's Eyes.* She lives in New Mexico, where she's currently at work on another novel.

Stephen Donaldson, born in 1947 in Cleveland, Ohio, lived in India (where his father was a medical missionary) until 1963. He graduated from the College of Wooster (Ohio) in 1968, served two years as a conscientious objector during the Vietnam War doing hospital work in Akron, then attended Kent State University, where he received his master's degree in English in 1971. After dropping out of his Ph.D. program and moving to New Jersey in order to write fiction, Donaldson made his publishing debut with the first "Covenant" trilogy in 1977. That enabled him to move to a healthier climate. He now lives in New Mexico. The novels for which he is best known have received a number of awards. However, the achievements of which he is most proud are the ones that seemed the most unlikely. In 1993 he received a Doctor of Literature degree from the College of Wooster, and in 1994 he gained a black belt in Shotokan karate from Sensei Mike Heister and Anshin Personal defense. Having recently completed the five-book, seven-year Gap sequence of science fiction novels, Donaldson spent quite some time "on vacation." However, he has now returned to work. His most recent books is a second collection of short fiction, *Reave the Just and Other Tales.*

Gary A. Braunbeck is the author of the acclaimed collection *Things Left Behind*, as well as the forthcoming collections *Escaping Purgatory* (in collaboration with Alan M. Clark) and the CD-ROM Sorties, Cathexes, and Human Remains. His first solo novel, *The Indifference of Heaven*, was recently released by Obsidian Books, as was his Dark Matter novel, *In Hollow Houses*. He lives in Columbus, Ohio, and has, to date, sold nearly two hundred short stories. His fiction, to quote *Publisher's Weekly*, ". . . stirs the mind as it chills the marrow."

Bonnie Jeanne Perry, an award-winning author, has sold four novels, written a column for the *Saint Louis Journal*, short stories, and a screenplay that took first place in a national writing contest. She belongs to Novelist, Inc., the Romance Writers of America, and the Published Authors' Network. She has spoken at national writing conferences and conducted manuscript critique sessions in Saint Louis, Missouri. Several of her novels have been published in Europe. She lives in Walnut Creek, California, with her husband, and is currently finishing her first romantic suspense novel, a historical novel proposal, and another screenplay.

Permissions

Printed in the USA
CPSIA information can be obtained
at www.ICGtesting.com
JSHW082150140824
68134JS00014B/170